THE MARRYING KIND

THE MARRYING KIND

A Novel

Heather Conrad

iUniverse, Inc.
New York Lincoln Shanghai

The Marrying Kind

iUniverse books may be ordered through booksellers or by contacting:

iUniverse
2021 Pine Lake Road, Suite 100
Lincoln, NE 68512
www.iuniverse.com
1-800-Authors (1-800-288-4677)

Because of the dynamic nature of the Internet, any Web addresses or links contained in this book may have changed since publication and may no longer be valid.

This is a work of fiction. All of the characters, names, incidents, organizations, and dialogue in this novel are either the products of the author's imagination or are used fictitiously.

ISBN: 978-0-595-48314-3 (pbk)
ISBN: 978-0-595-60402-9 (ebk)

Printed in the United States of America

Prologue

October 2006

It's only been ten years, Zooey thought, they can't have changed *that* much. Of course, she had herself. Who would have believed she would have a daughter? And at this late date?

Zooey's freshman roommate at Sanders College thirty years ago, Danielle, was hosting their reunion. Danielle owned her own vineyard; she and her husband were looking for something to do after he retired (at age fifty!). Their place was called Rivonnier, a made-up word, Zooey assumed—the kind of thing Danielle might come up with after a glass or two of sauvignon blanc. Zooey was looking forward to seeing their grand *faux* chateau atop a hill on thirty acres of prime Napa Valley land.

She shifted her Mini Cooper on the winding road. The green hills looked almost foreign, too green for California in October. Vineyards began to appear, twisted dark red leaves, rusty orange and yellow.

"Who's getting married?" Zooey heard as Danielle opened the front door and she saw her old friends sitting in an enormous living room. She hugged Danielle and followed her across the parquet foyer.

"Zooey!" Brenna smiled. Beautiful, sweet Brenna. Her once black hair was now silver but still set off her blue eyes that were filled with happiness. "It's so good to see you." She hugged Zooey tightly, as Patti watched with a dry smile.

"You'd think you'd just found her in a refugee camp, Brenna."

"Hi, Patti." Zooey laughed and leaned to embrace Patti, whose soft arms encircled her, briefly though not without affection.

"Where's Elizabeth?" Zooey asked.

"That's the mystery."

"She's getting married—can you believe it? In June."

"She was always so conventional," Patti said. "Although it is her first marriage."

"I thought she joined an ashram a few years ago."

"I couldn't believe her phone message saying she wasn't coming and not a word about why. I thought, did she take a vow of silence?" Danielle said.

"Didn't she get enough religion in high school?" Patti looked at Zooey. "She went to Holy Name High with you and Brenna, didn't she?"

"Oh the Catholic thing." Danielle waved a dismissive hand as a strand of sleek blonde hair, loosened from her chignon, fell fetchingly across her forehead.

Brenna flushed slightly. She was still a practicing Catholic and Zooey gave her a sympathetic glance. Sometimes when Danielle and Patti got going no one was spared. They needed Elizabeth to round them out. She was more reserved—not secretive exactly, but self-protective. Her presence had a calming influence on their group.

Zooey missed Elizabeth and wondered, suddenly, if she herself should have come. Then just as quickly a decades-old memory came to mind and it still troubled her—after all these years—that particular memory of Elizabeth.

"That was my first husband," Patti was saying. "You'd think I'd have known a guy named Trevor wouldn't have a libido."

"Ladies," Danielle's husband called from the dining room. "Dinner is served."

"Aren't second husbands the best?" Danielle said to Patti.

Sanders College
1971

Name: *Zooey James*
Birthdate: *October 7, 1953*
Birthplace: *Glendale, California*
Father's Name: *Carter James*
Mother's Name: *Evelyn James*
High School: *Holy Name High School*
Grade Point Average: *4.0*

Why I want to attend Sanders College:

I first visited Sanders College with my best friends, Elizabeth and Brenna. I immediately knew I wanted to study at Sanders. The beautiful campus and hills and trees felt so alive, like a foreign land, especially compared to the parking lots and shopping malls of my hometown. And the academic choices at Sanders are even more important...

Name: *Elizabeth Riordan*
Birthdate: *November 24, 1952*
Birthplace: *Pacific Palisades, California*
Father's Name: *Dr. Martin Riordan*
Mother's Name: *deceased*
High School: *Holy Name High School*
Grade Point Average: *3.8*

Why I want to attend Sanders College:
    Sanders College offers an excellent liberal arts education in an exquisite setting. I am particularly interested in the English Department and the highly qualified professors as well as advanced classes in English and American poetry. I hope to pursue a career in English Literature ...

Name: *Brenna Donovan*
Birthdate: *June 21, 1953*
Birthplace: *Pacific Palisades, California*
Father's Name: *Frank Donovan*
Mother's Name: *Maureen Donovan*
High School: *Holy Name High School*
Grade Point Average: *3.3*

Why I want to attend Sanders College:

I am so excited about applying to Sanders College! I want to become a valuable member of the Sanders community. I'm hoping to join service organizations like The Children's Day Project which helps children in the nearby towns, or any other …

Name: *Danielle Delacroix*
Birthdate: *April 17, 1953*
Birthplace: *Tiburon, California*
Father's Name: *Lucien Delacroix*
Mother's Name: *Sandrine Delacroix*
High School: *Marin Preparatory Academy*
Grade Point Average: *3.7*

Why I want to attend Sanders College:
I would like to attend Sanders College because it is ideal for my educational plans. The Junior Year Abroad program will allow me to study in Paris as I have always wanted. The emphasis on romance languages and classes in French literature are of interest to me ...

Name: *Patti Hammond*
Birthdate: *January 6, 1953*
Birthplace: *Tiburon, California*
Father's Name: *John Hammond III*
Mother's Name: *Marie Hammond*
High School: *Marin Preparatory Academy*
Grade Point Average: *3.1*

Why I want to attend Sanders College:
   I'd love to go to Sanders. I know the teachers and classes are the best. My father and brothers went to Sanders and they got a great education. My best friend Danielle will probably be at Sanders as a freshman and we'd be great studying together because we both went to MPA together. I like the extracurricular clubs like the Debs....

PART I

October 1971

Zooey ran against the red light, her black tights sagging beneath her miniskirt as she breathlessly dodged traffic and landed on the curb at the other side of the street. She kept running. She hadn't known she could run this fast. It felt reckless and made her laugh. Her light brown hair blew behind her as strands fell across her eyes and she brushed them back.

"Zooey, what are you *doing*?" Patti called as she came up the path.

"Nothing." Zooey ran past.

At the portico she turned and took the inside stairs two at a time. She had ten minutes to change, pack and meet Danielle.

"Zooey, you're not even ready." Danielle stood in the doorway.

"Give me two minutes. They just let me out of there. The dishwasher overflowed. Everybody had to help."

"Meet me downstairs, then. I have that extra pair of skis for you."

"Thanks! Where's Brenna?"

"On the phone. Come on! We're waiting for you. We have to pick Patti up at the store."

Zooey searched through the heap of things on the chair by her bed for the snow clothes Elizabeth had lent her. She'd been to the snow with her family, in the mountains east of the Southern California suburb where she grew up, but all they had done was build snowmen. She had never been on skis and had no idea what it would be like. This daytrip was Danielle's idea. She'd been skiing since she was a kid.

It was a two hour drive and Danielle had wanted to leave at 7:00 a.m. but they had to wait for Zooey to finish her breakfast shift in the dining hall. She worked 5:30–7:30 a.m. every weekday morning. That plus her scholarship paid her way at Sanders.

They piled into Danielle's car laughing and shoving their stuff into every available space. The skis were on a rack on top. Danielle had her Peugeot which she often brought to school. Her parents were French and although her father was born in California he still had something of the Old World about him. He was from an aristocratic family who chose to live in the United States after a Paris banking scandal threatened, but did not diminish, the family fortune. Danielle's mother, Sandrine, was very reserved, beautiful and thin; she felt displaced in America and doted on Danielle, her only child. They lived a half-hour away in Tiburon, but Danielle boarded at school like the rest of the girls. Sanders had few day students. Almost everyone, certainly all the freshman girls, lived in dorms.

Zooey, Elizabeth and Brenna sat in back. They stopped at the campus store and honked the horn, shrieking and leaning out the windows. Patti came running out with a horrified face, waving her arms like she'd seen Godzilla and jumped in the front seat. Danielle put the car in gear and took off heading for the highway as they all screamed out the words to *Here Comes the Sun* on the radio.

The snow was beautiful. It fell in great feathery flakes and was absolutely silent. The girls watched it wordlessly a moment as they got out of the car at a rest stop. There was no one else there. It was 9:00 a.m. on a Friday morning and the weekend ski traffic hadn't yet started. Each of them was cutting a class or two so they could come today. No one's parents knew.

Brenna and Zooey stood at the edge of the carpark, bundled in hats and scarves, looking into the woods.

"Wow, Zo. Isn't it incredible?" Brenna whispered. "Can't you feel God here?"

"I know what you mean."

The tall pines' dark boughs were draped with mounds of shapely, soft snow. A gray chunk of granite thrust up from the blanketed forest floor, covered in a crust of white. Still the soft flakes fell gently, light as air.

"*Whose woods these are I think I know,*" Elizabeth said, coming up behind them.

"*His house is in the village though,*" Zooey said without turning around.

"*My little horse must think it queer—*"

"*He gives his harness bells a shake,*" Zooey broke in.

"No, no, that's not how it goes." Elizabeth picked up a handful of snow and threw it at Zooey.

"Oh, whoa!" Zooey shouted brushing it off then using both hands scooped up a mound of wet powder and flung it at Elizabeth.

Patti ran over from the car and landed a better-made snowball on Brenna's back and then they were all shouting and laughing and hurling ineffectual snowballs, tumbling over and getting wet.

"Whose idea was that?" Patti said, back in the car. "I'm freezing."

Danielle turned the heater up full blast. The snow still fell as they drove up the mountain. "Of course, we don't have any extra hats. We can get some at the lodge."

"These'll dry." Patti waved her hat briskly in front of the heater vent on the dashboard. "We can't all buy new clothes every time we spill something, Danielle."

There was a momentary silence. They knew Patti must be annoyed because ordinarily they avoided the issue of money, at least in comparing each other's wealth or lack of it—at least to each other's faces. Although Patti came from a wealthy family, her father was more restrictive than Danielle's. Patti and Danielle had known each other since they were toddlers. Patti's father made a fortune in the shoe industry in St. Louis in the '40s and then moved his family to Tiburon where eventually Patti and her four brothers were born. Patti enjoyed the rowdy, male environment of her family home where servants maintained the household and her parents entertained lavishly when they weren't taking cruises. She had developed a knack for fending for herself.

"You could make your own hat, Patti," Brenna said. "You could crochet a scarf like you made for Rick."

"You could make a toga," Zooey added.

"Oh god. The toga party! Who's going?" Patti asked.

"You mean the beer brawl." Elizabeth wrinkled her delicate nose and brushed her thick dark hair from her face, clasping it neatly into a barrette at the back of her neck.

"I'm not," Zooey said. "What about you, Brenna?"

"Drew really wants to." She gave a little shrug and turned to gaze at the pristine banks of snow outside. Brenna was a middle child in a very large Irish family and during her elementary school years her father ran for state senator and won. Her parents were away much of the time on the campaign trail or in Sacramento. A strict nanny ran the household and the smaller children hardly knew their parents. They looked to Brenna for maternal warmth and she gave it happily. She loved her "little ones" as she called her younger siblings and devoted herself to them, until she came to live at Sanders and met her boy-friend Drew.

"Sean and I are going," Danielle said. "It'll be fun!"

"We'll have a great time!" Patti said.

They tromped into the lodge and ordered coffees and hot chocolates.

"Who's going up The Sky with me?" Danielle called out.

"Brenna and I are taking a lesson on the bunny slope." Patti stuffed her red curls into her wool cap.

"I'm going to sit over there." Elizabeth pointed to an overstuffed couch by the fireplace near the window overlooking the slopes. She pulled out a paperback book from her bag.

"Oh come on, I drive all the way up here and no one's skiing with me? You will, won't you, Zooey," Danielle said.

"Well. I've never skied before."

"It's easy. I'll show you what to do. I know you can do it."

Zooey hesitated. She looked out the window up the steep slope as a figure came schussing down in a crouched position, poles straight out behind. It didn't look that hard. Zooey remembered running as fast as she could that morning, how she surprised herself with how well she could run.

At the chairlift there was already a short line. Zooey watched as each skier maneuvered into position. Danielle had spent fifteen minutes after they put on their skis showing Zooey how to turn and stop.

It wasn't that hard to sidle up and let the lift swoop her into the air. It was fun. The two of them dangled their skis side by side looking below them and laughing. The light snow had stopped. They were quiet as the cables creaked and carried them higher up the mountain above the treetops. Danielle had her neck craned to look behind them. Her pale blonde hair fell straight down her back beneath her jaunty pink ski cap. "I think I see them. Patti's waving her ski pole at the instructor. She's such a flirt."

"They look so little." Zooey took a breath of the thin, cold air. It felt heady, like her brain was crystalline. Her eyes glittered. She could see forever. The cables creaked again. You could hear a pin drop, she thought, as she looked down at the trees and snow and then saw a flash of red and heard the schuss of skis below. She looked up the mountain. There was a wooden structure with an Alpine roof.

"We're getting off in a minute. Remember what I told you," Danielle said.

Zooey focused intently on the grinding gears and platform ahead and swiftly planted her skis down then got out of the way with an assist from the lift worker and clomped out onto the snow. She swished her skis along the flat ridge using her poles looking for Danielle and found her on the other side of the platform at the top of the run.

"Ready?" Danielle asked. She looked happy.

"Well." Zooey looked down. It was very steep. "Now … what do I do?"

"Just go down. Follow me. Do what I do. If you go too fast, fall over."

Zooey watched as Danielle slid her skis forward and then took off in that semi-crouched position. Zooey took off after her. Within seconds she was going faster than she had running that morning; she was going so fast she couldn't believe it—it didn't seem right. She couldn't turn—the wind was freezing as she flew down bent over her skis, too fast, and she said now or never and fell on her side to stop herself but didn't stop and lying on her side kept hurtling down the mountain, her skis out front, her arms splayed as she lost her poles and kept sliding and then she hit a tree.

Elizabeth turned a page of her novel, *The Razor's Edge*. She loved Somerset Maugham. But she'd never read anything quite like this book about an American man who was so un-American—a wanderer seeking some inscrutable meaning instead of money or success.

Elizabeth's father was a busy doctor who, after his wife's death, worked incessantly. Elizabeth was ten when her mother died. Her older brother had been away at college at the time, and Elizabeth stopped speaking for nearly a year. It wasn't until she went to Holy Name High School that she began to open up again, and much of that had to do with her friendship with Zooey. Zooey's quirky sense of reality often caught Elizabeth by surprise, and helped her to take life a little less seriously. Zooey sensed something exceptional occurring each time Elizabeth spoke at all much less revealed her feelings. She was fascinated by Elizabeth's reserve and then those rare moments when she would open a small, guarded door to her inner truth. It was in complete contrast to the busy, crowded household Zooey grew up in where feelings were expressed easily and explosively. Zooey's father was a high school basketball coach; her mother worked in the office of the local elementary school, and her aunt, whose husband had left her and two boys younger than Zooey and her sister, stayed with them for what was called a temporary visit but had been for as long as Zooey could remember.

Elizabeth and Zooey sought each others' company often in high school as well as Brenna's kind and dependable friendship which rounded out their threesome. They were thrilled when all of them were accepted to Sanders.

Elizabeth glanced up as she heard a commotion outside. Two skiers with red crosses on their vests were attaching a gondola to the chairlift going up. A small group of people at the bottom of the slope stood watching. Elizabeth closed her book and followed a couple other curiosity seekers out the door of the lodge onto the deck.

"Someone's fallen up there."

"Hit a tree."

"That's what some guy who just skied down said."

Elizabeth overheard these remarks from the bystanders next to her and her hazel eyes narrowed. She lifted a hand to brush the light snow off her face then shaded her eyes and gazed intently up the mountain.

"How far up is it?" she asked.

"Near the top."

Elizabeth stopped breathing for a second. She had a feeling—though what really were the chances, but—She bit her lip and kept trying to see up through the trees.

The chairlift stopped. They must have finally gotten the gondola to the top and were taking it off. What was happening to the poor person under the tree all this time? Maybe other skiers had stopped to help?

"Elizabeth!" Danielle skied over near the steps up to the deck.

Elizabeth looked down at her and waved.

"Have you seen Zooey?" Danielle yelled. "We started off together but I was out in front—"

Elizabeth walked across the deck and down the icy wooden steps, moving carefully in her leather boots. It took her a few minutes and then she was standing on the bottom step and Danielle slid forward on her skis to stand next to her.

"Aren't you freezing? Where's your jacket?" Danielle asked.

"That may be her." Elizabeth pointed up the slope where the gondola with its large white circle and red cross was sliding slowly between the trees with two young men in ski patrol jackets guiding it.

"Oh my god. What are you talking about?"

"I don't know. It's just a feeling—"

"Don't be ridiculous!" But Danielle's pale blue eyes looked worried now.

They watched in silence as the little caravan became larger, slowly traversing between the trees, making its way to the lodge.

"It can't be that bad, whoever it is, or they wouldn't be going so damn slow." Danielle jammed her poles into the snow to propel her forward and took off, saying, "I'm going to find out."

Elizabeth watched as Danielle maneuvered herself to the lower slope and side-stepped up ten yards, approaching the gondola as the ski patrol man in front waved her away. Then Elizabeth could see the body in the gondola, the green jacket. Zooey. Danielle started to follow along behind them and Elizabeth turned and rushed up the icy steps to get her coat. She felt a grim calm as she put it on. Pulling her gloves from the pockets, she ran back out to the deck. They were still in sight, going around to the back of the lodge, as she made her way down the steps again and tromped through the snow to follow.

The first aid station had several cots, two of which already held injured skiers. There was a doctor in a white coat tending one of them who seemed to have a head injury. A nurse stood nearby.

"They won't let me move but I'm perfectly fine," Zooey was saying from the other cot as Elizabeth closed the red wooden door behind her. Danielle was standing over her shaking her head and frowning.

Elizabeth felt her eyes well with tears when she heard Zooey talking, slightly impatient, slightly embarrassed, totally Zooey. "How do you know?" she asked her.

"Hi." Zooey greeted her. "Can you believe it? I broke one of Danielle's skis."

"How about any bones?"

"No. But they want the doctor to check it. My ankle might be a problem."

"As in broken?"

"Just sprained probably."

"What were you thinking!" Danielle asked.

"Well, I guess I just don't know how to ski."

"I guess not."

"Danielle, why did you take her up there?" Elizabeth asked.

"I don't know. I thought she'd figure it out."

"Acing a midterm isn't the same as skiing down a mountain," Elizabeth said and walked out of the station.

"I know that," Danielle said, but the color had drained from her cheeks.

At lunchtime Zooey sat on the couch in the lodge near the fireplace, her wrapped ankle propped on a low burl table. Her crutches lay on the floor.

Elizabeth put a paper plate with a sandwich and fries in Zooey's lap and sat down with an identical plate for herself. "Slim pickings."

"This looks pretty good." Zooey picked up a french fry.

Elizabeth looked at her then turned and silently took a bite of her processed ham sandwich with distaste.

"Those skis I broke belonged to Danielle. My parents will have to pay for them, and it's not like they need any more problems—they don't even know I'm here."

"How much are they?"

"No idea."

Elizabeth turned and watched Zooey who stared gloomily at the fire burning low in the large stone hearth. "What was it like?"

"You mean...." Zooey turned to her.

"Falling?"

"Oh." Zooey shook her head. "It wasn't like falling at first. It was like being out of control—fantastic, a thrill ride!" She laughed. "Until I realized I couldn't stop. I was going faster and faster and there were trees and people, so I fell over, on purpose, but that didn't stop me. That's when it was weird, I kept sliding and sliding, but," she narrowed her eyes, remembering, "I kind of didn't care."

"You didn't care? I'm sure."

"I wasn't even thinking. It was just happening. I could've been anybody then—or a log, or a boulder sliding down a mountain really fast. That's all there was. I was never scared. Until I was lying there, and my ankle started to hurt."

"So you were scared—then? Did you panic?"

"Well, I thought. Now what? I can't move. It's freezing. There's snow in my face, and I started thinking about frostbite and that book we read—*Anna Purna*."

"The Frenchman who lost all his fingers."

"Yeah. But my ankle hurt so much, I wasn't really thinking that much about my fingers."

"Did you see the ski patrol coming up?"

"No, I didn't know they existed. I thought some skier would have to help me but they were all whizzing by like I was a dead squirrel or something."

"Well ... did you pray?"

Zooey looked at Elizabeth, then smiled. "Yes."

"To whom?"

"Just God. No saints, is that what you mean?"

"Remember what Sister Lourdes told us in high school? There are no atheists in the foxholes in a war. Was it something like that?"

"Well." Zooey looked perplexed. She gazed at the fire. "I guess. It was hardly a war. I mean this is a ski resort."

"Zooey. Obviously." Elizabeth pushed her dark brown hair back from her face. She picked up her book from the couch. "How far have you gotten in this?" She held it up.

"*Razor's Edge*? I haven't even started—" Zooey bit the inside of her cheek as she stared at her ankle. "I guess I'll have plenty of time to study now."

"This man, Larry, the hero, was in World War II. His best friend was killed, and then he felt like there was no meaning to his life."

"Hey, don't tell me the whole story."

"It's just—I can so understand what he felt."

Zooey looked at Elizabeth.

"Zooey! What happened?" Brenna rushed up to the couch, her black hair glistening with snow. "Danielle told me. Oh Zo—Your ankle. Does it hurt?"

"Hi, Brenna." Zooey returned her quick hug.

Brenna looked sadly at Zooey. She made the Sign of the Cross and sat down on the couch between her two friends. "When I think what could have happened."

"Well it didn't," Elizabeth said. "Where's Danielle now?"

"Oh, she's still skiing. Patti's with her. I think they met a couple guys."

January 1972

Early Sunday morning Brenna came by Zooey and Danielle's suite to pick Zooey up for church.

"Where's Elizabeth?" Zooey asked as she adjusted her black lace veil in the mirror. She wasn't usually very happy looking in the mirror. Her hair was not manageable. Her features were not perfect. Though a boy she'd danced with at a "mixer" recently told her—from a distance—she looked like Jane Fonda in *Klute*. She didn't ask him what she looked like close up. It was dark in the college gym where the dance had been. She decided it meant she looked sexy because, although she hadn't seen it, she knew *Klute* was about a prostitute. Was this a compliment? She decided it was. Although right now, she felt she looked ridiculous with the little veil perched on her head like a beanie, anchored with large, dark bobby pins.

"She's not coming." Brenna smiled at her. "That looks cute."

"Thanks, Brenna." Zooey laughed. "How come? Is she sick?"

"She didn't say. I don't think so."

Brenna, Zooey and Elizabeth had gone to Holy Name High in Los Angeles and applied to Sanders College in Marin County to get away from their families, hoping to room together and eventually get an apartment. Freshman girls weren't allowed to live off campus, although freshmen boys could have their own apartments. So the rule wouldn't even prevent anyone from getting pregnant, Zooey told Patti when Patti complained about how unfair it was. "Oh my god, you're such a Catholic," Patti had said, although Zooey couldn't see the relevance. Patti's parents were atheists. As it turned out they all had assigned roommates freshman year. Zooey wasn't even in the same dorm as her high school friends. But they saw each other often and went to Mass together every Sunday.

Brenna and Zooey walked the mile to Our Lady of the Immaculate Conception, a suburban church of angular cement blocks and a yellow glass cross embedded in an upthrust, gray slab. It was a cold morning and Zooey, having forgotten a jacket, walked quickly. Brenna, who was shorter than Zooey, gallantly strode along with her as they discussed their Psych 101 test. "I didn't think there would be so much about rats." Brenna adjusted her royal blue beret, pulling it forward, which made her blue eyes even more striking.

Zooey pulled open the heavy door and they went into the vestibule. Dipping their fingers in the tepid holy water they crossed themselves and entered the nave, sitting in a pew in back.

Zooey preferred the mission style church she attended at home with its tiled arches. As a girl she was an ardent Catholic and even wondered if she should become a nun. Freshman year at Holy Name High, she and Brenna belonged to the girls' club, Sodality. Every Saturday at 8:00 a.m. they went to Mass and afterwards ate glazed donuts and drank hot chocolate and discussed the Blessed Virgin and how each of them could be more like her, more pure. Brenna continued through all four years of school but Zooey abruptly dropped out that first spring. Her mother was in the hospital with a heart problem and Zooey lost interest in Sodality.

Now Zooey remembered those meetings as she murmured the Latin responses to prayers led by the priest at the altar in his elaborate brocade vestments and white surplice. She and the other girls in Sodality had worn "scapulars" under their blouses, plastic holy pictures of Mary on a thin ribbon necklace which they never took off. The plastic stuck to her sweaty chest during gym class and the white ribbon became dingy and gray. She couldn't believe she'd worn such a thing—it made her laugh now, a small breathy sound, and Brenna looked over at her.

Zooey looked away. This had happened to them before—out of nowhere one of them would laugh in church and the other would start and they would be in actual pain trying to stifle their laughter. For some reason Zooey remembered what Elizabeth said about *The Razor's Edge*, about—what was the point of anything? She wondered if that's why Elizabeth had not come today.

The priest finished reading the gospel and Zooey realized she hadn't heard a word he said as she sat down in the pew. Oh well. Now he began his sermon and Zooey decided to listen. He was a young priest, good looking and blond, sure of himself.

He began with a lengthy tale about a husband and wife who had wanted to divorce, but in the end were saved by their faith in Christ. Then he elaborated on the gravity of the sin of divorce. In closing, he recited the marriage vows with carefully enunciated authority: "For better or for worse." He said "worse" darkly, evoking depravity. "In sickness and in health," he delivered more hopefully, and then with a stentorian flourish, "Until death do us part!"

This could have set Zooey laughing again but when she glanced at Brenna she seemed rapt, almost tearful. Zooey felt suddenly irritated. For one thing, this priest never had nor ever would be married. What could he possibly know about it? About sex, or living with someone, fighting.

Now he was saying with the same absolute certainty, "God wants you to live within the family. God wants children created in His image. God wants you …"

A sudden sensation chilled Zooey—like a freeze frame, or a flipped switch. She saw with perfect clarity: There was absolutely no way this man knew what God wanted. He was completely deluded. And with that realization, the house of cards fell. All of it—she looked around—the stained glass windows, stations of the cross, statues, candles—a movie set. It meant nothing. It was nothing. She felt panic as tears came to her eyes.

"I've gotta go," she said to Brenna and edged past her and the others in the pew to leave. In the vestibule she saw an elderly priest of the parish standing in his black cassock, waiting for someone or something, but alone at the moment. In her confusion, she rushed to him. "Father." She started to cry. "I've lost my faith."

He looked at her as if she'd said she lost her purse. Startled, then impatient, finally fatigue settled in his eyes. "Say your prayers then. Go along." He looked away.

Dismissed, Zooey walked outside to the front steps of the church. *How's that supposed to help?* His indifference cleared her head. She checked inside herself. Yes. It was still gone. Vanished.

She began the walk home alone—she'd explain to Brenna later, she couldn't think what to tell her now—and a memory filled her: At the beach with friends, she had taken off her scapular and put it under a beach towel before going to the changing room to put on her swim suit. At the end of the day, in her friend's parents' station wagon going home, she realized she didn't have her scapular. It was gone. She'd had it for years and now it was gone. That's how she felt now.

When Zooey walked onto campus it felt odd to her how everything looked exactly as it had an hour ago. As if nothing had changed.

She walked into the suite she shared with Danielle and saw her sitting in bed reading the Sunday paper.

"Hi," Danielle said without looking up. "I made some coffee."

Zooey glanced at the coffee maker on the hall shelf between their two rooms. She felt she had something monumental to tell Danielle and, yet, also that there was nothing to say.

"Thanks," she said and although she didn't often drink coffee she poured herself a cup and stood looking at the bare tree branches through the high hall window.

Danielle and Zooey had met in September when they were assigned to share a suite. Zooey remembered sitting in her bedroom the first night of school with her door slightly ajar half-watching Danielle unpack her two large trunks. It had taken her hours. She smoothed every garment before hanging it up and refolded some for drawers. On her desk she aligned a silver letter opener, pen and paper weight in perfect symmetry. In her drawer she arranged pencils by length. She stopped only for a long phone call from her mother about her father missing a dinner at the country club. Then she alphabetized her books. Her make-up in the bathroom was arranged by color. Now, she had the newspaper stacked neatly in front of her by sections she had or had not read.

"Did you hear about the demonstration in San Francisco next Sunday, about the war?" Danielle asked Zooey, still without looking up.

Zooey turned and brought her coffee into Danielle's room and sat at the end of her bed.

"Elizabeth said something about it."

"Sean's going to go, I can't believe it. He better not get beaten up."

Zooey raised her eyebrows and looked at the wall. It was possible but hard to imagine. Sean, Danielle's boyfriend since the first month of school—she came, she saw, she conquered—was a Greek god on his way to becoming class president and a basketball star. And miraculously he was kind of sweet. Zooey had a crush on him, partly because he always smiled and said hi to her when they crossed paths even though she was not in his league. That she knew Danielle and they were becoming friends was purely the luck of the draw. Danielle seemed to want to take Zooey under her wing sometimes, like Auntie Mame or Pygmalion might.

"Look at this." Danielle spread out the newspaper so Zooey could see photographs of police in riot gear with billy clubs pushing a chaotic crowd of demonstrators. Zooey was more aware of the anti-war movement now that she was at Sanders. They never discussed Vietnam at Holy Name. Her response was to wear black at all times—black sweaters and skirts. Girls weren't allowed to wear pants at Sanders. But Elizabeth said she was going to go to the next demonstration. Maybe she should, too. Instead she found herself saying, "Sean would never get drafted."

"I know, he's got a deferment. He's just against it. The war is wrong." Danielle gave her an open, flat look that said how obvious can it be.

Zooey nodded. "Are you going to go?"

"No, it doesn't look very organized. I wish Sean weren't going."

"Hi girls!" Patti walked in. "Oooh, coffee."

Danielle got up and stretched then walked to her closet. "It's freezing today." She opened the door and looked at her sweaters, each in a transparent plastic bag stacked on the shelf. As she took down a blue cashmere cardigan Zooey saw a bottle peeking out behind the empty bag, clear liquid, a black and white label and red screw cap with a paper seal. Danielle closed the closet door.

"The Jefferson Airplane are at the Fillmore next Saturday," Patti said.

"Sean and I are going. His cousin is here from Berkeley. Oh of course! That's why Sean's going to go to that demonstration. His cousin is trying to turn him into a communist."

"But you just said the war is wrong," Zooey said.

"Well." Danielle shrugged. "I guess his cousin is cool, in a hyper way. You know what?" She looked at Zooey. "He's coming with us to the Fillmore. Why don't you come too, Zooey?"

"Ooh, a double date!" Patti said.

"A blind date, you mean." The thought made Zooey slightly ill, although she was flattered. Having gone to a girls' Catholic high school, she'd rarely dated.

"Come on, it'll be fun!" Patti said. "I'll do your make-up. Rick and I are going."

"There you are!" Brenna walked in. "What happened to you?" she asked Zooey.

"Oh, I—"

"Brenna, tell Zooey she has to go with Sean's cousin to the Fillmore Saturday," Danielle said. "Are you going?"

"Oh. No." Brenna shook her head. "Drew wants to see the new Bergman film."

"I'd like to see that," Zooey said.

"No way! You're coming with us." Patti laughed. "We'll get all dressed up."

"No black, Zooey. You have to look hip, not beat," Danielle said. "You'll like Mark. He's a real brain. He goes to Cal."

It seemed late to Zooey to be getting ready for a date. Seven o'clock. But they weren't even going until 8:00. She sat in front of Patti's vanity mirror. It was Saturday night. Somehow Patti had a single room, one of only two available to freshmen girls at Sanders. Something about her father's name on a donor plaque in the dining hall, Danielle had surmised to Zooey at the beginning of the year.

"Don't move." Patti was breathing lightly in Zooey's face, her parted lips an inch from her nose as she leaned in applying black eyeliner to Zooey's eyelid and making a little black tail where a laugh line would eventually be. Danielle stood on the other side trying to do something with Zooey's shag haircut.

"Well, tell Danielle to quit pulling my hair." Zooey wanted desperately to squirm but was also intrigued by the proximity of Patti's face and the fact that her breath didn't smell at all.

"Danielle, get us something to drink." Patti backed up to look at her work. "Oh my god! The new you."

Zooey looked in the mirror. She didn't think she looked that different. Except for the ridiculous jacket they gave her—white with gold brocade and buttons. There was a towel draped over it while Patti applied the makeup. She was putting on beige eye shadow a shade lighter than the brown of Zooey's eyes. The thick eyeliner did make her eyes look bigger, Zooey thought, or more intense. She stared into the mirror dramatically.

"Yes, yes!" Patti laughed. "Though don't go crazy. Boys don't like crazy."

"Oh, Mark might," Danielle said. "He's so intense. On the other hand, he'll probably just want you to listen to him talk."

"What if he wants sex?" Zooey asked.

"They all do. Just play along," Patti said.

"What do you mean! I don't want to have sex with this guy."

"You don't have to. Are you still a virgin?"

Zooey blushed. Of course she was, weren't they? Then she shrugged.

"She is, she is!" Patti crowed.

"Well, so am I, Patti, you're the only slut in the room, as far as I can tell." Danielle had pulled a paper bag out of her purse and was getting three glasses from the bottom drawer of Patti's dresser. Her pale blonde hair formed a silk curtain as she bent to her task.

Zooey could see Patti's green eyes narrow then harden and she braced herself for something bad. She had never seen Patti and Danielle behave so—sophisticated. Usually they just studied together and joked around or ate together in the dining hall.

But Patti had decided to let the slut comment pass, it seemed. So, she was sleeping with Rick, Zooey thought.

"You've just never been in love, Danielle," Patti finally said.

Danielle handed Patti a glass of vodka and orange juice. "Oh, drink up, Patti. Here's to love." Danielle took a large sip of her drink then handed one to Zooey.

Zooey had never drunk alcohol before. She took a small sip. It had a sharp taste and was too warm. Oh well. She took another sip.

"What should I do with her hair?" Danielle ran her fingers through Zooey's thick uneven hair as Patti started on Zooey's other eye.

"Tease it up, make it big. Here." Patti handed her a comb.

"How about you, Zooey. Where were you for your first kiss?" Danielle asked. Zooey saw her smile at Patti in the mirror. Zooey decided to help them make up after their near argument.

"Oh let's see. I was at a drive-in theatre in the Valley with this guy. He was going to go to Vietnam so we were seeing *True Grit*. He was nice, sort of, though he didn't have a lot to say. He worked at the restaurant where I was a waitress."

Patti made a face at Danielle. Waitress, drive-in. It sounded like a B movie. They knew Zooey was on scholarship and worked in the dining hall but had tried to ignore it.

"He was a fabulous kisser."

Now Patti looked attentive. "What do you mean?"

"His lips were soft but with a sharp little force sometimes."

Danielle and Patti burst into laughter.

"But when I tried to talk to him he would never say anything. Just—'yep,' 'nope.'"

"Well. A lot of guys are like that." Patti laughed again.

"It's so boring," Zooey said.

"You'll love Mark, Zooey, he never shuts up." Danielle set the comb on the counter.

Patti stepped back to look at their work and they all took sips of their drinks. Zooey realized she looked different but wasn't sure if it was good or bad.

"It's not really hippie enough. I think a headband—around her forehead, you know?"

"I don't—" Zooey began.

"If I can wear a granny dress, you can wear a headband." Danielle started going through drawers in Patti's vanity. Zooey watched her and then in the top drawer saw a round diaphragm case. She knew what it was because she'd seen one in a magazine. Zooey reached for her drink and sipped it until it was gone.

"Perfect." Danielle held up a blue paisley ribbon.

"You really think it goes with this majorette jacket?" Zooey asked. "I think I should carry a baton."

"Oh, did you do baton?" Patti asked. "No, I can't see you—"

"Patti, not everyone needs to be a cheerleader." Danielle started to smooth Zooey's hair over the ribbon in a protective way.

"It was drill team! You should have seen us strutting our stuff." Patti put her hands on her hips and pranced across the room, her red pony tail whipping around as she turned her head sharply side to side.

Danielle hooted with laughter. "I remember!" She and Patti had gone to a private high school in Marin together.

Patti started doing jumps and then nearly did the splits.

"Wow," Zooey said. Danielle freshened their drinks.

"Remember Mikey! Talk about a good kisser." Patti picked up her glass. "Did you know he and Janice were fucking their brains out senior year. I walked in on them once! I was walking by the TV room and I don't know why, I turned the doorknob and they were on the floor—"

"What did you do?"

"I laughed so hard. Their faces!"

Zooey started laughing. It sounded like one of the funniest things she'd ever heard. She was feeling so happy. This was really fun.

Patti and Danielle were laughing too, gasping for breath.

"Oh my god!" Patti pointed at Zooey and fell back on the bed laughing harder now. Zooey looked in the mirror and saw her eye make up was smeared down her cheeks. She started laughing again but for a second thought she might start to cry.

"Hurry up! They're going to be here in ten minutes." Patti jumped up and ran to the sink to grab a towel.

Zooey sat in the back seat with Mark as Sean drove his blue Chevrolet across the Golden Gate Bridge at seventy miles an hour. The front windows were open and the radio was blaring *Procol Harem*. Danielle was singing along. Mark smoked a cigarette as he told Zooey about Tom Hayden and SDS.

Zooey was listening and also looking up at the monumental bridge tower silhouetted against the dark sky. She felt like she was in a movie, with her hippie costume, her can of beer and Mark's intense brown eyes bearing down on her as he talked passionately about the importance of stopping the war. She believed him, although she was having trouble keeping the facts straight. Danielle's singing was like the background music. *Dating is fun*, she thought, though she hadn't said much since their introductions in the lobby of the dorm. Sean was sweet to her as always and once Mark established where she was from and what her major was, it was all politics from then on. "He's a Leo," Danielle told her in a loud whisper on the way to the car, teasing Mark who apparently hated astrology.

"Hey, man, you have the tickets?" Sean called back to Mark now.

Mark stopped what he was saying and with his cigarette stuck between his lips patted the sides of his Nehru jacket. "Yeah."

Zooey glanced at Mark's faded jeans, the tear in the knee. He wore Doc Marten boots. He was kind of good looking, though not as good looking as Sean who had thick black ringlets and green Irish eyes. Mark had straight black hair down to his collar in back and a dark strand falling over his forehead. His face was thin with good cheekbones and a straight nose. He hadn't batted an eye at Zooey's wacky outfit when they met under the fluorescent lights of the dorm lobby. She had on flowing harem pants and espadrilles with her majorette jacket and the paisley ribbon on her head, her hair fluffed out all around it. Sean wore sneakers, jeans and a purple tie-dye shirt, and Danielle had on a floor length *huipile* she'd bought in Guatemala on Christmas break which Zooey thought didn't really qualify as a granny dress. But Zooey had lost all self-consciousness halfway into her second screwdriver back in Patti's room and was smiling a lot. She loved how she felt.

The beer she was sipping now was her third drink. She might never have felt quite this good before. Except when she rode her bike downhill really fast when she was a kid. But this was lighter, airier, euphoric.

"Hey, man, you have any grass?" Mark said to Sean.

"No, man. We can score there though."

"Sean." Danielle gave him a disgusted look.

Sean shrugged. "Hey, I'm not into it, man. Basketball season."

"Oh right. Superjock. That's cool, man." Mark gave the side of Sean's head a little punch like a junior would give a freshman.

Sean swerved the car playfully. "Hey, man, I'm driving!" A station wagon in the next lane honked. Danielle had stopped singing and started pushing the buttons on the radio with sharp little jabs.

There was a mass of bodies in front of the Fillmore auditorium, boys and girls swirling around, it appeared to Zooey. The building itself seemed to pulsate as Mark showed their tickets and they squeezed into the crowd at the entrance.

The sound was deafening. The bass alone could have brought down an airplane, Zooey thought. A sudden shrieking guitar riff made her cover her ears then immediately put her hands to her sides. No one had seen her. Sean, Mark and Danielle were all looking around like she was. Projected green amoebae covered the walls. A group of shirtless girls and boys gyrating in a circle just in front of them made it hard to move forward. Zooey watched the white tender skin of the girls' breasts bobbing double-time under the strobe light, and beyond, lying on the floor among carnations and daisies, more half-nude bodies glowed in ultraviolet light.

Mark took Zooey's hand and started forward as she trailed behind him. He made their way like a ship captain forging through shoals, his thin body moving decisively. Zooey appreciated his competence. She couldn't even hear herself think. Sean and Danielle were following in their wake. They threaded through the semi-nude dancers and flower children painting each other. Mark seemed to be heading toward the serious dancers by the stage, but then he veered off toward a side door where there was a blast of fresh air as someone ran out into the dark night. Zooey looked behind her and to her dismay Danielle and Sean were gone. She looked all around but it was hard to see anything clearly with the constant flashing of dark and light. She called Danielle's name and couldn't hear her own voice. She turned to Mark who had let go of her hand and was leaning up against the wall looking around. Then he jerked his head toward the side door and she nodded and they stepped out onto a stone balcony alongside the building. Zooey's whole body relaxed when the door closed behind them and the crashing sound of the band was cut in half.

Mark perched on the cement balustrade surrounding the balcony and lit a cigarette. "Kind of a scene."

"Yeah."

"Want a drink?" He pulled a pint bottle out of his jacket pocket.

"What is it?"

"Southern Comfort. In honor of Janis."

"Oh. She died last year. Wasn't it from drinking this?" Zooey made a face.

Mark looked shocked. Then half smiled. "Heroin. And maybe some of this." He took a swallow and handed Zooey the bottle. She took a gulp. It was sweet.

"You know she had it down about class. That song. *Dialing for Dollars.*"

"*Oh Lord, won't you buy me a Mer Say Deez Benz,*" Zooey sang in a raw voice and laughed at how real her impression sounded. She took another sip from the bottle and handed it to Mark.

He gave her another surprised glance, then laughed, too. "She was one of the greats."

"Yeah." Zooey looked down at her espadrilles. One of them seemed to be coming undone. But then she forgot about it.

"Who I really like is Dylan, though. You heard of the Weathermen?"

"You mean. Like on TV?"

"No, no." Mark took another drink. "Remember how SDS split up?"

Zooey nodded although everything Mark told her on the long drive from Marin was a blur in her mind now. All she saw was an image of how incredible the bridge looked.

"The guys who are escalating against the war—they call themselves the Weathermen. They got it from a Dylan song." He looked off into the trees surrounding the balcony where they stood. "They're going to make it happen," he said, then looked at Zooey. "Are you going to the demonstration tomorrow?"

"Probably." It made sense to her at the moment.

"Cool. You should come with Sean and me."

"Okay."

Zooey looked down the length of the balustrade and saw for the first time bodies in the darkness at the end of the balcony, two it seemed, intertwined.

"*Lay Lady Lay,*" Mark was saying as he followed her gaze. "That's such a great song too." He looked back at Zooey. "You've got such pretty eyes. They're so big."

"Thanks."

He reached an arm out and brought Zooey so she stood face to face with him, standing between his legs as he leaned back against the balustrade. He cocked his head and brought his lips to hers, then brought his other arm up to hold her closer to him. She let herself lean into him, her breasts pushing against his chest as his warm lips kissed hers. She laid her hands on his thighs. After awhile, he brought one hand down her lower back to the base of her spine, inching downward. She felt something give, some liquid melting. A delicious feeling. A thundering roar drowned out the band music as a jet flew low overhead. Zooey startled at the sudden noise and her left foot fell off the high-heeled sole of her espadrille. She jerked to her right then straightened up unsteadily and started to giggle.

"What? What?" Mark said trying to pull her gently and firmly back to him.

"Whoa!" Zooey said as she took a step back stumbling again on her shoe as it remained tied to her ankle but off of her foot. Then she clomped her foot up and down and took a few silly steps. "An octopus has my foot," she said and laughed some more.

Mark looked confused then looked down at Zooey's foot and the half-attached shoe at her ankle. He seemed nonplused. "Your shoe fell off?"

Zooey leaned over and tried to unlace the complicated webbing then giving up she sat on the stone floor and crossed her legs. "I can hardly see," she said, leaning close over her ankle and laughing again. Her harem pants billowed out around her.

"Let's see." Mark knelt down in front of her. He untied the laces and got her shoe all the way off.

The side door opened and a group of people came and stood beside them on the balcony, ignoring the two of them as they focused on the glowing tip of a joint they were passing among themselves while they talked and laughed. Mark looked up as he smelled the musky scent of marijuana. Zooey was putting her espadrille back on, concentrating on the laces and saying "oh my god" under her breath and laughing as she found she couldn't tie a knot.

Mark stood up. "Just a sec," he said to Zooey. He stepped over to join the group. "Hey, man," he nodded at the guy next to him. "Peace."

"Cool," the guy said. He passed Mark the joint when it came by. Mark took a long deep puff and held it as he passed the joint on. He stood affably, smiling and nodding as the group talked and he waited for the joint to come back around to him.

"What's your sign?" a girl in a felt hat and embroidered overalls asked him.

"Leo."

"Groovy."

After his third hit Mark suddenly turned to see if Zooey had fixed her shoe. She was gone. "Oh man." He looked around the balcony then back to the group. "Did you see that chick sitting over there, right there?"

The girl in the felt hat turned to him. "What?"

"The chick. Right there. Putting a shoe on?"

She shook her head.

Zooey was looking for a restroom. Her shoe was on her foot again though a little loose. Back in the auditorium her head started to pound with the throbbing bass and she thought it might explode. Or she wasn't sure what she thought. Her brain seemed on overload all of a sudden, like it was giving off static. It wasn't working right and she wondered if she were going crazy. But maybe she just needed to pee and then find Danielle and Sean.

She headed toward a staircase hoping it led to a restroom. She wondered what Elizabeth would think about all this. She wondered if Elizabeth would think it had a point or if she would be able to make sense of it. The thought of Elizabeth helped calm her down a little. Because being with Mark made her nervous although it was only because he was a boy and boys didn't care, generally, about what girls thought. Where were Danielle and Sean? She looked behind her as she walked up the stairs on her precarious espadrilles but saw only a blur of bodies heaving in the flashing lights.

In the restroom someone was vomiting. There was an empty syringe in the sink. Zooey looked at herself in the mirror and saw her eye make-up formed ghoulish circles around her eyes again. She was no longer in a giggling mood and frowned at the mess. She had to get out of this place. She remembered suddenly last Sunday in church, how she had walked out. How she'd had to get out and now she felt that fuzzy low level static in her mind, like a radio between stations.

Or maybe what would really help is another drink of something. She'd been so happy! It was only a little while ago everything was so great. She turned to wait for an empty stall.

"Then I wandered around for hours looking for them. Danielle finally found me feeling sick in the bathroom," Zooey said.

"Are you serious?" Elizabeth looked shocked.

"Oh, Zooey. How sad." Brenna put her arm around her and gave her a hug.

They were sitting in the cafeteria after Zooey's breakfast shift drinking coffee.

"But it was kind of fun, up until then."

"Until the guy left you sitting on the floor with your shoe."

"I'm not sure why, he just walked over to these kids and started hanging out with them. I really had to pee and didn't want to go up and announce it. Then I couldn't find him. The music was so loud I feel like it etched into my brain, like if you put a needle on my scalp and spun me around it would play back."

Elizabeth laughed. "That's original."

"He should have paid more attention to you," Brenna said.

Zooey began to relax. She had felt ashamed of her failed date.

"He was really apologetic later." She shrugged. "He didn't say much on the ride back, though, he seemed to be sleeping. Anyway. So much for my *blind date*."

"He sounds like an ass." Elizabeth dismissed him with a look of distaste.

"Oh Zo," Brenna said, sounding mournful. Zooey knew why—she was hopeless with boys. Their personalities just didn't fit with hers. Mark was cute, she liked kissing him. But he bored her. It was like going out with her employer, she thought, someone she couldn't talk to. Though she couldn't say this to Elizabeth and Brenna.

"How was the Bergman movie?" she asked Brenna.

"Heavy. I don't like that sinister feeling. But you know, Zo, Drew loved it."

"Wasn't *Nausea* his favorite book?"

"I love Sartre," Elizabeth said.

"I remember when you hated Sartre." Zooey looked at her. "Because you thought you were the first person to think up existentialism. Until you read him in tenth grade."

Brenna laughed but Elizabeth simply shrugged.

"And now you're back into—'life has no meaning.' Why?" Zooey couldn't help worrying that Elizabeth, who lost her mother at age ten, was still searching for an explanation.

"You guys are nuts. I bet if I told you Mark and Sean just walked in," Brenna was looking behind them and waved, "you'd find some meaning."

Elizabeth and Zooey shot around but there was no one there and Brenna laughed.

"Brenna. I wanted to see this odious Mark." Elizabeth was disappointed.

"Maybe you will. Are you going to the demonstration?" Zooey asked.

"I am. Danielle's lending me her car."

"She probably wants you to keep an eye on Sean."

"Oh I don't think so, Zo. Danielle can be so generous," Brenna said.

"Who's coming with me?" Elizabeth stood up.

"I am. I hate this war," Brenna said to Zooey's surprise.

"Where's Drew?"

"He's taking his parents to Mass. He does every Sunday. He's so good to them." Brenna seemed as if she might be about to cry. "I don't want him to get drafted. I couldn't stand it. And he's been talking about joining the Navy."

"What? Let's go. Coming?" Elizabeth looked at Zooey who nodded.

"We're never going to find a place to park." Zooey was driving. She had never seen so many people in one place in her life. People streaming into Golden Gate Park, stopping traffic as they walked in front of cars on busy Lincoln Avenue and then disappearing into the dark cypress trees. It was a day of glittering sunlight, stark lights and darks. She made a sudden left turn and pulled the car to a red curb and parked. Elizabeth objected but Zooey promised it would be alright and she would pay the $20 if they got a ticket.

On the sidewalk they were caught up in a group carrying signs. Zooey saw Brenna look stricken as she read one held by a nun, HOW MANY DEAD? A man in a suit with long side-burns held a banner: U.S. OUT NOW and beside him a barefoot woman in Indian beads carried a flag saying PEACE.

"We should have brought something," Brenna said. The three of them were dressed in skirts and sweaters. Elizabeth had a "Stop the War" button on her cardigan. Zooey wondered where she'd found it.

They followed the stream of people into the park heading toward "hippie hill." Zooey felt with either relief or disappointment she would never see Mark and Sean in this crowd. It was almost frightening how many people there were as they approached the center gathering and saw a small wooden stage at the top of the hill and heard guitar music and a high, beautiful soprano voice that gave Zooey a sudden thrill, a visceral sensation. She stopped a second and Elizabeth glanced at her. Her own eyes were filled with tears, whether for excitement at the huge crowd or the sound of the magnificent voice … Zooey smiled at her. They looked around. Brenna was behind them going through her purse for a few bills to put in a bucket a man with one arm held in front of her. He, too, was barefoot on this brisk January morning, with ragged camouflage pants and an olive drab jersey. The thrilling soprano continued to silence the gathering.

"Let's get closer," Zooey said when Brenna caught up to them.

"I don't know, Zo."

"Come on, Brenna, I want to see the stage." Zooey was already starting ahead.

They snaked through the onlookers in front of them and came to an open patch where people had spread blankets and were sitting and lying in the chilly sunlight. Everywhere on the vivid green grass were sharp black shadows of people's heads, children, picket signs. The singing stopped.

The scene on the stage changed as they got within viewing range. There was a slight man in a priest's collar next to a stocky man in khaki with his thumbs hooked in his belt loops and another man in a pea coat. Someone was speaking into the microphone, a loud angry voice. "Ain't gonna study war no more." The crowd took up the chant. "Ain't gonna study war no more!" Then the young priest set something on fire and was waving it in the air as a roar went up from the crowd. He held it aloft until it seemed it was burning his fingers and the crowd kept roaring.

"What is it?" Brenna asked.

"His draft card," Elizabeth said.

The two veterans on the stage gave the priest rough hugs.

"Who's next?" the loud voice bellowed into the microphone. There was a tense silence as thousands of people waited expectantly and then like a dancer a young man leapt onto the stage. He was tall and wore faded jeans with a tear in one knee and a jean jacket with tin slogan buttons. Someone shouted, "Welcome, brother!" as the young man pulled his wallet from his back pocket. The microphone was put in front of his face as he extracted his card and he looked up at the crowd. He said into the microphone, "We've got to stop this war. Stop the killing of innocent children. Stop the lies! Stop the liars in the White House!" He started waving his draft card and someone gave him a lighter and he set it on fire. He held the burning card high and chanted, "Kissinger lies, thousands die! McNamara lies!" The crowd joined him.

"What do they mean?" Brenna asked.

"The Pentagon Papers," Elizabeth said as she joined in the chant. "Thousands die!" Her voice was angry and her eyes seemed riveted on the young man on stage who was waving his burning card and with his other hand brushed a strand of long black hair off his forehead.

As the flames disappeared the chanting slowed. Zooey looked stunned as she said in a near whisper, "That's Mark."

"What?" Elizabeth said.

"Mark. Sean's cousin."

"Where?"

"On stage."

Zooey pointed at the young man who was moving to the back of the stage now to stand with the others. "That was him."

"You're kidding!"

Zooey shook her head as if in shock.

"Wow," Elizabeth said.

It was nearly 7:00 p.m. when they finally got back to Sanders. The fog had come in, gray, cold and windy.

"I'm starving," Brenna said. "Let's go in the Student Union."

"I've got to give Danielle's keys back," Elizabeth said.

"I'll give them to her later." Zooey pulled open the glass door to the Union.

"Don't forget. You know how fussy she is."

"Sshh," Brenna said. "There she is, give them to her yourself."

Elizabeth and Zooey looked around the student cafe and saw Danielle's long blonde hair as she sat with her back to them at a table in the corner with Sean and Mark.

"Oh no," Zooey said as Elizabeth said, "Oh wow."

"Go on." Brenna shoved them forward.

"I'll go and order our food, what do you want?" Zooey said quickly.

"Grilled cheese and a coke. And you're a chicken," Brenna said.

"Chicken—chicken salad and coffee." Elizabeth still looked at the group and now, Sean, glancing up, waved at her. Zooey went to order as Brenna and Elizabeth smiled and waved back. Danielle turned and, seeing them, made urgent waving motions for them to join her.

When Zooey arrived with a tray piled with food and drinks she was relieved to see the only empty seat was next to Danielle at the opposite end of the table from Mark. The lights felt so bright as she put the tray down but no one seemed to notice her as they talked excitedly about the demonstration.

"I was so pissed!" Danielle was saying then looked up. "Hi Zooey." She smiled.

"Hi there, Zooey," Sean said. Zooey smiled at them and then at Mark who nodded at her with a smile. "Hi."

She sat down and turned to Danielle. "Pissed about what?"

"Mark here," Danielle waved her arm at him, "almost got himself *and Sean* in jail."

"Not Sean—" Mark started to protest.

"No, it was all him," Sean said. "I wasn't throwing any bottles at the cops."

"Cops?" Zooey asked.

"A bunch of them left the demonstration and started marching through the streets," Danielle said. "Then of course the cops came and there was a big confrontation."

"We missed the best part," Elizabeth said dryly. Then she smiled at Mark and Sean.

Mark laughed then sat forward. "I don't know best. We were trying to get to the recruitment center, shut it down." His eyes narrowed. "Then the pigs came like always and, man, I was sick of it."

"We saw you on the stage," Brenna said.

"When he burnt his draft card?" Danielle said. "Guess what. That's the third time he's done it. It was probably an old ticket stub or—"

"Danielle, it's the second time and it was a new card they sent me last year. I burned it the first time when I was eighteen."

"You're going to end up in prison, Mark." Danielle pressed her lips together.

"What happened in the fight with the police?" Zooey asked.

Mark looked at her. "We were saying—it was so intense—they had all this riot gear and clubs, coming at us—"

"It was bitchin', man, Mark picked up this bottle out of a garbage can and hurled it at 'em, bounced off of this guy's helmet." Sean laughed. "He looked like 'whoa! whoa!'" Sean leaned back rolling his eyes in his head.

"Yeah, man, that was so funny." Mark and Sean looked at each other, laughing hard.

"And they didn't do anything to you?" Zooey asked. She glanced at Elizabeth who was studying Mark like he was an unusual shell on the beach.

"No," Sean laughed again, "we were runnin' like hell, you should've seen us!" He and Mark started laughing again, howls and then snorts of laughter.

"I can't believe you, Sean." Danielle was glaring at him though it wasn't all anger. She seemed a little thrilled, to Zooey, charged up.

Zooey took a bite of her hamburger and glanced at Brenna who looked over at her and smiled, then raised her eyebrows as if to say 'can we get out of here?' She had finished her sandwich. Zooey nodded. She ate quickly as she watched the boys do more imitations of police and demonstrators and now they had Danielle laughing and even Elizabeth looked amused. Zooey wiped her mouth with her napkin and stood up. "Got to study," she said vaguely to the group as Brenna said, "Me too."

"Bye, see ya."

"What do you think, Zo? About Mark now?" Brenna asked as they headed to the dorms.

"Well." What could Zooey say. She didn't feel much of anything toward him, sadly. Though he would probably be cool to have for a boyfriend. "I can't believe how intense he is, fighting with the cops and everything. Can you?"

"I think he likes you."

"No he doesn't. After last night."

"He was looking at you when you didn't notice and his eyes got kind of soft—"

Zooey laughed.

Brenna shrugged. "Well." She linked her arm through Zooey's as they crossed the main quad. "You'll find the right guy for you, Zooey."

Zooey felt as if she might cry, a little pull of despair in the bottom of her heart, and then she looked up at the sky. It was still thick with gray fog.

"What would Drew think of that thing with the draft cards?" Zooey asked.

"He would be so mad if he knew I went to this. Don't ever tell him, Zo."

"Doesn't he know you're against the war?"

"But it's not like anyone is really for the war. Except his father, of course. Because he was a Navy pilot."

"Is that why Drew wants to join the Navy?"

"I don't think he wants to. He just thinks he should."

"For his dad?"

"Drew is so sensitive, Zo. He feels it's his duty to serve and he keeps talking about it, since he turned eighteen. He would die if he knew I went to this demonstration."

Brenna stopped as they came to the path to her dorm. "Want to come to our room and study?"

Zooey glanced back toward the Student Union. She didn't want to see Elizabeth or talk anymore about anything that happened this weekend. "I think I'll just go to bed. See you tomorrow, Brenna."

"Sleep well, Zo."

Zooey went further up the hill, following her own path as she listened to the fog horns sounding miles away over the hills where the Pacific Ocean lay. She could see the blurred lights and forms of buildings far ahead. The gray hopelessness she felt inside her seemed mirrored everywhere in the air.

March 1972

The path to the dining hall was lined with blossoming trees. Each intricate pink flower tiny and complex, hundreds and thousands of blossoms in a bright blue sky.

Patti trotted up and fell into step with Zooey. "Hey, brainy, want to pull an all-nighter tonight?"

Zooey looked at her then groaned. "You mean the biology midterm."

"I certainly do. Elizabeth and Brenna's room. Eight o'clock." She glanced at Zooey. "Come on, Zo. Danielle will be there, too."

Zooey nodded and Patti said, "Where you going—Lunch?"

"Film class."

"Oh yeah. I heard it's good. That Mr. Baxter's pretty cute, huh?"

"He's so smart. He gets everything. He—you know, the subtext—what's going on that nobody's really saying." Zooey's eyes lit up and she was smiling now. "Like what people are thinking but don't know they're thinking. That's what the great films show, in the end. You get the audience to think it before the characters figure it out, or you trick the audience into thinking they know but the characters surprise everyone, including themselves."

Patti crinkled her nose. She looked at Zooey, who seemed much happier than she had a minute ago. She thought a second. "You mean, like in *Vertigo* when Kim Novak realizes Jimmy Stewart already killed her, or—how does it go?" She glanced at her watch. "Oh my god! I've got a midterm." She turned and ran across the grass.

"Good luck!" Zooey called after her. She stood a second and looked above her at the pink-white blossoms. The air was soft and warm and for a moment she felt comforted, glad for her film class which was the best thing that happened to her this semester. She wished Elizabeth were taking it, too, as they'd planned but she'd decided on American Literature instead—"something more substantial". Zooey wasn't sure why, they were just freshmen.

She continued up the path, frowning now. She hadn't seen much of Elizabeth since she'd started dating Mark six weeks ago. Every single weekend Elizabeth went to Berkeley or Mark came to Sanders to pick her up, though she never stayed away all night—she wasn't sleeping with him, Zooey didn't think, but she didn't know because it was a touchy subject between them. Zooey didn't have a crush on Mark or care that much, but she still might have gone out with him again if Elizabeth hadn't moved right in on him after that demonstration. It was like she got star struck when he waved his burning draft card, or ticket stub if Danielle was right—up on the stage. Zooey remembered it so vividly—like a scene in a movie, perfect light, all sharp lights and darks and he was so tall in that jeans outfit, the black hair. She could see why Elizabeth had been taken with him—she hadn't yet talked to him and didn't know he could drone on without ever registering if you were listening. You had to nod and say, Oh really? Oh yeah! with even a little inflection, that's all he needed. Even Danielle said he was arrogant, though she wouldn't say that to Sean because Mark and Sean were close. Still, Zooey had a hard time believing Elizabeth had fallen for him. A really hard time. She'd thought Elizabeth was a little more savvy or—what?—too realistic to go for Mark. That she would have the same flat non-feeling about him she herself had. She could not picture Mark *listening*. And she couldn't picture Elizabeth doing the fakey interested thing as he talked on. But maybe Mark really dug Elizabeth. Maybe he did listen to her. Maybe they had deep, intense conversations like Elizabeth and Zooey used to have, where their minds thrilled each other sometimes. Zooey slowed her steps, thinking about it. That joy she could feel talking with Elizabeth—a joy at being understood in your soul. It was something Zooey had never experienced with any boy and, frankly, she didn't believe Elizabeth had either. She didn't believe it—that it was happening for her now, with Mark. Zooey looked up at the blossom tree above her, it was so exquisite, she felt a catch in her heart.

Since she and Elizabeth didn't talk about Mark—because Zooey didn't want to seem like she cared, and she didn't care—about Mark; and Elizabeth seemed to feel a little guilty and want to be breezy and ignore the Mark issue around Zooey—the result was all their conversations were superficial now. Zooey bit her lip. She knew she missed Elizabeth but there was no way to do anything about it. There was no way of telling anyone about any of it.

At ten after eight Zooey knocked on Elizabeth and Brenna's door. Patti swung it open. "Where the hell were you? I thought you were standing us up."

"It's 8:10."

"Listen, you're even more punctual than Danielle and she's been here since 7:45."

Actually, Zooey had wanted to be sure they were all there before she arrived. "Hi! Hi hi hi." She smiled at Brenna, Danielle and Elizabeth and plopped on the end of Brenna's bed with her books in her lap.

"Want a coke, Zo?" Brenna asked as Zooey smiled and took one from her.

"Let's get going, girls. Questions One through Nine at the back of Chapter Six." Danielle started thumbing through her textbook.

"I've got some notes on those," Zooey said.

Elizabeth looked up. "I knew you would."

At 10:30, Patti raised her arms high, drawling "oh my god," as she yawned. "Why is there so much goddamn Latin in biology? If I wanted that I would have taken a foreign language."

"If we want coffee, somebody has to get to the Student Union before 11:00."

"We can use the vending machine."

"That dishwater?"

"Then you go, Danielle."

"I'll go with you, I need to take a walk." Brenna got up.

"I'm going to my dorm and get that notebook I forgot." Patti turned and hurried out the door.

Zooey looked after them as they left then back at her book.

"Well, we may as well take a break until they all get back," Elizabeth said.

Zooey shut her book. "Yeah." She lay into the pillows and looked at the ceiling. Then she sat up. "How's it going with Mark?"

"Oh. Well." Elizabeth smiled. "What do you mean?"

"Are you in love yet?"

"Oh. Well." Elizabeth looked at the open door of the room, then back at Zooey. "I think so, Zooey."

"Really!"

"I know you didn't like him when you went out with him, but—"

"Well, I didn't really get a chance to know him." Zooey picked a piece of lint off her black sweater.

"Meaning?"

"What?"

"Meaning I prevented you from getting to know him?"

"No, no." Zooey couldn't believe they were finally having this conversation and glanced anxiously at the door, afraid the others would come back. "I never would have fallen in love with him."

"Why not?" Elizabeth sounded offended.

"Well, he … he … What is it about him you're in love with?"

Elizabeth looked into the middle distance, her eyes gleaming in a way that made Zooey's heart sink.

"He's so smart," she finally said.

"Something more than that, Elizabeth." Zooey laughed.

"He's good looking."

"Yeah, he is. I like the black hair, how that one bit comes over his forehead."

"He's sexy," Elizabeth said.

"Like?"

"Well, didn't you kiss him that night? You said you did."

"I did."

"And?" Elizabeth looked at Zooey as they sat across from each other on single beds. She raised her eyebrows slightly, as if in challenge, and held her gaze.

Zooey pressed her lips together then smiled. She was thinking of that night, standing between Mark's thighs and leaning into him as she looked at Elizabeth's face. She felt herself warm slightly and licked her lips. "Sexy."

"How? Tell me exactly how." Elizabeth's eyes glittered.

They heard footsteps running down the tiled corridor toward the open door and Patti came in. "Found it."

"That's how I feel," Elizabeth whispered intensely to Zooey then turned quickly to Patti. "Finally. Are you prepared now?"

Patti narrowed her eyes. "What's with you two?"

"Oh we're bored stiff. Where are Brenna and Danielle?" Zooey said. "Did you see them out there?"

Patti made a doubtful face, then turned as they heard footsteps clattering down the corridor. "Here they come."

"Coffee. *Au lait* for you Elizabeth." Danielle handed her a huge Styrofoam cup. "Black for Zooey, of course."

"Where were we? Oh my god. Question fucking Five," Patti said as they all settled back on the beds.

"Patti," Brenna said.

"Pardon my French, dear. Or should I say Latin."

"I like the phylum, species, order—"

"You would, Danielle."

They looked up as a large girl wearing pajamas and big fluffy slippers peeked in their open door. "Oh hi," she said and shuffled on down the hall dragging her feet.

"Sounds like a bean bag chair going down the hall," Patti said.

Danielle laughed.

"She's probably just lonely," Brenna said. "She's a very nice girl."

This set Patti and Danielle laughing so hard Brenna smiled then she and Elizabeth and Zooey started laughing, too. They were snorting and gasping after a minute. Zooey got up to make sure the girl wasn't still in the hall.

"Is she gone?" Patti asked guiltily. Zooey nodded.

"So is it true about her?"

"What?"

"Lesbo," Patti said.

"That's what I heard. Sean said the guys call her Jimmy," Danielle said. "Her name's Ginny, though."

"That's so pathetic," Patti said.

"I wonder what makes people do that." Brenna wrinkled her nose in repugnance. "I mean it's so sick."

"Lez be friends," Patti said ogling Brenna and pretending to reach for her.

"Stop!"

"It is sick," Elizabeth said.

"How do you know?" Zooey asked. "Why are they saying that about her?"

"Sean said a guy saw her kissing that dorky girl—what's her name, she's always shooting baskets in the gym?"

"Kissing her! Where?"

"Behind the gym. Where else?"

This set them all off again. Danielle reached for a tissue to wipe away her tears of laughter.

"You guys, it's past 11:00 and we're only on question Five," Brenna said.

"Wait, wait. I've got this great idea," Danielle said. "You know my dad has that beach house in Mazatlan."

"What are you talking about?" Zooey asked.

"Zooey. My dad has a beach house in Mazatlan. Mexico, dear heart. And listen—Why don't we all go down there for spring break!"

April 1972

The house was bright white stucco, so new it seemed still under construction. It had five bedrooms, three baths, funny villa-esque archways here and there and tiled verandahs as if it couldn't decide if it were in Italy or Spain. The plumbing didn't always work. Two maids came every day, one to clean and one to cook. The views of the Pacific were breathtaking. The water was blue and calm. Not the roiling ocean the girls remembered crashing onto the shores of Northern California this time of year.

Danielle, Zooey and Patti arrived in the morning on an early flight from San Francisco, and Brenna and Elizabeth came from Los Angeles in the afternoon. Now they all sat on an upstairs verandah in hand-painted chairs eating fresh shrimp from a ceramic bowl. Patti was mixing tequila sunrises at the outdoor bar.

"I can't believe it—we're actually here!" Patti gave Danielle a drink. "All of us!" Suddenly she grabbed Brenna's hands and danced her around the patio in a wild polka laughing and Elizabeth grabbed her drink off a side table yelling "Watch out!" as they careened by.

"Earthquake!" Zooey shouted, shaking the center table and rattling the handblown glasses ominously as Danielle laughed and shouted, "Dive for cover!" when Patti and Brenna danced past and fell into their chairs breathless, laughing.

Then Patti jumped up and sat in Elizabeth's lap and sang *Oh Solo Mio* at the top of her lungs. Elizabeth looked shocked but then joined in and all of them started singing *La Cucaracha* in loud raucous voices. Brenna stopped mid-note as she saw a small young Mexican woman standing in the doorway from the verandah to the house.

Danielle looked around. "Oh, Maria. *Ola*." The girls fell silent.

"*La cena*? The dinner?" the Mexican girl asked.

"Oh. In an hour? *Una hora?*" Danielle made a circle with her forefinger. "*Si?*"

"*Si.*" The girl disappeared.

"I can't believe you have a cook—and maids!" Patti said. "We don't have to do *anything.*"

"Except figure out how to talk to them. They speak about three words of English," Danielle said. "Did anyone bring a Spanish dictionary?"

"I did," Zooey said.

They all laughed. "Did you bring your biology book, too, Zo?"

"Don't mention biology," Brenna said.

"Wait until chemistry—my one bad grade in high school." Danielle turned to Zooey. "I suppose you aced it."

"Not really." Then she sat forward. "But you know what I realized. If you think about the elements—the periodic table—it's like its own astrology."

"What?"

"You know how the elements are in columns based on the number of electrons each has? To bond, each one needs to total eight in its outer ring, so, for example, carbon has four and needs four more. It can combine with itself, or four hydrogens, which each have one electron—hydrogen is the exception—the oldest, truest element, so to speak."

"Zooey, Zooey," Patti said.

"No, let her talk," Danielle interrupted. "How is it like astrology?"

"Well, instead of being a Leo you could say someone is Carbon—kind of needy, half complete, giving off a lot of heat and able to link up with all different kinds of people. A needy extrovert. It would describe how someone is in relationships."

"I love it. So what am I?" Danielle asked.

"Hmm. I think Lithium."

"An inert gas?" Elizabeth said. "It self destructs, its half-life—"

"I don't know the future—I meant Lithium only needs one more electron, it already has seven. It's self-sufficient. It can take care of itself."

"Should I say thanks?" Danielle said.

"You are truly bizarre, Zooey," Patti said.

"Well, I think it's interesting," Brenna said.

"So what's Brenna then?" Danielle asked.

"Gold." Zooey got up to get herself another drink. "Anyone ready for another?"

Brenna glanced at Danielle with concern. Danielle shrugged, then said, "I'm still on my second. I think I'll wait."

"What am I, Zooey," Elizabeth said.

Zooey turned around. "Uranium."

"Oh my god, Zooey. The atomic bomb?" Patti spluttered with laughter. Elizabeth regarded Zooey narrowly.

"No, no. Uranium doesn't really bond with anything, but it lasts forever." Zooey took another sip of her drink.

"You never should have discovered booze, Zooey," Patti said into the tense silence.

"Well I guess this is a good time to tell you guys, guess what!" Danielle said. They all looked at her with relief and renewed interest.

"I talked to Sean last night and it turns out he and Mark are driving down here in his dad's Jeep. They left last night and they'll probably get here tomorrow night!"

"So they're going to do it," Elizabeth said.

"Bitchin'," Patti said, though she didn't look happy.

Brenna laughed a little guiltily. "Drew's going to fly down here tomorrow."

"You're kidding. That's cool," Danielle said.

"He's staying at the La Mirada."

"Are Sean and Mark staying here?" Patti asked, looking around. Each of them had taken a bedroom for herself.

"No way, are you kidding? My dad barely agreed to us staying here without a chaperone. Actually … he doesn't know Sean and Mark are coming and I know he'll check with the maids, so we will be seeing them off the premises."

"What about Rick?" Zooey asked Patti.

"He's not coming. We're the spinsters here, Zooey."

The walk to the beach in the morning took only minutes. They passed a hotel painted aqua-blue, then took a little dirt path by a coral tree and magenta bougainvillea to the white sand and blue sea. The girls carried beach towels, baby oil and straw bags with magazines and candy bars from home, each of them in a two-piece suit and flip-flops, laughing and talking about how tan they would be when they got back to Sanders.

As soon as they stepped onto the beach two dark-skinned children in worn shorts came up mumbling inaudibly and holding out copper plates and colorful woven hammocks—a load that seemed to topple them over. Their skinny legs had scabs and their bare feet looked caked in mud.

"Oh my god," Patti said. "The real Mexico. How dare they!"

Brenna was digging in her purse and pulled out some paper money. "How much?' She pointed to a copper plate.

"Brenna, wait a minute, they'll all be on us like a horde of locusts. Don't buy anything."

"I have to, Danielle. Look at them, they're so cute."

Zooey had found her dictionary. "*Quanto es*?" she said to the boy.

"*Vente pesos.*"

Zooey started thumbing through her book.

"It's twenty pesos," Danielle said, resigned, and Brenna pulled out a brown bill.

The little boy grinned and handed her a beautiful engraved copper serving plate.

"It's pretty." Brenna admired it as she followed the others to the water's edge and plopped her stuff in the sand.

"Are you going to use that for a pillow? Or how about a sundial?" Patti asked.

"Won't this look great in our room, Liz?" Brenna said.

"Actually, yes." Elizabeth slathered baby oil on her white legs as she sat on a lavender beach towel.

"We do need a sundial, I forgot my watch. Thirty minutes each side max," Danielle said. "By the way, when did Drew tell you he was coming? What was the secret?"

"Well." Brenna dug her hand into the warm sand, lifting it and letting it trickle down. "There's more to it."

They all looked at her.

"Drew's going to transfer to Annapolis in the fall."

"What? The war might be over—"

"Is this for sure, Brenna?"

"Yes. He only told me after he got his acceptance."

"Will you stay at Sanders?"

"For now. I can still hardly believe it. And so, that's why he's coming." Brenna's eyes filled with tears.

"Oh, Brenna." Zooey patted her arm.

"I can't believe he's voluntarily joining the military," Elizabeth said.

Zooey gave her a warning look. Then she wondered how Drew and Mark would get along.

"It's so hard to imagine the future." Zooey looked around. "Like, what any of us will be doing in five years."

"I better be married," Danielle said. "And I'll probably be pregnant."

"Me too," Patti agreed.

"Drew and I want a lot of kids. We're talking about getting married senior year."

"Oh my god, that's rushing it. I want to party senior year. Then settle down."

"I can't picture you settling down, Patti."

"Listen, I want that ring on my finger." Patti held up her left hand and waggled her ring finger.

"I thought you were going to get a teaching credential," Zooey said.

"Plan B."

"I might go to graduate school. In art history. Did I tell you I'm going to Paris for junior year?" Danielle asked.

"About ten times," Patti said.

"I'm definitely going to graduate school to get a Ph.D.," Elizabeth said.

"Professor Elizabeth Riordan."

Elizabeth smiled.

"What about you, Zooey?"

Zooey bit her lip. An image of herself working in the dining hall sprang to mind. "Well, what are the choices? Nurse or teacher. I hate the sight of blood, so … I'll probably be a teacher."

"Gee, don't get too enthusiastic."

"What about a professor, like Elizabeth?"

"Or what about getting married?"

"First she'd need a boyfriend," Patti said.

"Yeah, Zooey," Danielle said. "When are you going to get together with some guy? When's the last time you even went on a date?" Then she remembered Mark and glanced at Elizabeth, and rushed on, "Anyway, who do you think is cute?"

"Yeah, Zooey," Patti said. "Which guys turn you on?"

Zooey put a finger to the side of her face and said, "Hmm," as if concentrating. Her mind was blank.

"I think Zooey likes gin more than boys these days," Patti said, giving up.

"Can you believe how hot it is? I'm actually sweating! It never gets this hot in Marin," Danielle said.

"Let's go in the water." Zooey jumped up.

"I'll go, just a sec," Brenna said.

"Maybe in a little bit," Patti said as Danielle said, "Never."

"Liz?" Brenna asked.

"Okay. Go ahead. I'll come in a minute."

Zooey looked around as she waited for Brenna and saw more tourists arriving down the beach in front of highrise hotels. They sat on white lounge chairs under thatched-roof canopies Danielle called *palapas*. Others lay on towels by the water. Wandering among them were dark children selling colorful wares. People were splashing in a shallow aqua lagoon scooped from the beach in front of one of the hotels.

"Let's go!" Brenna patted Zooey as she ran past her toward the water. Zooey smiled and ran after her.

"Yikes!" Brenna shrieked as she ran in up to her shins.

"Brenna, it's *warm*." Zooey laughed and swooped her hand across the water sending a big splash Brenna's way then ran ahead and hurled herself headfirst into a wave, jumping up on the other side, waist deep. She looked out to sea, to the hillock of water forming twenty feet in front of her, then swam toward it, then away, then back and waited as it crested showing a thin edge of white foam. As it curled she swam along the front knife edge and felt the breathtaking drop of the wave as it took her and hurtled her toward the shore, her arms stretched out in front of her, she rode the surf all the way to the wet sand of the beach. They were perfect waves, smooth even curls.

Brenna was standing ankle deep in the water laughing as Zooey stood up, her hair straggly and wet, pulling her suit back in position.

"Incredible, Zo! That's looks so fun—teach me!" Brenna said. Her black hair waved around her face, backlit by the sun and her blues eyes reflected the sea as she smiled.

"Come on." Zooey ran back toward the waves. They laughed and splashed their way through the surf feeling the cool water's spray and the dazzling heat of the sun on their skin. The pale blue sky was enormous. Zooey dove through a wave and Brenna followed and soon did catch a wave, shrieking all the way in with delight, then ran back out to the break.

Elizabeth watched as she stood at the edge of the water letting the tide slowly cover her ankles and recede, burying her feet in soft wet sand. She could see the flash of Brenna's green-flowered suit in the high waves. Zooey wore a black suit and looked like a water nymph, her long arms aligned perfectly above her head, hands pointed as she caught a wave.

"Go on, go on!" Patti yelled. Elizabeth turned around. "Get in there!" Patti waved at her to go in the water. Elizabeth laughed and turned back. She took a step forward then hesitated. She heard someone yelling and looked back at Patti and Danielle, but they were sitting talking and it looked like they were eating a candy bar. Elizabeth heard someone yell again and looked in the other direction down the beach toward the hotels. Someone was shouting and pointing and people were standing up looking at the water. No one was in the water, except Zooey and Brenna. A Mexican boy was running toward her on a tear, shouting and pointing. Elizabeth started to run toward him, looking out at where he was pointing. She saw it, about fifty feet beyond the surf break, the black fin. Then she heard him yell, "*Tiburon! Tiburon!*"

Elizabeth started shouting, "Zooey! Brenna! Zooey!" She ran out into the water to her knees but their backs were to her and nothing could be heard above the sound of the waves. The black fin was circling back and Elizabeth dove and swam hard, scrambling against the breaking waves until she finally got close to Brenna. Zooey was further out. "Brenna!" she screamed. Brenna turned around and Elizabeth waved frantically for her to come back, come to shore, "Shark!" Brenna looked at her, confused, but started swimming toward her. Elizabeth was panting and was suddenly knocked over by a wave. Zooey, she thought. She stood up and stared hard at Zooey who was treading water thirty feet ahead and willed her to turn around, to see her. *Look at me Zooey*, she said with her teeth clenched boring her eyes into Zooey's back. Abruptly, Zooey turned her head around. Brenna had reached Elizabeth, shouting, "What's going on, Liz?" as Elizabeth was waving Zooey in and Patti and Danielle had run to the water's edge screaming and signaling them to come in.

"A shark," Elizabeth shouted to Brenna above the surf and pointed at the black fin circling again, ten feet closer and it appeared to be heading toward Zooey. "Oh no!" Brenna screamed, "Zooey!" She started to swim toward her but Elizabeth grabbed her back and then Brenna saw Zooey swimming toward them. They both waved at her and in that second Zooey caught a small wave and swept past them as they turned and half swam, half ran to shore.

"Oh my god!" Patti screamed as the three of them ran from the shallow water and into Patti's and Danielle's open arms. There were hugs and screams as the Mexican boy who had come to warn them stood watching in amazement. Brenna gave him a hug and he laughed then frowned. They insisted he come back to their little camp with them and gave him a candy bar and some pesos, they didn't know how many. They were all talking at once about sharks, swimming, Elizabeth saving them, not realizing that Tiburon meant shark and anything else that came into their minds. They flung themselves back on their towels. Elizabeth was breathing hard and she felt the sun burning into her wet skin finally start to calm her down.

"They're here!" Danielle yelled as she hung up the telephone. "They're staying at the *Buena Vista*. It's half a mile down the beach—we can walk there," she said as she ran onto the verandah where the others were finishing dinner, except Brenna who had already taken a taxi to meet Drew at the airport late that afternoon.

Elizabeth looked slightly stunned and glanced at Patti and then Zooey.

"Oh, well …" Zooey was saying.

"No you don't, Zooey. I'm not going to be the fifth wheel and I want to go out tonight. You're my date, honey." Patti draped an arm across Zooey's shoulders.

Zooey had been picturing the thick novel in her suitcase. The last thing on earth she wanted was to go out with Elizabeth and Mark.

"There'll be six of us Zo, it'll be fun!" Patti said as if reading her mind. "We'll even let you wear all black."

Zooey laughed. She felt a little trapped but she didn't want to be a spoil sport. "Okay." She did want to see more of the town. "Only you have to stick with me, Patti."

"I will, I will!"

A light breeze did little to alleviate the humidity as the four girls walked along the wet sand. The hotels were brightly lit but above them there was no moon in the black sky. They felt soft and warm and damp. Danielle's silky blonde hair was on top of her head, it was driving her crazy, she said. Patti offered to cut it off. Her own red hair was pushed behind her ears and she looked like a pretty elf. Elizabeth's thick, dark hair frizzed slightly, giving her an electric look with her yellow cat's eyes. She wore an iridescent green blouse. Zooey wore a black blouse and linen pants Danielle lent her and *huarache* sandals she'd found in the outdoor market where they went that afternoon. Danielle wore a smocked white shift and black flip flops.

"There are so many stars," Zooey said looking up. "I wonder if we can see the Southern Cross here."

"We should be able to." Elizabeth followed her gaze.

"It's so romantic." Patti sighed and hugged herself and twirled around. "If only Rick could have come."

They heard laughter, tinkling silverware and glasses as they neared the first large hotel and its patio restaurant set under trees and hanging lanterns. On the beach the tide was out and the sound of the surf was gentle compared to that morning when they'd had the scare with the shark. That seemed so long ago now, Zooey thought as she looked out at the waves breaking. They had a hypnotic sound that stirred some kind of … in this heat … the air was so soft. Some kind of longing.

"That's the *Buena Vista*." Danielle pointed ahead. "That big coral tree and the patio, that's the restaurant." *Palapa* roofs on bamboo poles surrounded the tree.

As they approached they could see a swimming pool beyond the orange flowering tree. Blue lit water surrounded a tiny island bar where people in bathing suits sat on submerged stools, drinking. Zooey nervously scanned the patio diners for Mark and Sean.

Heads turned as the four girls appeared from the dark beach, illumined by lantern light—a blonde, a redhead and two brunettes—young, attractive, beautiful.

"*Senoritas, bien venidos!*" A handsome Mexican man in a black suit rushed to greet them, extending his arms as if to embrace them. Zooey looked up and saw there were two parrots sitting in the coral tree, bright yellow, blue and green.

"You like a table? By the sea?" he asked them.

"Thank you." Danielle smiled. "We're meeting someone." She looked around and then saw Sean coming toward them.

The *maitre de* turned as he saw Danielle's eyes light and Sean walk up to her and envelop her in a long embrace.

"Ah. The love. Is a many splendor thing, *si*?"

Patti and Zooey giggled. Elizabeth looked tensely around the restaurant. Then she saw him in the shadow of a *palapa* away from the pool. He smiled and made a beckoning motion with his hand. Sean and Danielle were still gazing into each other's eyes.

Zooey was watching Elizabeth. "I guess that's our table," she said more dryly than she felt.

There was some rearranging and scraping of chairs as the group gathered. Mark had stood and given each of the girls a kiss on the cheek. Elizabeth sat next to him and he took her hand but kept his eyes on the group. "What've you ladies been up to?" he asked.

"Shark hunting," Patti said and the other girls groaned.

"It was so scary," Danielle said as Patti said "My first shark!" and they told the boys the story.

Mark and Sean told how they'd caught someone breaking into their jeep when they slept on the beach in Guaymas the night before but they'd scared him away. "Poor bastard," Mark added. "He's probably starving."

"Hey, man, tell that to my dad," Sean said. "That jeep has to come back perfect. Hey, I hear old Drew's down here."

"Yeah, one look at him and that'll send these people running for the hills."

"Patti." Zooey sounded pained.

Mark glanced at her. "Who's Drew?"

"Brenna's boyfriend," Zooey said. It was the first time she'd actually looked at his face. He looked exactly the same.

"Is it true he's going to Annapolis?" Sean asked. "Some guys said he got a letter."

"Annapolis? Are you kidding me?" Mark's jaw dropped in disbelief.

"Yep. His dad's a Navy man, poor old Drew," Sean said.

"So?" Mark said.

"You guys, you guys. We're in Mexico. The night is young," Patti said. "Let's go dancing!"

Sean laughed.

"Yeah, come on. Have you finished eating?" Danielle took a glass with a little umbrella from in front of Sean's plate. "I want one of these." Then she took a fork and started eating the rest of his dinner.

"Let's go to a club. You can get a drink there, Danielle."

Mark was talking in a low voice to Elizabeth. Zooey thought she heard the word Vietnam. She wondered if Drew would go there.

La Cucaracha was on the main street near the hotel. "Dancing" and "Fiesta" it said in red neon above the door. Inside it was air-conditioned and Danielle swore she wasn't going anywhere else that night. There were café tables and a shiny black dance floor in front of a small stage. It was a thoroughly modern place, Zooey thought, and only half full.

A man in an embroidered gaucho shirt and tooled cowboy boots who looked both slick and handsome came on stage. A keyboard and trap set were behind him and two musicians took their places. "*Bien venidos, señors y señoras, me llamo Carlos …*" He introduced himself and his small band.

The boys were drinking beer and the girls margaritas and they were talking about the differences between Sanders and Cal Berkeley where Mark went to school. Mark seemed to be winning the comparisons contest. But they were silenced as the soft, jazzy background music gave way to an operatic burst of song from Carlos. He held the microphone to his mouth and gazed skyward with closed eyes as he sang truly from the heart, an amazing tenor, about the love of his life. Even Zooey could understand the lyrics, although they were in Spanish. When he sang the words *mi amor* he swept his hand from his groin to his chest as if he were lifting the weight of the world and held the note for what seemed like a full minute. Then he slipped into the next number, *Girl from Ipanema*, soft and sexy.

"He's pretty good," Patti said.

"*Très romantique*," Mark said.

"That's French, Mark." Danielle gave him a disapproving look.

"What's wrong with romance?" Patti wanted to know. There was something about the way Mark had said it.

Zooey sat back in her chair with her eyes closed. The beautiful voice was all she could hear. He was singing about love again, this time in English. *Killing Me Softly*.

She felt it again, as she had on the beach only now it felt unbearable—the longing. It was somewhere deep in her heart, a well of sadness, something breaking and weeping. What she yearned for, deeply, and would never, ever have. And suddenly she saw herself kissing her, she saw her lips on Elizabeth's mouth and sat up abruptly, terrified.

No one seemed to notice because Sean and Danielle were slow dancing and Patti, Mark and Elizabeth were talking in low tones. Zooey was sweating. But no one had read her mind. No one knew. She was still safe. She picked up her drink and held onto it. It wasn't guilt she felt. She'd suspected—known she was like this since seventh grade. She had no doubt her love for Elizabeth was as true and pure as anyone's love. There was nothing wrong with it except she would be destroyed for it and she could never let anyone know or even think about it.

Carlos finished his set. Sean and Danielle came back to the table. "Awake now, Zooey?" Danielle said to her and Zooey blushed.

"I want the Supremes," Patti said. "Where's the dance music? Let's move on."

Just then Carlos pulled a chair up to their table and sat beside Zooey. "May I?"

"Sure, man," Sean said as everyone smiled at him and they made a round of introductions. But he seemed to have eyes only for Zooey. He'd seen her mooning over his singing, Patti would later say. Meanwhile *C.C. Rider* blared out from the stereo system and Patti leapt up to dance, grabbing Sean's hand.

Carlos asked Zooey to dance but they were no sooner on the dance floor than he asked her if she'd like to take a walk, it was so noisy. Zooey assumed he had to be back on stage soon. She said okay.

Outside they walked across the street and through a passage that led to the beach. The tide was coming in and Zooey immediately heard that hypnotic sound of the surf as they strolled slowly along the sand, Carlos talking to her in his charming English. He asked where she was from, how long she would be staying. They talked about his music. His father had been with the Mexican opera and had been grooming him for the opera too, but he had rebelled. Did he regret it? Zooey wondered. Life is not for regrets, he said.

"May I?" He took her hand, and Zooey let him hold it as they strolled along. His speaking voice was as beautiful as his singing voice. Even in the sea air she could smell his cologne or maybe it was the pomade for his hair which stayed so perfectly in place despite the light breeze. She worried for a minute about his expensive boots. He was telling her about his life in the town of Patzcuaro where he'd grown up with his family in the state of Michoacan. It sounded beautiful. Zooey tried to picture it. She looked around and realized they were past the highrise hotels and were coming to a more secluded part of the beach.

"Don't you have to go back?" she asked him.

"No, not yet." He stood still a moment and put his hands on her shoulders to turn her toward him.

"You're not going to sing again?" she asked.

He leaned forward and kissed her, then slipped his arms around her back. She let him. As she felt his lips on hers, his tongue pressuring her to open her mouth, she could hear the rhythmic wash of the waves but now she felt oppressed by the scent of his cologne, by the gently demanding tongue pushing her lips open and the taste of mouthwash. The words *très romantique* passed through her mind. As he began to slip his hand under her blouse searching for her breast she felt numb. She supposed she should go through the motions. Isn't this what she was supposed to do? Shouldn't she try to get used to it? She wasn't quite drunk enough though. She stepped back a little.

Carlos loosened his arms but still held her, whispering into her hair, "Zooey, Zooey, you are so beautiful. When I saw you I knew, this woman, she is for me. She understands my music. She—come on, Zooey—where are you going?"

Zooey had wriggled out of his arms and laughed breathily. She wondered if he did this every night during his break. "When do you sing again?" she asked cheerily.

"In an hour, more … we have time."

"For what?"

"No, no, I mean—you like to walk? Let's walk again." He took her hand and again she let him though she made sure they were going toward the club.

When they returned the others had gone. She could hardly blame them, she hadn't told them she was leaving. Luckily, Carlos' second set was about to begin. Zooey began to wave good-bye to him with an affectionate smile but he dedicated his first song to her so she stood at the door listening and smiling as everyone watched them gaze at each other. When she could, she slipped out and walked back to the house.

She thought she would be glad to be alone and was looking forward to reading her novel between the starched white sheets the maids put on the beds everyday, but as she entered the empty house it felt dark and cavernous. She felt alone in a way that made her understand—she was already ostracized. Pretending was its own exile. She walked out to the verandah overlooking the beach and poured herself a drink.

There was a loud knock on her door. Zooey sat up. "What!"

"Zooey—are you in there? Open up," Patti said.

"It's open." Zooey fell back into the bed. Her head ached and her mouth felt like an empty gin bottle. She put her arm over her eyes. She'd stayed up drinking by herself but still had gone to bed before the others came home.

"I wanted to make sure you weren't in here with Carrrrlos." Patti laughed. Zooey groaned.

"He's pretty cute." Patti plopped on her bed. "In a lounge singer way."

Zooey snorted and took her arm off her eyes and opened them.

"Have fun?"

"It was okay."

"Gee, Zo, enthusiastic as ever."

"He's nice. His father was an opera star." This was true, Zooey thought as she sat up.

"Listen, Zo. I don't want to hang out with the lovebirds anymore. It was kind of a bummer after you left."

"I'm sorry, Patti. The whole thing took me by surprise."

"Oh never mind, I'd do the same, but listen. Last night some people were talking about a cool beach near here, off the beaten track. San Blas. Why don't you and I take the car we rented and go there today. I already asked Danielle—they have the jeep and Brenna has not shown up. She called and she's staying at the hotel with Drew. Chastely, I'm sure."

"Okay." This sounded like fun to Zooey, an adventure with just Patti—getting away from the group.

"You have to drive, though. Have you seen how people drive in this country? I'm surprised we made it from the airport."

At breakfast Danielle greeted Zooey, "*Señorita! Como esta? Donde esta Carrrlos.*" Even Elizabeth laughed. Zooey wondered if Elizabeth was relieved Zooey had finally gone out, so to speak, with another guy, besides Mark.

"So? Tell all, Zooey, don't think you're getting away with the silent thing."

"*Très romantique.*" The words were out before Zooey could stop them.

"I see you didn't learn any Spanish," was all Danielle said, but Elizabeth was studying Zooey's eyes.

The rental car, a blue VW bug, stalled occasionally but Patti said there wouldn't be any stops once they got to the highway outside Mazatlan. Still, it was a challenge in the town traffic to keep the car going. Once they left the beach hotels, any sign of affluence disappeared and the neighborhoods became poverty-stricken. First there were tiny stucco houses with curtains for doors built on high cement curbs lining the pot-holed road. Then dirt alleys with scrap-wood shanties twisted out to distant fields where there were occasionally cows, or garbage. Little children in ragged clothes were playing ball in the dirt streets or just sitting. They were all thin and barefoot. Sometimes when the car stalled a flock of children surrounded it but scattered as soon as the engine re-engaged and the car lurched forward.

"We're not making a lot of progress," Zooey said grimly after the fourth stall.

"Oh, never mind. It's just good to be going somewhere. But, Jesus, look at how these people live," Patti said.

"It makes you wonder." Zooey picked up a little speed as they got out to a more open road.

"What?"

"I mean the difference—people, us, back at the hotels—and then all these poor people. It's their country, supposedly. It's like rich tourists come and take over the only nice part of town. And then all the real people are living in huts wearing rags. Don't you think it's weird?" Zooey turned to Patti.

"Of course. It's awful. I don't know. Danielle says they're used to it."

"Oh. Well that makes it okay." Zooey didn't say more because she knew Patti's family was very wealthy.

"Anyway, I'm glad we're out of there." Patti opened her window as they finally pulled onto the strip of highway leading south.

"But yeah," Patti said. "Danielle can be a snob. It's like, someone can collapse in the street in front of her and she'll just shrug. But if she has a run in her nylon she'll call 911 to bring her a new pair."

Zooey laughed. "She's not that bad. But yeah. She hates to get snags in her nylons."

"Or any imperfection."

"When I move her toothbrush one inch in the bathroom she has a hissy fit."

"Oh my god. I know. That's why I didn't want to room with her and I asked to get my own room."

"I love Danielle though," Zooey said.

"Oh I know, me too. Are you rooming together again next year?"

Zooey shrugged. "Don't know. Haven't talked about it yet."

"I'm keeping my single. Plus, Rick will have his own apartment next year."

Zooey looked at her. "Are you getting married?"

Patti gave a coy smile. "Don't say anything. But we might just live together."

"Wow." Zooey watched the road ahead and then rolled her window down as the day was already very warm. The tropical vegetation bordering the highway was becoming more lush and an occasional burst of orange flowers from a coral tree or a profusion of lavender from a jacaranda made her feel as if they were entering paradise.

"I wish Rick could've come," Patti said. "It's would've been such a blast."

"Why didn't he?"

"He couldn't afford it, and he wouldn't let me pay. He's got a job roofing houses this week. He doesn't really have to be doing that. It's so annoying." Patti glanced at Zooey. "Did your parents help you come here?"

Zooey felt heat rise from her neck to the roots of her hair as her face turned red. "Well. Speaking of 'don't say anything'—Danielle lent me the money." In fact, Danielle had given her the money but Zooey had every intention of paying her back.

"Isn't she funny. She can be so nice sometimes."

"I know."

"Anyway, Rick didn't want to drive down with Sean. They're not friends. Rick isn't a jock. He's more into cars and building stuff—it would've been weird. Especially with that Mark guy. You were smart to hand him off to Elizabeth, Zooey."

Zooey half laughed. "You think so?"

"Oh yeah, he's so full of himself. I'm surprised he even knows anyone else is in the room."

Zooey looked at her. "What does she see in him?"

"He is kind of sexy. In a know-it-all way. But not my type."

"You think he's her type?"

"Who knows what Elizabeth's type is. You should know. Who did she date in high school?"

"She didn't."

"I can see that. She's, like—"

"What?"

"In her head all the time. She's not a sensualist, that's for sure."

"Oh, she is too. She loves nature."

"Nature. I'm talking about sex, Zooey."

"There's sex in nature—haven't you seen *National Geographic*?"

Patti laughed. "Now, Carrrlos. I bet Carrrlos knows about sex." She waggled her eyebrows at Zooey.

"Nope. Still not talking."

"You Catholic girls, I swear. You're like a bunch of nuns. I'd heard Catholic girls could get down and dirty like nobody, but if you guys are any example—"

"I haven't seen Brenna since Drew got here. What kind of nun is that?"

"And she's probably not using birth control because the Pope won't let her."

"I think she's probably really not having sex with him."

"Oh come on."

Zooey shrugged.

"Hey, is that it?" Patti pointed at a small brown sign with the words San Blas and an arrow pointing to the right.

Zooey slowed down and turned on the little rutted road heading through the jungle. As they drove more slowly they could feel the heat envelop them. Patti helped Zooey strip off her blouse as she drove so that she wore just a halter top and wrap-around skirt. Patti wore a white sleeveless sundress and her curly red hair pulled back. She brushed it up off her neck and fanned herself with her hand.

It was at least forty minutes before they finally saw another sign saying San Blas and a little arrow pointing straight ahead.

"Like there's anywhere else to go," Patti said. But they could see tall palms rising above the low green jungle in the distance and Zooey imagined she smelled salt water in the air. After a few miles they saw a small house in a clearing and then a cluster of shacks made of wooden poles and thatched palm-frond roofs. Then ahead the domed, arched towers of a colonial church rose in the sky above the jungle canopy. There was a fork in the road and they headed toward the church. Soon the road turned to cobblestone and a small town square. There was an open air market at one end. Two Indian women with long black braids sat on a bench near the church, one weaving on a hand loom the colorful cloth of Nayarit.

"It's so different here." Zooey slowed the car to creep along the bumpy street.

"Where's the beach?" Patti asked, craning her neck around. "Let's take that road over there?"

"You don't want to stop here?"

"Later. We can come back. Do you want to see the church?" She gave Zooey a puzzled look.

"You mean because it's Catholic?" Zooey laughed. She turned on the road past the church and they drove out of the little village as quickly as they'd arrived. The cobblestones turned to gravel then dirt and they were back in the thick vegetation, surrounded by palms, banana trees, mangrove and flowering vines. Zooey bumped the car along and then brought it to a stop in a clearing where the jungle abruptly fell away to a white sandy beach and they saw a perfect crescent of turquoise bay before them. To the south were marsh and inlets—they could see a wooden canoe disappearing on a narrow waterway into the jungle. But just ahead fine white sand stretched far out to the water and nearby was a restaurant on the beach—tables under a canopy of thatched fronds held up by thin palm poles painted green and yellow.

"Food!" Patti jumped out of the car and slammed the door shut. Zooey gathered up her bag and keys and stood a moment looking at the exquisite sand and pale blue water, the hundreds of coconut palms ringing the bay. She felt her entire body relax in the soft, embracing heat.

"Isn't it gorgeous?" Patti said and headed toward the open-air restaurant on the beach.

It wasn't yet noon and there were only a few locals at one end of the long restaurant. Patti sat down at an empty table in the middle and stretched out her legs, kicking off her sandals as she gazed at the sea. Zooey did the same.

"*Señoritas.*" A thin young man in black shorts and a white shirt came up to their table. "*Bebidos?*"

"*Cerveza, por favor. Dos equis,*" Patti said. Zooey nodded, the same. She was impressed Patti was such a quick learner after just one night on the town.

They had drunk only half their beers, staring at the ocean in a desultory way and murmuring how fabulous it was, when three young men in swimming suits and open cotton shirts came in the restaurant and sat at the table next to them. Their dark skin and hair was glistening as if they'd just been swimming and they were speaking in rapid Spanish, something about fishing—Zooey thought she heard the word *pescado.* But it turned out they were going to eat fish, because when the waiter returned and they ordered she heard the word again. When he came to their table Zooey said she wanted what the young men were having. She hadn't meant it as an invitation but soon they were all sitting at the same table and there were more bottles of beer. Zooey and Patti saw the waiter send a young boy off down the beach toward a man by a wooden boat and realized they may not have even caught the fish yet. But now they were on their second beer and the girls were amazed by how much Spanish they could speak, or at least how they could make themselves understood as Jorje, Miguel and Chema talked to the *gringas* about the beach, the waves, the United States. Chema offered Zooey a cigarette and she took it and put it in her mouth. He lit it for her and she took a puff as she had seen hundreds of others do. She inhaled. It tasted disgusting and made her head feel full of acrid air. She took another puff. Patti was laughing, saying, "Zooey! You don't smoke." The boys were laughing too and cheering her on. "*Que bueno. Mire, mire!*" Soon both girls were smoking *El Capitans* and the boys taught them to blow smoke rings—Patti looked so funny trying to puff out her cheeks, making huge billows of smoke as they laughed until they could hardly speak.

On their third beers, Zooey saw the young boy coming back their way with five silver fish hanging from a small piece of line. Smoke was coming from a grill at one end of the restaurant. By the time the waiter came with five plates of vegetables, rice and the tender grilled fillets of fish, the girls had agreed to go surfing after lunch. The heat was stunning. It was well past noon and the hottest time of day, although a hint of breeze off the water occasionally cooled their sweaty skin. Zooey felt she had never tasted anything as delicious as the barbequed fish she was eating now, covered in lime and salsa, a perfect, succulent flavor. Patti groaned with pleasure tasting the first bite. The boys laughed as they ate quickly.

When Patti and Zooey emerged from the dirty little outhouses set back under the palms in their bathing suits and flip flops the boys were waiting for them, each with his surfboard, and escorted them to the water's edge. Patti would tell everyone back at the house later how Chema had first taught Zooey to smoke and then how to surf. Patti did eventually catch some waves with the help of Jorge and Miguel though she never could stand up on the board, but after an hour or so, Zooey rode her first wave half kneeling, half standing and felt ecstatic. She had never imagined herself on a surf board. They spent hours in the transparent aqua water riding the perfect gentle curls of waves. But after awhile Patti tired of surfing and she and Jorge walked off down the beach together, leaving the three boards for Chema, Miguel and Zooey. After another hour, Zooey was riding the waves standing up with the two boys cheering her loudly, loving that they had taught this *gringa* to surf. Finally, the three of them clambered out of the water and plopped down in the sand. Zooey was exhausted. For the first time, she realized they would have to drive all the way back to Mazatlan and it was a long drive on those bumpy roads. She sat up and looked down the beach for Patti. Nowhere to be seen. She couldn't imagine Patti would actually go make out or something with Jorge, would she? What about Rick? She remembered Danielle calling Patti a slut that time they were getting ready for the Fillmore. Zooey lay back down. She felt a numbness dulling her body as she stared up at the empty sky.

"*Donde esta tu amiga?*" Chema asked her. He laughed, looking around.

"*No se*," Zooey answered. She couldn't imagine how she was going to escape Chema making advances now that Patti had disappeared and she didn't want to hurt him. She liked him and Miguel. They were fun and kind of sweet. And she didn't want to go along with it either. It had hardly been twelve hours since her last boring make out scene. She sighed. That damn Patti!

But then she heard someone calling her name. "Zooooooey!"

Chema touched her shoulder and pointed behind them. Patti and Jorge were walking out from the jungle palms toward the restaurant and Patti waved at them to come and join them. She had her white sundress back on and looked like she was wearing some kind of necklace.

Zooey jumped up and she and Chema and Miguel walked to the shade of the open-air restaurant.

"Jorge and I walked up to the village," Patti told her when they sat at their table and ordered more beers and tortillas. "Look what I got from that woman who was weaving."

"It's beautiful." Zooey felt guilty for her suspicions about Patti and went on at length about how pretty her new necklace was. They were smoking cigarettes again. Now they tasted so good, Zooey thought. She loved inhaling the smoke then letting it flow out in a smooth stream from her lips. She liked holding the cigarette between her two fingers and resting her elbow in the palm of her hand. She wished she had her sunglasses to complete the picture. She knew she had found a friend—*El Capitan*.

By the time Patti and Zooey were in the car heading toward the highway, they had invited the boys to visit them at the house in Mazatlan and given them elaborate instructions on how to get there.

On the long drive the two of them discussed everything that had happened, the fabulous food, the surfing, the town, who was the cutest boy. Patti liked Jorge a lot and started joking about wanting some "papaya"—referring to how the crotch of Jorge's tight bathing suit looked. She loved this joke and moved on from there to Carrrlos jokes. "Carrrlos. He has the 'pa*paya*' for Zooey. Come and taste!"

"Patti. Are you sure you and Jorge just walked to the village and that's all?" Zooey turned to her. To her surprise, Patti's face turned pink. "Patti!"

"He's such a cute guy, Zooey. Do you think only you can have a fling. With Carrrlos?"

"What about Rick?"

"If you tell Rick, I'll kill you." She almost sounded serious. "Do you think Rick doesn't fool around sometimes? I know he does. It'll be different when we're living together. We've got to get it out of our systems now. We're only nineteen, for Christ's sake."

Zooey could see her point—she was only eighteen. But what had they done?

"I didn't give him a blow job or anything," Patti said as if reading Zooey's mind. "I just wanted to kiss him and that was about the extent of it. So let's drop it, okay?"

"Sure."

Their last night in Mazatlan, Zooey was alone at the house reading her novel. She was almost finished, having spent every evening reading while the others went out. Chema and Miguel never came to visit them, happily for Zooey. But Jorge had borrowed his cousin's motor scooter and ridden all the long way to see Patti two days before and he still hadn't gone home. He was staying in their living room but Zooey couldn't help thinking Patti was doing more than kissing to keep Jorge so entranced. Who knew though. Who knew how it really worked. She looked up from her book at the calm blue water. The ocean did seem pacific from here. Zooey felt so happy. There had been some wonderful things about this vacation. The ocean was the best part—swimming in it, watching it, eating the fresh fish from it. And the people here, Mexican people, seemed more friendly than Americans, or relaxed—something different. And the warm sun and water. It did something, something good, to your mind.

Bright, fluffy clouds had blown in along the horizon and now they were turning pale pink, spreading up from the sea until soon the whole sky was rose-colored and then golden. Zooey took a sip of her beer and lit another cigarette. She wished it wasn't supposed to be shameful to be alone because it was such a relief sometimes. She could feel the others feeling sorry for her though. They thought Carlos had dumped her, and then Chema never showed up although Jorge did. But most days she went with the group to the beach and a few would split off to go shopping or on a drive, and in the evenings they all had dinner together here at the house. The cook made great chicken *mole* but nothing yet compared to that grilled fish in San Blas. Tonight though, their last night, everyone wanted to go to a restaurant and Zooey had opted to stay here. Partly because she didn't want to run into Carlos in town, not that he would do anything or even care. It was just awkward. Things were getting harder, now that each of her friends had a boyfriend. How much longer could she make excuses or act like she hadn't met the right guy. She felt herself getting hot and sweaty and took a sip of her beer. She decided to make a drink and walked to the bar on the side of the verandah.

The sky above the flaming red horizon turned dark blue then indigo as the last strata of light disappeared. Stars twinkled, twenty and then a hundred. Zooey stood leaning back against the bar, sipping her gin and tonic as she watched the sky. The air was so warm and lush. Again the words sounded in her head. *Très romantique.*

She closed her eyes, and an image appeared in her mind, she and Elizabeth, arms linked, walking in an orchard on a soft spring day when they were fifteen. Blossom petals, pink and white, were fluttering and falling in a light breeze. They were at Holy Name but alone in the orchard, talking about the Bronte's and who they loved best, Charlotte or Emily. Suddenly Elizabeth recalled the movie, *An Affair to Remember*, and turned to Zooey and said no matter what happened to them, they must meet exactly ten years from that very day at the top of the Eiffel Tower, and they solemnly swore to it. Zooey wondered now if Elizabeth would remember that.

She looked at the sea, at the white line of surf that shone in the moonlight. She wondered why she couldn't have felt more for Mark. He was sexy. She had liked kissing him, though she had been drunk. But she'd never know if she would have liked it anyway, sober. She might have. But then, that wasn't really the issue. Sex wasn't love, being in love. And she had never been in love, for even a second, with a boy. She'd never even had a crush on a movie star, unless she were a woman. That had been her first inkling, back when she was twelve. Her friends were excited about the Beatles or Paul Newman, but she liked Sophia Loren, and even then she'd known not to tell anyone. She took another sip of her drink. This was the most she had let herself think about this in a long time and it was much, much better never to think of it at all. She remembered in high school, feeling agonized, realizing she was homosexual, and almost telling her favorite teacher. Thank god. Thank god she never did.

Zooey jumped a little as she heard the front door downstairs open. She stood perfectly still, listening. Someone was walking across the tile floor, alone. She could hear the clip clip of his shoes. Instinctively she looked out toward the ocean. Then she ran over to the verandah wall to see how far down it was to jump. Twenty feet, but it was sandy below. She thought she heard the footsteps coming up the winding staircase through the center of the house. He must think no one's home, she thought; she hadn't turned on any lights yet. She felt tipsy and couldn't think straight. Was there another way out? How could she escape? She decided to climb onto the wide stucco verandah rail just to be ready. She boosted herself up with her hands and crouched on it, eyeing the sand below. It didn't seem it would be that hard.

"Zooey, what are you doing? Stop that!"

Zooey turned around. It was Elizabeth.

"Oh." Zooey hopped off the rail back on to the verandah. "I thought you were—I don't know, I thought you were a burglar."

Elizabeth gave her a doubtful look. She sat in one of the leather-backed lounge chairs. Her thick dark hair draped over her shoulders like an ermine stole. "That's ridiculous."

Zooey thought she slurred the word slightly. She shrugged and found her drink on the railing beside her. She took a sip. Then she held it up and said to Elizabeth. "Want one?"

"Sure." It came out 'shrrrr'. It wasn't like Elizabeth not to enunciate.

"Where is everybody?" Zooey asked.

"You mean Mark?"

"Well, okay—Mark."

"At his hotel."

Zooey walked over and handed her a gin and tonic and sat next to her in a leather-backed lounge. They both looked out at the starlit ocean. The air was still hot.

"It's over," Elizabeth said.

Zooey took a sip of her drink. Well, well, she thought. But she wasn't sure what to say.

"He's an s.o.b.," Elizabeth said.

"You think?"

"Oh, yeah." She took a long swallow. "So arrogant."

"But, you've been seeing him for three or four months," Zooey said, only implying *and you just now figured that out?*

"I thought he'd—I thought he was different." Elizabeth's face crumpled a little and Zooey thought she was going to cry, but then she lifted her chin, still staring at the sea. She took another sip of her drink and then held it in her lap.

"Different how?" Zooey asked.

"Sensitive. You know."

"You mean, poetic? Artistic?"

"No. He's a poli-sci major. Mr. Rational."

"Well then ..."

"I thought—" Elizabeth glanced at Zooey then back at the water. "That we'd get to know each other. I thought, eventually, he'd be ..." She seemed to be having a hard time clarifying her thoughts. "I don't know. Softer. That he'd be more ..."

"Like a woman?" Zooey asked.

"No!" Elizabeth shouted. "Don't be stupid, Zooey." It sounded like doan-bestooopedzooooey.

"I thought he would *care*," she said and then she did start to cry.

Zooey said nothing.

Then she said, "I'm so sorry, Elizabeth. I'm sorry he hurt you."

Elizabeth stopped herself and held her chin high again. "It's not that. He didn't hurt me. 'Cuz I never really cared about him either. That's the real truth."

"It is?"

"I wanted to care," she said in a hushed voice. "I wanted him to be someone who would make me care."

"Care about … living?"

"I wanted to be in love with him, Zooey! Don't you know why? You of all people should know what I mean."

Zooey narrowed her eyes. She was listening hard. She thought she knew exactly what Elizabeth meant.

"And why couldn't you be in love with him?" Zooey finally asked.

"I told you. He never saw me. He never even saw who I am. And that got boring. Really a damn bore." She looked at Zooey. "He's a bore," she repeated. She seemed to be getting weepy. "You see me, Zooey. You know who I am."

"I know." Zooey's voice was a whisper.

Suddenly Elizabeth got to her feet, swaying slightly. "I'm going to bed." Without looking at Zooey again, she walked carefully and purposefully into the house.

Zooey listened to her footsteps on the tile floor as she went down the hall to her room and closed the door.

June 1972

"You're a natural, Zooey," Danielle said. There were small beads of perspiration on her forehead.

Zooey smiled.

"I mean this just comes naturally to you. You absolutely have to join the team with me next year." Danielle folded down a pleat in her white tennis skirt. "And we have to get you something else to wear." She looked at Zooey in her denim cutoffs and black t-shirt, a wood racquet dangling from her hand.

"Danielle, are you nuts? I've only played a few times." She laughed and reached for some water.

"Listen. Come and stay with me this summer. We'll go to the club every day—you can take lessons from the pro. And we'll play in the fall. When the season starts you will definitely be ready. We'll play doubles together."

Zooey didn't say anything. She did love how she felt right this minute. Her head seemed lighter and clearer than it had in months. She felt almost … happy?

"You'll have to knock off the booze though, Zooey."

Zooey had her head back, drinking the last drops of water from her cup and her eyes saw thin cirrus clouds in the western sky. "Completely?"

"Just a lot less. And less smoking. You should anyway, Zooey, you're turning into a mess. Since Mexico, you seem like a truck going downhill with no brakes. I've been meaning to talk to you about it." Danielle stood still now, looking at her.

Zooey tossed her paper cup in the trash bin next to the iron bench by the net-post where they stood. Her eyes prickled as she fought back whatever she was feeling—dismay, embarrassment, gratitude that Danielle noticed or cared.

"What is it? Was it something about Carlos? Or that thing with Elizabeth and Mark?"

Zooey longed to unburden herself but not only was she too taken by surprise—she felt almost ambushed—but she knew better. "Oh. Stuff is happening at home," she finally said. "My parents. They're fighting."

"Oh." Danielle sat on the bench. "Tell me about it." To Zooey's surprise, she suddenly looked as if she might cry.

Zooey watched her with concern. "What do you mean?"

"Mine. They're awful." Danielle sounded tight, as if the words were costing her.

"They're talking about divorce."

"Really?" Zooey sat down next to her. The noon sun cast short stubby shadows of the two of them on the green court. Zooey studied the grid of stunted lines in the net's shadow.

"I can't stand being at home with them. They don't talk."

"But they might get a divorce?"

Danielle nodded. "I'm sure they will. It's just a matter of months, probably. I guess they were just waiting for me to go away to college. Now they go at each other. It's hell. I hate it. I absolutely hate it." Danielle slammed her racquet against the bench.

"I'm sorry," Zooey said. "It must be so hard on you."

Danielle turned and looked at her, her eyes appeared as light blue as the sky and her pupils were tiny points. "Come and stay with me this summer. We can go to the club every day and play tennis and swim and read. We can go to the movies and restaurants. It could actually be fun, Zooey. And you could get away from your parents, too."

"What about Sean?"

"My father would never let him stay with us. Anyway, he's going to be a camp counselor in Yosemite for eight weeks."

"Okay," Zooey said. Danielle really seemed to want her, or even need her, to come. And it did sound like fun. Her parents would let her go. They weren't really fighting, just working a lot. Her mother's health was better now. If she learned to play tennis, Zooey thought, she could think about that and forget about everything. Maybe it would help. And then she wouldn't have to get a job this summer. It could be good, something good.

"Terrific," Danielle said. She leaned over and gave Zooey a quick hug then stood up. "Let's go get something to eat at the Station." She put the racquets in her tennis bag.

"This is great, Zooey," Danielle said as they walked off the court toward the Student Union. "We can play tennis all summer and then be on the team together next year. We'll room together again, too, right?"

"Yeah, sure." Zooey smiled.

They'd just sat with their hamburgers when Brenna and Elizabeth walked in and waved at them as they went to order food.

"So Elizabeth is going to church again," Danielle said before taking a small bite of her burger.

"I know. Brenna is happy. She hated walking there by herself all the time and Drew's never here on Sundays."

"And you? Are you going back, too?"

Zooey shook her head. "It's gone. I don't believe any of it anymore."

"I never knew how you could in the first place. I wonder what's going on with Elizabeth."

"She said it gives her a sense of belonging."

"I think it has something to do with Mark."

"What? How?"

"You know how she mopes about him—he was the love of her life, she doesn't know what went wrong."

"I know she says that."

"I'm sure she would go out with him again if he weren't with Jill now." Danielle took another small bite then pushed her plate away.

Zooey thought about it. In a way, Elizabeth's going back to church was the same as her saying now that Mark was the love of her life. Both were the delusionary behavior of someone determined to be conventional. Although she doubted that's what Danielle meant.

"Hi you guys." Brenna set down her tray and pulled out a chair. Elizabeth followed with her own tray. They had eggs and toast and juice.

Danielle sat back a little and lit a cigarette. She took a sip of her diet coke.

"How was tennis?" Elizabeth asked.

"Zooey's a natural." Danielle exhaled a thin plume of smoke in an upward direction. "We're going to play all summer at the club and join the team next year."

"I thought you'd never played, Zooey."

"I'm going to learn. It's fun. I love it really." She looked off a moment, remembering how great she felt right after they played.

"You're really going to stay with Danielle?" Elizabeth glanced at Danielle.

"She is. We're going to have a great time."

"What's Sean doing this summer?"

"Camp counselor. Yosemite," Zooey answered for Danielle.

"I can't wait to see you in a little tennis dress," Brenna said, giggling. "Do they have black ones?" They all laughed.

"You're not going to Yosemite to see Sean?" Elizabeth asked Danielle.

"And sleep in one of those tents in the dirt?" Danielle looked at her as if she were demented. She turned to Brenna. "What are you doing this summer?"

Brenna glanced at them shyly. "Drew and I are going on a retreat at Marymount Loyola."

"A retreat. Now, what exactly is a retreat?" Danielle asked.

"There'll be a lot of silent time, and prayer. And discussions on Catholic values in marriage, and the family."

"Oh," Danielle said. "And what will you be doing for fun?"

Brenna laughed. "We're going to Annapolis before school starts, with Drew's parents."

"I repeat, what will you be doing for fun, Brenna? In Mexico we never saw you, and now you're either in the library or with Drew. You guys are getting way too serious. You are coming back to Sanders next year, aren't you?"

Brenna glanced at Elizabeth.

"Brenna!" Zooey cried. "You told me you were."

"I am. But, well—if Drew asked me to marry him now I would. I just want to have his baby. I want children so much, it's all I think about. Drew and his parents think we need to wait until senior year." She looked forlorn. "I'm going to miss him so much. I don't know what I'm going to do."

"I can just see your room next year. One side will be a shrine to Drew and the other a memorial for Mark." Danielle laughed but Elizabeth gave her an angry look. "I'm sorry, Elizabeth, but the two of you are so mopey. Sean's going to be gone all summer and I'm just making other plans. What *are* you going to do this summer, Elizabeth?"

Zooey watched Elizabeth as she drew in on her own cigarette. They all smoked now except Brenna.

"I'm going to a poetry workshop at the University of Iowa."

"Impressive," Danielle said. "Congratulations. Isn't that hard to get in?"

"So you heard from them," Zooey said. "That's great, Elizabeth!"

"You should have applied, too, Zooey," Elizabeth told her.

Zooey wondered now why she hadn't. The thought of going to the poetry workshop at Iowa with Elizabeth seemed thrilling. And yet that's why she hadn't.

"I've got dibs on Zooey for the summer," Danielle said laughing. "We're going to be the stars of the tennis team next year."

July 1972

Zooey curled her toes as she stretched her legs on the chaise lounge, tensing her calves, then relaxing them. She lay on her back, one arm flung over her eyes. Cold droplets of water from the pool dried on her skin, evaporating in the hot sun. Her body had never felt so strong before. Playing tennis three and four hours a day for a month had made her feel incredibly alive. Or maybe it was staying off booze. Probably both.

The sun felt like a narcotic. It burned into her skin. Pinpricks of intense heat penetrated her flesh all over until her brain finally just shut up. She lay perfectly still. A blue jay's raucous noise set off chirping and a fluttering of wings as a songbird was displaced. Zooey flopped her arm at her side and looked up at the sky. Blue, of course, bright blue with the tall palms on the north of Danielle's family estate looking like a post card of Hawaii. Or a film clip because a slight breeze set the huge fronds swaying just noticeably. Danielle was still in the house—the mansion, Zooey thought of it—talking to Sean on the phone. She and Danielle had eaten lunch at the club after four hours of tennis this morning. Ordinarily they would have stayed for the afternoon but Danielle had arranged this call with Sean who didn't often get near a phone in Yosemite.

They spent as much time as they could at the club, or else at the shopping mall or movies. They didn't stay out late or party, though, because they were "in training" as Danielle liked to call it. But they stayed away from the house as much as they could because the tension there was unbearable. You wouldn't think a place with seven bathrooms and god knew how many other rooms could feel so small sometimes. Or so bursting at the seams with the unspoken. It wasn't exactly like hatred, Zooey had decided, because it wasn't violent in that way. It was a sort of rageful disgust she thought. That's what Danielle's mother felt about her husband. As for him, he wasn't there much but when he was, he seemed to feel "who gives a fuck about you" toward both Danielle's mother and Danielle. It was shocking to see how upset Danielle really was because she was always so cool and in control. But Zooey had heard her crying one night in the bathroom. And once when Zooey had her period in the middle of the night and was looking for Kotex she thought she heard Sandrine, Danielle's mother, pacing back and forth in the living room downstairs. In fact, Zooey had stood there and listened for a long time, compelled by some blend of curiosity and sympathy. She could hear the pad-pad-pad-pad-pad of Sandrine's quick footsteps across the sixteen-foot Persian rug, first one way, then the other. Then all of sudden a click-click-click of heels on hardwood and then a cabinet door opening. And then a gurgle-gurgle of liquid, a lot of liquid, being poured into a glass. The click-click-click, and then the pacing on the carpet started up again. Zooey thought she might have listened for as much as an hour. When she heard the click-click-click and then the gurgle-gurgle again she decided to stop her vigil and go back to bed. But the next morning, Sandrine was up at 6:00, in the kitchen, drinking a bottle of Slimfast. Maybe she had never gone to bed.

Sometimes, at the beginning of the month, Sandrine joined Danielle and Zooey at the club for lunch. She knew a lot of people there and seemed to enjoy running into them. She always had a vodka collins with lunch. On these occasions the girls discussed tennis with Sandrine, who took a lot of interest in their progress and the game itself, although she no longer played. She had hurt her knee years ago and it seemed to give her pleasure that Danielle was taking up the sport. Zooey even wondered if this whole thing—Danielle's sudden devotion to tennis, joining the team at school, training Zooey to take it up with her—wasn't something Danielle was doing out of consideration for her mother. Or even with the hope of somehow saving her mother, because although you couldn't really see it—except perhaps in how very thin Sandrine was—her mother seemed to be falling apart. Or falling in on herself. You had a sense of her flailing and clinging to the railing of a sinking ship, even though she never had a single hair out of place and her linen slacks had neatly pressed creases at all times. Her silk blouse tucked in, she looked like she had stepped out of *Vogue* magazine. And Danielle looked just like her, only the collegiate version. Maybe *Mademoiselle*. It was always a shock to Zooey when Danielle broke a sweat on the tennis court and actually had perspiration dripping from her face. She seemed a little desperate in her own right and this made Zooey sad. For one thing, she had come to rely on Danielle—Danielle's total confidence. It was hard to see her getting rattled, for both of their sakes. And they were becoming best friends. Zooey knew she filled some need for Danielle, although she wasn't sure exactly what it was.

Zooey flipped over onto her stomach. She wondered if she should bother to go find the baby oil. But she was already so tan she looked like she might be a different race. She'd had her hair cut shorter, a kind of modified pixie and it was getting so sun bleached it was at least two shades lighter than it had been at the end of school. It was a really good haircut, supervised by Danielle and Sandrine. And Sandrine had given Zooey two tennis dresses from the club shop as a gift when she first arrived. The only way she knew how to repay them was to work as hard as she could on the tennis court. This seemed to really please them. And Jim, the pro they worked with every day, said she had "what it takes". She already was an advanced intermediate, a "4.0" player, he said. That was good enough for the team at Sanders and she hoped by the end of the summer to be a 4.5. In fact, this morning she woke up with an exciting glimmer of hope—what if she did really well on the team and got a tennis scholarship for junior year at Sanders. She knew a friend of Sean's had a tennis scholarship on the men's team. And then she could quit her job at the dining hall! This had so motivated her she played incredibly well this morning. Jim said he was going to start playing her against more people to get her used to different styles of play and to become "match tough". She was ready.

Zooey ran her flat hand down the front of her thigh, smoothing the pleats of her white tennis skirt then looked up across the net. A woman twice her age was bouncing the ball repeatedly in front of her and then began her service motion as Zooey bounced up and down on the balls of her feet. She saw the white orb speeding, spinning toward her and turned her shoulder, racquet back and let it rip, whipping the ball into the back corner of the opposite court. The woman scrambled back, lifting her racquet to slice a backhand return but Zooey was at the net and pounded it cross court for a winner. Game point.

"That's it. That's it!" Jim called from the sideline. "You're looking like Billy Jean King."

Zooey grinned at him. For the last two weeks he had taught her strategy and how to play the net. She preferred to stay at the baseline and whip the ball long and deep to the back corners of the court, but she was getting better at rushing in and attacking a weak ball. Her terry cloth headband was damp with sweat.

As she walked to the side of the court for the change-over, she was panting slightly. But her mind was clear and empty. It's what she loved most about the game, she realized as she took sips from her cup of water at the courtside cooler. There was no place else in the world right now. Just the court, the ball, and herself. She didn't even see her opponent. The goal was to hit the ball with all the speed and power she possibly could. It never happened exactly right, or rarely so, but each ball was another chance. Let me try that again. Again. Again. She couldn't get enough of it. She loved it!

"Are you winning?" Danielle walked up to the low fence at the side of the court where Zooey stood.

"Don't jinx me."

"I'm starving. Hurry up and beat her so we can go to lunch."

Zooey walked back onto the court to serve for the match. She was aware of Danielle watching her and hoped it wouldn't distract her. She tried to close her out of her mind but as she bounced the ball with her racquet on the way to the baseline she couldn't help thinking of watching Danielle serve. Danielle had such an elaborate ritual. She always ran her hand across her forehead once while looking across the net, then she leaned over and bounced the ball one-two-three times, never more, never less, then started her serve. Danielle once told Zooey the thing she loved most about tennis was that everything had to be within the lines—no mess.

Zooey stood at the baseline and began her own service motion, a quick bounce or two then a high ball toss; she leaned back and lunged at it as if cracking a whip. The ball kicked out at a sharp angle but the woman across the net was there and smacked it back. Zooey drove a backhand slice to the opposite corner which the older woman simply couldn't reach.

In a few minutes Zooey won the game at love, and the match. As she shook the woman's hand at the net she saw her for the first time—a less starkly thin version of Sandrine, really. She looked annoyed. This was the part Zooey hated about winning, but the woman barely gave her the time of day as Zooey said, "Good game."

"Great job, Zooey. You're really coming along," Jim said.

"Thanks."

"I'll go with you while you change," Danielle said as Zooey packed up her gear. "We'll see you tomorrow, Jim."

It always came as something of a shock to Zooey how Danielle talked to the people who worked for her family. It wasn't rude or condescending—it was just a "taking for granted". She wondered how Jim felt about it. And how much Sandrine was paying him to train them, to train her, Zooey. She didn't want to think about it. She would just keep working really hard.

As Zooey got dressed after her shower, Danielle sat on the oak bench in the locker room waiting for her with her eyes slightly averted.

"You know what?" Zooey was putting on a clean blouse and not looking at Danielle either. Her voice was almost shy, and Danielle looked up.

"I had this idea a couple weeks ago. Maybe if I did okay, or I mean pretty well on the team this year—maybe I could get a tennis scholarship for junior year." She started rummaging quickly through her locker.

"Zooey. They don't have tennis scholarships for girls. Just for the guys."

"Oh." Zooey shrugged. The dream vanished. She laughed. "You'd think I would have known that."

"Maybe some school somewhere does, but you've got to stay at Sanders. With me. Promise?"

"Sure." Zooey smiled and slung her purse over her shoulder. "Onward."

They walked along a stone path across a lush green lawn to the club restaurant. Inside, a wall of glass windows looked onto the Olympic swimming pool and terra cotta deck where chaise lounges neatly lined each side. Scarlet bougainvillea draped the high wall beyond the pool, a brilliant red in the midday sun.

"I'm thinking of the Cobb salad. I'm so hungry." Danielle pushed her long white-blonde hair behind her shoulder.

"That sounds good." Zooey often ordered whatever Danielle did. It all went on some bill or tab Zooey never saw.

"And iced tea." Neither Danielle nor Zooey touched alcohol since Zooey had arrived in June. Danielle was looking very tan and healthy and her tennis was excellent. She tended to take fewer risks than Zooey but was more consistent. They never kept score when they played with each other though.

"I should have peed in the locker room—I'll be right back. Tell him what I want if he comes," Danielle said.

"Sure." Zooey looked out at the sparkling light in the blue water as she waited for someone to come and take their order. The afternoon crowd hadn't arrived yet and only a few people were swimming, although the restaurant was beginning to fill up.

"Billy Jean King!" someone at the next table said.

Zooey glanced over. Two men her father's age were drinking martinis.

"She's a dyke if I ever saw one."

"Oh come on."

"Tell me," he said matter-of-factly, "what would you do if you got into bed and found her there."

"Oh jeez. If you put it that way."

"All this stuff about women's rights. She's a lesbian."

"Isn't she married?"

"You know Jim, the pro? He knows a couple guys on tour and that's the word. He heard it from them. The husband—he's her beard."

"If that's true it's disgusting. She should be kicked out of the game. All those young girls she's around all the time."

"That's what my wife says."

"Ready to order, Miss?" A middle-aged Mexican man stood on Zooey's other side. She swung around.

"Oh, yes. Thank you. There are two of us. We'll each have a Cobb salad and iced tea." Zooey smiled at him as he jotted down their order. She saw Danielle making her way back across the room between the tables. She looked like a model. Or an actress. Like Tuesday Weld only more formal. Zooey tried to frame her in her mind, how this would look in a movie, the background of bougainvillea and blue swimming pool through the glass, the white-table cloths and well dressed diners, Tuesday Weld moving slowly into the fore-ground, a mysterious look on her face, ready to impart some terrible secret to her companion waiting at the table—something that would change all their lives, all the characters' lives but especially her companion's.

"Where is your mind now, Zooey? You look like you're in a trance." Danielle sat down.

Zooey looked around nervously. She didn't want to embarrass Danielle. "I don't know. Just thinking about … a movie."

"Have you ordered yet?"

"Yeah, he just came."

"Should we see a movie tonight? We deserve one night out this week. We have been so utterly pure, I can't believe it."

Still, it was only 9:30 p.m. when Danielle and Zooey got back from the the-atre. They threw their purses on the living room coffee table and plopped down in two catty-corner stuffed chairs.

"Paul Newman is such a stud," Danielle said. "I am starting to really miss Sean."

"When's he coming back from Yosemite?"

"Two more weeks. I should've gone up there. I could have stayed at the Ahwahnee Lodge, I found out, it's like a real hotel."

"You still could."

"No, no, Zooey. It's all tennis all the time. What's the point now, anyway. He'll be here in thirteen days. Did I tell you he's grown a beard? I told him—that has to go."

"Why?"

Danielle gave her a look both incredulous and kind. "Zooey. Have you ever kissed a guy with a beard?" Then she remembered. "Oh. Mark."

"No, he didn't have a beard then."

They heard someone outside rattling the front door handle then a clattering sound. Zooey jumped up as Danielle turned her head sharply and looked toward the foyer. Then the door opened and Sandrine appeared. She seemed slightly breathless.

"Mom? Where were you? I thought you were upstairs."

"Oh thank god you're back." Sandrine came in the living room and they could see immediately she had been crying. Her eyes were red and she had a smear of mascara dripping from one. "I was driving all over looking for you."

"What?" Danielle stood now. "Mom, you shouldn't be driving."

"Your father's left me." She started sobbing. Danielle walked to her and led her to the couch to sit down. She said nothing but sat rigidly next to her mother and looked straight ahead, her eyes glittering with something Zooey hadn't seen before, a kind of bright, compressed zeal or terror. Sandrine turned to her and Danielle put an arm around her and held her. It was rage. That's what Zooey saw in Danielle's eyes.

Sandrine was trying to pull herself together. She suddenly sat up straight, away from Danielle and pulled some used tissues from the pocket of her culottes. She dabbed at her eyes, blew her nose, and stood up. She began pacing back and forth on the other side of the coffee table as the two girls sat immobile, watching her.

"He left. He left today. He left a note. I found it at dinner. On the dinner table. Anyone could have read it. Jeanine probably read it. Probably had a good laugh. I hate him. I hate that man." She was walking quickly back and forth.

"Mom, Mom. Jeanine's not even here today. It's her day off."

"What do I care!" Sandrine nearly shrieked. "Let him go! Besides, fifty years ago most people were dead by the time they reached his age! She can have him! She can have his nasty little smirk, his sweaty, stinking feet—"

"Mom, Mom. Please!" Danielle was near tears herself. Zooey felt paralyzed.

Sandrine had walked over to the walnut cabinet where the liquor bottles were kept. She fumbled with the skeleton key in the lock and then wrenched it open and started to make herself a drink. She was mumbling something about

ice. Zooey risked a glance at Danielle but Danielle was sitting perfectly still gazing at her mother with a blank stare.

Sandrine took a sip of her drink and then set it down and found her tissues.
She patted her eyes again and was visibly trying to calm herself. She picked up
her drink and turned and faced them. "I'm leaving too."

"Mom."

"We're leaving tomorrow for Paris, Danielle."

"What?"

"We can look at places you might stay for your junior year. It's never too
soon to plan. Your father certainly won't be helping us." She started to pace
again but more slowly. "I've thought this through, Danielle. I've seen it coming, all right."

"Mom."

"This won't be the first night he hasn't slept at home. Hardly." She scoffed.
"Well, he's all hers now." She seemed as if she might cry again but then shook
her head. She stopped and looked at Danielle. "You'd better go pack. Our flight
is at noon."

"Mom!" Danielle cried out the word with a desperation Zooey never
dreamed she would hear from her. She could see it—imagine the awful task of
traveling to Paris with this crazed, distraught woman. Taking care of her for
weeks, months … years. Zooey suddenly felt such relief, such good fortune,
that it was not her job. And just as quickly she realized she had better pack too.
And call her own parents and tell them she was coming home.

"Come upstairs with me, Danielle," Sandrine was saying. Her voice seemed
more pleading than commanding. "We need to find our passports, wherever
your father keeps them, in the study, I don't know." She was starting to pace
again.

"Mom, Mom. Come on. Let's go upstairs." Danielle stood from her chair.
Her eyes were less startled. She was pulling herself together. She turned to
Zooey. For a moment, she looked mournful again. "I'm sorry, Zooey." Then
she turned and walked toward her mother.

At midnight, Zooey still lay in the chaise lounge, the one she realized she
had come to think of as her own, by the pool. It was a beautiful night, moonlit
with the palms silhouetted against the blue-black sky. It was unusually warm
and she could smell the fragrant, sweet jasmine on the picket fence separating
the pool from the grounds. It had been a great summer. With a bad ending.
She felt so terrible for Danielle. Although maybe it was better to have all the

awful tension finally explode. They had tried to ignore it, but really, it was always there. It had probably been driving Danielle crazy. Tennis was their great escape, their great dream. Zooey shrugged as she took a sip of her vodka collins. It had been fun while it lasted, there was no denying. But poor Danielle.

September 1972

Zooey held her own gaze in the mirror. She didn't look as hungover as she felt. Her brown eyes were only slightly bloodshot and she hadn't lost her tan from all those hours on the tennis courts, although weeks had passed since she left Danielle's. She used her brush to tease up her pixie cut. It had grown out well as expensive haircuts often do.

She had their dorm room to herself. Danielle was going to be late coming back to school. She was still in Paris with her mother who had actually been in a hospital there briefly, Danielle's last letter said—malnutrition. That didn't make sense, Zooey thought. Wasn't malnutrition something only poor people in Africa had?

Elizabeth said Sean came back yesterday. He had been in Paris with Danielle the last two weeks and told Elizabeth Danielle was "a wreck". He seemed sympathetic, though, according to Elizabeth. He was still her boyfriend—still in love with her.

Zooey sat at her desk and started looking through the text books she had bought for this semester. She and Elizabeth were taking American poetry together from Mr. Grayson. Elizabeth had written to her often once Zooey went back to her parent's house for the rest of the summer. She absolutely loved Iowa and planned to go to graduate school there after Sanders. She said Zooey should come, too. She seemed to have recovered from the slump she'd been in after Mark.

Zooey half laughed. It was as if that conversation about Mark the last night in Mexico had never happened. Elizabeth was still saying now he was the love of her life, but that she would devote herself to art because love was a lost cause. Zooey's eyes narrowed. She didn't believe it. She couldn't have made up what she felt between Elizabeth and herself. She knew the difference between feelings that went one-way where the other person had no idea, and feelings that went both ways. And then she felt the terror, that it *was* just her and she must never ever tell anyone.

She looked at the anthology for the poetry class. It would help, to read poetry. To write it. To discuss it with Elizabeth. It was something.

"Hey, Zooey, are you in there?" Patti knocked on the door.

"Yeah, come in." Zooey turned and smiled as Patti came to sit in the easy chair next to Zooey's desk. She slumped back into it, stretching her legs in front of her. She was short and the chair seemed to engulf her.

"Are you going to lunch?"

"In a little bit. Are you?"

"I don't know."

"What's wrong?" Zooey looked at Patti's face more closely. She looked as if she could have been crying. Or maybe she was hungover, too. The beer had flowed at the back-to-school party last night. Zooey stayed just long enough to drink a lot of beer but had seen Patti there and they screamed and hugged, happy to see each other. Patti talked about her summer at Lake Tahoe, how great it was when Rick was there and did Zooey miss Carrrrlos, although they could hardly hear each other over the rock band.

Now she looked morose.

"Have you seen Rick?" Zooey asked.

"Oh yeah. He got here this morning."

"What's going on, Patti?"

"Zooey, I can trust you, right?"

"Of course."

"You can't tell anybody. Especially not Elizabeth or Brenna. They're so religious, it's like Elizabeth is more devout than ever—"

"I won't. What is it?"

Patti scrinched her face as if she tasted acid. "My period is late."

"How late?"

"Four weeks."

"Four!"

"I know. But I couldn't deal with it at the lake. My parents, their friends. Rick. I couldn't!"

"What are you going to do?"

Zooey waited but Patti said nothing. "I guess you haven't told Rick."

Patti shook her head.

"Do you want the baby?"

"I kept telling myself, this is not happening, but if it is—I'll just have it. But at school—it's crazy. No. I don't want a baby. It's freaky. I'm freaked. What am I going to do?" She put her head in her hands.

"Have an abortion?"

"Oh god. Oh god. Oh god."

"Why don't you talk to Rick about it, Patti? You guys can figure it out."

"He'd leave me, Zooey." Patti started to cry. Zooey was startled. She thought Rick and Patti were planning to get married. She was silent. Then she stood and found a box of tissues and put it next to Patti on the arm of the chair.

"You've got to help me, Zooey." Patti looked at her. "I can't do it alone. I don't even know where to go. And *nobody* can know. Rick can never find out about this. He thinks I'm on the pill. I couldn't get a refill—I tried but it's not San Francisco up there, this little town. I thought, okay, be careful, you know? And then—I can't believe I fucked up like this! What am I going to do?"

Zooey felt like Patti was handing her a very heavy suitcase to carry indefinitely, but of course she would be there for her, right now. "We could call Planned Parenthood."

It was only the fourth day of the fall semester, a hot, sunny Thursday in early September, when Zooey and Patti drove across the Golden Gate Bridge in Patti's new red Corvette. Her mother had given it to her over the summer. Zooey was driving so she could learn the five-gear stick shift in case Patti was completely out of it when it was time to drive back to Sanders.

They had decided not to go to a private doctor. Patti was terrified of anyone finding out, including her uncle who was a prominent obstetrician in San Francisco. They chose the clinic at the University of California medical school where they hoped she would be anonymous. Zooey glanced at Patti now. Her eyes were closed and her hands clenched in anxiety, about the procedure along with everything else.

Zooey looked across the bay. The city seemed white, all white. Coit Tower looked like a lighthouse amid white houses tumbling down Telegraph Hill, then tall, boxy highrises, also white. The sun was glittering white gold on the blue-green water of the bay. It was a day that could exist only in September, the early autumn light.

Zooey glanced at Patti again. She was taking tiny short breaths. "Patti. It'll be okay. Really. Millions of women do this. It's okay." Though in fact, Zooey would not want to be in Patti's position. Not for anything. Pregnant at age nineteen—it seemed untenable.

They drove through the park and headed up the hill to Parnassus and the UCSF medical center. There was absolutely nowhere to park. The streets were crowded with patients, doctors, students bustling among the tall buildings. Patti's appointment was in fifteen minutes.

"Just park anywhere." Patti seemed to have passed from near panic to dull resignation.

Zooey pulled into a bus stop and cut the engine. Getting out of the car they looked around, a little bewildered. "I think it's over in that building." Zooey pointed ahead. As they approached they saw three picket signs and a small cluster of people. A war protest? Zooey wondered. Up here? But as they got closer she saw one of the signs: a blown up photo of a bloody, gory mass and block letters: Baby Killer. She took a sharp breath. Patti hadn't seen it yet but then she did and stopped where she stood.

"Oh my god." Her voice was small and frightened. They simply stood where they were and then Zooey thought to take Patti's hand. One of the women in the protest group saw them and approached. She seemed to have her church clothes on including a small brimmed hat and a gold cross around her neck.

"Hello girls. Do you know what's going on inside this building?"

A man in a suit stood next to her and handed Patti a leaflet. She took it and she and Zooey stared at it wordlessly. It said "Life and Death" and showed a garbage bag full of late-term aborted fetuses. Patti started to cry. Zooey put her arm around her. The man was quoting statistics to them about murder and babies. To Zooey's amazement, Patti pulled away from her, raised her head and walked toward the glass doors of the clinic, the leaflet still in her hand. She never looked back although the man in the suit followed her, badgering her in a quiet way. Zooey hurried to catch up and followed Patti into the building.

"I think the elevator's over there," she said gently to Patti, pointing down a fluorescent-lit hall to a set of double doors.

When they entered the clinic Patti went to the receptionist and gave her name. Then she laid the leaflet on the desk in front of the young woman.

"Can't you get rid of those religious freaks out there?" She sounded as if she might cry again.

The receptionist sadly shook her head. "First amendment," she said simply. Then, "Would you like me to find a counselor?"

"I just want to get this over with." Patti's voice was tight.

"Someone will be with you shortly to start your paperwork." The receptionist seemed sympathetic and Patti nodded and found a seat on one of the orange plastic chairs.

Zooey was standing by a window at the end of the narrow waiting room. It looked to the north, over dark cypress trees in the park, and the ornate twin-domed spires of the USF basilica, across Victorians and bungalows in the Lake district and on to the bay, still beautifully blue-green and bright, and then across to the Marin Headlands beyond which was Sanders, their school, their dorm. It seemed a million miles away—a foreign country. She glanced back at Patti who was sitting perfectly still, slumped slightly in her chair. She had retreated totally within herself now. She didn't look up at Zooey but Zooey went and sat next to her saying nothing.

It was like a waiting room in a doctor's office anywhere but Zooey felt there was one big difference. They weren't sick. For a moment she wondered, what if she were Patti, what if she had something inside she couldn't even feel. Patti said she didn't feel different at all. It wasn't about her own body, it was some-thing put in there by sex with Rick, and now those people down on the street thought they had a right to it somehow, like Patti owed that thing in herself to the world, or to those people in particular. Zooey could feel her own mind looking down on her self, her body as she sat in the orange chair. She saw her forearms, tan and covered with tiny fine hairs and her hands folded on the small protrusion of her stomach as if she were looking at a doll's stomach or a mannequin's. She swallowed, a gulp of air, because her head felt light.

"Patti Hammond?" A woman had opened a door and stuck her head out.

Patti looked up and stood. As she leaned over to pick up her purse she whis-pered, "Remember, Zooey. This never happened." She turned and followed the woman behind the door.

It was a sunny, late September Saturday, when Sean dropped Elizabeth and Zooey at the bus station in San Rafael.

"I'm glad you and Sean are friends now," Zooey said as they waited in line for the express bus to San Francisco. "He seems lost without Danielle, don't you think?"

"I do. I think something happened in Paris."

"What do you mean?" They moved forward as their bus drove up and Eliza-beth found her ticket in her purse.

"I think they became very close—because Danielle needed Sean for once. She's vulnerable now. He told me her mother had attempted suicide."

Zooey nodded, Danielle had written her about it. In the letter she sounded in control but Zooey remembered her face that last night at home with her mother.

"And now here he is at school and she's on the other side of the world. It must be a terrible loneliness. He comes over to talk about her."

"He's such a sweet guy, too," Zooey said.

They boarded the bus and found two seats. The air-conditioning made them feel they'd entered a refrigerator with loge chairs.

"Well. The one bus with a ventilation system."

"I hope it's not foggy in the city, I forgot a jacket."

"Zooey."

"I woke up late. It's strange to have that suite to myself. I really miss Danielle."

"You and Sean should get together, too. Next time he calls let's meet for coffee."

"Sure."

"Are you trying out for the tennis team next week?"

"Yeah, though I haven't played in a month. But it must be like riding a bicycle."

"Shouldn't you practice?"

"I don't know anyone who plays." Zooey shrugged.

"Brenna and I could try. We're bound to get it back sometimes. It's better than nothing." Elizabeth laughed.

"Would you? I mean, it is better than nothing." She smiled at Elizabeth who said, "Tomorrow. After church we'll meet and you can hit or serve or whatever you do. Patti told me you're very good. Even Danielle's mother told Patti's mother et cetera."

"Really?"

"I never see Patti now. Does she still have the flu?"

"Yeah. She is so bummed. I mean to be sick at the beginning of school and miss her classes." Zooey thought of Patti, who for the past week and a half slept most of every day. She had lost blood during the procedure and they had brought her out in a wheelchair. Zooey helped her to the car and then into the dorm when they got back. Luckily her room was down the hall from Zooey and Danielle's and Zooey looked in on her frequently. But it wasn't loss of blood that was keeping Patti in bed for ten days, Zooey knew. She was depressed.

Elizabeth was looking out her window as the bus sped across the Golden Gate Bridge, at the bay and the city beyond.

"It's so white. Like a white Shangri-La. What is it about the light?" Elizabeth said in wonder.

"I know." Zooey had often thought the same. She asked, "Are you studying in Europe next year, too?"

"I think so. I'm thinking of London."

Zooey felt a sudden sorrow. It would be lonely at Sanders with Danielle and Elizabeth in Europe next year. "Do you think Brenna will make it to senior year before getting married?"

Elizabeth shook her head. "I really don't know. She's like Sean the way she misses Drew, don't you think?"

"It's like she's not really here. She's so sad and preoccupied."

"She joined a pastoral ministry group at Church."

"What?"

"It's a group of mostly older women," Elizabeth explained. "They help poor people in the parish, taking them food and clothing."

"Good for her. I mean, Brenna is a really good person."

"She's a bit of a purist."

"You mean—no drinking, no smoking."

"No sex before marriage even when you're staying in the same hotel room in Mexico with your fiancé."

"So you got that out of her."

"I had to know."

"Did you sleep with Mark?"

"Yes."

Zooey said nothing and Elizabeth was quiet, too. Zooey wondered if Elizabeth had gone to confession and told the priest when she started going to church again but this was a subject on which they remained silent.

"She and Drew are going to be model Republicans," Elizabeth said.

"Except Brenna isn't political and she's too nice to be Republican. Leave that for Drew."

"He's become so much more conservative at Annapolis. He writes long letters about staying the course in Vietnam and justifying all the bombing. It's nauseating."

"How can she stand it?" Zooey asked.

"I think she ignores that part of him. She likes the wounded part of his personality. The part that's hurt and angry at his father."

"Wow. You think?"

"She said once that no one really understands Drew and it breaks her heart, and she loves him so much, et cetera. Brenna likes to save people."

"I know. She's really a good person."

"She is." Elizabeth looked out the window of the bus as they sat at a traffic light on Van Ness Avenue in the city.

"Zooey." She turned to her. "It's your birthday next month. Let's go shopping for your present." Elizabeth's face lit up. "Let's get you a jacket. Then you can give it back to me after today and I'll wrap it up."

"No, no—"

"I know Brenna will go in with me, and Patti too. Come on. It'll be fun."

The bus finally stopped at Market Street and they stood up. Elizabeth gave Zooey a little push out into the aisle. "Let's go. Let's go to the City of Paris and send a post card to Danielle."

Zooey laughed. "Okay."

Off the bus, they immediately headed toward Union Square. The mica in the sidewalks glittered in the bright sun as they walked quickly laughing and thinking of what to say to Danielle and planning to write more cards to their high school friends in Southern California. They stopped at a shop with a post card rack and began spinning it around looking for the most touristy cards they could find. Zooey picked one of The Grotto, a restaurant specializing in crab. "Dear Sister Lourdes, We looked for you to appear here." They burst into laughter, and finally they bought half a dozen and then walked to the beautiful beaux-art building in Union Square.

Stepping inside, they were illuminated by shafts of sunlight in the rotunda. They looked up, high above at the intricate gold, black and white stained-glass dome.

"We're in Paris, Zo," Elizabeth said and for a moment they felt as if they were, gazing at the exquisite work of art backlit by the midday sun.

They strolled around the store and Elizabeth finally spotted what she was looking for and took Zooey's arm to lead her to a display of suede jackets.

"No," Zooey said. "I can't, Elizabeth."

"Please, Zooey."

"I know, how about a sweater? We could go to Macy's and have lunch at Blum's."

Elizabeth looked at Zooey for a moment, reading her. "Okay," she said and smiled.

"Nineteen feels so old." Zooey was examining a french fry on her plate as they sat a table at Blum's.

"I know. And I'll be twenty in November," Elizabeth said. "Time to get married. My aunt says if you're not married by age twenty-two, there's something wrong with you." She laughed and then looked away.

"How old was she when she got married?"

"Twenty-one." They both laughed then.

"I do think Brenna will get married next year. And Danielle, too. It's a definite possibility."

Zooey shrugged. She didn't want to feel the hopelessness that suddenly came over her. She picked up her chocolate shake and sucked on the straw. It was cold and syrupy-tasting, good. But it didn't seem to fill her. She took out the straw, sucked the end, then put her lips to the glass and gulped more down.

"I don't know." Elizabeth picked up her coke and took a sip. "I think I'll join the convent if I don't get married."

"You're kidding, right?"

"No, actually." Elizabeth gave her a steady look. "Think about it, Zooey, it's not a bad life. Remember Sister Mary Angelus?"

"No."

"The pretty one who came senior year to teach music? She told me how much she loved playing the piano and organ and she spent hours every day—"

"Wearing white cardboard around her face and long robes—"

"That's changing—"

"Not fast enough. The rules, Elizabeth. How could you even breathe?"

"It's a disciplined life. A good life. Not good like Brenna, saving people, though I suppose you could be a missionary. But—" Elizabeth looked away for a moment at the noisy diners, the clinking of glasses and flatware, two women erupting in laugher, a child at another table crying.

"Good in what sense?" Zooey asked.

"Good in … the life of the mind."

Zooey looked at her blankly. Then she narrowed her eyes. "Oh. You mean—like Sartre. An intellectual life. I don't think there are many existentialists in the convent." She lifted her napkin to her mouth then put it on the table.

"There are a lot of writers, poets."

"Those are the monks. The nuns are doing the menial work."

"They are not, Zooey. Look at Marymount or Dominican or all the Catholic women's colleges."

"Oh I guess. But couldn't you be a poet without living in a convent?"

"Who'll support me?"

"Your father?" Zooey asked in all seriousness.

Elizabeth shook her head. "Not a chance. I couldn't tolerate that. Believe me, it would be worse than the convent."

For some reason that reminded Zooey. "The post cards. Let's write to Danielle."

After lunch, Elizabeth bought Zooey a sweater for her birthday and a skirt and shoes for herself. Outside again, in Union Square, the day was still bright and warm. They followed the path among flower beds and tall palms toward Powell Street to catch a cable car to Fisherman's Wharf where they planned to have dinner and then take the ferry back to Marin. A block from the huge wooden turntable where the cable cars turned to climb the hill they saw picket signs raised above the crowd of people in line. Zooey felt a catch in her throat as Elizabeth shaded her eyes with her hand to see the crowd better, looking for Mark, Zooey assumed. But Elizabeth said, "Doesn't it seem like you can't turn a corner anymore without somebody demonstrating about something."

"What is it? The war?" Zooey tried to read a sign, silently hoping it did not have pictures of dead babies.

As they got closer they saw that, separate from the line of people waiting for a cable car, the protesters were gathered in a circle and they were women, all of them. Mostly young but some Zooey's mother's age. One sign said, "EQUAL RIGHTS FOR WOMEN NOW!" And before she could read the other signs, Zooey saw one woman at the center waving a flaming bra over her head. She had actually set a bra on fire. Zooey burst out laughing. She looked at Elizabeth whose lips were set in a grim line as she took in the sight. Then they heard the rumble of the cable car as it appeared from up the hill and rushed to get in line. In seconds they bustled into the crowd and managed to jump on and grab a pole as the cable car finished its 180 degree turn while the conductor ratcheted the huge lever in the floor and another rang the bell frantically for everyone to get out of the way. They lurched forward and Zooey, perched on the outside running board, turned to watch the women. Some had very short hair and wore jeans, sandals and flannel shirts while others looked like hippies or women at anti-war demonstrations. Zooey peered at one woman in jeans, boots and a colorful vest over her cotton shirt. She had long curly black hair and looked so familiar—Zooey couldn't believe it—it was Molly, from her film class last semester, wasn't it?

"Look, look," she said to Elizabeth, but Elizabeth was looking ahead toward Nob Hill and the Fairmont Hotel with her back to the crowd on Market Street and didn't seem to hear her. Zooey was gripping the pole to stay on board the lurching car with one hand and holding her purse and sweater bag in the other so she couldn't nudge Elizabeth or get her attention. She wanted Elizabeth to see Molly, to verify it was her—she had met her once after class. "Elizabeth!" Zooey screamed at her and was sure she could hear her even though the women were chanting now, E.R.A., E.R.A., and the cables were grinding and groaning under the tracks and the tourists were all talking and laughing. Elizabeth kept her back to her, looking straight ahead as the car climbed the steep hill block by block and people jumped on and off at the intersections, the bell ringing noisily and the conductor clanging his change machine collecting fares. Zooey watched the demonstrators recede further and further into the distance until they looked like miniatures in a distant tableau.

At the top of Nob Hill Elizabeth finally turned to her. "Fog," she said. Zooey turned to look at the western horizon and saw the white massive fog bank lying across the coastal edge of the city, rolling just perceptibly toward them. "Aren't you glad you have a sweater?" Elizabeth smiled at her, a warm, caring smile. Zooey smiled back. "Yes."

October 1972

Zooey stacked one more syrupy plate on the white plastic tray then hefted it to her chest, cradling it in front of her, and headed to the kitchen. The aluminum carts with wheels were in short supply today for some reason. Still she thought she would get out by 11:00. Though there was no reason to hurry, she had no plans. Brenna and Elizabeth were going to an annual celebration at church. And Patti, who seemed more herself lately, was going to a football game in Berkeley with Rick. Zooey thought she might take the bus to town and see a movie. She clattered her tray down on the steel counter and Manolo started spraying the dishes and stacking them on the conveyor belt running to the dishwasher. He nodded at her, a nod she was familiar with that meant she could go now and she smiled and reached behind her to untie her apron.

Outside she headed across the quad toward her dorm. It was definitely an autumn day, breezy and cool. Bright light cut stark shadows of golden-leafed maple trees onto the perfect green lawn.

"Hi Zooey." Sean walked over to her from the adjoining path. She hadn't seen him and looked up, surprised.

"Hi." She smiled at him as he fell in step beside her.

"Where you headed?"

"Just back to the dorm."

"I talked to Danielle last night. She wanted to know if you made the tennis team?" He grinned at her. "She was sure you would. How'd it go?"

"I did. I was nervous at first but it went fine. Once I started playing I forgot it was a test."

"Yeah. Isn't that cool? That's how I feel playing basketball, once I start, the game's on, there's nothing else in my head."

"Yeah, exactly. That's one of the things I love most about playing."

"Me too. Especially if you've got a problem or something. You go on the court. Boom. It's gone."

"How are you doing?" Zooey asked. "I mean. Any idea when Danielle is coming back?"

They had reached the library where the paths diverged to the dorms and they stood for a moment.

"Hey listen," Sean said. "I'm driving over to the headlands for a little while to hike around. Want to go?"

"Sure."

They switched direction and headed toward the parking lot.

Sean had a maroon Ford Falcon that used to be his older brother's. He opened the passenger door for her and she got in.

"Oh wow," Sean said as they were pulling out of the lot. He stopped the car and looked at her. "Do you care if we pick up my cousin, Mark? He's in Sausalito, it'll just take a minute. But, I forgot—"

"Oh what. You mean that time we went out a year ago? That's so over." She laughed.

Sean smiled, relieved, and put the car into gear. He started to tell Zooey how Danielle was doing, that it looked like she wouldn't be back until after the holidays since she'd already missed so much of this semester. Her mother still wasn't well and they were going to stay with her mother's sister in Massachusetts for awhile. Her father had filed for divorce. Most of this Zooey already knew from Danielle's letters. She was a little shocked and preoccupied with the idea she was suddenly going hiking with Sean and Mark, of all people, and she was also very curious, excited. She wondered if Elizabeth would want to hear about it or not.

Mark was sitting on the deck of Ondine's drinking a beer. Zooey realized he was a senior now, twenty-one, and could actually buy a drink legally. What a luxury. For the first time since she and Danielle stopped smoking last summer Zooey was dying for a cigarette. Sean drove through the parking lot and honked the horn and waved until Mark looked around and saw him. He downed his beer and put some money on the table. He hadn't seen Zooey yet. He peered at the windshield as he came up to the car to see who was sitting next to Sean and then jumped in the backseat.

"Hi." He grinned at them both. Zooey realized he either didn't recognize her or didn't remember her name which was a relief of sorts. She turned around and smiled at him.

"Mark, do you remember Zooey? Danielle's roommate?" Sean glanced at him in the rear view mirror as he drove back onto Sausalito's main street and headed south.

"Sure. How's it going, Zooey?"

"Pretty good. How's Berkeley?"

"Oh man. There's some heavy shit coming down. Smoke?" He pulled a pack of Camels from his shirt pocket.

"No thanks." Sean and Zooey passed. Zooey glanced at Mark as he lit his cigarette. He was more good-looking than she remembered. Maybe it was the hollows in his cheeks as he inhaled on his cigarette to light it. The strand of black hair still fell across his forehead and he had a beard but it was neatly trimmed, not the shaggy kind. She could see a little why Elizabeth had tried—or believed herself—to be in love with him. But now he was telling them in detail about a demonstration he had been to the day before and what some of the speakers said and what he did and didn't agree with.

"Bobby Seale, though, man. He is so right on. It's a crime what the FBI did to the Black Panther Party. He's going to run for Mayor of Oakland now, man. I guess that's cool." Mark blew out a stream of smoke. "There has got to be more white support for the Black Liberation Movement, though, man. They are the vanguard of the left in this country."

"Aren't you still in that group?" Sean asked. "Prairie Fire?" He glanced at Zooey. "Mark's getting more and more radical. I can hardly hang out with him anymore, he keeps trying to convert me."

"Listen, man. This country is on the verge of armed struggle. You have got to choose sides one of these days."

Zooey turned and looked at Mark. His brown eyes looked serious, sad. "Armed struggle?" she asked.

"Absolutely. The contradictions are intensifying. It's not only this country, it's around the world. The FUPI in Puerto Rico. The BLM here. Cuba. Mozambique. The people's liberation movements, and we have to get behind it, man. We can't just sit around on our asses living off our white-skinned privilege."

"Mark. You gave me this rap a couple weeks ago, man." Sean laughed. He had taken a road south of Sausalito winding through the Marin headlands. Now he pulled the car into a small dirt lot high on a bluff with a view of the bay and the ocean. He cut the engine. "You said you wanted to cool out, right? Go on a hike?"

"Yeah. Yeah, man. That's cool." He ran his hand through his hair.

Sean and Zooey opened their doors and stood outside. They waited while Mark rustled in his pockets, looking for something, and then got out of the car. The wind off the ocean whipped through Sean's long black curls, blowing them back from his face and he looked like Jason the Argonaut gazing out to sea as he sat on the hood of his car waiting for Mark. Zooey felt the wind lifting her short hair straight up on her head. She imagined she looked like a scarecrow. Their jackets fluttered and billowed in the wind as Mark joined them and they started off along the trail. No one said anything—it was as if words would be blown away in the wind before they reached anyone's ears. Zooey looked out at the Golden Gate Bridge which appeared monumental, as always, above the choppy bay and sea. They fell into single file, Sean, then Zooey followed by Mark, and took a side trail, no more than a foot path, going steeply down toward a small cove below. The boys were wearing sneakers but Zooey had on loafers and she stumbled a little on some loose rock. Mark shot out a hand from behind to steady her and she said thanks as she righted herself. She was careful not to slip again. The wind abated as they got off the high, exposed ridge and she felt she could finally hear herself think. She wondered where exactly they were going.

The path evened out two-thirds of the way down the incline then dropped again in a sharp hairpin turn to the small sandy beach below. There was a pile of rocks and rubble at the bottom and Sean turned and took Zooey's hand to help her down. He let go after she'd hopped down safely onto the sand. Mark followed her and they walked over to the sunny side of the tiny beach and sat against the cliff wall.

"Good thing you're not afraid of heights." Sean grinned at her.

"No kidding."

"I love this place," Mark said. "It's like, a million miles away. We're so lucky." He looked out at the surf breaking in wild, foaming cross-currents thirty feet in front of them. Again, Zooey thought he looked sad. She wondered where his girlfriend was. Her eyes scanned the horizon and she realized he was right. They could be anywhere in the world. The bridge and San Francisco weren't visible beyond the cliff walls surrounding them, only the slice of wild ocean and bright blue sky directly ahead.

Mark was rummaging in his jacket pockets again and took out a tiny tin foil packet. He opened one end and extracted a hand-rolled cigarette, a joint, Zooey realized. The ocean breeze, much milder here in the protected cove, ruffled his hair. It took him a few seconds to light the joint. He inhaled on it deeply and held his breath for what seemed like a full minute. Then he held the joint out to Sean who, to Zooey's surprise, accepted it and inhaled a deep drag in a practiced way. Zooey knew Danielle would be angry he was smoking grass and as if reading her mind Sean passed the joint back to Mark and said to her, "Practice doesn't start for a couple weeks. I never do grass in the season."

"Sure." Zooey shrugged and smiled. It wasn't her business. The tennis team didn't start for a couple weeks either and she intended to quit drinking again when it did although it seemed much more daunting now than last summer with Danielle. Not that she drank much, just weekends when someone in the dorm had a bottle or there was a party somewhere she'd go to with kids she hardly knew.

Mark had taken another toke and now held the joint out to Zooey. She reached and took it from him and put it to her lips and inhaled. She knew not to take a huge puff and start coughing and choking and also cigarettes had inured her to the burning sensation she felt as she pulled in the harsh smoke and held it. She passed the joint to Sean, who smiled at her as if to say, "What the hell. For now." She smiled her agreement. They knew they wouldn't tell Danielle.

"I met a black chick," Mark said to Sean out of nowhere after his fourth toke. His voice was tight and choked as he tried to keep the smoke in his lungs and talk at the same time while putting a serrated clamp on the end of the joint. He passed it to Zooey who was staring at him spellbound and suddenly burst out laughing. His voice sounded so funny! She was trying to stifle it but another splutter erupted from her closed lips and she bent over, her head nearly in her lap and her hand over her mouth. At the sight of her Sean started laughing, a funny wheezing sound as he too tried to stop and couldn't. He had tears in his eyes. Mark stared at one of them, then the other. "You guys are nuts." He started to laugh too though he didn't know what was funny but the sight of them was ridiculous. "How fucked up are you?" He shook his head, laughing. "You novices."

Sean finally straightened up and wiped his eyes and Zooey had gone silent although she couldn't look at either of them. "Where's Jill, man?" Sean asked.

"She's moving to Boston. She got some internship and, anyway, it was over." Mark took a long last drag on what was left of the joint. Then he shrugged.

Zooey could hear them talking about Jill but while she was staring at the sand she'd found an incredible thing, a sea shell that must have been hundreds—thousands of years old. She held it up to the light and gazed at it. It had swirl after swirl after swirl going around and around and around and she realized that, beyond a doubt, she was seeing infinity.

"Whatcha got, Zooey?" Mark had glanced over at her.

"This incredible thing." She still held it up in front of her face, looking at it in awe against the backdrop of the ocean.

"That shell?" Sean asked.

"Can you believe it?" She looked over at him and handed it to him. He held it up to the horizon as she had, looking at it.

"Wow. Oh man." He sounded awe struck.

"Let me see," Mark said but Sean was transfixed by the shell. Zooey was looking at a piece of seaweed now, a dark amber bulb glistening in the light. She picked it up, too. It was slimy and gritty where it was covered by sand. She dropped it.

Sean finally handed Mark the shell and he held it up to the light. "Cool.

"So I met this black chick," Mark started again, looking at Sean who seemed to be listening now. "And we went to get a beer after that demonstration on Telegraph, some bar. We're sitting there. She's cool. A groovy chick, man, and I'm kind of getting into her. Then these cats walk up. Four black guys. And they, like, surround the table and tell her she needs to come with them, she ain't got no right bein' with no white devil son of a bitch, blah blah. It was sick, man. It freaked me out. What is that about? Here I am, doing all this shit for the BLM. I was so pissed."

"Did she go?" Sean asked.

Zooey was looking at Mark as he spoke. She couldn't understand what he was saying. His lips were moving up and down, up and down, and then into a terrible grimace like he had a toothache. And another grimace. Her eyes narrowed as she tried to see if he were sick or what was wrong with him. A ship appeared, a dark shape on the horizon far behind Mark. And for a split second she wondered if she should try to flag it down. Were they stranded here? She looked behind her at the sheer cliff wall going a hundred feet up. Oh my god. My god. They would never get up that.

"How did we get here?" she asked.

Sean heard her and pointed behind her. She turned and looked at the other end of the little cove where there was a pile of rubble and a foot trail heading up a steep incline. She felt immense relief, laughing, it was so ridiculous. Terror. Then nothing.

"I am so hungry, man," Sean said, amazed at himself.

"We could flag down that ship." Zooey started waving her arm at it. Then she started laughing again.

Sean turned and looked, laughing too, then gazed at the ship as it moved so slowly across the horizon it seemed to be still. "I wonder where it's going."

"Asia," Mark said. They all watched it in silence until it passed completely beyond their view.

Zooey felt herself becoming chilled and realized she was sitting in shade now except her left foot which was still in the sun. She watched her black leather shoe change color as she slowly drew her foot in and sat cross-legged, completely in shade. Half of Mark was shaded and half in sun and Sean was still completely sunlit. His green eyes seemed lit from within as he still gazed at the horizon. He was breathtakingly beautiful. She felt Mark's eyes on her, watching her stare at Sean and she looked over at him. He smiled at her. It was the sexy smile he was so good at, a slow lifting of the left side of his mouth, the slow revealing of his white straight teeth. She looked at him. She'd never noticed before how much he looked like Sean and then wondered if he actually was Sean and she had gotten them mixed up. She smiled at him and they looked at each other.

"Whoa!" Sean said. Zooey and Mark looked at him. Zooey heard a wave crash, louder than the others, and followed Sean's gaze to see another wave break and flow toward them stopping five feet away.

"The tide's coming in," Mark said, raising his voice as the third wave in the set crashed and they could see the tideline less than fifteen feet from the cliff face now. They listened to the crashing waves until the set finished and the surf fell into a calmer rhythm.

"I wish I had a cheeseburger," Sean said.

"Yeah," Mark said. "Let's go." But they sat still watching the ocean which had gone from blue-green to dark gray as a bank of clouds drifted in front of the sun. The breeze picked up and blew their hair back from their faces in a tangle. Finally Mark stood up. He reached a hand down to Zooey who took it and he pulled her up. Sean got up too and wordlessly they headed single file, Mark in the lead, across the sand to the path.

It was easier going up than down. Zooey felt her feet fall naturally into perfect places on the path like a mountain goat. She wished Mark would move faster in front of her, he was slowing her down but then she looked back at the ocean, waiting for him to get ahead, and saw the Golden Gate Bridge. For the first time in her life it was a gloomy sight to her. Civilization, school, work. Her life. She did not want to go back to it. Sean was waiting for her to move ahead and she turned back to the trail and climbed but she felt sad now.

They stopped in Sausalito to get something to eat though they had to hurry so Mark could catch a ferry to the city for a meeting he was going to that night. The boys barely spoke as they devoured their burgers and fries. Zooey ate some fries and sipped on a coke. She felt so strange. She did not feel normal at all. Mark asked Zooey if she wanted to go out sometime and she wrote her phone number at the dorm on a napkin for him before he walked over to the ferry dock. On the ride back to Sanders Sean talked about Danielle again, more intimately now. He told Zooey he loved her so much. He didn't know what he'd do if she was in Paris all junior year. He'd have to try to go, too. He wanted to marry her. He needed her. He sounded so sad.

Back in her dorm room Zooey sat at her desk. She knew she should study chemistry for the quiz tomorrow and she pulled the book out of a pile on the floor. It was late afternoon and she felt she could hardly see in the dusky light. She felt so sad, so sad for Sean, like a weight in her chest. She turned on her desk lamp and leaned forward, opening the book, she flipped through some pages trying to find the chapter they were on. For a minute she lost track of what she was doing. Her mind felt blank. She focused on the page numbers and then the text on the page and realized she couldn't really make out what it said. The letters and symbols were all there in lines but they didn't say anything. There were no words there or she couldn't make out the words. She tried harder but, in fact, she couldn't read. Her brain wasn't working. The letters were just jumbles. She closed the book and sat in silence, afraid. Then she stood up. She felt so strange, like a blank. Something was really wrong and she still felt high but it wasn't fun. It was scary. She left her room, walking slowly down the hall. She needed to get outside.

The setting sun cast a gold glow on the brick of Elizabeth and Brenna's dorm as Zooey approached it. She felt if she could just find Elizabeth, maybe then she could feel okay. She knew she was still high from the joint and was afraid she might never come down because it wasn't supposed to last so long and at the same time she felt like a zombie, a catatonic as she slowly climbed the steps to the second floor and walked down the hall. She knocked on their door.

Elizabeth opened it. "Hi," she said. But Zooey found she couldn't talk. She stood there.

"What's the matter, Zooey? Come in." Elizabeth shut the door behind her as Zooey walked in and sat down on the chair by the door.

"Brenna is having dinner in Ross at Drew's parents." Elizabeth looked at Zooey, who still said nothing. Then she turned and walked back to an ironing board and picked up the hot iron and pressed it to the white collar of a blouse. It made a spitting sound as a puff of steam erupted. Elizabeth carefully ironed the collar, the long sleeves, the cuffs, the front panel between every pearl button. She glanced at Zooey who sat in the chair still listless, silent.

Although Zooey felt less afraid, being there; she simply could not talk. Words had stopped holding together for her. They would not form in her mind.

Elizabeth ironed a long skirt. She glanced at Zooey occasionally. Finally she said, "What is it, Zooey?"

Zooey knew she had to say something. She couldn't lie about it because words didn't work anymore for her.

Elizabeth waited, then turned to the closet to hang up the pressed skirt.

When Elizabeth turned to look at her again, Zooey said, "I'm in love with you, Elizabeth."

"No you're not." Elizabeth turned back to the closet and hung up a blouse. "You just think you are."

Zooey was crying into her hands now, quietly weeping. Elizabeth closed the closet door, and then found a box of tissues and brought it to Zooey and walked back and stood behind the ironing board. She was calm but kept her distance. Finally she said, "Zooey. Do you want me to make an appointment with the school psychologist for you?"

Zooey nodded, yes. Elizabeth told her she would call her tomorrow and tell her when the appointment would be and that neither of them should talk about this to anyone, at all. Then, gently, she suggested Zooey go back to her dorm.

Zooey sat in a small green room on a vinyl chair in the student health building waiting to be shown into another room to take some tests. An MRT or something and something else. Even though she felt she didn't really have control over her life now, it was better this way, to be here.

Yesterday, Monday, she worked through her morning shift in the dining hall with an unbearable dread. Elizabeth had made her an appointment with the psychologist, Dr. Reynolds, for 11:00 a.m. She must have told them it was an emergency. Zooey still wasn't talking—couldn't talk. After her shift she had gone back to the dorm to change her clothes and sat at her desk and torn off a strip of binder paper. On it she wrote, "I'm in love with a girl." She would show him this. She couldn't say it out loud. She had walked across the campus to the health services building as if on her way to receive a death sentence. Still, somewhere inside her she prayed for a miracle, prayed he would pronounce her normal, heterosexual after all. But she knew better. She knew. She knew she would receive the opposite sentence: You will never have a normal life. You are the shamed thing. A freak of nature.

In his office at 11:00 she had sat down in the chair across from his desk and handed him the piece of paper. Then she cried into her hands for the entire hour without stopping. She heard very little of what he said, just mumbled yes or no to some of his questions. Eventually he set up appointments for her to come today and take the tests, and to pick up a prescription.

At one o'clock, a young woman called her into her office and asked her to take a seat at a desk. She explained the first test was multiple choice with 500 questions. Zooey took the number two pencil and the stapled packet and waited for her to leave the room.

She worked quickly, the test required little thought. "Are you shy around others?" "Do you enjoy a challenge?" After forty questions, one asked, "Do you love your father?" Then "Do you think there is poison in your coffee?" Zooey wondered if anyone in their right mind would answer yes to that. But of course, she realized, this test was for crazy people. And one thing Zooey did know. She was scared and exhausted and unhappy. But she was not crazy.

By the time she left the clinic at 5:00 p.m., Zooey had three bottles of pills: Milltown, Stelazine and Seganol. She felt drained and profoundly sad. She took a back way to her dorm not wanting to see anyone and for once she was glad Danielle was gone.

On Thursday evening, Zooey was sitting in bed reading. She hadn't left her dorm since the afternoon at the clinic, except for an appointment with Dr. Reynolds that morning. She had been taking the pills and eating food from the vending machines in the basement laundromat. She had called the dining hall manager and told him she was sick and wouldn't be back until next Monday. Today, she found she could read again. She felt much calmer and yet still couldn't face the world. What would she say?

Dr. Reynolds told her to try to date boys more often and try to behave like the other girls. Get some new clothes and make-up. When she used the word "extrapolate" describing something she'd read, he told her to stop trying to sound smart. Be more fun-loving. She would feel better.

She did want to feel better. She did want to be normal and he seemed to think if she tried harder she had a chance. She hadn't seen Elizabeth since last Sunday night, when she'd said those words. And she didn't expect to see her, not any time soon. Unless somehow she could convince her she was normal. So it was probably better not to see her.

Zooey stood up and went to the mirror and looked at herself. She didn't look any different. That was so odd because her entire world had changed. Or what had been inside had all come out and now she needed to somehow get it back inside. But at least she had help. She leaned forward, her eyes close to the mirror, staring hard, trying to see—to see what was going on. She felt someone looking at her and turned abruptly.

"So, you finally had your nervous breakdown." Patti laughed. "What the hell are you doing?"

Zooey stared at her, her mouth open. Had Elizabeth told her?

"Didn't you hear me?" Patti was asking. "I knocked and came in and stood here. Do you have something in your eye?"

"Oh. I thought so. But I don't see it." Zooey went and plopped down on her bed. "How're you?"

Patti sat in the easy chair across from her and slumped back. "Pretty good. I flunked that fucking chemistry quiz. How about you?"

"I didn't go."

"What? Miss A student?"

"I didn't study for it. It's just the weekly quiz." Zooey shrugged. "I've had a cold."

Patti looked at her, remembering her own "flu".

"You still have it? Brenna said she hasn't seen you at all this week."

"Yeah, it's been bad. But I think I'm getting over it. I need to read all this stuff and catch up, I guess." Her voice sounded tired. Then she herself remembered Patti's "flu" the first ten days of the semester, after her abortion. And somehow this gave her hope, because Patti was fine now. Had been fine for weeks.

"So, I guess you don't want to walk over to dinner with me?"

Zooey shook her head. "No. Thanks though."

"How about if I bring you something? And then we study chemistry together?"

Zooey took a breath. But it sounded better than staying alone any more, she was so tired of being alone with herself. It sounded like a good distraction. "Okay. Sure."

"Good." Patti stood up to go, then turned. "Next week's homecoming you know."

"I know."

"Did you know Drew's coming for the weekend to take Brenna to the dance?"

"That's cool. She must be ecstatic." Zooey smiled. Talking to Patti was making her feel more normal than she had in days and days.

"Are you going?" Patti asked.

"No."

"Yeah, I didn't think so, but listen. Rick's friend Ben really wants to and he doesn't have a date. I know you don't know him but, I told him I'd ask you." Patti shrugged. She knew Zooey rarely dated—too studious, Patti assumed—and imagined she would say no but she didn't say anything. "So think about it, Zo. I'll be back."

Nine days later Patti knocked on Zooey's door again. This time Zooey heard her and yelled, "Come in." She was in front of the mirror again, only now she had a silver eyelash curler clamped on one of her eyelashes and was holding it steady there with her other hand. She didn't look around.

Patti had a black cocktail dress on a hanger. "Finally!" She hung it from Zooey's bookshelf. "I waited in line for practically an *hour* to get our dresses. Half the kids at Sanders were at the cleaners picking up stuff for tonight."

Zooey unclamped her eyelash and turned to her. "Thanks, Patti. Are you going to have enough time? When are they coming?"

"Oh in awhile. The dinner's at 7:00. I already got my hair done this morning, can't you tell?" She turned her head side to side.

"Yeah. It looks great!" Zooey turned back to the mirror and clamped her other eyelash. "So—what? In an hour?"

"Yeah. You want a candy bar? I'm going to get one."

"No thanks."

Patti left and as Zooey unclamped her other eyelash and picked up her mascara she suddenly remembered that evening Danielle and Patti dressed her up for her blind date with Mark. Her last blind date. It was nearly a year ago to the day. Mark had actually called her last Sunday morning, one week after their hike with Sean at the headlands. He wanted to know if she could meet him in Sausalito that afternoon. It was not because she wasn't feeling well that she'd said no. She had already decided to follow Dr. Reynolds advice and date more, but she knew if Elizabeth found out she would assume Zooey was going out with Mark to hurt her or get some kind of sick revenge, and, in fact, that would be true. And it was tempting. But not worth it. She'd already gone out with Mark once and figured out what Elizabeth had finally figured out, too—and admitted to her that night in Mazatlan—he never really saw who you were. He never saw you as a person. It would not be healthy to go out with Mark. This made Zooey laugh, a short, quick exhalation.

"What are you chuckling about?" Patti walked in with a Nestles Crunch and gave her a piece.

"Oh nothing. Thanks." Zooey popped the chocolate into her mouth. It tasted delicious. She let it melt against her tongue as she held her face perfectly still and lightly brushed the gooey mascara onto her curled eyelash. The good news was, Patti had told her Rick would have a flask of Johnny Walker Black in one suit pocket and a flask of Smirnoff's in the other. They just had to order cokes and 7-ups at dinner and they would be all set.

At 6:30 Patti and Zooey were smoking cigarettes when they got a call that they had guests in the lounge. Patti had on a midnight blue dress that came sharply in at the waist and emphasized her generous bosom. Zooey looked trim and lithe in the simple black cocktail dress she had borrowed from a friend of Patti's. She wore black pumps and a black silk jacket her mother had wired her money to buy last weekend when she told her she was going to the Homecoming dance.

"Still in your native black, I see," Rick said to Zooey as he greeted her in the lounge and then introduced her to Ben, who was shorter than Rick and possibly an inch shorter than Zooey. She smiled at him. He had thick blonde hair that stuck up a little and freckles. He was nice looking and smiled at Zooey in a way that made her relax.

They took Patti's car to the hotel hosting the dinner dance in San Rafael. Ben was an engineering major which explained why Zooey had never seen him before; he took classes on another part of the campus. He was interested in hearing about her American poetry class and said he liked poetry in high school, especially Robert Frost. Rick passed a flask over the back seat and Ben and Zooey each took a swig of scotch. Zooey wondered if she might actually have a good time tonight.

As soon as they walked into the dining room they could see Brenna and Drew at a table near the middle of the room because Drew was in full Navy dress although he had put his white brimmed hat on the table.

"Oh my god," Patti whispered to Zooey as they waved at Brenna and started to make their way over. "I hope he doesn't get assaulted by protestors. Jesus." Patti looked around. "Can we sit somewhere else?"

Zooey laughed, then smiled at Brenna who had stood to wait for them and Zooey walked up and hugged her. She gave Drew a stiff little hug, too, and glanced around. She didn't see Elizabeth anywhere. She was disappointed.

The table was set for eight, but there were only six of them sitting there when the salads were served. People seemed to be giving Drew a wide berth, or maybe Zooey was only imagining that. Still. Would any of them sitting here have chosen to eat dinner with a Navy officer? Except Brenna, that is. Her heart went out to Brenna when she thought how she would feel if Drew were shunned by her own friends.

"Where've you been, stranger?" Brenna said to her now and Zooey turned from Ben who had been telling her about his rugby team.

"Where've you been, you mean," Zooey said. She couldn't think what else to say.

Rick and Ben got up to go the men's room. Zooey wondered if they were going to refill the flasks. She wouldn't put it past Rick to have a hidden stash somewhere.

"Did you have a fight with Elizabeth?" Brenna was looking closely at Zooey's eyes.

Zooey felt exposed and she couldn't lie to Brenna. "Kind of."

"Oh you two," Brenna said disapprovingly. "You two get too intense. You need to make up, I miss you, Zooey."

"Well, let's do something. Let's go to the city next week."

"That would be fun. But, Zo. You need to make up with Elizabeth. I'm sure she really misses you, too."

"Sure." Zooey smiled.

Drew put his arm around Brenna's shoulder and pulled her toward him. "What are you girls gossiping about?" He smiled at Zooey.

"Dorm life," Zooey said. "How's Annapolis, Drew?"

"I'll tell you, Zooey, I finally feel like I've got my head screwed on right. I didn't realize I didn't have my values in place here. It's hard to be clear here."

Zooey looked at him quizzically. "What do you mean? Clear about what?" She glanced over at Patti but she was talking to two of her friends who had stopped by the table. People were milling around even though dinner was being served. It seemed to Zooey some people were already drunk.

"It's like a free-for-all," Drew said. "There're too many choices at Sanders and in the Bay Area in general. Every time you turn around somebody's demonstrating—women's lib, black people, poor people, animals—everybody's got to get their two cents in. Everybody's on drugs. It's like a circus."

"It's not like that in Maryland?"

Drew shrugged. "Maybe in some neighborhoods but generally, no, it's not. The East coast is more reserved, for one thing. But definitely Annapolis is not like here." He laughed.

"What is it like?"

"People are serious about their lives. They're responsible. They know life isn't just about what mood they're in today. We have a responsibility to our families. To our parents, to our spouses and children once we've formed families of our own. To our community. To our country. That's what holds societies together. It starts with the institution of the family, our own families. And then our extended family in our schools or churches, our towns. Otherwise, things start to unravel. Threads come loose and things start to fall apart."

"You mean, kids think like that? Students?"

"We do at Annapolis. I'm telling you, Zooey, it was such a relief when I got there. I felt so conflicted here. I knew my dad wasn't all wrong when he said this country would be nothing without its institutions. But the culture here is so—free-for-all, like I said, and I couldn't get past that. I couldn't find anyone who took themselves seriously or had any sense of responsibility." He looked lovingly at Brenna, "except Brenna. And the people at Our Lady of the Immaculate Conception."

Brenna looked up at him lovingly and he kissed her. They seemed absolutely happy. Sure of themselves. Zooey watched them. She couldn't deny it. They seemed so solid and good.

Drew looked back at Zooey. "I hear Elizabeth is back in the fold. When are you coming back to church, Zooey?"

Zooey shrugged and smiled.

"Think about it, Zo," Brenna said. "Remember how much fun we had walking to Mass and having lunch afterwards? Didn't it feel more like family? You and me and Elizabeth." She sang, "Together again," in an operatic voice and clutched her heart. Drew and Zooey laughed.

"It's like there's no core here," Drew said, looking around. Zooey followed his gaze and it was true, people were wandering about, some were smoking cigarettes, there was a lot of laughter. No one was eating much or sitting at their tables although waiters were serving entrees. Mostly, everyone was partying.

"I mean, what do you really believe in now, Zooey? What would you stand up for. Or even give your life for?" Drew asked her.

She thought a minute, looking off from them a second as she realized there was absolutely nothing she felt that way about. Except perhaps, Elizabeth. And that made her feel empty. And it wasn't what he meant.

"We all need to have something we believe in with our whole hearts. That's what I couldn't find here, at all. Except for Brenna, of course," he said again and seemed about to kiss her once more.

Patti was listening to them now, Zooey saw, and she said, "Sorry to interrupt, but I'm going to the powder room. Coming, Zooey?"

Drew and Brenna were gazing at each other so Zooey stood up. "Be right back."

"Whoa," Patti said as they headed toward the foyer where the restrooms were. "Has he been brainwashed, or what? Where's the part about napalming Vietnamese children? That's what I want to know."

They ran into Sean who was there with the sister of a basketball teammate and a group of friends and their dates. He seemed a little tipsy, Zooey thought.

"How are you two beautiful ladies?" He gave each of them a kiss on the cheek.

"Fine, except for the Admiral over there." Patti nodded her head in the direction of their table.

"Yeah, what's with the get up? He's so straight, man. What a trip."

"He was about to start singing 'Oh Fatherland'—" Patti turned as Rick and Ben appeared from the foyer and joined them.

"Sean." Rick grinned and Ben asked Sean when the first basketball game would be and they began talking sports. Patti took Zooey's arm, "Come on, Zo. Let's find the little girls' room."

November 1972

Zooey and Ben walked in silence, holding hands, across the moonlit quad to the dorms. Zooey had worn the flattest shoes she had, an old pair, and her left foot had a blister, she could tell. Even so she was a tiny bit taller and she knew it bothered Ben so she often cocked her head to one side when she was with him to make up the difference. This was their third date since homecoming and she had to admit he was a very nice guy. At the moment she felt a little woozy although they'd only had two drinks after the movie, but every time she drank since she started taking those pills, it was different than it used to be. She hadn't mentioned it to Dr. Reynolds, who she was seeing twice a week. Part of what kept her interested in going out with Ben was the effect it had on Dr. Reynolds. Usually he was pretty unreadable, but she could tell when she spoke positively about Ben he was pleased. He looked like a person who thought he was actually curing someone of a horrible disease.

"What're you doing for Thanksgiving?" Ben asked.

"Oh. I haven't thought about it."

"It's in a couple weeks."

"Yeah. I'll go home, I'm sure. To my parents."

They had arrived at Zooey's dorm and Ben held the door open for her as they went into the lobby. He had very nice manners and was always respectful of her. He didn't pressure her too much about sex, or at least he always took no for an answer. Zooey didn't want to do much more than make out for the requisite half hour every time they got together. This always occurred in his car, where they had a couple drinks, at the very end of the Sanders parking lot under a big oak tree, if that spot wasn't already taken by another couple. All three dates had been pretty identical, in fact. First they went to dinner and talked about school, classes, sports. Sports was one of their favorite topics and Zooey tried to follow some of his favorite teams in the newspaper and even watch the games on TV because it was fun. After dinner they would go to a movie, then to the parking lot, then he brought her home. It was fine.

"Let's sit down a minute," Ben said and gestured at two cushioned chairs by a big ashtray in the corner of the lobby.

Zooey squinted at him. This was a departure from their usual routine and she took a quick breath, then said, "Sure."

The smell from the ashtray was disgusting but even so Zooey wished she had a cigarette. She'd quit smoking again now that tennis practice had started.

"Did you know there's a professional women's tennis tournament in Oakland next week? The Virginian Slims? There's going to be a lot of top stars," Ben said.

"Oh yeah, some of the girls on the team were talking about it. It sounds like fun." She had been thinking of going to it with them.

"How would you like to go on Friday night, and then maybe even stay over and watch the semifinals Saturday, too."

"Oh, wow, Ben. Our team is going as a group and I said I would go."

He looked crestfallen and she knew it had taken a lot for him to make this proposal. "I'm sorry," she said.

"Oh, that's all right. It'll be fun to go with your team."

She felt grateful they had this one true link, a love of sports and teams. Because his hand in hers right now—he was holding her hand—felt simply like a stranger's hand or like a generic hand you would pick off a shelf and put in your grocery cart, and tomorrow night it would be just another hand. She couldn't tell Dr. Reynolds this. But this was her feeling as she sat there and wondered when she could go upstairs to her room and go to sleep.

"Well," he said, since she hadn't responded to his last remark. He plowed ahead. "I was thinking maybe we could get together sometime over Thanksgiving break. You know, like you could come back early or I could visit you in Glendale. San Diego's not that far away."

This took her by surprise, too. She immediately saw in her mind how happy her parents would be if a boy from Sanders visited her at home, and how happy Dr. Reynolds would be that things had gone so far, that such a happily normal event might occur. She could see it as if it were a scene in a movie but—and this made her realize what she would have to say—she simply could not see herself playing the part, her acting was flat, uninspired, awful. She could not do it. She could only do these dates like they had been, once a week.

"Oh Ben, I'm sorry. My mother's very ill." At least this was partially true, her mother had once been very ill although she was fine now. But this made Zooey feel especially sad because it would make her parents so happy if they thought Zooey had a boyfriend. She wished she could at least do it for them. "I don't know."

"It could be an afternoon or something. It wouldn't have to take away from her. We could go into L.A., see a show or a Lakers' game."

"Okay. Okay, sure." She smiled at him.

Ben grinned. "Cool." He leaned over and gave her a long slow kiss. Then he smiled and looked in her eyes for a few seconds. She felt so incredibly sleepy but she smiled back at him and then finally he said he'd call her later in the week and got up to leave.

Zooey pulled her racquet back and zeroed in to hit the ball down the line but was a half-second late and her shot went wide. As she walked to the ad court to receive serve she felt a twinge in her elbow again. It was getting so she couldn't hit returns down the line because she was so late they were going out, and failing to hit the ball in front was straining her elbow tendon.

She pushed her hair back from her forehead and waited for the serve. It was a topspin down the T and she blocked it back in the middle giving her opponent a good chance to rush the net and smack a volley winner.

Zooey glanced over at her coach, Jenny, on the sideline who nodded at her to keep trying her best. Zooey hopped up and down on the balls of her feet waiting for the next serve, a slice out wide she barely got her racquet on and slapped back cross-court. Her opponent whipped it down the line but Zooey ran fast enough to get there and then hit her backhand late so it went to the raised racquet across the net and the girl pounded it for a winner.

Zooey stepped back and felt frustration simmering inside although something seemed to be quaffing it, dulling it, and instead of anger she felt weariness. Her playing was hopeless lately and no matter what she tried to do she couldn't fix it.

When she lost the next point, too, Jenny pulled her out and put another girl in to finish the set. They were working out their rankings for the matches next weekend against Pomona College.

"Zooey," Jenny said to her as she left the court and Zooey turned and walked over to her. "I'm just wondering if you've been getting enough sleep lately?"

Zooey hated to tell her just how much sleep she was getting, more than she ever had in her life. "Yeah, I'm pretty sure."

"You're not partying a little too much—" Jenny looked her in the eye.

Zooey shook her head. "I'm not. I don't know what it is."

"Well if it isn't physical, it's mental. This is a mental game, anyway. Is something distracting you? You seem ... slowed down."

Zooey shrugged. Jenny had said it and now she had to admit it to herself. She wasn't as fast or alert as she was before she started taking all the pills and she couldn't tell Jenny or anyone about the pills. No one knew, not even Elizabeth. And the fact was, they were affecting her play.

"Maybe I should take a break from the team?" she asked Jenny.

"No, no, Zooey. I'm not criticizing you. You're a very good player and we need you—we need you at your best. I just want you to think whether anything off the court is interfering with your game. Your focus isn't there like it was at the start of the season."

"Okay. I'll work on it."

"That's a girl." Jenny patted her on the back and turned to watch the two girls playing on the court.

Zooey walked away to find her gear and as she moved to the benches she felt her eyes brim with tears. She would have to drop off the team. She felt so sluggish and inept, like she could hardly even play the game anymore. She had thought at first, when she was making more errors these past few weeks, if she concentrated harder she could compensate but, evidently, she couldn't. It wasn't her body that was slowed down. It was her brain.

Sunday morning Brenna knocked on Zooey's door. "You ready?"

"Come in a sec," Zooey called. She was standing in front of the mirror putting on eyeliner and mascara.

Brenna walked in. "You never used to be a minute late, Zooey." Brenna caught her eye in the mirror. "We used to take bets on who would show up earliest, Danielle or you."

"Well, too much is made of punctuality."

Brenna said nothing and plopped down in the easy chair near the door. She was so glad Zooey had agreed to come to church with her again she wasn't going to pressure her. It didn't matter if they were a few minutes late. Elizabeth was meeting them at church and then they were all going to lunch together like old times and as far as Brenna knew it was the first time Zooey and Elizabeth had seen each other in a month. No one was talking about what went wrong but Brenna assumed it had something to do with Zooey going out with Mark and Sean, which she had heard about through the grapevine. Although when she asked Zooey about it, Zooey said that day had been a fluke. Then later Patti told her Sean said Mark wanted to start dating Zooey and she told him no. Brenna had heard plenty about Mark from Elizabeth and how much she loved him last year and she thought Zooey was being a really good friend to Elizabeth by not seeing Mark. After all, it was Zooey who'd gone out with him first. Anyway, it was all sad and she didn't like to think about it. She was glad things were so clear and good with her and Drew.

"Ready!" Zooey grabbed her purse as they left the room. She sounded so cheerful to Brenna, which was not Zooey's usual mood for church. Maybe it was a relief to her to finally come back. Brenna smiled happily at her and took her arm as they walked down the hall and out into the cold, gray November day.

Elizabeth was waiting for them on the steps of the church and she smiled at Zooey, a bright, cheerful smile. Brenna realized then that maybe all this cheerfulness was about getting through something, a hard thing.

"Hi there," Zooey said and the three of them went inside. Zooey faithfully dipped her fingertips in the holy water font, crossing herself and genuflecting to the altar before they slid into their pew in back. Brenna sat between her and Elizabeth and Zooey relaxed a little as it all came back to her. She went through the motions, standing, kneeling, sitting, but when she tried to murmur the responses to the prayers she found her lips frozen. The words just would not come. It wasn't that she couldn't remember them. One year of absence would not erase eighteen years of weekly repetition but she could not speak the words: "Oh my God, I am heartily sorry for having offended Thee … *mea culpa, mea culpa, mea maxima culpa* …" my fault, my fault, my most grievous fault, because she was born this way and her very existence was an offense according to this place and despite the barbiturates she was taking she felt herself shut down completely to the idea that it was her fault.

She should not have come here. But as she sat for the sermon and decided not to listen as the droning voice of the priest made her sleepy, she realized it would be simple to sit quietly and pretend she was somewhere else. In her mind she went to Danielle's house, last summer, to the sparkling blue water of the swimming pool and the warm feeling of sun on her skin. The happy days of playing tennis and training for the team, the steady, kind friendship of Danielle who always made Zooey feel safe. She remembered those weeks with happiness and then, for an instant, she wondered if there was a way out of where she was now. What was the way out? And yet, it seemed hopeless. She didn't have to go to church—she didn't have to be Catholic—but she did have to live alone for the rest of her life, because she couldn't, she realized, live with a Ben or a Mark or even a Sean. After Ben asked to visit her at her parents' Thanksgiving weekend she felt she was sure she could not go on dating him. He was nice and good looking. But the idea of getting more involved with him made her realize, the next time they went out—although everything went well in a hollow way—that she simply felt hollow with Ben.

She hadn't told Dr. Reynolds yet. She hadn't told Ben either. She supposed she could just keep going through the motions until Christmas break. It was only three more weeks. She would try. Then over break she'd figure out what to do.

Danielle would be back after Christmas and it wouldn't be as lonely, not seeing Elizabeth and Brenna much anymore. And she had fun studying with Patti sometimes and hanging out in the dorm. But being here now, in the church, listening to prayers and hymns she had heard thousands of times, she knew she couldn't come back. Maybe she couldn't go forward, where she wanted to go, but she could not go back. Not to this.

As the organ struck the chords of the final hymn, Elizabeth, Brenna and Zooey gathered their things and followed the parishioners slowly making their way out of the pews down the aisles to the vestibule. Brenna smiled at Zooey and took her arm as they walked out. Zooey felt like a traitor. What would she tell Brenna?

"Should we go to Zell's?" Brenna looked happily at Zooey and Elizabeth once they were outside the church. Zell's was around the corner, a coffee shop where they often had lunch after Mass freshman year.

"Sure," Zooey said and Elizabeth smiled the odd, bright smile again.

"I thought that was a really good sermon," Brenna said as they headed to the restaurant. "I liked the part about listening to your heart."

Zooey looked up from studying the pavement and glanced at Brenna. Maybe she should have listened.

"What did you think, Zooey?"

"Yes. I agree with that." Although, did she?

"How God is in our heart and will tell us right from wrong," Brenna went on. "We just have to listen."

Elizabeth was looking at Zooey now, trying to read her, but Zooey said nothing.

They sat in a red vinyl booth and all of them ordered the same things they always had—burgers, grilled cheese, cokes.

"I've got something to tell you guys," Brenna said after the waitress left. She was brimming with nervous excitement like a child about to blow out the candles on her birthday cake.

"What?" Zooey was filled with curiosity and Elizabeth, who sat next to Brenna, turned and looked at her with surprise.

Brenna took a breath. "I'm getting married in June! Drew and I decided last weekend, we've talked to our parents—everything."

Although it shouldn't have, this came as a surprise to Zooey and Elizabeth looked as if she hadn't expected it either. Both of them said "That's great!" and "Congratulations, Brenna. That's so exciting!" Brenna lifted her shoulders in a blissful gesture, thrilled with her friends' good wishes.

The waitress brought their cokes in curved frosty glasses. Zooey ripped the paper wrapper off her straw and balled it up then stuck the straw through the ice in her drink. "Will you move to Annapolis?"

"Yes, of course. I'll get an apartment, and a job, and Drew will stay with me every time he has leave and liberty. Then in two years, it depends on where Drew gets stationed where we'll live." She looked confident and happy. Zooey glanced at Elizabeth but she was looking at Brenna, smiling.

"Now you two are going to be my bridesmaids, you know, so start getting ready!"

"Of course, Brenna. Where will it be?"

"In San Francisco. We want to be near Sanders so our friends can come. It's going to be so fun, you guys. You're coming, right?" She turned her head back and forth looking at each of them as they nodded, yes, yes, of course!

On the next Tuesday, Zooey was late to her American Poetry class. But it was the first time since October she hadn't dreaded seeing Elizabeth there. Lunch with her and Brenna Sunday had eased things between them. Zooey slipped into a desk in the back. Mr. Grayson was talking about the Beat poets. Zooey had missed a test a few weeks ago and was hoping she could still manage a B. She saw Elizabeth sitting up front by the windows. Then she saw her lean over and say something to a guy Zooey had never seen in class. He had light brown hair half-way down his back and when he turned to listen to her, Zooey saw he had lines around his eyes and mouth. He couldn't have been a student.

Then Mr. Grayson was saying he wanted to introduce Lucius McPhee, a friend of Elizabeth Riordan, who generously made time to come and speak to them today about Jack Kerouac. Zooey searched her mind for a poem by Jack Kerouac—didn't he write that novel *On the Road* in three days and that was it?

Who was Lucius McPhee? Elizabeth had never mentioned anyone like that. Zooey sat up straight trying to see better as Lucius walked to the front of the room. He shook Mr. Grayson's hand then stood at the podium with the ease of an experienced speaker. He seemed to be about forty years old. He spoke very fondly of Jack Kerouac whom he apparently knew slightly and said he himself had been inspired by Kerouac to become a jazz poet. Then after reading from Kerouac's last work, *Vanity of Duluoz*, he invited everyone to come to a poetry reading of his own work Saturday night in San Francisco. He thanked his good friend Elizabeth Riordan for the opportunity to speak to them today. The class applauded happily, he had been an interesting change from Mr. Grayson. Then everyone stood and began gathering their books to leave. Zooey sat a moment and waited for Elizabeth and Lucius to go but they stayed to talk to Mr. Grayson. She slipped out the back door of the classroom and headed to lunch.

Zooey hoped Patti would be at lunch because she was feeling consumed with curiosity and Patti always knew the gossip, although Patti saw as little of Elizabeth these days as Zooey did. Zooey wondered if he were a friend of Elizabeth's father—but why would he know a poet in San Francisco? Elizabeth's father was an endocrinologist in Pacific Palisades. It didn't make sense. Oh! Maybe someone she'd met in Iowa at the poetry workshop. Of course. But she'd never mentioned him in her letters last summer.

Zooey pulled a tray off the stack at the lunch counter and plopped her purse and books on it, then turned and glanced around the dining hall for Patti. She saw Rick with Ben and some of their friends and turned quickly back. She didn't usually come to the dining hall anymore because she didn't want to eat with Ben. She often just grabbed food on her shift in the morning and took it to her room. In fact, she thought right now she might have better luck finding Patti at the dorm and glanced at the door of the dining hall and at that moment saw Elizabeth and Lucius come in. He had his hand on her back, steering her toward the line. Zooey turned back around. She couldn't believe it. He was her boyfriend. No. It couldn't be, it must be some kind of avuncular gesture. But she grabbed her tray and went to the front of the line and cut in.

"Hey!" a senior boy complained but Manolo was working the line and looked up. "Zooey. What can I get for you?"

"A turkey sandwich. Thank you." She pointed to the prewrapped sandwiches. He handed her one and she turned to the cashier line paying quickly and, grabbing her things, went out the rear exit and headed toward her dorm.

She felt so agitated as she walked quickly, eyes straight ahead, her mind buzzing like it hadn't in a very long time. If it were true. If Elizabeth were dating that effete old jazz poet … it was such a betrayal! She couldn't say exactly why but it felt outrageous, ridiculous … But wait a minute. She calmed herself. She needed to find out first what was really going on. Her eyes brimmed with tears. Nobody had even told her about this. Why hadn't Brenna … but maybe that meant it was nothing. Of course, she was being ridiculous to jump to conclusions. He was just some older poet whom she had met in Iowa, possibly, and he was being gentlemanly escorting her into the dining hall. That's what made sense.

She went straight to Patti's room when she got to the dorm and caught her just as she was about to leave.

"Patti!"

"Hi, Zo. What's happening? You look bent out of shape."

"Oh no. I'm just behind on stuff, but listen—do you have any cigarettes?"

"Yeah." Patti headed back into her room and Zooey followed her.

Patti shook two out of the pack and gave Zooey one. Then she perched on her desk and lit hers. Zooey sat on the bed, dropping her books and purse on the floor and Patti walked over to give her a light. "Behind on what?"

"Oh. Studying. Like American Poetry, I was in there this morning and I missed a test awhile ago."

"That doesn't sound like you."

"It's the only class I've missed a test in."

"Except chemistry. We should start studying for the final. I know it's way off but I'm freaking already."

"Maybe tomorrow."

"Okay, after dinner."

"You know what?" Zooey said. "Do you know a guy named Lucius McPhee?"

"Elizabeth's new boyfriend?"

"Yeah. Him." Zooey took a long pull on her cigarette. She blew out the smoke.

"I just met him once. Haven't you talked to her? I thought you and Brenna went out to lunch with her last weekend. I never even knew why you guys weren't talking in the first place. What's happening?"

"Oh." Zooey blew out another long plume of smoke in an exhausted sigh. "You know sometimes, things just don't go right."

"Oh that explains it, Zooey. Come on. Give. What's the deal?"

"In a way, it was about boys, Mark, you know. That kind of thing."

"You mean even though she hasn't seen Mark since last year she was mad he asked you out?"

"Not really that. We just had an argument about—the nature of love. You know. How she says she loved him so much …"

"That's a landmine, Zooey. You can't tell someone they aren't really in love."

"Exactly. That's what happened."

"So, is that why she didn't tell you about Lucius?"

"I guess." Zooey took a last drag on her cigarette and put it out in the ashtray on the bedside table. "Who is he?"

"A poet she met in the city. Brenna said she went to some readings with kids from your poetry class. Didn't you go?"

"Oh, that's when I was out, maybe."

"It was at City Lights in North Beach. He read his poetry and Elizabeth went up to him afterward all ga-ga and they went for coffee, and it's been hot and heavy ever since. Brenna says she's really into him. Like Mark, only more."

"And you met him, right?" Zooey looked levelly at Patti.

"I know. I couldn't believe it. I mean what is he, forty years old? And skinny—I thought when I met him—oh my god, I hope you're not sleeping with this guy because he is *gross*! What is the appeal?"

"Escape."

"What?"

"You know. Escape through art. Haven't we talked about that?"

"No. You and I don't talk like that Zooey, that's how you and Elizabeth talk. And he looks real to me—scary real."

"Wow. So." Zooey shook her head. She felt the buzzing in her body subside and a great weariness take its place.

Patti stood up from her perch on the desk. "Let's go to lunch. I'm starving."

"Oh, I already got something. I'm going to my room to study."

"Okay. But listen. Tomorrow after dinner—chemistry."

"Chemistry." Zooey laughed.

A loud knock on her door at 10:00 a.m. woke Zooey. "Yes?"

"Phone call!"

Zooey hurried to get out of bed. She was still wearing the plaid cotton shift she'd had on the day before. Raking her hands through her hair, she walked down the hall to the telephone on their floor. She prayed it wasn't something bad.

"Hello?"

"Took you long enough."

"Danielle!"

"Were you still asleep?"

"Yes." Zooey yawned. "Sorry." She realized she'd missed her ten o'clock class.

"I couldn't remember your schedule. You don't have classes this morning?"

"Well. I've already missed it."

"Zooey. That doesn't sound like you. Cutting classes. They won't give you straight A's anymore."

"Well." Zooey couldn't think what to say, especially since she would be lucky to get C's now that she had missed so much. She stayed in her room most of the time now, sleeping a lot. Sometimes she read novels. Twentieth Century Novel was the one class she was getting an A in. "I'm getting an A in English."

"That's good. How's tennis?"

"Okay." She couldn't tell Danielle she'd dropped off the team. "But listen, how are you? Any idea when you're coming back? We miss you."

"Oh god. You have no idea how much I miss Sanders. I am going crazy here, Zooey."

"You mean—your aunt's house? Or Boston?"

"All of it. It's fucking freezing here, for one thing. And it's so gray and dark. It is unbelievably depressing."

"How's your mother?"

"A little better. I think she made it through a whole day without crying yesterday." Danielle sighed.

"That's pretty good." Zooey meant it.

"I have got to get away from her, Zooey." Danielle was speaking in such a low whisper Zooey strained to hear her. "I am going to end up crazy, too, I swear to god."

"Oh, Danielle. It's so hard. I'm sorry."

"I'm counting the days. Mother promised we would fly home the day after Christmas. Twenty-seven days and I hope I can make it."

"But you've made it this far—it's been months."

"It's harder at the end and I'm afraid she'll change her mind."

"But can't you come back yourself? Can't your aunt take care of her?"

"Aunt Jeanne cannot *wait* for us to leave."

"Oh."

"Listen, Zooey. Have you seen Sean lately?"

"No. But I haven't been out much. Why? Haven't you heard from him?"

"Oh yes, every day, he calls, he writes. But Patti told me Rick said Sean's started smoking grass. A lot."

"Oh."

"Do you think it's true?"

"I don't know. Maybe he's tried it once or twice? I don't know if he's smoking a lot. I never see him, Danielle."

"If he is, I swear, I will not marry him."

"Are you talking about getting married?"

"Just recently, we've talked about it. When he was here at Thanksgiving he said he wanted to get married and he didn't want to wait until graduation."

"What did you say?"

"I said I couldn't think about anything until my mother was all right and I was back at school."

"That makes sense."

"So obviously you've heard about Brenna and Drew."

"Yeah, a couple weeks ago. She seems happy."

"And we all get to be her bridesmaids! That'll be fun."

"I know."

"You don't sound that happy, Zooey."

"No, I am. We'll have a blast."

"It's hard to imagine anything being fun again right now."

"I'm so glad you'll be back soon, Danielle. I can't wait to see you."

"I hope you're keeping our room clean."

"It is so tidy." Zooey thought of the unmade bed, the piles of clothes and books and papers everywhere.

"Listen, what's this about Elizabeth's new boyfriend?"

"You mean the illustrious Lucius McPhee?"

"I guess. Patti said he's the skinniest guy she's ever seen and old enough to be her father."

"He actually is. I think he's got to be forty."

"What is with her?"

"You tell me."

"Well, I haven't talked to her in months. She did write me in September and I wrote back and I haven't heard from her since."

"She's off into a poetry thing and he's a poet. That must be it."

"I don't understand it. Elizabeth is very attractive. She's so strange about guys."

"I know."

"And how about you, Zooey? Are you still going out with Ben?"

"Not lately."

"Because?"

"He wasn't doing it for me, Danielle."

"Oh. Well, Patti said she was surprised you went out as long as you did. He had a thing for you though, apparently."

"He's a nice guy. I mean, I tried."

"Who is going to do it for you, Zooey?"

Zooey found she couldn't say anything.

"Have you ever been in love?" Danielle asked.

"Yes."

"With whom?" Danielle demanded.

Zooey almost said Elizabeth's name, it was on the tip of her tongue and then she saw the shock and fear that would be in Danielle's eyes—the fear in Elizabeth's eyes that evening in October.

"Somebody I knew in high school." That wasn't a lie at least.

"You never told me about him."

"It was kind of short-lived. Anyway, we have to have a big party when you get back. Wouldn't that be fun? Like a New Year's party or something."

"I can't even imagine that right now. It is so dreary here it's like a mausoleum. My mother sits in the living room and chain smokes and my Aunt Jeanne keeps fanning the smoke away with her hand. I've started smoking again. We watch a lot of TV. I try to take my mother to museums and restaurants but it's like entertaining a cadaver."

"She's not getting any more together?"

"A little. Like I said, finally she's not crying as much and she even smiled at something on TV last night. I think if we can just get through Christmas, she might come out of it. Keep your fingers crossed, Zooey."

"I will. I'll be thinking of you Danielle."

December 1972

Zooey lit a cigarette as she stood on the steps of the student health center then stuffed the pack in her purse and walked, head down, toward her dorm. It was a dark cloudy day, threatening rain. She was thinking about what Dr. Reynolds said. For one thing, when she finally told him she'd been skipping classes and hadn't gone to any at all for a week, he told her she should ask for incompletes. Somehow she'd thought she could squeak by, just take the finals and see what happened, except for chemistry which she couldn't fake. But now she wondered if she was kidding herself. And he'd said she should consider not staying the two and a half weeks until break but go home now and try to rest, then see old friends over the holidays, go to parties, have fun. Try to be normal, was the idea. And it would be a relief, she thought, to leave school and quit pretending, except going home to her parents would be worse. She couldn't possibly tell them what was going on, it was going to be hard enough to be there over break. A month would kill her. She felt like it would, unless she could keep doing what she was doing: sleeping, watching television—simple shows, nothing scary—and reading novels. That's what was working for her and although she could do that at home, pretending to be happy for her parents would be much harder than pretending at school where no one really knew what she was up to. Her friends were busy with their boyfriends and studying. She could hide here. But she felt too uneasy now to go to the dining hall and pick up some lunch and she was running low on supplies in her room. She thought she'd better walk into town and get some food. She could buy a lot of it and get a taxi back. She could stop going to see Dr. Reynolds and he would think she had taken his advice. That was a possibility.

She smoked another cigarette and then another as she walked along the winding tree-lined road the two miles to town. It was better, really, not to think too far ahead because it was very hard to imagine what was next. What she would do. It was better to just keep on doing what she was doing. Which was what? She started to have the hollow feeling again as if she dwelt in less than three dimensions, a flat suffocating plain. She looked around trying to shake it off and kept walking but it felt as if she were barely present, only eking out a presence by keeping her feet moving forward. Where was she heading? Oh yes, the grocery store. This made sense. She could do this. Pick out some food, put it in a cart. She calmed down. She would go to the grocery store. She could see the first small shops at the beginning of town just ahead.

As she turned the corner on Grant Street it started to rain. She hurried on but at the end of the block a downpour began. She stood under the awning of a shoe repair store for some time and then noticed she was across the street from her favorite bookstore. Cars were going by on the dark rain-slickened street with a swooshing sound, sending up a spray. She waited for a break in traffic and dashed across the street and into the store. A bell rang as she stepped on the indoor mat but no one looked up. Zooey ran a hand through her hair, brushing off the moisture, and walked to the nearest display table. She dried her hands on her denim jacket and picked up the first book she saw. She focused on the title. Yes. She could read. It came as an enormous relief. A woman at the magazine shelf on her left caught her eye.

"Zooey. Hi! How are you?" She walked over to where Zooey stood.

"Molly! I haven't seen you around school at all this year."

"Oh I'm not a student at Sanders. I was auditing the film class. It was good, I thought."

"Yeah, I loved it. Mr. Baxter didn't come back this year, though."

"I know—he's teaching at the Film Institute in the city now. I took another class from him this year."

"You go to the Film Institute?"

"Just taking some classes there." Molly laughed, a throaty, ironic laugh. "I might get a degree by the time I'm thirty. But probably not."

"What classes are you taking?"

"One of them is great. A woman director, she does independent films—" Molly looked around the quiet store. "Do you want to go get a cup of coffee? There's a café around the corner. Corelli's?"

"Sure."

They sat in soft, cushioned chairs at a low wood table in the back of the café. A Boston fern hung from the ceiling above them next to a print of Van Gough's *Starry Night*.

"Do you live near here?" Zooey asked after they had discussed Molly's classes at the Film Institute.

"No, I have an apartment in the city. I met my brother for lunch here today. He's a lawyer. His office is down the street, by the bank." Molly's long black hair was even more curly after walking in the rain and she pulled it back off her face and fastened a hair band around it in a practiced way as she spoke. Her eyes were light brown with long dark lashes.

"Where in the city?" Zooey could not imagine having an apartment in the city. It seemed amazing. She wondered if Molly was older than she looked.

"Near Washington Square. On Vallejo."

Zooey had no idea where that was.

"What year are you at Sanders?" Molly asked.

"Sophomore."

"Well, I would be a senior if I hadn't dropped out. You know, in '70 when Nixon bombed Cambodia? I was going to Cal and the entire campus shut down. I got involved in the protests and—" She laughed. "That was it for me. It didn't seem relevant anymore."

"Do you know Mark Landry?" Zooey asked, then wished she hadn't.

"Oh, I've seen him around. He's hard to miss."

Zooey laughed. "I thought I saw you a few months ago. At a demonstration in the city, about the ERA."

"On Market and Powell?"

"Yes."

"That was me. I'm more into feminism now. The left—well, you know Mark?"

"A little. Not well."

"The left is run by guys. You know, I told you when Cal shut down all the students went on strike, and I went to one of the headquarters with a friend to see what we could do. There was this guy running everything, he was phoning all over the country sending guys to speak at high schools and do security, and when my friend and I showed up, he looked at us, two women, and told us—I promise you, this is the truth—to clean the bathroom."

"I believe you."

"That kept happening—women doing clean-up jobs and sitting at meetings listening to guys make the decisions. There are very few women in leadership in the antiwar movement. Only the ones whose boyfriends put them there. A lot of us got sick of it. We've started working for the ERA. It's more interesting than cleaning bathrooms for the male left." Molly laughed again.

Zooey had never heard anyone refer to girls as women. She took a sip of her cappuccino. It was delicious.

"Why didn't you join us?" Molly gave her a challenging, teasing look.

"Oh, I was on the cable car. With a friend. Going up the hill," she said a little weakly. "Or I would have." Was this true, she wondered.

"Well, listen—this is short notice but—do you want to come to a conference tomorrow? There's going to be a lot of workshops, feminist issues—the ERA, equal pay, the right to choose. I'm doing one on film and the 'male gaze'. The keynote speaker is Shulamith Firestone."

It was as if she were speaking a foreign language.

"Yes," Zooey said. She wrote down the time and place.

Zooey sat in the packed auditorium next to Molly, joining in the uproar of applause as the keynote speaker finished her remarks and gathered her papers.

"Oh, there's Fiona." Molly was craning her neck to look behind her. "I've got to talk to her." She stood and worked her way to the aisle and in the direction of her friend while Zooey sat still, digesting what she had heard. Her grandmother had not been allowed to vote! Women were the property of their husbands, like a horse, until the 1880s. Today women earned half what men did for an identical job. In 200 years there had been only 10 women senators.

How had she made it to her second year of college without knowing this stuff? Well. They didn't teach it in school. She sat perfectly still, not seeing the activity around her because her mind was focused inward. She felt *finally* what was within her had been seen. It was so validating, an amazing feeling. The speaker had articulated all the societal causes of the inchoate rage and longing Zooey had been feeling her entire life. So, she might not really be a freak after all. It actually was true: it wasn't her fault.

She glanced around. The auditorium was empty, only a few people lingered in back or near the stage. She looked at her program. She and Molly agreed to meet in the courtyard for lunch because Zooey didn't know what workshops she would go to. Alone now, she looked at the list, her eyes scanning the words. "Freedom to choose." She felt a moment of hope—choose what—then remembered that was about abortion. Something she would never have to consider. Then to her amazement, she found what she was looking for: "Lesbians...." She didn't even register the rest of the workshop title, something about rights. But the word: lesbian. She had never seen it written outside the context of disease.

It was a classroom on the second floor in the old high school the conference had rented. The door was ajar and Zooey pushed it open slightly and looked in. There were twenty women seated and four people sitting on chairs in the front of the room, facing them. Everyone was still getting settled and Zooey slipped in the door and sat in the back. She studied the four women in front so bravely displaying themselves. She knew they must be girls because of the title of the workshop but to her deep dismay she would have sworn one was a guy. She had short slicked-back hair, a barrel-shaped body and was dressed in a man's button-down shirt, khaki chinos and clunky men's shoes. She seemed to be in her forties. The two women next to her might have been difficult to figure out, too, although Zooey could tell after a quick scan they were girls, they had breasts and hips beneath their flannel shirts and corduroy pants. One wore denim overalls. Their hair was very short but more in the style of bad pixie cuts. None of them wore make-up—even the girl on the end who was pretty and had a lot of frizzy hair and a blouse that looked like something Danielle bought in Guatemala only faded, and jeans and boots. They all looked nervous and sad. Zooey felt shame for them and sadness. The liberated feeling she had moments ago was lost. Again, she had that sense she couldn't even put in words, that lesbians were not really girls—they were something else. Look at them! Except for the one with long hair and the blouse, they didn't even look like girls. The long-haired one introduced herself as Marla; she was the moderator. At least, Zooey thought, they had the sense to make the pretty one their spokesman.

Marla was saying lesbians deserve respect. They didn't hurt anyone and should be allowed to live their lives without the threat of illegality or harassment and assault. The woman in overalls told a story of being taunted and pelted with garbage by teen-age boys in front of the house where she lived with her lover who, apparently, was the woman in corduroys next to her. Then the woman dressed in man's clothes with the man's haircut told a story about a lesbian dance at the neighborhood community center held by a lesbian group she was in. It was a long story of how they paid for the hall and a women's band was playing and women were dancing with each other when the party was crashed by some guys who yelled obscenities and taunted them. One woman who stood up to them was beaten up. The police took forever to come and were not very friendly when they got there. Marla started talking about how "straight" women discriminated against lesbians, too, not just men. Then things started getting heated and an argument between Marla and some of the women in the audience began during which Marla said feminists often discriminated against lesbians even though lesbians had started the current women's liberation movement. The older lesbian and the two lovers just looked on, although the woman in corduroys called someone a bitch at some point and her girlfriend started to cry. Then she said in a plaintive, bewildered voice, "Why can't people let us be who we are?" This caused a momentary silence and Zooey felt her heart go out to her. When she looked at her closely, Zooey saw she was just a normal looking girl with overalls and short hair and no make-up. But why did she do that to herself? Wasn't she kind of asking for it? An attractive woman with shiny dark hair gathered in a silver barrette at the base of her neck and wearing jeans and a stylish jacket lit into Marla again about lesbians damaging the feminist cause and the need for them to recede from the limelight. Zooey saw the defiant expression on Marla's face, the silent seething of the girl in corduroys and the crestfallen, shamed look of the other two. They were such a small little group, so isolated. It was terrifying. Zooey got up to leave.

She didn't know why she had come here. She hurried down the corridor trying to remember where the entrance to the school was. She looked for a sign with directions but only saw something saying, "This building is condemned in the case of an earthquake."

She saw a staircase and headed down the cement stairs. Most of the conference was on the first floor and women were crowding the halls now that the first workshops were ending. Zooey wondered if she should try to find Molly to tell her she was leaving. It would be rude not to, so she started walking through the crowd looking for Molly's curly head of dark hair. Finally, in the courtyard she saw her standing in the sunlight with a girl who looked like one of the saints on a holy card from church, her skin was such a creamy white and her eyes so pale they looked like they were made of glass. She had long dark auburn hair and a heart-shaped face. Molly was talking to her in an agitated way and Zooey stood back, waiting a moment. The girl was holding an expensive, large camera in one hand and gesturing with the other, her thumb and forefinger in an L-shape extended in front of her as if to frame something. Molly laughed then and nodded. They seemed to be joking about something now. Then Molly looked up and scanned the faces in the courtyard. Zooey emerged from the shadows and made a slight waving motion in case Molly was looking for her. Apparently she was because she smiled and waved at her to come over.

"Zooey. There you are," Molly said as Zooey walked up and smiled. "Fiona, this is Zooey." Close up, Fiona's eyes were even more startlingly clear, transparent.

"Hello, Zooey." She had a confident, assertive voice for someone so unusually pretty. She smiled and Zooey saw she had a small thin line, whiter even than her skin, a scar on the left side of her face.

"We're starving. Let's see what's for lunch," Molly said. "It's in the cafeteria." She headed across the courtyard and Fiona and Zooey walked with her. "What workshop did you go to?" Molly asked Zooey who found herself speechless. But what had she thought? That Molly wouldn't ask.

"Oh, something upstairs …"

"Lesbians and the Women's Movement?" Molly asked and glanced at her.

Zooey nodded, blushing. She wondered if she would ever see Molly again now. Probably not. Molly was meeting her boyfriend tonight, she'd said, when she'd offered Zooey a ride to the Ferry Building after the conference. And thanks to the workshop, Zooey now knew being a feminist didn't necessarily mean you thought lesbians were okay.

"What'd you think?" Molly asked but just then a friend came up to ask her about the film workshop she was giving after lunch. Fiona stood back and lined up the scene of Molly talking to her friend and worked with the adjustments on her camera. After a few minutes, she shot several photos. Zooey waited, watching. She was impressed with Fiona's lack of self-consciousness and complete concentration as she performed her work. Since she would likely never see these people again she decided to ask Fiona if she was taking pictures for Molly, or for the conference as a whole. Fiona told her she was one of the photographers shooting the conference and was going to Molly's workshop to shoot that and was Zooey going to it, also?

"Sure," Zooey said.

Molly finished her conversation and they joined the crowd at the food table buying sandwiches and sodas. There was a lot of talking, people running into friends, hugging and laughing. Fiona had put her camera back in its case and suggested to Zooey they get away from the crowd and go to a store around the corner to buy something for lunch. Zooey gratefully agreed.

"So you're not really here to attend the workshops," Zooey said as they walked down the front steps of the school.

"I participated last year," Fiona said. "It was very academic and I get tired of that, you know." She gave Zooey a knowing look.

Zooey felt disconcerted. No, she didn't know. "You mean. A lot of facts, and—"

"A lot of academics. Upper class and middle class women who lord it over anyone who isn't like them."

Zooey thought of the woman in the stylish jacket badgering Marla.

"This is a gig for me this year, that's all."

"Oh. Sure," Zooey said.

Fiona smiled at her and said in her confident voice, "And what are you here for, Zooey?"

"Oh well—" They had come to the little store and Zooey changed the topic to which sandwich she might order.

Back on the sidewalk as they headed to the conference, Fiona gave Zooey an intent glance and repeated, "And what are you here for, Zooey?"

Zooey gave a breathy little laugh. Fiona wasn't going to let it go. She wasn't used to this—directness.

"Molly just told me about it yesterday. And it sounded interesting."

"Interesting?" Fiona repeated as if this were a truly empty word.

"Yeah," Zooey shrugged and then made an encompassing gesture with her hand. "It's so … different for me."

Fiona's eyes questioned her.

"Well. Really I never heard of feminism, basically, until today. I mean, I've heard the word but …"

"Oh. As a put-down?"

"Yes." She thought of remarks she'd heard, on TV or even in the women's dorms at Sanders. "Bra-burning women's libbers." "Ball-breaking feminists." But for the most part, she hadn't heard of feminism at all.

They were back at the conference and women were heading to the next set of workshops.

"I'm going to Molly's room to set up," Fiona said.

"Can I help you?"

Fiona gave Zooey that intent glance with her startling eyes again. "Yes, you can."

Zooey sat in the back of the classroom finishing her sandwich as Molly began her workshop. Fiona had only a few bites in between walking around the perimeters of the room, checking her light meter, setting up a tripod. Zooey had never seen quite the quality of attention Fiona brought to her work. Or at least, not in someone like Fiona. Not in a girl who could have been homecoming queen but Fiona didn't seem to be going to college as far as Zooey could tell—that talk about academics. But she seemed to be her same age, or Molly's age at the oldest. But then Molly had dropped out of school, too.

"Every scene in Hollywood movies you see today is filmed from the point of view of a man—the male gaze. The camera pans a woman's legs, her skirt flaring up in the breeze revealing a tantalizing bit of thigh—it can be several minutes before we see the woman's head, or face, or eyes. The entire film can go by and we will never see the woman as a person, a subject, a doer, or as anything other than an object of male desire."

Molly's speaking voice was very pleasing, melodic. And yet what she was saying was so … different, Zooey felt. The same word she had said to Fiona to describe this conference. What did she mean by that? She had been so inarticulate. Especially because, Zooey felt, Fiona had been prodding her. It was as if she knew something Zooey knew, except that Zooey didn't know what it was. She glanced over at Fiona. She was in her own world now, intent only on her work. Zooey recalled, viscerally more than with her mind, what it felt like to have that intent gaze focused on herself—the disconcerting thrill of it. She looked back at Molly and tried to pick up the thread of what she was saying while at the same time running clips from movies she'd seen recently through her mind and realizing how totally they were from a male point of view. It was astonishing, really. It was truly astonishing.

Zooey ate dinner on the ferry back to Sausalito. Patti was out with Rick tonight but Brenna had Patti's car and would pick Zooey up at the ferry dock at 8:00 p.m. It was very cold on the water and Zooey sat inside at a table by the window eating a sandwich and drinking a coke. The lights on the deck illuminated the swirling water rushing by the hull as the ship cut through the dark, windy night. Zooey was glad Brenna would pick her up because she felt unfathomably alone and yet she had no idea what to say to Brenna about this day. There was nothing Brenna would want to hear. There were so many feelings swirling in Zooey's mind, the icky feeling she had about the lesbians in their weird clothes and the pathos when the pretty feminist grilled them and the angry look on the tired, pretty face of Marla, and the "academic" information that was thoroughly enlightening to Zooey at the keynote address and in Molly's workshop but faded now that she was out of the classrooms and sitting on this ferry going back to Sanders and the norm of life there. She glanced around the ferry at tourists, couples on dates, business men who worked on Saturdays, reading the *Wall Street Journal* in their suits and ties, and all the information she learned today didn't seem to make a dent in their world—they would swat it away like a fly. But there was that Fiona. So unusual. She hadn't seen her again after Molly's workshop. She was like a rare tropical butterfly or an iridescent flower in a stack of books. Zooey had looked for her later in the afternoon but she was somewhere doing her "gig", Zooey assumed. Zooey had gone to two more workshops in the afternoon and then Molly gave her a ride to the ferry. There were three other women in the car so she hadn't talked to Molly much, but Molly had been very nice and said she would call and they would have coffee again next time she visited her brother. Zooey looked up suddenly at the shriek of the ferry whistle and saw they were near the dock.

Brenna was waiting for her at the edge of the wharf wrapped in a red wool jacket and white knit scarf waving happily at Zooey who walked down the plank to the dock. Zooey grinned and waved back.

"Now, where were you?" Brenna put the car in reverse and looked over her shoulder to back out of the parking lot.

"At a conference."

"A conference? About what?"

"Well, remember that film class I took last year?"

"Mmhmm." Brenna was concentrating on pulling out into the busy traffic on the main road.

"Things about that."

"Oh. Was it fun?"

"Very interesting."

"Good, Zo. I'm glad you had a good time." Brenna had been worried about Zooey recently but was so busy planning her wedding and spending weekends either at her own home or with Drew's mother making plans—and Drew would be home soon for the holidays.

"Did you see anyone you knew from the class?"

"Yeah. Molly. Did you ever meet her?"

"No. I don't think so." Brenna sped up as she merged onto the freeway. She looked in the rearview mirror and changed lanes. They were quiet a minute.

"Zooey. Do you think pale blue or pale green is better for the bridesmaid dresses? Patti says pale green and Elizabeth says pale blue and Danielle says she doesn't care. Do you think she's depressed?" Brenna glanced at Zooey.

"Danielle?"

"Yes. I've only talked to her once this whole past month. I feel so bad. I feel like I'm losing touch with you guys kind of." She looked over at Zooey. "Zo, I don't want us to lose our friendships. I feel like I hardly see you anymore either. I don't even know what you're doing, it seems like."

"Well, Brenna. I mean, Danielle is in Boston. You're getting married. Elizabeth has a new boyfriend."

"Oh, I know. Lucius."

"Lucius McPhee."

They giggled, mildly at first, then more out of control. Brenna had tears in her eyes and told Zooey to stop it or they would crash. "Anyway, we should be nice," Brenna added. "He's a perfectly nice guy."

This made Zooey give a snorting laugh but they didn't giggle anymore and they were silent for a few minutes.

"It's like we're all going our separate ways, Zo," Brenna said mournfully.

"I know," Zooey said, although she wondered what way she was going and where.

On Sunday Zooey woke up late again. She had taken her pills the night before but on Friday, the night before the conference, she had purposely not taken any because she hadn't wanted to sleep through her alarm and miss the ferry to the city. Then she and Brenna went to the Student Union for a coke last night when they got back to campus and talked about Brenna's wedding plans and what Danielle was going to do, and then Zooey had said she was tired and had to go to bed. She had been overcome with anxiety suddenly, afraid if she didn't take her pills that minute she might have some kind of outburst or who knew—whatever it was the pills were supposed to keep her from doing. She hugged Brenna good-bye and thanked her so much for giving her a ride because she wanted Brenna to know she would always love her and not think she was anxious to get away from her or being rude, but she felt she was going to jump out of her skin. Back in her room she had taken a double dose of the pills to make up for Friday night and then made herself a vodka collins with the small remaining stash of alcohol she had. It was noon Sunday when she awoke.

She felt so groggy she wasn't sure what day it was. Then she remembered it didn't matter because she didn't go to classes anyway. She lay back down. Her mind felt too fuzzy to even read. She gazed at the ceiling for awhile thinking nothing, feeling nothing other than a vague buzzing, a nervousness shrouded in fatigue. An image from the conference flashed in her mind—the lesbians, the stylish woman attacking Marla, the sad look on the face of the one in overalls—she turned to her side trying to shut out the image. She wondered if she should have another drink. She looked at the clock. It was two in the afternoon. She got up and started opening drawers and found a box of crackers that was nearly full. She sat down and began eating them, robotically, as she looked out the window at the lawn below. The maple trees had lost nearly all their leaves. The bare branches looked stark against the overcast sky. There were no shadows, only a foggy dull light that made everything look gray. Zooey put down the box of crackers and walked over to her bookshelves looking for something to read. She heard a knock on her door and stood perfectly still. Luckily she had locked it. She heard Patti's voice say, "Zooey. Zooey? Are you in there?" After a minute, she left. Zooey relaxed. She turned and went back to bed and lay down and soon she was asleep again.

At six o'clock there was another knock on her door, louder. "Zooey! Open up!" It was Patti again.

Zooey dragged herself out of bed and ran her hand through her hair. She went to the door and opened it.

"Oh my god. Are you rehearsing for Lady Macbeth?" Patti pushed her way into the room.

Zooey looked at her own upturned palms.

"Very funny. Out out damn spot!" Patti shouted.

Zooey knew enough to smile but she wasn't sure what was going on.

Patti plopped onto the bed and stretched out her legs, leaning back against the wall.

"You look like a fucking wreck, Zooey. What is your problem?"

"I'm just so tired." Zooey sat in the easy chair.

"Or hungover?"

"I guess."

"Does that mean you don't want to talk about pale blue or pale green dresses?"

"Kind of, I don't."

"Well, that's not what I'm here for anyway. I haven't seen you in chemistry class lately."

Zooey shook her head and shrugged. She really didn't know what to say. She couldn't get her mind to clear.

"Zooey. Snap out of it!" Patti sat forward. "Are you even going to classes anymore?"

"Not chemistry. I'm getting an incomplete."

"What? You're kidding."

"No, I just—Maybe I have mono."

"What? Have you been to a doctor?"

"I'm going to have a test." So, finally, she was out and out lying. Burning her bridges.

"When?"

"Next week." Maybe she could stall until break and then figure everything out, get back on track. Start over next semester. Danielle would be back, starting over too. At least Patti had helped her get her brain to start working again. Zooey smiled. "It's not so bad. I'm just really tired and I decided to take an incomplete in chemistry."

"Mono. The 'kissing disease'?" Patti was looking at her. "Does Ben have it? Rick didn't say anything."

"No, no. It's not from Ben and I don't even know if that's what I have."

"I can't believe you dropped out of chemistry. Why didn't you tell me?"

"I just decided."

"Now I'll never pass the final. Who will I study with?" Patti looked upset. Then she looked back at Zooey. "So are you taking any medicine? What are you supposed to do to get better?"

"Rest."

"That's all?"

"Pretty much."

"What about eat?" Patti looked at the empty box of crackers on the bedside table and the crumbs on the floor by the window. "Great, Zooey. The cracker diet."

"I know."

"I don't want to be seen in public with you, Lady Macbeth, so I'll bring you something back from dinner." Patti got up from the bed.

Monday morning Zooey woke at 10:00. She had taken only her normal dose of pills the night before and felt more herself now, the self she had been the past two months since seeing Dr. Reynolds. She had tried to help Patti study chemistry after Patti had brought her some hot food from the dining hall, but after an hour Patti saw Zooey wasn't really up to it and went to the library. Zooey had gone to sleep as soon as she'd left. Now she sat up in bed and tried to talk herself into taking a shower and getting dressed. It was hard to come up with a compelling reason to do it, though. She thought of going to the grocery store to get more food, or the bookstore—she hadn't got any books last Friday when she met Molly. Molly. The whole interlude at the conference felt like a strange dream. She lay back down. Brenna. Patti. Sanders. Pretending to still be in school. Hanging on until break and hoping for a miracle, as if somehow next semester she would be back to normal. Except she wasn't normal. This is what kept her stuck in the bed. She couldn't fake it anymore. She couldn't walk the fine line of pretending without lying. Now Patti would tell everyone she had mono. It was a good excuse but would ratchet up the level of pretense she had to maintain and she had already lost her ability to perform at level one. But she couldn't face leaving Sanders. Losing her scholarship. Moving back with her parents. She couldn't conceive of going out and getting a job and an apartment in Los Angeles. In Marin? In San Francisco … It seemed so daunting at the moment. But Molly had done it. Or did Molly have a trust fund. She was going to the Film Institute. Maybe she could call Molly and ask her. Do you have a job? How did you get it? Zooey supposed she could be a waitress. She had cafeteria experience. But where would that lead? She would never be married. Could she be a food worker for the rest of her life? Living alone, hiding. It seemed so lonely. More lonely than she even felt now. She turned over in bed, closed her eyes.

"Zooey!" There was a knock at her door. "Telephone." Zooey sat up. She had the familiar fear that it was something bad. She got out of bed and found her robe in the closet and walked down the hall.

"Hello?"

"Hello, Zooey."

She recognized that confident, rich voice.

"Oh. Hi." Zooey felt a slightly off-balance feeling. That disconcerted excitement.

"Molly gave me your number. I hope you don't mind my calling."

"No. It's fine."

"I didn't know if I'd find you at home or if you'd be in class."

"No. I'm not going to any classes today."

"Good. I was going to ask if you wanted to have lunch. Are you free?"

"You mean, in the city?"

"I could pick you up at the ferry."

"Oh". Zooey looked at the clock in the hall. She could be there by 1:00.

Fiona drove an old green mustang convertible she said her sister had given her when she moved to New York. The top was stuck in the down position and Fiona wore a scarf, gloves and beret with her camel colored jacket. Zooey wore a black jacket but had no hat or gloves. She laughed as they drove down Van Ness Avenue and the cold wind blew through her hair, longer now than it had been in awhile. She pushed it back from her face but strands kept whipping around her cheeks and getting in her face.

At a stoplight Fiona leaned over and opened the glove compartment to pull out another beret and give it to Zooey. "Try this." Zooey took it gratefully and tucked all her hair up into it. Then she pulled down the visor and looked in the little mirror. To her surprise, she looked good with her hair all on top of her head, a few strands whisping down at the sides of her face. Her brown eyes looked huge. She looked at Fiona whose translucent pale green eyes glanced back at her. "Warmer?" Zooey nodded feeling an odd kind of déjà vu.

"There's a photography exhibit at the deYoung. Some are stills from old films. Would you like to go?"

"Sure."

"Molly said she took a film class with you at Sanders. I didn't realize you went to Sanders. I hope I didn't offend you with what I said about academia."

"Well no. I didn't think you meant the students."

Fiona laughed and glanced at her to see if she were putting her on, but Zooey's expression appeared guileless. "What are you studying?" she asked her.

"Oh not much right now."

Fiona glanced at her again, a direct, unsettling gaze.

"I've had a hard time with classes this semester. I've pretty much stopped going." Zooey surprised herself by this revelation and stopped talking. She took a breath.

"To classes? Or to college at all?"

"I'm not sure."

Fiona said nothing.

"Were you in college—and dropped out, or you never went in the first place?" Zooey asked.

"I got a job after high school in a photo shop, right in this neighborhood." Fiona slowed down looking for a parking place on the southeast side of Golden Gate Park. "And then I got into photography. I'd taken a class in high school, but I went to some at a Junior College, too." She pulled up alongside a Volkswagen and began to parallel park.

Zooey was silent as she watched Fiona maneuver her car into the spot with the same focused concentration Zooey found so compelling in her last time they'd met.

"Why did your sister move to New York?" Zooey asked as they walked briskly down the sidewalk toward the park.

"To be an actress, of course."

"Isn't that Hollywood?"

"On the stage. My mother loves the theater and took us to plays when we were kids, we were always going to the Curran and saw everything ACT did. Even when my father was still alive she took my sister and me to Saturday matinees almost every weekend."

They headed up a path toward the deYoung Museum. Zooey dug her hands deep in her pockets. Although the sun was breaking through the clouds the air was cold.

"Even plays that weren't for kids?"

"Yes, everything. She thought it would be a good education for us. If it was too sophisticated we didn't understand it anyway, most of the time. Sometimes we would go home and spend a lot of the time with the dictionary, though." She laughed.

Zooey thought of the Curran theatre, the play she and Elizabeth went to last year, the excitement and rustling of playbills before the velvet curtains went up, the drama unfolding onstage lifting everyone into it. It seemed magical to have your childhood education take place in theatres, watching plays. "That's wonderful," she said then looked up as Fiona led them into a cave-like tunnel with stalactites descending in crusty odd-shaped sculptures. At the end sunlight splashed across blooming rosebushes. For an instant Zooey felt she was in a storybook and Fiona was the fairy godmother taking her on an outing. She smiled at Fiona who looked at her and held her eyes a moment before she turned to find the path leading up to the concourse at the entry of the deYoung.

At lunch in the museum café Zooey told Fiona about Holy Name High School and the nuns, Sister Lourdes and Sister Agnes. Fiona could hardly believe Zooey's stories of how the nuns lived and what they told the girls about life, the rules they set.

"And did the nuns wear those long robes and—"

"Habits. They're called habits."

"—even when they were by themselves?"

"I'm sure they did. Though I don't think they slept in them."

"And when class started every morning," Zooey went on, "we all had to get out of our desks and kneel on the ground and if your skirt didn't touch the floor you were sent home."

"Really!"

"Absolutely."

"But didn't you say it was an all girls' school?" Again the direct, startling gaze.

Zooey faltered a second, then said in a mock British accent, "Modesty is the highest virtue."

"My mother didn't have any patience for religion, Catholic or Protestant, coming from Ireland, so we never went to church at all," Fiona said.

"Do you still live with her?"

"I moved to my own apartment a few years ago."

"Oh. Weren't you kind of young …"

"I'm twenty-one now. Old enough to be legal." She laughed.

The exhibit was wonderful, Zooey thought. Perhaps it was looking at the photographs with Fiona and discussing them, the composition, the light, the ironies. Each photograph seemed to have buried riches they could unearth if they looked long enough.

The stills from old films reminded Zooey of her film class and Mr. Baxter, and that Molly said he taught at the Film Institute now. She asked Fiona if she ever went to the Institute, if she knew him.

"I went to a lecture he gave on cinematography," Fiona said as they left the exhibit and walked to the lobby. "He's brilliant. I learned so much in that one evening."

Zooey believed he was brilliant, too, although at Sanders he had been—the whole class had been—on the outside, somehow. "I thought so, too."

"His lover's a playwright," Fiona said.

"What's her name?"

Fiona looked at her. "Are you serious?" And seeing she was, said, "His name is Ivan Stone."

Zooey blushed and Fiona said, "Zooey. Zooey. What are they teaching you at Sanders? Ignore the obvious? No one ever said a word about Ivan Stone?"

"Not really. Well, not that I heard." Zooey tried to think if there had been something she missed. They entered the Arboretum and watched a fountain shooting up geysers of water and hundreds of droplets exploding in the sun.

Fiona turned to her and said quietly, gravely, "Do you really not know a gay person when you see one?"

Zooey blushed again and felt that disconcerting, slightly thrilled sensation. She didn't know what to say.

"I'll tell you what," Fiona said in a brighter tone. "Let's go have a drink. I know a place near here."

"But I'm only nineteen," Zooey said. They passed a large pond where seagulls swam with geese.

"Oh, they're not fussy about legalities there." Fiona led them up a little trail between shrubs and plants Zooey had never seen before. She tried to read some of the small green signs identifying them. *Labiatae. Salvia. Labiataceae.*

Down another narrow path they ran into a chain link fence but Fiona knew where there was a hole just big enough for them to squat down and squeeze through. After a few minutes they were in a forest of giant ferns with green fronds the size of bedsheets blanketing the sky over their heads. It was late afternoon and the glade was nearly dark.

"I forgot my machete," Zooey said.

Fiona laughed. "We're almost there." And in fact, in a few more minutes they were on a busy urban street with cars speeding toward Ocean Beach and the setting sun, trying to beat rush hour traffic.

It was another fifteen minute walk to Geary Boulevard where Fiona stopped in front of a nondescript stucco building and opened a heavy wooden door. Although it was dusk outside it was darker inside and Zooey peered at the small round tables with votive candles flickering in red glass globes. To one side she saw a bar with bar stools and then the patrons began to come into view. And hadn't she really known this all along. That this is where they were headed and yet she felt she was walking into the very taboo itself. Here she was—the bad place. She followed Fiona to a small table by the wall. It was terrifying, it was thrilling. As she sat down she tried not to gape openly. She thought she saw everyone on the lesbian panel at the conference or at least their twins and more women who looked just like them. And then Fiona. She dared to look at her. The stunning eyes. Even in the dark, she was beautiful. In fact, she didn't really know about Fiona.

"What would you like?" Fiona asked.

Zooey couldn't think.

"I'll buy the drinks up at the bar, no problem. I'm having a scotch and soda."

"The same," Zooey said.

As they sipped their drinks, Fiona asked, "Have you never been in a gay bar before, then?"

"No!" Zooey looked shocked.

"Somehow I thought you might have been." Fiona smiled at her.

"No, no." Zooey shook her head, looking around again. "Why would you think that?"

"Oh, Zooey, you can relax. I'm not going to put the make on you."

This sent another thrill through her, though Zooey simply raised her eyebrows and said, "I should hope not."

"Who have you been dating over there at Sanders?" Fiona asked.

"Oh. A guy. Ben."

"Your boyfriend?"

"In a manner of speaking." Zooey realized she was feeling slightly panicked. She sipped on the narrow little straw in her drink sucking up the last drops.

"Another?" Fiona asked.

"But my treat this time." Zooey opened her purse.

After their second drink Fiona told Zooey about the boyfriend she lived with after high school for six months and how they had drifted into a platonic roommate relationship because Fiona discovered she preferred women. She had an affair with a friend of Molly's from the Film Institute, Gabrielle, but it ended because Fiona realized she wasn't really in love with her.

"Then maybe you're not really gay," Zooey said.

"I'm not straight. Maybe bi," Fiona said simply.

Zooey gave her a blank look.

"Bisexual?" Fiona laughed. Zooey didn't know if she was being teased, but she'd heard that word before. It seemed, somehow, less dangerous than "lesbian." "Bi." It was almost a possibility.

They decided Zooey better take the express bus down Geary to the Ferry Building because it would be faster than walking back to Fiona's car. Fiona waited with her at the bus stop. The wind was blowing hard down the corridor of Geary from the ocean a few miles to the west and it was bitterly cold as they watched headlights stream by on the dark, busy street.

"Oh," Zooey said as she put her hand in her jacket pocket and felt Fiona's black beret, the one she had borrowed in the car. She pulled it out and handed it to her. "Thanks."

"Put it on." Fiona said. "It's freezing. The ferry might be colder. Don't you have any gloves there at Sanders?" Fiona laughed.

On the walk to the bus stop Zooey had felt for a minute as if she and Fiona were like two friends—the disconcerting tension gone, and so now she was happy when putting Fiona's beret on brought it back—the thrill, the thought of seeing her again.

The noisy bus came careening up to the curb but Zooey didn't move with the others to crowd aboard. Suddenly, she could not leave.

Fiona grabbed her hand and gave it a squeeze. "I'll call you," she said, and quickly turned and walked down the street, her long auburn hair forming a dark curtain down her back.

On the bus ride and then ferry ride and then a cab ride back to Sanders, Zooey thought of nothing but Fiona, reliving every moment of their day that seemed more like a dream with every mile away from her she traveled. It was close to 10:00 p.m. when she finally opened the door to her room and switched on the lights. She flung her wool jacket on the chair by the door then went to the mirror and carefully took Fiona's black beret off and examined it under the bright light. She rubbed the felt between her thumb and forefinger softly thinking nothing in particular, only the old longing, in a new way.

In the morning Zooey was awakened by a vivid dream. Her heart felt light as if a weight had been lifted and she felt like smiling. What was it? She scrunched the pillows to sit up and tried to recall exactly … It had started in a village—there were gabled rooftops like Wind in the Willows and two elves inviting her into their storybook house. Inside it became a dark tunnel, a tunnel of love at a carnival and she was in a boat with Fiona traveling on an underground stream surrounded by fountains and powerful geysers of water spraying upward and waterfalls magnificently lit in the colors of the aurora borealis. It was an incredible dream. She felt entranced, joyful.

Even after she got out of bed and made her way down the hall to take a shower, then back to her room to dress, brushing her hair and teeth, the feeling stayed with her. She glanced at the clock. It was only 8:00 a.m.! She realized she'd forgotten to take her pills the night before. And yet she didn't go find the green plastic bottles hidden in the back of her top dresser drawer because she didn't want to take those pills and obliterate this feeling inside of her now. She decided to walk into town to get some breakfast and go to the bookstore. Then she would decide what to do.

At nine o'clock that evening Zooey was laying on her bed reading when she heard the knock on the door she was waiting for. "Zooey! Telephone." She knew it was something good. She knew it was Fiona.

They decided to meet Thursday in Sausalito and take the ferry to Angel Island. Fiona would bring a picnic lunch from the deli near the photo shop where she worked three days a week.

It wasn't until that morning, Thursday, that Zooey realized she had forgotten her appointment with Dr. Reynolds the day before. Instead she had gone to a double feature at the arthouse cinema in Mill Valley. She couldn't wait to talk about it with Fiona. She was sure Fiona said she'd seen *L'Enfant Sauvage*.

It was a crisp, bright winter day when they hiked in the green hills of the island. They sat under a wild oak on a cement bunker built during World War II, when Angel Island was an outpost, and spread out their sandwiches and drinks. They watched the sailboats go by on the choppy blue bay and Fiona asked Zooey what she planned to do after Sanders. Zooey realized she wasn't thinking much past this very day. She felt a moment of panic, the dread again, and wished she had taken her pills after all.

"You don't have to decide anything soon," Fiona said in that confident way that soothed Zooey and she relaxed a little, looking out at the whitecaps dancing across the water.

"I was going to be a high school teacher," Zooey said.

"Was going to?"

"Well. I realized I didn't really like high school when I was there. Why would I like it later?"

Fiona laughed. "It might be different as a teacher. But it's true, if you don't like the setting, you probably wouldn't be happy there."

"How did you know you wanted to be a photographer?"

"All the plays we went to as kids—my favorite thing was the setting, the lighting and how it altered the mood. It seemed like magic—that the way a thing was illuminated could change its entire character."

"Have you ever seen those drawings," Zooey asked, "where if you look at it one way it's a river in the forest and then you look again and it's a snake on a rock?"

"Right. You realize you and someone else can be looking at the same thing and see it very differently. But when you photograph it your way, you interpret it as *you* see it. I love that because I hate being misinterpreted—I hate people assuming I'm something I'm not. They have no idea."

Zooey looked away from the sunlit water to Fiona. Her pale green eyes were hard, angry as she watched a ferry making its slow crossing to the city.

"You mean, like the 'male gaze'?" Zooey ventured.

"Sort of. Yes." Then she looked over at Zooey and her eyes had returned to that transparent clarity that was almost ethereal. Zooey felt spellbound by them. She said nothing.

That evening, reading in her room again, Zooey realized she hadn't talked to a living soul other than Fiona for almost a week, except a clerk at the movie theater. It was even harder to say good-bye to Fiona at the ferry late this afternoon than it had been the other night in the city. Yet, it still wasn't clear what they were doing. They were friends. But Zooey knew much more was going on, wasn't it? The only allusion to anything had been when Fiona said she wasn't going "to put the make" on her. And that was fine with Zooey because it was terrifying and yet, what was she waiting for? But in fact Zooey didn't want anything to change how they were right now because—seeing Fiona, being with Fiona—was like another reality, like diving in an undersea kingdom. She couldn't wait until Saturday when she would be able to spend the entire day and evening with Fiona. She startled when there was a knock at her door and froze hoping it wasn't a call from Fiona changing their plans. But it was Patti who knocked again and then opened the door and walked in.

"Hello stranger." She stood just inside the doorway looking at Zooey who sat up and swung her feet down from the bed.

"Hi. How are you?" Zooey smiled.

Patti walked in and pulled out Zooey's desk chair and sat down. "What are you up to, Miss Zooey?" She tilted her head to one side as she looked at her.

Zooey felt full-fledged panic and then realized she hadn't done anything. She had not done a thing anyone could gossip about or criticize her for—except that lesbian bar but no one she knew had seen her there. She had checked at the time.

"Look at you!" Patti laughed. "The cat who swallowed the canary. What is going on?"

"I've been hanging out with some people from my film class last year that I ran into. In town. At The Bookshoppe. Last week. I've seen a couple movies. Did you ever see *The Wild Child*? It is incredible."

"What? No, I never saw that. Is Robert Redford in it? If not, I haven't seen it."

Zooey laughed. "No. Just French people. What have you been up to?" She relaxed back into her pillows a little.

"Not so fast, Missy. I have been sent here as an emissary by Danielle, Brenna and Elizabeth and I am going to perform my mission."

Zooey felt a twinge of guilt or sadness. Her friends, whom she loved, felt so far away now.

"For one thing, do you know next week is finals week? Huh?"

"Yeah, yeah." Zooey waved it off as if she had it covered.

Patti leaned over and picked up the open book on Zooey's bed. "*Sexual Politics* by Kate Millet? What class is this for? Who's Kate Millet?"

Zooey couldn't think fast enough. Fiona had talked about it and so Zooey bought it. Finally she said, "I'm looking up some stuff in there for my lit course."

"I knew I should've taken that class. There is zero sex in any of my classes." Patti sighed. "I am so bored with studying. How come we don't have our all-nighters anymore? Just because Danielle isn't here?"

"We don't all take the same classes like we did freshmen year. You and I have chemistry, but I'm getting an incomplete …"

Patti remembered what she came for. "Elizabeth hasn't seen you in American Poetry for over a month. What's that about? You're never at meals." She looked closely at Zooey again.

"I'm working that out with Mr. Grayson. I have to do some make-up."

"But where have you been, Zooey? You said you had mono and how you had to stay in bed, so Brenna came over here with flowers and—I don't know—tissues, and she knocked and knocked and you weren't here. We've all been looking for you and you've been gone all day every day this week. Do you really have mono?"

"Maybe not!" Zooey said brightly. "I told you I didn't know for sure yet."

"You're lying to me, Zooey."

Zooey felt the panic start to rise in her again. She hadn't taken her pills in days. What could she say to Patti?

"Who are these film people you're talking about? Is that it? Are you doing drugs?" Zooey had been so spacey, for weeks and weeks.

"We smoke grass sometimes." Maybe that would suffice, Zooey thought.

Patti nodded. So that was it. Then she said, "Well what is that about? Is it worth flunking out of school? When you were getting straight A's? What about your scholarship?"

What *was* she doing, Zooey wondered. She hadn't thought about her scholarship. Though she had called in sick to the dining hall the past two weeks. She should have stuck with the mono story, with everyone, she realized wearily. What was she doing?

Patti realized she was finally having an effect when she saw Zooey close her eyes and sink back into her pillows, defeated somehow. It wasn't really the effect she wanted to have.

"Zooey, maybe you should talk to someone. You can get help. You can get yourself together and start over next semester."

Oh right. That was her plan. Zooey sat back up and looked at Patti. "That's my plan. I'm just getting through the next ten days, and then I'll go home and next semester I'll be back to normal." Normal.

"You'll stop smoking grass."

"Yes, absolutely. How am I going to get any grass at my parents' house."

"That's true." Patti sounded relieved.

"I'll go over and see Brenna tomorrow."

"Promise?"

Zooey nodded.

"Okay." Patti stood. "Rick's waiting for me at the library. He is a really crappy study partner, though." She walked to the door and before she left she turned and said, "We miss you, Zooey." As she shut the door Zooey's eyes filled with tears.

Brenna wasn't in her room when Zooey went by and neither was Elizabeth to Zooey's great relief. She borrowed a piece of binder paper from a student next door and scribbled a note saying she had come by to visit. "See you later!" she wrote and signed it and then added a cheerful squiggly line under "see you". She shoved it under their door and then walked into town to buy more groceries and another book. She was running low on money but soon she would be home for Christmas. Her parents had sent her a bus ticket. At home she would start taking the pills again—or the night before she left—so she could get through the visit and then … Her mind refused to go that far ahead. She had to assume she would figure things out over break.

She was on her way now to Mr. Grayson's office to make sure he would give her an incomplete instead of flunking her although she was also wondering if she could talk him into giving her a C. She had some poems she had written in the past few months with her and she had even written a short essay on Denise Levertov—although Levertov wasn't on his syllabus.

In fact, these days her mind was so resistant to looking at the future she hadn't even thought about her plans to see Fiona on Saturday, tomorrow. Something about her conversation with Patti last night had paralyzed her—her feelings had frozen. Now she was vaguely trying to take care of practicalities. Food, reading material, grades. She knew she should visit her advisor and talk about salvaging her scholarship, too. Maybe next week. After all, she wasn't going to be taking any finals so she would have time. She noticed her mind also refused to let her take the pills. She hadn't taken them for almost a week. She meant to take them last night after Patti left and she felt so sad, but she hadn't.

She was glad now she wasn't feeling sleepy when she had to make her case to Mr. Grayson. But as she got close to his office she found her mind also didn't want her to go there. She didn't want to see smarmy Mr. Grayson and kiss his ass and give him all her deeply personal poems. Was she crazy? She was surprised by how angry she suddenly felt. It wasn't like Mr. Grayson had done anything to her. It wasn't his fault Elizabeth got involved with Lucius McPhee, for example. Although Zooey found she didn't care terribly about that any more. It seemed distant, like an event from her high school years although it was just a few weeks ago, wasn't it, that Lucius McPhee had spoken to the class?

She was walking more quickly now, having left the humanities building and Mr. Grayson's office behind. She was thinking of catching a bus in town to Mill Valley and going to a movie. She knew it would all end soon, this doing her own thing. It would end next week, but for now, who cared? And tomorrow? She would see Fiona.

They spent the afternoon at Aquatic Park and walked to the end of the pier, turning back to look at the city. It was a cold, clear day and the bay was rippled with silver and very blue. A group of hippies and black guys were sitting on the wide stairs of the amphitheatre in front of the Maritime Museum playing conga drums. People gathered to listen and some were dancing with their colorful clothing flowing in the wind as they swayed their arms.

Walking on the narrow beach by the amphitheatre Zooey felt the intense beat of the drums in her chest as if it could alter her heartbeat—boom-ba-ba-boom-ba-ba-boom-boom, louder and louder and then a sudden change in rhythm and a ringing cow bell, then a new rhythm over and over until bursting, it shifted again. She and Fiona listened and watched the dancers then walked further along the beach where swimmers wearing bright red bathing caps swam long laps to and fro in the frigid water. Tiny wavelets lapped at the wet sand in a hypnotic rhythm.

"I feel like I'm in a Fellini movie," Zooey said.

"Which one?"

"*Eight and a Half*, I guess."

"Falling to the beach?"

"No ..."

"Oh, like—everyone existing in their own world, but simultaneously."

"Right." Zooey nodded. She was used to this, already. Fiona knowing her thoughts.

They watched a little girl in a fluffy pink jacket playing in the sand at the water's edge. A collie walked up and sniffed her then meandered on down the beach. A gull above them cried out then swooped down to the water and sat bobbing on the surface. The sun would set soon although it was only half past four.

"Should we go to the Buena Vista and have an Irish coffee?"

They had two. They were discussing the books they had been reading all week. Zooey realized she hadn't really given up studying. She was studying with Fiona. And Fiona was more educated than most college students—she knew more about theatre, film, politics and art, even if she hadn't read *Beowulf*.

They drove back across town in Fiona's convertible in the dark, cold evening. The fog had come in. But Zooey had a hat and gloves and she loved watching the misty glowing lights along Van Ness and then Geary as they headed out toward the beach. They were looking for a little café Fiona heard about in the avenues near the Surf Theater. But they never saw it and the next thing they knew they were at the ocean. The sound of the surf was enormous as Fiona idled the car in the parking lot a second before turning around.

"Listen to it," Zooey said.

Fiona turned off the engine and headlights and they sat a minute looking out toward the sound of the crashing waves and at the ghostly fog all around them. Far off down the beach they saw the yellow diffused light of a bonfire and another farther on.

Zooey turned to Fiona to smile at her and then felt herself leaning toward her and felt her lips on Fiona's warm half-parted lips and raised her hands to hold Fiona's face between her palms and kiss her, letting the kiss become everything.

Late Sunday afternoon Zooey walked slowly across campus heading away from her dorm to the small woods and creek at the western edge. She still wore the same wool skirt and sweater she had yesterday in the city. Fiona had driven her to the Ferry Building at noon after they had spent the night in Fiona's apartment, in Fiona's bed. Even now Zooey could see Fiona's remarkable eyes looking at her as they lay together, she could remember feeling she finally knew what everyone was talking about, *this* is what sex is. It was as different as night and day, to actually feel it, instead of only going through the motions.

Zooey sat on the ground near a tree at the edge of the creek. It was cold and she took off her scarf to sit on, her legs stretched out in front of her. She gazed at the winter sunlight on the silver streams of water rippling over rocks and branches in the creek bed. Her mind was empty but her body sang. Images of Fiona, sensations of Fiona filled her. It was simple, she realized. She was in love with Fiona and would be with Fiona. She would be gay, a lesbian. That was her future. Finally her mind reached out and met it—her future. And then, she told herself, if Fiona ever left her, she would commit suicide.

April 1973

"Zooey, it's for you," Fiona called. She heard Zooey call, "Okay," from the bedroom and laid the phone on the table and went back into the little pantry she used as a dark room.

Zooey came into the kitchen and set her cup of coffee on the table. She took a puff on her cigarette before she picked up the receiver. She didn't get many phone calls, almost none, and was frowning as she said, "Hello."

"Too early in the morning for you, Zooey?"

"Danielle!" Zooey couldn't believe Danielle had found her number. She felt both happy and wary.

"I finally tracked you down. Your mother said you had an apartment in San Francisco, though she didn't say you had a roommate—who is she?"

"Fiona."

"Never heard of her."

"A friend of a friend. Of Molly, remember? From film class?" Zooey's palms were sweating. She snuffed her cigarette out in an ashtray on the counter.

"Not really. Zooey why didn't you tell me you were flunking out last semester! Why did you stop calling?" Danielle sounded like her mother had when Zooey told her she wasn't going back to school and had lost her scholarship. Then Zooey felt overwhelming guilt and sadness but now she felt only confusion. What should she tell Danielle? The truth was unthinkable. Instinctively she resorted to the half-truths that had been her habit at Sanders.

"I realized I didn't really want to be a teacher. I needed time to think about everything, so I decided to live in the city and get a job for awhile. My friend Molly sublet her place to me while she was gone after Christmas and … now … I'm roommates with my friend Fiona. I'm fine. I'm learning a lot." She relaxed. "What are you up to Danielle, are you back at Sanders? How's your mother?"

"But don't you miss Sanders? Yes, I'm back. We've all been looking for you and talking about you and no one knew where you were. Brenna called your mother in January and she said you were subletting somewhere but you didn't have a phone. What kind of primitive place was that? Some hippie pad in the Haight?"

"No, I told you, Molly's flat. It's in North Beach." There was a phone but at the time Zooey had not told her parents or anyone. She needed to be totally alone, except for Fiona whom she saw every day, and when Molly came home in February, she moved into Fiona's apartment.

"North Beach," Danielle said. That sounded interesting. "Where are you now?"

"Stanyan Street. Near the park."

"The Haight. I knew it!"

"It's up the hill a little."

"Hmmp."

"How's your mother?"

"Oh, she's fine now. After dragging me all over the place, Paris, Boston. Now she's back at home and it's like nothing ever happened. She's at the club every day, swimming, playing bridge. The only difference is my father is one hundred per cent out of the picture. He's living in Mazatlan with his girlfriend."

"At the beach house?" Zooey could see the white stucco walls and scarlet bougainvillea in the sunlight. She moved to sit down on the cushioned seat in the bay window, stretching out her legs.

"Yes. She's twenty-seven."

"Wow."

"My secret hope is she runs into Carrrrlos and goes off with him." Danielle laughed.

"I think she'll choose your dad."

"You seemed to think Carrrrlos was cute enough."

"How's Sean?"

"He's a sweetheart. He called me every single day last semester. It kept me sane, you know."

"He really is a sweetheart." Zooey pulled her feet up under her and reached for her coffee. "How's Patti?"

"She broke up with Rick."

"You're kidding!" Zooey saw the waiting room of the abortion clinic vividly in her mind and then Patti having the 'flu'. "Oh no."

"It's not that bad. Well it was at first. They broke up over Christmas and Patti was a wreck for a month, until she met Trevor."

"Trevor?"

"He transferred in last semester. He'd been in a seminary. Is that what you call it?"

"You mean, to be a priest? Patti with a priest?"

"Yes." Danielle snorted with laughter and Zooey started laughing too.

"But, is she okay?" Zooey finally asked.

"She loves it. You know how Rick always ran the show with them. Well, now Patti's in charge. He's kind of an innocent. And he looks like Troy Donahue."

"Oh. That's pretty good."

"Zooey! He's gorgeous! She's thrilled."

"Good!"

"I cannot *believe* you disappeared on us, Zooey. Why?"

Zooey caught her breath and sat up straight glancing around for her pack of cigarettes. "I—was just sorting things out. I knew I'd miss Sanders ..."

"So you just cut us off?"

"I'm sorry, Danielle. It's great to talk to you—" Zooey looked around the kitchen nervously as if she could escape.

"Anyway, you're coming to Brenna's wedding in June, aren't you? You're not going to hurt her by not showing up?"

"Of course."

"Good," Danielle said with finality. "We're meeting at City of Paris in two weeks for a fitting for our bridesmaid dresses. What did you vote for, pale green or pale blue?"

"Oh."

"Pale blue, right? Well that's what it is, just for you, Zooey. We're going to have lunch at Blum's at one o'clock and then walk over for our appointment. Write this down, Zooey. I'll call you to remind you."

"Oh." Zooey could not envision this event. She wasn't even going to go to Brenna's wedding but when Danielle mentioned it she pictured herself slipping into the back of the church and leaving as soon as it was over, just showing up out of loyalty to Brenna.

"Zooey!"

"I'm thinking. In two weeks? What day is that?"

"Saturday. Come on. Brenna is counting on us. Don't you want to see us?"

Of course she did. But she wasn't the same person now. But then, they all had gone through changes. She realized she hadn't asked about Elizabeth.

"Zooey. One o'clock. Blum's. Two weeks from today. Wear a slip and stockings for trying on the dress and shoes."

It sounded impossible. But how could she say no? "Okay. One o'clock. Blum's."

"Right." Danielle sounded relieved—mission accomplished—and then pleased. "I can't wait to see you."

Monday morning Zooey sat at their sunny kitchen table smoking a cigarette. Fiona had left for work at the photo shop. Earlier Zooey had run down the three flights of stairs to buy a newspaper and two cups of coffee and they had sat in the kitchen talking, then Zooey followed Fiona to the front door and they kissed good-bye as if Fiona were leaving for a month. It was still hard for Zooey to part from Fiona, even just for the day. It scared her sometimes how much her life had become about Fiona. Yet the idea of seeing her old friends was equally frightening. Pretending to be straight all the time had taken such a toll on her and now that she really was a lesbian, living the life of a lesbian, how much harder was it going to be to talk to them? The half-truths would be total lies and it made her weary to think of it. But she had to go to Brenna's wedding. They had been friends since they were ten years old. And everyone would believe that Fiona was simply her roommate because no one could conceive of having a close friend who was actually a lesbian. The idea of anyone knowing made Zooey want to die. She tried to catch a breath.

She pulled out the classified section of the paper. More than anything right now, she needed a job. She flipped through the help wanted ads. Part of the reason she decided not to go back to college was because gays couldn't be teachers anyway. She had the feeling there would be a threat at any job. She was even afraid Fiona's landlord would evict them but Fiona said that was silly. Fiona always thought everything would be okay. Zooey smiled, thinking of Fiona's easy grace. But Molly said she knew two women who were turned down for an apartment because they were lesbians. When Zooey told this to Fiona she just shrugged.

The fact was, Zooey felt paralyzed when she thought about getting a job. She could type but didn't have the clothes for downtown offices and, too, would they hire a dyke? Not that she couldn't pass—but she felt it was written all over her. And there was something scary about being in that situation again—having to be someone she was not. She hadn't taken any pills since before Christmas, months ago. When she was staying at Molly's in North Beach looking out over the spires of Saints Peter and Paul she wrote a letter to

Dr. Reynolds saying she was better now and would not be seeing him again. She never wanted to have to go back to that. The pills, the appointments. Fiona said she should never let anyone pathologize her again. But people did. Wouldn't working full time in a downtown office be similar to Sanders? The dress code. The obedience. The pretense.

Fiona said there was no hurry for Zooey to find a job because she had been paying the rent herself long before she met Zooey who had made her life so much happier. But Zooey knew she had to contribute more than just her existence. A few days before, she had used the last of her savings. She was starting to feel desperate. She went to interviews at five restaurants and a steak house downtown but had not got a job. The dining hall didn't qualify as waitress experience they said. While she was there she overheard two girls talking about "food stamps" and "general assistance". Welfare. Jobs were scarce, it seemed.

Zooey read the headlines of the newspaper. OPEC, the price of gas. Threats of rationing, recession. Jobless rates up. Welfare. She thought of the hour she spent yesterday going through the pockets of every piece of clothing she owned. Seventeen cents. She couldn't live like this. She couldn't be totally dependent on Fiona. She would have to get an office job but first she had to get at least one new dress and some shoes. She just couldn't ask Fiona for that.

She looked for the phone book in the hall closet under a stack of magazines and pulled it out. It would be a long walk, all the way to the Civic Center. She found her purse and key and left the flat.

It was two hours before she was called to a cubicle for her interview. She had sat in a plastic chair in the welfare office looking around the room wondering if she had a right to be here. There were a few hobos with scruffy hair and beards, missing teeth and the stale scent of alcohol. There were many more young men wearing camouflage pants with canes or missing limbs. One man kept swatting at imaginary flies and muttering. A few women Zooey assumed were prostitutes wore dayglo hot pants and big dyed hairdos.

"Zooey James." Her name was called and she hurried to the interview counter. She felt the others looking at her plaid skirt and black sweater. She really didn't fit in.

Zooey handed a woman behind a Plexiglas window the forms she had filled out. The woman, who reminded Zooey of Dr. Reynolds' nurse, reviewed them.

"Nineteen years old?" She looked at Zooey who nodded. The woman looked her over for a moment. Then she glanced back at the forms. "Where are your parents?"

This took Zooey by surprise. They weren't going to call her parents were they? "I'm an orphan." Her palms were sweating and she blinked a couple times.

"Where are your parents buried?"

Zooey's mind raced. She couldn't think of a thing. Then she remembered a place she'd heard of in Los Angeles. "Forest Lawn."

"I see. Just a moment." She left her desk.

It seemed like she was gone forever. What was she doing—calling the police? Was it illegal to apply for welfare when you came from the middle class?

The woman returned and sat down. "There are no records of your parents at Forest Lawn," she said, not unkindly. "I'm afraid you don't qualify for general assistance. You'll have to go to the Employment Development Department and use their listings to apply for a job. In the meantime, I am giving you a voucher for food stamps for one month."

"Thank you." Zooey smiled and stood. She felt grateful it hadn't been worse.

It was noon when she left the Employment Development Department after an hour sifting through clerical listings. She had picked three small neighborhood businesses so she could go to them dressed as she was. The social worker had set up an appointment for her that day in an hour on Divisadero Street, a half-hour walk. She looked at the listing again: "Business Assistance Unlimited."

It turned out to be a doublewide trailer in the parking lot of a gas station. A group of black men in front of the mechanics shop were listening to the radio. Zooey stopped across the street and got a tissue out of her purse, patting at her forehead. She crossed the street to the parking lot and walked up the three little aluminum steps and knocked on the trailer door.

"Come in," a voice said. Zooey walked into the small room and looked at the woman sitting behind a large mahogany desk. She had a pretty round face with dimples and dark eyes and was wearing an enormous wig, swirls and swirls of dark brown hair with two or three steaks of iridescent blue.

"Hello. I'm Velma Davis." She stood and held out her hand. She wore a tailored forest green business suit and gold jewelry. She appeared to be in her thirties.

Zooey shook her hand. "Zooey James."

"You're from the agency?" Velma seemed a little surprised.

"Yes. About the assistant job?" Zooey smiled. She felt her palms sweating and wondered if there was a bathroom.

"Have a seat," Velma said. She told Zooey the job involved typing, using a calculator and occasionally some photography. Had she ever used a Polaroid?

Zooey's eyes lit up. "A couple times. My … uh … cousin is a photographer."

"Well, that's fine. Now, how fast can you type?"

"Oh, fifty or sixty words a minute." At least she had once in high school.

"Why don't you take the test then." Velma pointed to a table with a type-writer.

"Oh." Zooey stood. "Okay." She sat at the table and put her hands over the keys, looking at the typewritten test on a stand. Velma was setting a hand-timer on her desk. "Begin."

Zooey typed as fast as she could. Her fingers were slippery with the moisture from her palms but she concentrated hard and finally heard the ding of the timer. She looked at her work: xgy[ajgnlssen nslubolsjm … "Oh my god!"

Velma came around from her desk to look at the paper.

"My fingers must have been on the wrong keys," Zooey said apologetically and turned to look at Velma. "Can I try again?"

Velma was looking at Zooey with a quizzical smile. "All right. You can take it again. Relax now, hon."

Zooey took the test again and scored fifty-five words per minute. She got the job. And to her surprise, when she asked when she could start Velma told her right then—she could work the rest of the afternoon. She would receive two dollars per hour.

Velma had a variety of clients, from people who wanted letters written for them, to an attorney who needed legal documents typed, to the production of identity cards for various people in the neighborhood. That's where the Polaroid camera came in, Zooey discovered. By six o'clock, she had taken identity photos for three different prostitutes, glued them onto wallet sized cards she typed with names, addresses and social security numbers they gave her, and laminated them. She typed a six page legal brief, and helped an El Salvadoran woman express herself in a letter to a priest about her depressed son. At some point a man with tight pink curlers in his hair and wearing a nylon drape came in from the other half of the double-wide, a hair salon, Velma explained. He had brought Velma a cup of coffee and they sat and gossiped and smoked cigarettes as Zooey typed. She heard them mention a famous musician who had come in for an ID card, she thought, but wasn't sure—it may have been to get his hair done.

When Velma closed at 6:00 she told Zooey she was very happy with her work and she should come in Mondays, Wednesdays and Fridays from nine to five.

Zooey smiled, delighted, and then hesitated. "Is it possible—" She paused.

"Do you need an advance? I'll give you the ten dollars you earned today, will that keep you until Wednesday." Velma smiled her pretty, dimpled smile.

Zooey ran up the street toward home. Ten dollars! She was ecstatic. A job. Her first real job. She was so grateful to Velma. It's true, Velma might find it a little strange, Zooey showing up like she did. And the job itself, it was a little strange. And maybe, she had to admit, some of it was illegal. But so was she. It was perfect.

"Business Assistance *Unlimited*, I guess so." Fiona was laughing. "Maybe you should make a couple of those cards for us. You know, just to have in case."

"Maybe. I'm kind of in Velma's sight all the time though. Our desks are catty corner."

They were eating halibut and salad. At 5:45 Zooey had told Velma she needed to call her cousin to tell her she'd be late. Fiona had roses, champagne and dinner ready when Zooey got home.

"That's nerve-wracking," Fiona said.

"I told her you were my cousin, when I called—that's why I sounded so weird on the phone."

"Kissing cousins, I hope." Fiona put her arm around Zooey and kissed her but they were laughing and then Zooey remembered, "It's time to go up!"

They stood quickly and gathered their glasses and the champagne. Zooey found her cigarettes and they went into their bedroom and onto the fire escape to the roof above their fourth floor apartment.

"It's freezing!" Zooey shuddered as they sat down and she filled their two glasses.

Fiona put her arm around her and pulled her close. "Tonight we'll *have* to see the comet. Your lucky night."

Zooey settled into the crook of Fiona's arm as they leaned back against the crates they had set there weeks ago. "If we haven't seen it by now, I don't think we're going to. Kohoutek—nobody's seen it." Zooey took a sip of champagne.

"Oh, I think we will. It's getting brighter every day."

"I love your optimism," Zooey said sincerely.

Fiona turned and looked at her. Even with only the stars and a half moon in the dark sky, Fiona's eyes were lucidly pale. "Think of how we met Zooey. It was purely luck. If it hadn't started to rain hard when you were across from the Bookshoppe that day, you wouldn't have gone in. And you wouldn't have seen Molly. And she wouldn't have told you about the conference the next day. And we never would have met. I've never been within twenty miles of Sanders. And do you think you would have ever come in the photo shop?"

"No." Zooey thought of that day, standing in the rain. How crazy and lost she had felt. "It was the worst day of my life."

"Were you feeling like the rain was the last straw? The worst thing that ever happened to you."

"Yes." Zooey looked out over the moonlit rooftops. "But it turned out to be the best thing that ever happened to me." She turned to face Fiona and kissed her while within she felt she suddenly understood—how it worked. Why you had to have faith.

"It was meant to be," Fiona whispered to her. "We are meant to be together."

Zooey believed this with all her heart.

"We don't know why things happen because we don't have all the information. We have to trust the universe." Fiona looked up at the stars. "They love you, Zooey. They love us."

Zooey felt awash in the emanance, it hummed within her as she listened to Fiona and watched the night sky and graceful shapes of white clouds wafting in from the ocean. It thrilled her to feel this sense of belonging, to believe in a universe that loved her. She had no faith in god, not the god she had prayed to all her childhood—Our Father, I am heartily sorry for having offended Thee—the god to whom her entire life was an offense. He no longer existed. But the universe that meant for her and Fiona to meet, an intelligence that blessed their love—this filled her with joyful awe and she did believe.

June 1973

"Here comes the bride, here comes the bride ..." The classic organ chords filled the gothic vault of the Church of Saints Peter and Paul as three hundred people stood and turned toward the vestibule. Brenna took a tentative step forward, her gown flowing in fold after fold of satiny white from her bodice to the twelve-foot train held by three little girls in blue velvet dresses. Brenna's father looked stiff and proud, his silver hair still full and his black tuxedo looking as polished and shiny as his shoes.

Zooey stood between Danielle and Elizabeth in descending height with Patti the shortest in their perfectly matched pale blue satin floor-length gowns. Zooey stole a glance at Drew, waiting at the altar in his full dress uniform, dark blue and white with brass buttons gleaming. He hardly looked like himself. Not the Drew who went to Bergman movies and drank beer and talked about symbolism and surrealism. He was all Navy now. There were at least thirty boys looking just like him sitting in the front pews on the groom's side. Zooey thought she saw Drew's father, too, looking like the captain of the ship they were on, stern and lordly. Not close to tears like Brenna's father who was slowly proceeding up the aisle with his daughter on his arm. Zooey felt a catch in her own throat as she saw Brenna's upturned face beneath her veil, her beatific smile. Everyone near her could feel the love emanating from her smile.

Zooey's eyes darted around the cathedral, the stained glass, the panels of carved wood, the hundreds of well-dressed, affluent guests, not a dark face in the crowd, she realized, except perhaps a child's nanny, and yes, one of the young naval officers. It was all pomp and circumstance but Zooey was happy she had come when she saw Brenna's face, to honor Brenna on this great occasion of her life. Although, when she thought of it, was it any greater than two people going to city hall and then moving in together? Or was it even any greater than she, Zooey, moving in with Fiona? What was the big fucking deal?

She was surprised at the surge of rage she felt although, now that she thought of it, hadn't Fiona warned her? Fiona who ended up having most of her "gigs" be weddings—she had shot so many weddings she said she didn't think she could stand much more. The gifts, the cake, the celebration, the joyful tears, the dancing and champagne. Everyone thrilled for the happy couple. Although Fiona was an optimist and rarely complained, all the weddings were getting to her.

The Mass began and they all faced the altar now. The interminable Mass that Zooey dreaded having to stand through. She fidgeted with her little bouquet and wished she were home with Fiona. She sensed Elizabeth, on her right, looking at her fidgeting hands and so stilled them. Elizabeth. It was strange to see her again, confusing. She didn't like the feeling, because it felt disloyal to Fiona to think of Elizabeth at all. It brought up all that intensity, that terrible time of longing. She still found Elizabeth beautiful in that electric way but if she had any feeling left for her it was anger. When they all met at Union Square in May to be fitted for their dresses, Elizabeth had been very aloof, or so Zooey felt. There was so much to do, getting lunch, trying on dresses, each of them being fitted by her own tailor. And Zooey hadn't seen Danielle since the summer before and wanted to hear all about Boston. The girls were tactfully not discussing Sanders. Patti wanted to tell Zooey about Trevor. Elizabeth didn't say much. And at lunch when Zooey told them about her job they all seemed momentarily speechless. It was Elizabeth who brought the conversation back to the wedding and Brenna and Drew. Danielle said Drew was becoming a know-it-all and bossing Brenna around more than he used to. Patti said he was becoming just like his father. And it was Patti who mentioned to Zooey, when they went to the restroom together at the restaurant, that Elizabeth had broken up with Lucius McPhee sometime after Christmas. She wasn't seeing anyone right now. Then Zooey hadn't heard from any of them again, except Danielle—who called a week ago to make sure she was coming and offer her a ride—until today, a cloudy day in the middle of June.

Zooey looked up at the altar as organ music filled the church again and she could hear the clattering and rustling and coughing behind her as hundreds of people stood up from the pews. The priest in his lacey surplice and brocade vestments was uttering centuries old prayers in a monotone born of years of daily repetition. She wondered what meaning the words held for him.

Then her mind drifted again to last night when she and Fiona went to the Full Moon Café, a new place near Castro Street run completely by lesbians—a "collective" they called themselves. There was a tiny bookstore, too, with magazines and books all about lesbians, by lesbians. Zooey had been astonished. The women sipping from ceramic cups at the round tables were that same mix Zooey was almost getting used to—like the women on the panel at the conference or in the bar that December evening with Fiona, and the women in The Study, a bar near their apartment where they had been a few times. Short hair—it seemed to be mandatory—blue jeans or overalls, also a must. Big boot-like shoes, no make-up or jewelry. They were lesbian feminists, according to one speaker who had given a rousing talk about "smashing the patriarchy" that drew hoots and wild applause.

Zooey was getting used to them although every time she came from the bustle of the outside world into one of these lesbian enclaves she felt split in two—the lesbian she was, allied in forbidden love, defiant, "revolutionary"—and the straight woman watching, repulsed by the mannish dress, ashamed and sorry for these rejects. She couldn't help thinking of what her friends would feel, their horror. Or what Rick or Ben or even Sean might think, their disgust and mockery.

She and Fiona had been the only two women in the café last night with long hair, although they did wear jeans and sweat shirts—they wanted to fit in. They had brought home a stack of the "radical lesbian" newspapers and stayed up late reading them. Zooey swore when they made love afterwards it was with a wild power. In the end it had been so exhilarating, the evening and night set her on edge in a way that made being here now in this masquerade feel insane.

She glanced up at the altar and to her surprise saw the priest coming toward her followed by his acolytes but it was Brenna and Drew he was coming to stand before. It was time for the vows. Zooey looked at Brenna's face turned to the priest in respect. She looked so young, almost like a child. Drew stood at her side in his erect military posture, serious and intent. Zooey tried to hear them above the coughing and shuffling and nose-blowing coming from the large audience behind her.

"Do you, Andrew Cabott, take this woman … to cherish … sickness and health …"

Drew's voice was strong and precise in response.

"Do you, Brenna Donovan … honor and obey … better or worse … death do us part."

Zooey had to strain to hear Brenna's tearful, "I do."

Drew gently put a ring on Brenna's finger and then lifted her veil and kissed her with perfect composure.

Then suddenly the organ burst into a triumphant hymn and everyone began to sing.

By the time the Mass was finally over Zooey's feet ached incredibly in their little dyed blue satin pumps. She and Patti were laughing and leaning on each other as they wobbled down the aisle to leave the church amid more triumphant music and the relieved, happy murmurs of the hundreds who streamed out from the pews behind them and filled the aisles, heading for the cool fresh air outside. "Welcome to Annapolis West," Patti whispered glancing back at all the midshipmen in their stiff white hats.

After a well-orchestrated photo session on the steps of the church, Zooey, Patti, Trevor, Elizabeth, Danielle and Sean rode to the reception in a white Lincoln town car with two bottles of champagne. Sean was driving and honked the horn the entire way as did carloads of friends and relatives in the caravan ahead of them.

The reception was upstairs at Tarantino's in Fisherman's Wharf, overlooking the fishing marina and San Francisco Bay. A swing band was playing a jazzy version of *Here Comes the Bride* when they arrived because Brenna and Drew had been sighted getting out of their limousine in the street below. It was hard to turn around without bumping into a dapper young waiter holding a tray filled with flutes of champagne. The sun intermittently broke through the clouds flooding the room with light and turning the bay bright blue, then receding, cooling the room and the bay to gray. Zooey sat at one of the round tables with the same group she had arrived with, although Trevor and Sean had gone off to do something to Drew's car. They were on their third or fourth glass of champagne and nibbling from little bowls of salted nuts. Occasionally, a young woman in a traditional maid's uniform arrived with a tray of canapés and they each took a few. On the dance floor two or three ambitious couples were doing the jitterbug. It was two in the afternoon.

"Here's to being the first!" Patti held her glass high above her head. It was their fourth or fifth toast, following here's to Brenna, to Drew, to us …

"Here, here!" Danielle clinked her glass and Zooey followed suit, having to stand and lean far over the table, as Elizabeth said, "First what?"

"Oh come on." Danielle gave Elizabeth a 'don't be ridiculous' look.

"First of us to get *married*." Patti said leaning forward and shaking her head at Elizabeth. "Who's next?" She looked around the table.

"Danielle," Elizabeth said as Danielle said, "Patti. For sure."

Patti looked pleased then said, "I say it will be Elizabeth. There was Mark, then Lucius, and the third will be the charm!"

"Prince Charming," Danielle said. They laughed.

Zooey wondered if, in fact, they knew—about her and Fiona, and that was why they hadn't even mentioned her. She felt her face redden.

"There they'll be, setting up their little house together," Patti said, "while we're over at Sanders studying for finals."

"Drew will only be there sometimes."

"Still. They're the first, to have their own place, their own bed ..." Patti sounded wistful.

"Not really," Zooey said. Her eyes glittered.

"What?" Danielle turned to her.

Zooey took another sip of champagne. She felt enraged—the same rage she felt in the church that had come and then quickly gone. Now, she felt it take over.

"I'm the first," she said, disdain in her voice.

Patti and Danielle looked at her as if she were crazy. Elizabeth looked away at the band playing *Begin the Beguine*.

"I'm the first to set up house and share a bed. With Fiona. Fiona and I are lovers. We're lesbians. You just don't want to count us." Her words were clipped.

"What are you talking about? Zooey, are you out of your mind?" Danielle said.

"Zooey, Zooey," Patti said. "Sssshhh! Don't do this."

"Oh fuck you." Zooey stood up. She grabbed her purse and walked barefoot out of the restaurant, leaving her satin pumps under the table.

March 1975

Ten women were in Fiona and Zooey's living room kneeling, leaning over large squares of cardboard with rulers and exacto blades. It was Molly's idea. She had been reading Saul Alinsky's *Rules for Radicals* anyway when Inez Garcia was convicted of murder. Fiona didn't sleep for two nights after reading how Garcia was raped in her apartment by a group of men and, when they left, picked up a .22 rifle and found them out in the street. One of the men who had held her down reached for his knife and she shot and killed him. She was put on trial for murder and the rape was not considered as evidence. Yesterday, Molly, Fiona, Zooey and the rest of their friends had gone to a demonstration on Market Street that turned loud and raucous. Afterwards, at Maud's, the bar that used to be The Study—Molly came up with her idea.

Each of the ten women made a small stencil in neat block letters saying "Stop Rape. Free Inez." The plan was to drive to the financial district early the next Saturday and spray paint the stencils on as many banks and highrises as they could in the half hour before dawn. Saturday would be March 8th, International Women's Day.

The phone rang and Molly, who was closest, picked it up. "It's for you, Zooey."

Zooey wondered who it was—almost all her friends were here in the room. As she took the receiver she picked up the phone, too, trailing the long cord after her and went into the kitchen.

"Zooey?"

Oh my god. "Danielle?" They hadn't talked in two years, since Brenna's wedding.

"I've been trying to call you, Zooey. Nobody is ever home—your phone just rings and rings. How are you?"

"Okay." There was a silence. "How are you?"

"Pretty busy. Mother got remarried after Christmas. And you know how she is, everything had to be perfect."

"She must be a lot happier."

"I think so."

Zooey stood nervously in front of the kitchen table and glanced back at the living room where everyone was working and talking.

"Are you still with Fiona?" Danielle asked.

"Yes."

"That's good. I'm glad you're happy, Zooey."

To her surprise, Zooey felt tears come to her eyes.

"Thanks. How about … Sean?"

"Sean's great. We're talking about, well—"

"Getting married?"

"Yes. After graduation. I've been studying like mad and taking extra classes the last two years making up for that semester I missed. So thank god, I'm graduating with my class."

"Next month!" Zooey realized they had all been in the class of '75.

"Finally. It's taken forever."

"How about Patti, and Elizabeth?"

"They'll be there. Elizabeth is graduating *magna cum laude,* of course."

"Have you heard from Brenna?"

"She's pregnant."

"Oh." Zooey pulled out a chair and sat down. Brenna with a baby. "I guess Drew is graduating now, too?"

"Yes and I think they're moving to San Diego."

"When is the baby due?"

"August."

The kitchen door opened a crack and Fiona peeked in giving Zooey a questioning look. Zooey held up her thumb and index finger meaning "a few minutes more." Fiona mouthed—we want more coffee. Zooey stood up to turn on the kettle and Fiona went back to work.

"Pregnant," Zooey repeated. "My god."

"Yes, she's the first," Danielle said.

Zooey thought of Patti, the clinic on top of the hill, and in the silence Danielle seemed to falter a moment. "I—I mean. Isn't it great? Brenna will be so happy, she's always wanted children."

"I know. She has," Zooey agreed. "She'll be such a wonderful mother."

"I just hope she doesn't let Drew boss her around too much."

"Does he?"

"Well, you know. He's a Commander or something and I guess he thinks that makes him God."

Zooey laughed.

"She loves him, though," Danielle said.

"To each her own."

There was a pause then Danielle laughed, a relieved, amused sound deep in her throat. "I'd love to see you sometime, Zooey. We need to catch up. Why don't we meet for a drink at Trader Vic's. I could come into the city this Friday, around 6:00."

The kettle started whistling and Zooey stood to turn it off. "Okay," she found herself saying.

"And listen, Zooey, just think about it—we'll talk more Friday. I want you to be my maid of honor. Sean and I are getting married in August. At the club. See you Friday." She hung up.

Danielle. Zooey could see her in her mind. And she hasn't changed, Zooey thought as she put a paper filter in the coffee maker. She remembered herself skiing into a tree, lying in the gondola on the way down the snowy mountain. And neither had she herself changed because whatever Danielle said Zooey always went along. Why? She couldn't believe she was going to Trader Vic's Friday. What would Fiona say about that? But Maid of Honor! Zooey laughed—she was out of her mind. Anyway, once she saw her on Friday—Zooey's short hair and black jean jacket with a lavender triangle sewn on the breast pocket, Danielle would change her mind. Although Zooey didn't want to hurt her. She loved Danielle. She wondered if Brenna and her baby would be at the wedding.

They met at Molly's at 4:00 a.m. to drink coffee and get organized. Zooey, Fiona, Karen and Ruth were going in Molly's car. Zooey would drive because she knew the financial district best from working temp jobs when she wasn't at Velma Davis's office. The other five women would go in Sue's car.

Everyone was wearing dark clothes and holding a stencil and can of spray paint. It was decided Sue's group would start at Union Square and do the department stores and Zooey would start with the financial institutions on Montgomery Street. Zooey could picture it, hundreds of identical one-foot-square messages saying Stop Rape, Free Inez. It would be so effective visually, like a Warhol painting of the same exact graphic repeated over and over. As they drove down Market Street there was an exhilarated tension in the car and then they were there, at the foot of Montgomery and Fiona, Molly, Karen and Ruth piled out. Zooey drove slowly up the block with the lights out waiting for them to do their work. Within fifteen minutes they had done four blocks and met up with the other group. They were all laughing and talking and then someone saw headlights on Market Street and they decided to get out while there was still no one around. Zooey waited for them to pile in the car and then she turned down California Street and Ruth and Karen said, "Wait, wait! We *have* to do that heart on the Bank of America. Let us out, just for a second. Go around the block." Zooey stopped the car and let them out then sped to the end of the street and around the corner. She turned the next corner and ran head on into a police car, the lights flashing. She slammed on the brakes. Four other police cars roared into the intersection and surrounded them. It was a matter of minutes before the police found the empty paint cans in the trunk and had Zooey and Fiona sitting in the back seat of the sergeant's car. Static and noise from walkie-talkies and black uniformed figures with holstered guns at their hips were everywhere—Zooey watched in a daze. The policeman driving the patrol car they sat in started the engine but before he moved forward one of the officers strode up to the car and flung open the back door where Zooey and Fiona sat. He was her father's age with a gray crew cut and he leaned his face into the backseat and looked them over.

"What the hell do you girls think you're doing!" he shouted. "Do you know this is property damage!" Fiona, who was closest to him, put her hand to her mouth, patting it lightly as she yawned largely. Zooey was stunned. The officer was enraged. "We're throwing the book at you!" he yelled and slammed the door. "Take 'em in," he commanded the driver with a jerk of his head.

At the station they were the talk of the morning. By a stroke of luck, at 5:00 a.m. the precinct changed shifts. Zooey and Fiona were the only ones in the holding cell. Even Karen and Ruth had somehow gotten away. But all the police beginning and ending their shifts came by to look at them. An officer had Zooey's driver's license with a picture of her at sixteen—long straight hair, a blue jumper—and he showed it around saying, "Can you believe this? That was her." He motioned toward Zooey who sat slumped against the wall in the cell—her short hair bristling up and her jeans and denim jacket faded and worn. She and Fiona hadn't exchanged a word. Fiona, probably because she didn't want to give the police the pleasure of eavesdropping on her. Zooey, because she was terrified. She still couldn't get over Fiona's yawn—the million dollar yawn, she thought of it, both with admiration and irritation.

It wasn't long before they were taken to the city jail and put in the day room, an enormous cage with a cement floor, a single toilet in the open and a metal picnic table in the middle. Twenty or more women, almost all black, were smoking cigarettes and drinking coffee out of tin cups. Zooey and Fiona sat down on the floor in a corner leaning against the wall.

"They think just the two of us did it," Fiona said.

"Yeah. What happened to Karen and Ruth, do you think?"

"Damned if I know."

"Now what?"

"We should call Molly. She's been arrested before. Maybe she'll know what to do." Fiona stood up and looked around for the matron. She saw her on the far side beyond the bars and turned to Zooey. "I'll be right back."

Surreptitiously, Zooey watched the other women in the cell. Most were gathered around the table in the center. Then she noticed a small group of white women coming into the open corridor. They wore nice skirts and sweater sets and stood in a row outside the bars. In a moment they began singing Christian hymns. Zooey wondered if they came every day. By the middle of the hymn, *Jesus Saves*, several of the women inside the cell were weeping. Zooey knew, from working at Velma's, most were prostitutes, maybe drugs, bad checks. Every single person in the cell was poor. Fiona with her job at the photo shop probably had more money than any of them.

"You won't believe it." Fiona sat down next to Zooey. "Karen and Ruth walked home this morning—no one stopped them, and now they're back down there with cameras taking pictures of everything we did."

"Oh great. While we're sitting here."

"It is great. I wish I were there, too."

Zooey put her hand on Fiona's arm to comfort her. They were already in jail, so she left it there.

"Molly talked to a law student she knows. We should get out on our own recognizance since we don't have records. Tell me you don't have some secret crime conviction."

"Hardly. This is too fucking scary."

"We'll be fine."

"All those buildings, Fiona."

Fiona shrugged.

Zooey put her head in her hands.

It was the next morning before they were released on their own recognizance. They spent the night in a small cell on ratty mattresses in bunk beds. Zooey lay awake much of the night. She couldn't believe two nights before she had been sitting on a bar stool sipping a mai tai and talking to Danielle about Sanders and the gossip from the country club where her wedding would be. She had thought Danielle would be put off by her new look but she made some dry comment like, "Who's doing your wardrobe," and then it was as if no time had passed since they saw each other, though it had been over two years if you didn't count Brenna's wedding, which, Zooey could tell, Danielle wasn't counting. Somehow Zooey found herself agreeing to be in her wedding, too, which seemed especially absurd now, but also it comforted Zooey to think of Danielle because when she thought of the mess she and Fiona were in she felt sick.

Molly and Sue were waiting for them when they got out of jail and Sue drove them to her flat on Sanchez Street. Molly's car had been towed away and they still had to figure out how to get it back.

As they climbed the steep flights of stairs to the narrow flat Zooey felt more agitated than exhausted. Their arraignment in court would be at 11:00 a.m. the next day and she had no idea what would happen. She plopped onto a gigantic floor pillow—Sue's living room furniture, and felt comforted by the sunlight streaming through two bay windows. The hanging ferns and coleus looked so fresh and green. Everyone was there except Ruth who had gone back downtown to survey the damage. They all began talking and telling their stories, filling in Fiona and Zooey on how they escaped and the TV news story about them last night. The newscaster had given both their full names and said the two of them had done it all.

"Did they tell Inez's story? How she was raped?" Fiona asked.

"A little, not enough."

Zooey felt as if her life were over. TV news. Arraignment. Tomorrow. "Throw the book at 'em."

The courtroom was crowded and Zooey could hardly hear the pleas of the accused as one by one they spoke in small voices before the judge sitting high on his bench, slapping down his gavel with what seemed to Zooey to be cold indifference. Even Fiona seemed cowed. They had been assigned a public defender who was busy and harried, her slip was hanging, and she was not favorably impressed with what they had done. She talked to them out in the hall only long enough to tell them to plead 'not guilty'. Zooey realized she had rarely felt so afraid—at the mercy of a power machine that would gladly grind her to dust. The women in the jail, the men and women in this courtroom now, so few of them white, almost all of them poor. She was one of them now herself. Their hearing would be in ten days.

They waited on Market Street watching the green streetcars trundling along the tracks, waiting for the N Judah, saying little. It was two in the afternoon.

"Let's go to Maud's," Zooey said.

"Okay. Get a transfer, though." Fiona had taken the day off from the photo shop for the arraignment.

At the bar, they sat in the back near the pool table drinking bottled beer. They had counted their money and still had four more dollars, enough for two more beers each. Zooey had a full pack of cigarettes she'd bought from the concessions cart at the jail, the high moment of the day for her and everyone else in the stark and odorous "dayroom". She lit two and gave one to Fiona.

"That lawyer's not going to help us."

"I know."

"How can we say we're not guilty when they found the paint cans and you even had paint on your hands?"

Fiona shrugged. Her clear, lucid eyes looked doubtful for the first time since she had known her, Zooey thought.

"Hey, you two."

Zooey looked up. It was Ruth. Zooey was a little angry with Ruth because if she and Karen hadn't insisted on doing the heart in front of the bank.... But Fiona had said "no what ifs."

"How'd it go?" Ruth asked pulling a chair out from their table and sitting down. "I thought I'd find you here." She lit a cigarette but she wasn't drinking. It was still afternoon.

"Our lawyer doesn't seem very enthusiastic about our defense," Fiona said.

"Well that's why I'm here. Guess who said she'd represent you?"

"Who?" Zooey's eyes brightened for the first time in two days.

"Marian Kyle. Roberta Stevens' protégé. I finally talked to her this morning. Molly's law student friend got me an entrée. She loves your case. She's done a lot of feminist stuff. She wants to see you tomorrow. Two o'clock."

Several days later, Zooey and Fiona sat with Marian Kyle in another court room. Marian had filed a motion for a show of evidence. She'd told them sometimes cops didn't show up for these and then the cases got dropped. Their arresting officer did show up, however, and although Marian later said he was lying, the hearing went against them. The good news was not many of the buildings' owners had filed charges. The D.A. met with Marian and offered them a deal. A plea of *nolo contendere*—no contest—and a fine of five hundred dollars. It would not go on their record because it would be a civil dismissal.

Zooey said, yes, yes, do it. She was thrilled it might be over, even though she didn't have a penny. It would have to be Fiona who paid. It would be almost all the money she had saved for new camera equipment.

But Marian thought they should turn it down. They should go to trial, it would be a political event and she would get them off completely. She told them to wait a minute while she went to a bank of telephone booths to call a well-known radical attorney and ask his advice.

Zooey paced back and forth across the speckled linoleum floor. She wanted it to be over. She didn't want to take risks. Fiona sat on one of the old wooden benches that lined the walls. It looked like a church pew. Zooey glanced at her but Fiona didn't want to talk. She shook her head. Zooey looked at her a moment and realized she had lost weight. Her face seemed thinner and her lucid eyes were even more startling now.

Marian came back. "He thinks we should go to trial. If we get a not guilty verdict, it's almost certain there won't be a civil suit. If you plead no contest, the building owners can still sue you."

"But if we wait for a trial more of the owners could come forward. Then if we lose we'll have to pay a lot more," Zooey said.

Marian said that was possible but they had a good chance of winning—feminist issues were in the news these days. They could get the press behind them …"

It sounded nuts to Zooey. Like people were going to carry signs: 'Free Zooey and Fiona'. "I don't think so. No. I just want it to be over."

"If you decide to accept the plea, I suggest you leave town for awhile, let it all blow over. If they can't find you, they probably won't sue you."

Fiona and Zooey looked at each other. Leave town?

"For how long?" Fiona asked.

"Six months. A year?" Marian shrugged.

Zooey looked at Fiona and felt herself wanting to beg, let's do it. Get it over with. Get out of here. She never wanted to see another jail or courtroom in her life. But she said nothing. She knew that Fiona knew what she was thinking.

Fiona bit the inside of her cheek. Her pale, pale eyes scanned the hallway. Zooey knew she was thinking of leaving her job, her apartment, her photography business, her mother—or of staying and taking a chance. And of her, Zooey.

"You want to do it, Zooey? Accept the plea bargain?"

"I do. But, you have more at stake. And I don't even have five hundred dollars."

Fiona turned to Marian. "We'll do the plea thing—no contest."

They started packing that night, although they had no idea where they would go. Fiona tried to call her sister in New York but she wasn't home. She only had a little studio apartment in Manhattan, anyway—they could never stay with her for more than a night or two. But Fiona hoped she might have some ideas. She hadn't decided what to tell her mother who, thankfully, had not seen it on the evening news.

When Zooey started looking through her clothes to decide what to get rid of she remembered Danielle's wedding in August. She really should call and tell her she wouldn't be her maid of honor. This made her unaccountably sad. It was the definitive end to her past, her old friends. She was sorry she promised Danielle because it was that much harder now. She decided to get it over with.

"I'm going to call Danielle and tell her I can't be in her wedding," she said to Fiona.

Fiona gave her an impatient look as if Zooey had a ridiculous sense of their priorities now. "Well when you're done, why don't you find those ID's you made us at Velma's."

"That's a good idea. They're in my dresser."

Zooey sat at the kitchen table while the phone rang at Danielle's apartment. She had a beautiful upstairs suite a few blocks from Sanders which she described to Zooey in detail when they met at Trader Vic's, a lifetime ago, Zooey thought.

"Hello?"

"Danielle. Hi, this is Zooey."

"Hi!"

"Listen, Danielle, I—"

"No backing out, Zooey."

"No, listen, I—I have to go on a trip for several months." Zooey realized she should have thought of what to say.

There was silence.

"My god, so it's true," Danielle finally said.

"What?"

"You're going to jail."

Zooey gasped, shocked.

"Patti said her mother saw it on the news two weeks ago. I was positive she hadn't heard the names right. I can't see it, Zooey—you're not a fighter. Do you know Patti's father owns one of those buildings?"

Zooey was silent now.

"I can't believe it really was you. What on earth were you thinking, Zooey? What are you going to do?"

"Uh. We're not going to jail."

"What do you mean?"

In her mind, Zooey could see Danielle's face as she asked this, cool now, curious, like a surgeon probing a tumor.

"I mean, we already paid a fine, the criminal charges are dismissed, and now we're going on a trip to, sort of forget about it."

"Where?"

Zooey was silent. She didn't know.

"Are you not telling me because I'll tell Patti and if she tells her father he'll find you and sue you? Patti would never let him."

Zooey was stunned by how astute Danielle was, but the fact was, she hadn't thought of that. She simply didn't know where they were going.

"I honestly don't know where we're going, Danielle. I really don't. This all—it all just happened."

"I don't think it 'just happened', Zooey," she said in a matter-of-fact tone.

"Look, Danielle, I didn't even know you knew about it. I just thought I should tell you, I'm sorry, I can't come to your and Sean's wedding. I should go now—" She stood up from the table.

"Do you have any money? What are you going to do?" Danielle's voice was still neutral.

"We're still figuring it out. Honestly. I don't know."

"Do you want to stay at the house in Mazatlan? You know, the beach house. I won't tell anyone. My father and his new wife are in Europe now."

Zooey sat back down.

"Danielle."

"You may as well. It's completely empty. He never uses it anymore. In fact, he said he was going to give it to me for graduation. Too many memories of Sandrine for him, I suppose."

August 1975

Zooey and Ruth pushed two empty shopping carts to an iron gate. Narrow cement steps led down to a basement under Karen's flat where Zooey and Fiona had stored the things they couldn't take to Mazatlan in May.

They were going to load Zooey's things in the carts and push them three blocks to the flat Ruth shared with Ginny on Guerrero Street. Zooey was renting a room in their second-storey flat. Fiona was in New York, staying with her sister, Caitlin. She was supposed to come back in a few weeks and move in with Zooey, Ruth and Ginny. Zooey was going to ship Fiona's portfolio to her, all the portraits of lesbians she had done, and the black and white photos of demonstrations and events. Caitlin was trying to arrange an exhibit of Fiona's work in New York. It was exciting for her, after a very hard summer.

Zooey pushed her cart single file behind Ruth, rattling over the bumpy sidewalk and trying to make sure nothing fell or blew out. She didn't have that much, all the furniture was Fiona's, except for a bedside table and a desk they bought together at Goodwill. Karen said Fiona's stuff could stay in the basement indefinitely, although Zooey knew it was damp and moldy down there. She would have to spend hours at the laundromat trying to get the smell out of the bedding.

Ruth had been telling Zooey about the Grand Jury hearings in San Francisco subpoenaing lesbians "by the truckload" because rumor had it Patty Hearst was hiding out with a lesbian group somewhere. Zooey wondered if she should have stayed in Mexico. But they couldn't have stayed another minute. She told Ruth how, at first, it had been fun, the gorgeous sea, the flowers, the white stucco villa. At some point along the line, though, it became a prison. Neither she nor Fiona spoke Spanish, although they did learn some from the older couple who Danielle's father hired as caretakers for the house. But they had almost no money. They couldn't get jobs without work visas and were using false ID as it was. They ran out of English language books and couldn't buy any. They swam and hiked and cooked a lot, but after four months they began to wonder if they could possibly last five or six more.

In the end, they simply ran out of money. Zooey felt terrible Fiona had spent the entire thousand dollars she had been saving since high school six years before. Fiona said it didn't matter, but how could it not? It was awful. They were down to a few dollars of pesos when Fiona called her sister in New York. She hadn't talked to Caitlin since the winter before, although she had written her letters and finally, when they spoke, Caitlin insisted Fiona come to stay with her. And when Caitlin told Fiona she might be able to exhibit her work, Fiona decided to go. Caitlin still worked as a waitress but she had been in several off-Broadway plays and had a lot of contacts. She said she would wire Fiona a plane ticket the next day.

When they sat on the verandah that evening watching the sunset, Fiona cried as she told Zooey her plans. But, on some level, Zooey was relieved. Finally some weird justice—something good coming out of this mess. Something good for Fiona. She reminded Fiona what she had said, almost three years ago—about lucky breaks—how if Zooey hadn't been going crazy in the pouring rain she might never have gone in the Bookshoppe and seen Molly and gone to the conference and met Fiona.

Fiona laughed through her tears and said, yes, but look where it got you now, and then she cried again.

Zooey had fleetingly thought of sitting in the very same spot on this verandah with Elizabeth one spring night years ago and felt a momentary chill. She looked at Fiona. Wouldn't they be seeing each other again in a month? Was it really such a tragedy? In fact, wasn't it good, in a way? Fiona might get a break—show her work, even get reviews or notice. Zooey would find them another apartment in San Francisco and get a job. Ruth had sent a letter saying Marian Kyle said the danger was most likely over.

Fiona looked so forlorn in the moonlight, gazing out to sea. Zooey moved to take her face in her hands, brushing her thumb lightly over the thin white line, the scar on Fiona's cheek. Just a bike accident when she was a child, she had told Zooey that first night in her apartment years ago. Precious Fiona, her precious face. "Don't you remember, Fiona? We're meant to be together."

Fiona nodded her head, yes, but her pale eyes continued to look out to the horizon.

In the morning—only a few days ago, Zooey called her parents collect and asked them to wire her a loan to buy a ticket home. The following day she and

Fiona hitchhiked to the airport outside Mazatlan and within a few hours boarded their separate planes.

Zooey missed Fiona terribly now as she and Ruth rumbled the overloaded shopping carts along the downhill side of Dolores Park. She had called last night and said nothing was happening about the exhibit yet, they were still making contacts. "I miss you so much," Zooey had said passionately. "Me too, but we'll see each other soon," Fiona reassured her.

"I think we can get the rest of your stuff in one more trip, don't you?" Ruth steered her cart to an old blue Victorian. Her flat was one flight up.

It was her home, too, now, Zooey realized as she took in its faded elegance—she had paid a month's rent with the loan from her parents. She was glad to have a real home again, and yet it wasn't real without Fiona. "We can do it tomorrow, Ruth."

"No, let's get you set up." Ruth knew this was a hard time for Zooey.

Zooey realized she was right and they unloaded the carts and set off again to Karen's place. Karen was home and offered them a cup of tea. They sat in her sunny kitchen overlooking the garden with her cat on the table in the middle of three steaming mugs.

"Did Molly tell you about her new job?" Karen asked. "She's putting on a women's film festival at the Castro Theatre in October."

"How cool."

"Yeah. And, Zooey, when I told her you were back she said maybe you could be her assistant. She needs somebody, like yesterday. She finally got the grant and now she has to jam."

Zooey sat forward. "You're kidding. Aren't there a million people who want it?"

"Not who can drop everything for two months and work nonstop on this."

"I'd get to see all the films." This was the best news she'd had all year. "I've got to call Molly. Wait until I tell Fiona!"

Two weeks later, Zooey stood on Mission Street with her overnight bag waiting for a bus downtown. It was ten in the morning but it would take hours to get to Tiburon. She was going to Danielle's house to get ready for the wedding. It would be a simple ceremony by the pool at the club and then dinner and dancing afterwards. Danielle didn't seem to know if the minister was Presbyterian or Episcopalian or what and she didn't care. It would be "small" she said, one hundred people. But Zooey, Patti, Elizabeth and Brenna were all in the wedding party. Zooey wondered if Danielle chose her to be maid of honor just to tweak the others. Her ironic sense of humor.

Zooey boarded the crowded bus when it finally arrived and as she stood in the crush of passengers and the bus lurched and crawled down Mission Street, she realized it felt much less absurd to be going to Danielle's wedding today than it had when she contemplated it months ago from a bunk in the county jail. Maybe it was something about the absence of Fiona—the constant emptiness Zooey felt which made everything else seem unexceptional, just what was happening on any given day. She was going through the motions. She prayed Fiona would come back soon because she didn't want that to start again. That foggy, mindless state she lived in before she met Fiona. She was drinking a lot, she knew. There was a bar called Kelly's not far from her flat with Ruth and Ginny that stunk of Lysol if you went too early in the day. Zooey played pool there for hours. The job with Molly had been postponed. Molly had applied for an extension to have the film festival next spring because two months simply wasn't enough time to put it together, she'd decided. But she promised Zooey a half-time job starting in December. Zooey had gone back to work for Velma, although business wasn't very brisk these days since the attorney had been disbarred. Still, she made enough to pay her rent. She had applied for food stamps and was getting them until December when she would have more work. She didn't have the clothes for temp jobs anymore. She used to borrow Fiona's. Fiona. Fiona. Zooey looked out at the crowded street as Saturday morning shoppers and workers and everyone else seemed to have somewhere to go. She hadn't talked to Fiona for nearly a week. The time change, Fiona had said, made it tricky and her sister's apartment was so small, there was no privacy. She still didn't know when she would come back. Somewhere inside Zooey remembered the promise she'd made to herself by the creek that last morning at Sanders, what she would do if Fiona left her and this thought also frightened her terribly and ordinarily when that feeling came over her she would have a cigarette or see if it was time to head over to Kelly's, but it was only 8:30 in the morning. She usually didn't get up early, because often she was out until 2:00 a.m., until the bar closed, playing pool, dancing, drinking. Although last week she had gone to a meeting with Sue about economic justice. She had wanted to because the sights of poverty in the back streets of Mazatlan, behind the luxury mansions, still burned in her mind. After the meeting she read their pamphlets and felt something she had not felt since the feminist conference years ago when she first understood the social injustice to women. As she read the appalling data with Sue about working conditions, military suppression, torture—obscene exploitation—she had a vision of committing herself, totally, of becoming a revolutionary. She knew Sue's friend went to meetings every day, organized demonstrations, raised money, called herself a "cadre". Zooey could imagine this devotion fired by rage at injustice and passion to change it—these feelings were the first to break through the numbness she'd felt since Fiona left. This was what she would do, if Fiona didn't come back—that was her new promise to herself that night.

But now, standing on the bus as it lumbered along on her way to Danielle's wedding, she couldn't summon it. She couldn't imagine living without Fiona.

If they just had more money. Fiona kept saying she wished Zooey could move to New York and they could rent a place but it was too expensive and they couldn't both stay at Caitlin's. Then she'd say she was coming back but she would never say when. Zooey looked up and hurriedly pulled the cord for her stop and started to slither through the crowd of bodies to the door.

It was 4:00 p.m. when Danielle, Zooey and Patti walked into the club. Zooey had finally arrived at Tiburon and Danielle's house at 2:00 and Patti was already there. They had daiquiris—just one each—and spent hours putting on make-up and dressing. The bridesmaids were not wearing matching dresses, just something simple and elegant from their own wardrobes. It was a casual wedding, Danielle had informed them, and she didn't want a big fuss. Still, they had fussed over their make-up and over Zooey who, once again, had to borrow something to wear from Danielle.

A large blue and white striped canopy was set up on the lawn by the pool. They needn't have bothered to prepare for rain because the sun was very hot in a hazy blue-white sky. The lawn was lush green although it was late August and hadn't rained for months. White and scarlet flowers bloomed in the terra cotta planters separating the pool area from the lawn and, on the verandah in front of the dining room, long tables were set in pink linens, silver trays and champagne flutes in readiness for the buffet reception.

As the three of them went into the women's changing rooms behind the pool to wait for the ceremony, Zooey looked around her, feeling not exactly nostalgia for that summer she nearly lived here playing tennis but, instead, a mix of regret and anger. She tried to focus instead on what Patti was telling Danielle about Trevor at the same time as she wondered when it would be time to start drinking. Did Patti say something about eloping? Danielle was saying, "Are you serious?"

"What was that," Zooey asked, "did you say elope?"

"Wake up, space cadet. I just announced the most important news of my life," Patti said. "Yes. Trevor and I are going to elope. Seriously." She passed her cigarette pack and they helped themselves.

"But—isn't that supposed to be secret?"

"It is, dummy! I'm just telling you and Danielle."

"Your mother's going to kill you," Danielle said. "Her only daughter. And she'll miss the wedding."

"My mother hates Trevor."

"Why?" Zooey asked.

"We have to get together more often, Zooey, you are so out of the loop. He's just not—" A look of pain crossed Patti's eyes and then she shrugged and in a mocking voice said, "athletic enough" at the same time as Danielle said, "rich enough."

"Nothing's enough for my parents, basically."

"That's hard," Zooey said. She thought she remembered, though, that Patti's parents had liked Rick. "When's the big event?" she asked, smiling.

"In two weeks. We're going to City Hall in San Francisco and my brother and Trevor's sister will be witnesses. Then we'll fly to Hawaii. I got tickets—"

"Two weeks!" Danielle turned around from the mirror where she was freshening her lipstick after putting out her cigarette. "How long have you been planning this? Why didn't you tell me before?"

"I probably shouldn't even tell you now. If this gets back to my parents—but you and Sean will be in Italy by this time tomorrow. Brenna will be back in San Diego and Elizabeth will be leaving for graduate school in New York."

"Where's she going?" Zooey asked.

"Columbia. Comparative Lit. Haven't you talked to anyone, Zooey? It's not just us you're hiding from over there in your illicit world."

"I'm not really hiding. Anymore."

"Patti." Danielle shot her a look, but Zooey was actually grateful some reference had finally been made to her real life. It seemed since she'd arrived they had done all they could to have a conversation and still ignore the scene Zooey made the last time she saw them at Brenna's wedding, or her life since then, including the graffiti incident.

Sandrine opened the door and put her head in. "Are you ready, Danielle? Do you need anything?"

"We're fine, Mother." Danielle was not the least bit nervous.

"I think your father's here," Sandrine said stiffly.

"Oh." Danielle turned to Patti. "Go out and find him, will you? And show him where to stand—you know, in the back of that tent thing?"

"She's making a mistake," Danielle said as soon as Patti was gone.

"Do you think she's still in love with Rick?" Zooey asked.

"Yes."

They heard the music start, an upbeat version of *Here Comes the Bride* played on a synthesizer. A small band had finished setting up on the deck by the pool.

"My cue," Danielle said.

She and Zooey walked out to the pool and all heads turned. Zooey saw Elizabeth and Brenna standing on the other side and waved at them. They smiled and Brenna waved back excitedly. Elizabeth wore a tailored pale green suit that looked very good on her and Brenna had on a flowery dress, both lovely and matronly. Patti was walking purposefully back from the tent and gave Danielle the okay sign. They all started walking toward the canopy under which a hundred folding chairs were set facing a dais.

Sean looked so handsome and endearing as he waited nervously at the dais, looking down the short aisle adoringly at Danielle. Zooey shouldn't have been shocked but she was to see Mark standing next to Sean as his best man. He was still very good looking in his raffish way. Another young man Zooey recognized from the Sanders basketball team stood next to him.

Zooey stood between Patti and Brenna and, as they watched Danielle and her father proceed up the aisle at a jazzy pace to match the music, Brenna nudged Zooey and dipped her head toward the front rows of seats. Zooey opened her mouth in surprise and delight when she saw Drew holding a little blue bundle, a soft blanket with a thatch of dark hair poking out. Zooey smiled happily at Brenna and gave her hand a squeeze, then they turned to watch the ceremony.

Danielle was true to her word, it was short and simple. She herself had edited the vows so that she and Sean said exactly the same phrases and Zooey could have sworn she left out "until death do us part." But there was something about "a lifetime" mentioned, in any case.

The mood was light and pleasant as the guests filtered out of the tent and onto the grounds. There were patio tables and chairs around the pool and more seating around a dance floor in the dining room. Six long tables on the verandah held the dinner buffet. The weather was still warm and almost balmy.

Zooey was standing with Brenna, who had taken her baby, Andrew Cabot III, from Drew as soon as the ceremony ended. Zooey was looking at the tiny little face, only two weeks old. It seemed miraculous. "He's so amazing," she said in awe.

"Hold him." Brenna handed her the little bundle and Zooey cradled him against her chest as she had seen Drew doing earlier. She looked into his dark little eyes as he gazed at the maple tree leaves above where they stood in its shade. She felt the warmth of his tiny being against her heart and in that instant she understood the magic, the desire Brenna had always had for a child.

Drew came up to them and put an arm around Brenna. He was wearing a dark suit but not his Navy uniform. "Don't be handing him around too much," he said quietly to Brenna. "We don't want him getting sick." Then he looked out at the crowd of guests and saw someone he knew from Sanders. "I'll be back in a minute."

Zooey handed the baby back to Brenna. "He's adorable, Brenna. You must be so happy."

Brenna was biting her lower lip but as soon as she took the baby and held him to her she softened and seemed to glow. She looked up at Zooey. "It's so incredible, Zo. He's everything I ever dreamed of."

"Brenna." Patti came up to them. "Let's see!" And as she and some other friends from Sanders started gathering around, Zooey scanned the guests and tables, looking for champagne. She saw waiters starting to circulate near the verandah and with a smile at Brenna turned and headed that way.

Having secured a glass she looked for the nearest seat and saw Elizabeth at a table alone. She walked over and pulled out a chair. "May I join you?" Although she hadn't intended it, there was irony in her voice.

"By all means." Elizabeth smiled at her warmly. "How are you?"

Zooey relaxed. "Okay. I hear you're going to Columbia. Congratulations." She sipped her champagne.

"It is pretty exciting. I'm just starting to realize I'll be living in New York." Elizabeth was drinking Perrier.

"It's a little intimidating, too," Elizabeth went on. "I don't know a soul there."

"Where are you going to live?" Zooey thought, for a joke, she should give her Fiona's number. She reached for her clutch bag and found her cigarettes and, lighting one, sat back.

"I'm going to stay in a hotel in the Upper West Side until I find an apartment. You know how impossible it is to find places to rent there."

"I've heard."

"That's the thing I'm most worried about, I haven't even thought about my classes."

A waiter came by and Zooey accepted another glass of champagne. Elizabeth gave her a sidelong look.

"You ladies shouldn't be sitting alone," Mark said as he came up and stood between them, putting a hand on each of their shoulders. Then he pulled out a chair next to Elizabeth and sat down. He smiled at each of them. "Some gig, huh?" He leaned back and managed to snag a glass of champagne from the tray of the waiter who had just served Zooey. "To the young marrieds." He raised his glass.

Zooey took a sip of champagne in half-hearted acknowledgement of him and his toast as Elizabeth eyed him with a sizzling look of interest and irritation.

"Hey there." A fit, tan man in his forties walking by their table had stopped suddenly. "Zooey!"

It was Jim, the tennis pro whom she spent so much time with three summers ago. Zooey stood and he gave her a hug. "How are you?" he asked. "How's your tennis?"

"Oh. A little rusty."

"You played for Sanders, didn't you?" He had perfect white teeth.

"For a little while, I left sophomore year. How's it going here? How're the leagues?"

By the time Jim filled her in on the gossip about all the players she might remember, she was on her third glass of champagne and Mark and Elizabeth seemed deep in conversation. Zooey sat back down at their table anyway. She thought she should go get some food at the buffet but she didn't feel like getting up again. She looked at the well-dressed guests milling about on the lawn, the pool deck, the verandah, and listened to the buzz of well-being and cheer as the wedding party progressed into evening. The manicured grounds, the silver service glinting in the sun, the starched, pressed pink table cloths, the fit, tan guests, the casual laughter and expensive jewelry—it was another world. The land of the rich. Richland, Zooey said in her mind. That's what it had felt like, over the years, these brief forays into Richland—like visiting another country and she had a definite feeling her passport was about to expire. She thought of the long trek back to her shared flat in the Mission district on four different buses tomorrow and all the people riding those buses who had never set foot in a private club like this except as a servant. She should consider herself fortunate, she supposed, in a way. But she found her lip curling slightly, that feeling—anger, disdain. Who were these people, anyway.

"There you are." Patti came up and sat down at their table. A waiter stopped and filled all their glasses except Elizabeth's because she had put her hand over the top.

"There she goes," Patti said. "Ms. Macrobiotic."

"Ms. *Ms.*" Mark hooted.

"You're not a subscriber?" Patti said in mock surprise.

"*Ms. Magazine.* Give me a fucking break. Who are those ball-busters?"

"You are gross," Patti said. "Male chauvinist pig."

"Okay. They're not all ball-busters. Gloria Steinem's a pretty good-looking chick," Mark admitted.

"Are you a subscriber?" Patti turned to Zooey.

"I've seen the magazine. It's interesting." Zooey gave them an impatient, annoyed look.

"Oh don't get all pissed off," Mark said. "Hey, how was Mexico, Zooey? Danielle told me you were down there at her dad's house."

Zooey took a little breath. Danielle had said she wouldn't tell anyone. But, she realized, Mark was family now.

"You remember. It's a beautiful house. We were all there." She looked around the table.

"Will you look at them? It's like he's glued to her side," Patti said indicating Drew and Brenna, holding the baby, standing on the other side of the pool talking to the minister. "I don't think she's been alone for more than a minute."

"He is proprietary," Elizabeth said.

"Oh, you don't like that, do you?" Mark said.

Elizabeth shot him a look that Zooey couldn't quite read.

"Talk about male chauvinist pig," Patti went on. She lit a cigarette.

Mark turned to look at Drew and his family and shook his head.

"Not the marrying kind, are you Mark?" Patti said as she watched him.

He turned back around and gave a charming shrug. The waiter returned to fill their glasses. Zooey watched hers fill as she thought, 'the marrying kind'. What was that? And she realized, she, Zooey, was the marrying kind. She would be loyal and in love with Fiona forever. She knew it beyond a doubt. If she could just get to New York or Fiona would come home. She felt a sick moment of fear. Fiona.

"… in Mazatlan?" Elizabeth had asked Zooey something.

"Mazatlan?" she said.

"Zooey. I hope you're not smoking grass now," Patti said.

"How long were you there?" Elizabeth repeated.

"Oh. Several weeks. We—were doing a project. Finishing a project."

"We?"

"My friend, Fiona. She's a photographer."

"You were doing a photo shoot?" Mark looked interested.

"In part."

"'In part.' Mysterious Zooey," Mark said, lightly mocking her.

"We—she did take a lot of photos." Zooey stopped feeling evasive and remembered suddenly and vividly the pictures, saw them in her mind. "She did a series on the back streets—away from the beach villas and hotels—where the real—where the people who actually work and live in Mazatlan are. Their houses are made of junk—scraps of wood and corrugated metal. They have dirt floors and the kids are wearing torn clothes and no shoes. They have hardly any food or clean water." She was getting angry as she spoke, looking at the affluence around her.

"What about that couple taking care of Danielle's house? They don't live like that," Patti said. "It's the hotels and villas that give those people jobs."

"Have you seen where they live?" Zooey asked her. "They have one room over a bar in town and there's music blaring until two in the morning. But at least they have a floor and running water. They don't live in that villa, you know. They don't even get a dollar a day for taking care of that great big place. How obscene is that?"

"Right on." Mark said.

Patti glared at him. Then she turned to Zooey and said with irritation. "So now you're a Marxist, too?"

The band had switched from playing jazz to Motown and Mark stood up. "Who would like the pleasure of this dance?" He smiled at each of them.

"I'm getting something to eat." Patti stood and walked toward the buffet.

Zooey looked at Elizabeth. "He's all yours." She took another drink of champagne.

Mark laughed and turned to Elizabeth and held out his hand. She took it, rather quickly, Zooey thought, and followed him to the dance floor.

Zooey sat alone at the table for awhile and then went to the buffet and filled a small plate with food. She noticed Elizabeth and Mark were still dancing together, a slow dance now. She would have liked to leave but had no way to. She had to go back to the house in Tiburon to return Danielle's dress and get her things. She walked toward the women's changing rooms and then around through a passageway to the tennis courts. As she sat on a courtside bench she was surprised by how much feeling it stirred in her. She had forgotten her love for the game. She had forgotten even who she was then, that summer, and all the years before. She had lost that self. And the self she was now felt lost, too.

PART II

May 1985

The sun was so bright, Danielle wore a Panama hat tied with a scarf under her chin and dark sunglasses. She sat beneath an umbrella at the glass table on her deck overlooking the bay, sipping a vodka collins. Patti sat across from her, her hot pink visor looking sporty with her bright red hair. She was drinking a glass of Riesling.

Danielle glanced at her watch. "Sean's picking them up today. Monday he called and said he was on the sixteenth hole and I had to get them. He won't do it again today. He moved up his tee time."

"And how many interviews have you done?"

"Six. It's impossible." Danielle aligned her drink stirrer and her napkin on the pebbled glass table but the little plastic stirrer wouldn't stay straight. She tried again.

"Did you ever think having kids would be so much work?"

"I don't know." Danielle looked at the bay. It was a breezy, crystal clear day and there were dozens of boats in full sail on the water. "Having two is so different. When we just had Jason I thought, if I have another child he'll have someone to play with, but now with Claire—Jason doesn't want anything to do with her."

"It depends on the kids. Sometimes Megan and Ricky will play together for hours. Still, I'd slit my throat if I didn't have Bettina. When she was in Mexico last month the cleanest thing in my house was the martini shaker."

"Oh my god." Danielle said and shivered. "That reminds me of Elizabeth. I still think about it all the time, even though it was six months ago."

"I know. I can't believe she did that. Over Mark! Anyway, she couldn't have really meant it because it didn't work."

"Only because one of her students came to her house and found her."

"I keep wondering how she got in the house. Why didn't she leave when no one answered the door?"

"She had an appointment. And Elizabeth is so reliable. Brenna said she looked through the window and saw Elizabeth on her living room floor. If they hadn't pumped her stomach an hour later, she would have died. Every time I think of it—it wasn't about Mark, though, Patti. That was over years ago."

"But there was no one after him. Remember at Sanders, the first time they were together? She mooned about him for the next three years—for a six month relationship. Then after your wedding they were together on and off—at least two years. So that would require ten years of mourning if you do the math. She had it bad for him. Is he an asshole, or what? I don't really know him."

Danielle shrugged. "I still don't think it was about him. I always had the feeling she had some dark secret. Though you're right, Brenna said she wasn't seeing anyone. She talks to her several times a year. I never do anymore. Elizabeth was always so—secretive, or self-protective. Don't you think?"

"It was hard to know what was going on personally with her. Though she had her intellectual opinions."

"She's a very successful professor. Brenna sent me an article she wrote for a journal. Did you get that? She must be so lonely, though. Brenna said now she's gotten involved in—not a guru thing—some group. I think it's Buddhist. Can you imagine?" Danielle scrinched up her delicate nose.

"No." Patti took a sip of wine. "What do they do?" She put her hands in her lap and closed her eyes. "Ommmm."

Danielle laughed. "Maybe it's soothing."

"Being alone is soothing enough. I can tell you that."

"You're not alone, Patti, you have two kids. That's the opposite of soothing."

"All right then, boring."

Danielle laughed. "But the kids aren't boring. I love being with my children. I just need more help. Since Maggie left—"

"Are you saying you are never bored?"

"Not with the kids."

Patti sat up slightly. "With Sean?"

Danielle looked out at the bay again and her shoulders drooped slightly.

"'fess up, Danielle. What's going on?"

"Nothing's going on."

"I see. And that's the problem."

"We still have sex, Patti, if that's what you mean."

"Well that's more than Trevor and I had. He should have stayed in the seminary. But at least now I don't have to listen to him snore."

"Oh, snoring. Isn't it awful?"

They heard a car pull into the driveway in front of the house.

"Speaking of. I guess he finished early." Danielle looked disappointed.

"Well. I better get going." Patti finished her wine.

"You said the kids won't be home for an hour and Bettina's picking them up. Stay and have a drink with Sean."

Patti hadn't heard Danielle sound anxious ever before and she stayed seated, curious. "All right."

The sliding glass door opened and Sean stepped onto the deck. To Patti he was as handsome as ever, though with just the slightest paunch, he was still tan and had those perfect features and curly black hair.

"Hi, Patti." He smiled warmly and walked over and kissed Danielle on the lips. "Looks like you girls need a refill. Shall I do the honors?"

"Sure, hon."

"Do you know Brenna is pregnant again?" Danielle said to Patti.

"Again? Her fifth?"

"They're Catholic."

"Oh. Well. She always wanted kids, now she's got them. Is she happy about it?"

"Yes but she's starting to sound a little tired. Drew doesn't lift a finger—women's work."

"Like our husbands ever did."

"Here you go, ladies." Sean reappeared with a tray of drinks and placed it on the table. "Gorgeous day." He sat down with them.

"How was golf?" Danielle said, rotely, Patti thought.

"Good, good." Sean nodded. "Had a great drive on five and then damned if I didn't four putt." He laughed. "Then on six I shanked it right into the trap. Two shots to get out. Then on eight I shot an eagle. Damnedest thing. This great tee shot over the water. I'll never be able to do it again. Hey, guess what, honey?"

"Hmmh?" Danielle glanced at him.

"Mark called last night after you'd gone to bed. He's bringing his new friend, Trish, over for dinner Saturday."

"Sean. You know we don't have any help right now."

"It's okay. I'm going to barbeque some steaks. Make a salad. Keep it simple."

"Mark. How's Mark?" Patti asked.

"Same old, same old," Sean said.

Patti waited for more, then asked, "Same old what?"

"Same old Mark. Not married. Living in Berkeley."

"Does he still go to those demonstrations?" Patti asked.

"Oh yeah. Honey, he said to tell you he saw your old friend Zooey last weekend. In San Francisco. One of those demonstrations. Something about—Nicaraga? How do you say it?"

"Zooey. Oh my god."

"I haven't seen her since your wedding," Patti said. "She was going on about Mexico then. Same old, same old, sounds like."

"I haven't talked to her since Jason was born. She was not in good shape then. She was drinking a lot."

"She was always kind of a boozer, wasn't she?" Sean asked. "I mean, she was nice but—she didn't seem very happy."

"Well she's a dyke you know, Sean."

"Don't mince words, Patti," Danielle said.

"Danielle told me. Is she still with that girl?"

"Fiona? She wasn't when I talked to her," Danielle said. "Fiona moved to New York before we were married. Then she came back for awhile—it was back and forth for a year or so and ended up with Fiona in New York and Zooey staying in San Francisco. Fiona had a show in New York of photographs she took when they were at our house in Mexico and I guess it was a success."

"Oh, I remember that. But no one knows what Zooey's doing now?" Patti asked.

"I'm glad to hear she's still alive, frankly," Danielle said. "She sounded so—alienated—when I talked to her."

"Remember how she and Elizabeth were into existentialism and Sartre—"

"I thought that was more Elizabeth's thing."

"You know we really should have a reunion. The five of us. Then we can get the real scoop," Patti said.

Danielle's eyes lit up. "What a great idea! You know it's our ten-year Sanders reunion in October. We can have a party for the five of us here that same week."

June 1985

"Mom! *Mom*." Jason came running into Danielle's bedroom as she stood in her dressing room surveying her clothes, arranged by season and category—evening dresses, suits, skirts, slacks—and within category by color.

"What is it?" Danielle asked, turning to her seven-year-old son, laughing a little at his urgency.

"Claire left the tops off my markers! They're all dried out," he sobbed.

"Oh dear." Danielle squatted down and embraced him. He cried a minute in her arms repeating, "They're all dried out."

"Let's go see." She stood and took his hand as they walked down the long hall to the playroom overlooking the bay.

Five-year-old Claire sat at her little roll-top desk diligently coloring. The pink tip of her tongue peaked out between her compressed lips and her pale blonde hair was pulled back in a French braid.

"Claire, honey, are you using Jason's markers?" Danielle walked over to the desk. "That's a nice picture."

Claire looked up proudly.

"Honey, are you using Jason's markers?"

Claire said nothing and went back to her drawing.

"Claire, you need to use your own markers. You can only borrow Jason's if he says its okay."

"She can never borrow them! Look at them!" he wailed and swept his arm toward a dozen topless markers strewn on the play table.

"Let's see which ones still work." Danielle sat down on a little painted Mexican chair and methodically tested each marker on a piece of paper, looking at Jason to see which were acceptable and promising to replace the rejects. She realized she should go down and make them dinner before she changed to meet Sean at the club and prayed the Danish *au pair* she was interviewing tomorrow would work out.

"Why don't you two come down and have some spaghetti."

"I'm not going anywhere with her!" Jason said as Claire said, "Yuck!"

"Come on, kids. You can watch TV while you eat."

Jason agreed but Claire stood her ground.

"Claire, if you want to have dessert with grandma tonight you have to have your dinner now." Danielle knew it was bad to offer bribes but nothing else ever worked. She called them "incentives" instead.

The children followed her downstairs and went into the family room to watch television while she opened a can of spaghetti and dumped it in a saucepan. She glanced at her watch. She was supposed to be at the club by 6:00. Sean would have a beer or two with his golf buddies and then meet her in the dining room for an early dinner.

As she quickly poured glasses of milk, she thought yet again of the tennis match she had played at the club yesterday morning. She was serving at five-three when they heard sirens. She didn't want to be distracted because sometimes she had trouble closing out a set, she didn't know why. She remembered how good Zooey had been at closing when it seemed to her it should be the opposite. Zooey was not a fighter—she didn't have the killer instinct. But she didn't choke in those final points when she, Danielle, sometimes did. It didn't make sense to her because she thought of herself as cool-headed. But sometimes she suddenly forgot how to serve. Yesterday, she was determined to close and she was up thirty-love when the sirens came screaming right up to the clubhouse and she looked two courts over at the doubles group hovering over someone. She and Sally stopped playing and watched as paramedics in dark blue uniforms came running with a gurney. She tried to see who it was—she saw Sylvia Bates, Todd Belmont and Christina Jacob all standing there and realized it must be John Vertig. He was always their fourth in mixed doubles. Then she saw them lift him onto the gurney and she and Sally realized he must have had a heart attack, or what? He was only forty-eight. She felt shell-shocked and stood there as Sally walked to the gate of their court and went to join the people on court four to find out what was happening. After a minute she turned around and nodded at Danielle. Yes. A heart attack.

"Oh god!" Danielle realized she was burning the spaghetti and turned off the stove. Then she found Claire's Miss Muffet plate and Jason's Spiderman plate and set them on the counter. Eighty per cent of the spaghetti was still edible and she scooped it out and took the plates into the family room, setting them on trays in front of the children who barely noticed her as they stared transfixed at a cartoon on the screen. She went back and rummaged in the refrigerator looking for carrots. As she sliced them into sticks she remembered standing on the court watching the medics put the gurney carrying John into the back of the ambulance. He looked absolutely still and white. She thought it was very possible he was dead and she stood absolutely still herself. John Vertig, a lawyer, wife, two children, house in Belvedere. Dead? She felt her breath quicken as if she couldn't quite catch it and was filled with a terrible dread. It had been a warm day, the sun was shining and the red cement under her feet beside the green court was bright and clean, the white lines so straight and clear cut. The air light and fresh. Could it be so sudden? she wondered. Everything—ended.

"Mom. *Mom!*" Jason was calling her.

"Just a minute!" She put the carrot sticks on a paper towel and took them into the family room.

"She won't let me watch Batman!" Jason was standing in front of the TV facing Claire, his arms outstretched blocking the screen. Claire had a firm grip on the remote control.

Danielle looked at her watch. When would Sandrine get here? Maybe she would call and ask her to come earlier. "Claire, how would you like to come and help me choose what to wear? Then Jason can watch Batman and after you can choose a show."

Claire thought about it. She hated to relinquish the controls just then and continued to hold the remote tightly with both hands.

"You can try a little bit of my lipstick," Danielle said.

Claire carefully lay the remote down next to her on the couch and jumped off.

At six o'clock, Sean was sitting alone at the mahogany bar in the club dining room drinking a Heineken. Danielle walked up and sat on a bar chair next to him, surveying the shelves of colored glass liquor bottles from around the world.

"Where are Ken and Gary?"

"Had to go." Sean took a sip of beer.

Ramon came over and asked Danielle what she would have. She ordered a vodka martini up, her father's drink, and lit a cigarette.

"How was your game?" Danielle asked as she did three evenings a week and then she nodded and said "oh" as Sean recapped each hole with enthusiasm and she looked out the plate glass windows to the pool where sunbathers still sat talking or reading and a group of teenagers were playing some game in the pool. She saw Sylvia Bates and her husband and thought she might go over and ask about John Vertig, how he was doing. She kept an eye on them as she scanned the other guests because if Sylvia started to leave she would interrupt Sean and go talk to her. She still felt so unsettled by what had happened—she could see it clearly in her mind, herself standing there starting her service motion, trying to ignore the sounds of the siren, her serve out wide to Sally's backhand and Sally's return just out. Then the sight of the ambulance pulling right up on the cement walkway between the clubhouse and the courts. The bright light of the morning sun, the red and green courts, Sylvia and Todd and Cristina hovering over someone—all of it right up to the dark-suited para-medic shutting the ambulance door.

"What do you think?" Sean was saying.

"You mean ...?"

"Shall we get a table? Before it fills up?"

"I thought we had a reservation."

"No, I didn't get in here to make one before tee time."

"Sure, then."

Danielle felt that quick, shallow breathing again as they walked over to the *maitre de* and he led them to a table by the windows overlooking the pool. She sat down and took her white linen napkin off the table, unfolding it and laying it in her lap and smoothing it out then smoothing it again once or twice more. She aligned her salad fork to perfectly parallel her dinner fork and then the same with her spoon and knife.

"How was your day?" Sean said after he ordered more drinks and accepted the menus from the *maitre de.* "Did you play today?"

Danielle shook her head. "Jean cancelled at the last minute and we didn't have a fourth." She felt so disconcerted. She had never felt this way before. When the waiter brought her second martini she took several sips then started to feel a warm melting in her chest and began to relax.

"How are the kids?" Sean asked.

"Jason was upset because Claire used his markers. He gets so hysterical. I thought girls were supposed to be the emotional ones."

"What do you mean—hysterical."

"He was sobbing about it. His markers."

Sean shrugged and looked off. "I guess we should tell him not to cry. He's getting pretty old to be crying about stuff."

"Fine. You tell him."

"Okay."

They ordered when the waiter reappeared, a steak for Sean and the filet of sole for Danielle. A bottle of white wine. Sean didn't care what kind of wine they drank.

They were silent in a companionable way as they finished their drinks and waited for their food. Danielle looked for Sylvia Bates and realized she must have left. Maybe she would call her. She glanced around the dining room and saw Cristina with her husband Dave. They were talking and laughing, Dave had a loud laugh that was more infectious than annoying. Danielle smiled as she watched them and wondered what they were talking about. They seemed so interested in whatever it was.

The waiter brought the wine and Danielle tasted it before he poured out two glasses for them. She smiled and gave a polite nod. She was just starting to notice the difference between various grapes and it was fun to try to describe it. She used to try to get Sean to say what he thought but he always took a sip and then simply said, "Nice."

Her sole was excellent and she hoped the new *au pair* could cook half as well.

"Too bad about John," Sean said, sounding grave.

Danielle's head shot up. She didn't even know he knew about it. Sean didn't know the tennis players at the club nearly as well as the golfers.

"John Vertig?"

"Yeah. When I was at the office yesterday his brother called about his life insurance policy. Wanted the particulars. He wasn't my client, I didn't know him very well but it's a pity. You ever play with him?"

"So he died." Danielle felt shell-shocked again.

"Yeah. Heart attack." Sean lifted the bottle of wine and refilled each of their glasses. "Forty-eight years old."

"I know."

"Damnedest thing. What a bummer."

Saturday morning Danielle met Patti at the field where Jason and Ricky, Patti's son, had a soccer game. Sean was taking Claire to visit his parents and Patti's daughter Megan had a play date.

Patti brought two folding beach chairs for them as she always did and Danielle had a thermos of coffee and two croissants. They sat down the sideline from the other parents. Patti said she had to stay away from them or she started cheering too much and Ricky hated when she did that.

"I talked to Brenna, finally," Patti said. "She's coming."

"Great." Danielle had almost forgotten about the reunion dinner they were planning.

"Do you know she voted for Reagan. Twice! I thought she was a liberal."

"How did that come up?"

Patti shrugged. "I was teasing her about having so many kids and she said it was great for their taxes. Taxes, Reagan, Republicans."

"Really? That doesn't sound like Brenna."

"I think she's parroting Drew."

"That's a little harsh."

"It's like she's in his thrall. I hope he's not abusing her."

"Patti. Don't be paranoid."

"Just because Sean is such a saint. Such a kitty cat. Men can be bastards, Danielle." She took a sip of coffee and scanned the field looking for Ricky. The game was getting started.

"Mark and his girlfriend Trish came to dinner the other night."

"What's she like?"

"Plastic. Her nails were so red and long. She could have used them for garden trowels."

"Too much dirt."

"No kidding. This girl wouldn't go near dirt. Or even outdoors."

"I can relate. I haven't been to a beach since 1972. Too much sand."

"Really? Mazatlan?"

"Probably. Weren't Mark and Elizabeth hot and heavy then? How many girls do you think he's slept with?"

Danielle shrugged. "Twenty?"

"More like fifty, I bet. Think of all the ones you probably never met."

"Can you imagine?"

Patti was quiet.

Danielle looked at her. "Well how many guys have you slept with?"

"That's for me to know."

Danielle sat forward in her chair to see Patti's face better. "Oh come on, Patti. How many? Trevor. And Rick. Who else?" Her eyes narrowed as she peered at Patti from beneath the brim of her straw hat.

"Oh, this one and that one."

"Jorge. In Mazatlan. I wondered. So that's three." Danielle was still looking intently at her.

"Listen Perry Mason, I'm not going to tell you, all right?"

There was a roar from the knot of parents further down the sideline and Patti and Danielle both turned toward the field and looked for their sons. Jason was running in a circle with his hands raised over his head and Danielle's heart sank that she hadn't seen whatever just happened. Usually she watched with a little more attention. She tried to watch now but her mind was buzzing. She really wanted to know just how many guys Patti had slept with. Because the fact was, she herself had never slept with anyone but Sean. Sex with Sean was so familiar now she could do it in her sleep and sometimes she felt that's exactly what she was doing. Sean was sweet but ... Danielle scanned the field and raised a hand to her mouth to stifle a yawn. She noticed Patti was ticking off something on her fingers.

"What's the score?" she asked her.

"Not sure."

"You're counting, aren't you! How many?" Danielle looked at Patti's hands and saw she was up to either nine or fourteen or who knew....

"But you know I never slept with Mark," Patti said. "Never even went out with him. And he made the rounds. Zooey. Elizabeth. Of course you were hands off, his cousin's girlfriend, and Brenna was under Drew's control. But why didn't he ask me out?"

"Obviously you were too busy elsewhere."

Jason came running by their end of the field and yelled, "Did you see my goal, Mom?"

"Great, honey!" Danielle yelled back clapping her hands loudly. "Go Tigers!" She was so sorry she missed it; although soccer was her least favorite sport, she loved to see Jason perform.

"My god, he kicked a goal," Patti said. They were both quiet and started to watch the game in earnest.

But after a minute Danielle found herself distracted again.

"A man dropped dead on the tennis court at the club last week."

"What?" Patti turned to her.

"There he was, a sunny morning, they were playing a tie-break and the next thing he was dead." Danielle looked at Patti soberly.

"How old?"

"Forty-eight."

"Eeeww."

"A heart attack. It made me feel so weird, Patti."

"Was he a friend?"

"No. Just someone I saw on the courts, or with his wife at the club." To her surprise tears came to her eyes.

Patti bit her lip. Danielle had never cried in front of her and she honestly hoped she wasn't going to now. She was relieved as Danielle looked away and irritably batted her eyelashes to get rid of the unwanted moisture. She ran a forefinger quickly beneath each eye.

"It was so sudden," she said now to Patti. "Suddenly, everything seemed so fragile."

"Hmm." Patti looked out at the soccer game.

"And I started to wonder, what have I done with my life?"

Patti looked at her. "Come on, Danielle. You have two gorgeous kids. And your perfect looking husband. You have those tennis trophies. A beautiful house. Do you know how many people would kill to have your life."

"It's boring, Patti. Except for the kids." She was quiet a second. "And tennis. But there are many more hours left in a day, you know."

"Do you realize what you're saying?"

"I need a hobby."

"Do you really not know what you just said by not mentioning his name?"

Danielle narrowed her eyes as she felt a cold probing sensation in her chest then a thud in her mind. "Sean," she said. She had to admit it. He bored her out of her mind.

"Maybe you should have an affair," Patti said lightly.

"Don't be ridiculous."

"That always spices things up." Patti had known for years, really, that Danielle was bored with Sean.

"Are you speaking from experience? When you were with Trevor?"

"Yes."

Danielle looked at Patti again. "You amaze me."

"It's not the end of the world, Danielle. It's just sex."

Danielle studied the screen of her new Apple computer and read the notes she had typed for Inga, their *au pair*. She scrolled to highlight a typo and corrected it. She loved writing notes and lists on her Apple. Finally, she hit print and checked her watch. Then she felt that quickness of breath again. It came over her for no reason lately, out of the blue. She got up from her desk and paced across the room then back again. She walked to the windows and looked out at the bay. It was foggy and she could barely make out the Bay Bridge in the distance. Inga had taken the children to the playground.

Danielle walked to her daybed and sat down, looking for her magazine. She remembered what Sylvia Bates had said about her five-year-old reading so well and how she found her reading *The New Yorker* the other day and was horrified. Danielle consoled her by saying she was sure it was well written. She smiled now and picked up her copy of *Redbook*. Sylvia Bates was such a snob.

She thumbed through a few pages then put the magazine down and gazed out the window. The fog was thicker than it had been a moment ago, she couldn't see any of the bridge now. She laid her head back against the cushion and counted the boats on the bay. Maybe she should take up sailing? Too wet, and windy.

She stood up and walked across the room then back. Her breath was still shallow. She stood at the window. She wished Patti weren't on vacation with her kids in San Diego. She would be seeing Brenna. Brenna's baby was due in December. Danielle contemplated having another child—a baby. She laid her hand on her flat stomach and imagined it ballooning out. She remembered the long months of pregnancy, the nausea and fatigue. Then the sleepless nights during the breastfeeding months. She was amazed, in a way, she'd ever done it at all. She wondered if her mother ever felt this disoriented. If that's why her father left her. But Sean didn't notice any difference in Danielle. If he did, he never let on. He was always so sweet to her. Everything was "keep it simple" for Sean. "Nice." It was amazing he and Mark were related.

Mark was even more of a cad now than he had been in college. He had already gotten rid of Trish after only a month and according to Sean she was heart-broken. He was momentarily without a girlfriend and had been calling almost daily to ask Sean to go have a drink or go for a hike in the headlands. Yesterday when he called and Sean wasn't home he had asked her to meet him for a drink at Ondine's. She had declined. She turned and paced back across the room and then back again and then back and forth again. But why had she—who would care if she and Mark had a drink at Ondine's? He was just bored. And so was she. She knew that. It was because the children didn't take as much of her time as they had when they were babies and especially now with Inga here, but she hadn't taken up her old activities—couldn't even remember what she had done before the children. When the phone rang she nearly jumped. She was really not herself. She glanced across the room.

What if it were Mark again? Patti, of course, would tell her to go out with him. What was the harm? She heard Patti's voice saying, "It's just sex." But that was *not* why she would go out with him. Just for a drink. What was the harm in that? She crossed the room and picked up the phone.

But it wasn't Mark. It was Todd Belmont from the club. He wanted to tell her there would be a gathering to dedicate a memorial plaque for John Vertig on the tennis courts Thursday morning and he hoped she would come. She said of course and felt her teeth clench and difficulty catching her breath. It had been terrible hadn't it, Todd asked her and for a moment she felt he was feeling exactly what she was. Yes, she agreed. She asked him what it had been like for him to be there at the time and he described the entire event in such detail Danielle knew he was reliving it in his mind on a daily basis. She listened sympathetically and then they began discussing what a sunny morning it had been and how fragile our daily routines really are, how they can shatter in seconds and nothing will ever be the same. When she hung up the phone she sat on the daybed and wept.

July 1985

Sandrine was coming to dinner and Danielle was checking to make sure Inga had followed her instructions. She walked around the dining room table aligning each salad fork parallel to each dinner fork, each knife with each spoon. It was shocking to her how Inga set the table in a haphazard way and didn't even see the disorder. She looked out the French windows to the bay and saw Claire or Jason had left greasy handprints on the bottom panes. Inga was in the middle of cooking so Danielle went into the hall bathroom and found the Windex and paper towels. She was carefully rubbing out each greasy mark when Sean came in with the children. She heard them laughing and squealing in the hallway. Sean was a great father, she thought as she had so many times. But now her shoulders tensed and she rubbed harder on the last smudge until the window pane glistened and then she had to do all the others so they were equally clean.

"Hi, hon," Sean called.

"Mom!" Jason came running into the dining room. "Dad got me some golf clubs!"

"Oh." Danielle stood up straight and looked at him. "That's fun, sweetheart." She smiled at him. She was wearing a cream linen shift and matching espadrilles. Her hair was piled up high and clipped in back with a platinum and diamond clasp.

"What are you doing?" he asked, seeing her with the bottle of Windex and wadded up paper towels in her hands.

"Just getting ready for Grandma." She looked back at the French doors and, satisfied, went to check on Inga. "Run upstairs and wash your hands and face, honey."

"They're already clean, Mom."

"Grandma won't think so," Danielle said absently as she opened the door to the kitchen.

Jason made a face then ran off to find Sean.

Just as the family sat down to dinner the telephone rang.

"Let the machine get it!" Danielle commanded. They sat and waited for Inga to serve the tomato bisque while the phone rang and rang and on the fifth ring Sean said, "It must not be on," and started to get up.

"Never mind!" Danielle jumped up and went into the kitchen to pick up the phone there.

"Mommy's so jumpy," she heard Claire say as the kitchen door swung shut behind her.

"Hello?" she said. Inga was back in the kitchen taking the roasted chicken out of the oven.

"Now's not a good time," Danielle said and after a moment she said, "Tomorrow. One," and hung up.

When she came back into the dining room and sat down Jason asked her who it was.

"Telemarketer."

"What?"

"A salesman," Sandrine explained.

Danielle found she couldn't look at her mother just then and instead smiled vaguely at Jason and with her spoon scooped her bisque very deliberately and raised it to her lips.

Danielle glanced at her watch as she sat on the deck at Sam's. Why did Patti always have to be at least five minutes late? True, she was a single mother but if you have a full-time *au pair* living with you, are you still a single mother?

It was almost too hot on the deck. Danielle took another sip of her vodka martini. It wasn't chilled enough. She couldn't remember exactly when she had switched from vodka collins to vodka martinis or even why. Oh, there she was—Danielle raised an arm and waved although Patti had spotted her right away. Danielle was wearing her straw hat with the scarf ties and her dark glasses. She had put on lots of sun block. She didn't know why Patti always wanted to sit out in the sun, although as she studied Patti approaching she thought she looked very good today. Her red hair was wavy, not frizzy, and even though she was tan she had absolutely no wrinkles. Of course, it did look like she had put on a few pounds. That may have flattened out any beginning wrinkles. "Hi," Danielle said as Patti sat down.

"Hi!" Patti sounded so happy. She never apologized for being late.

"Guess what." Patti said.

"You got caught in traffic."

"I met someone!"

This was news. "Who? Where?"

"On our trip. In San Diego but he's from here."

"Not a friend of Drew's I hope."

"Don't be negative, Danielle. He's a wonderful guy. Our age. And no, he's not a friend of Drew's. He teaches scuba diving and he was doing some kind of research. Brenna and I took the kids to the zoo and he was there with his nieces, his sister lives there. We were all in the restaurant sitting near each other and the kids were playing a game and he was making some cracks—he is so funny! I just love this guy."

"Did you go out?" Danielle found herself oddly envious and annoyed.

"Yes, the next night. Brenna took my kids for me. Brenna is still such a sweetheart, in a lot of ways she really is the same old Brenna."

"Wait. More about the guy." Danielle took another sip of her drink.

Patti looked around for a waiter. "I'm dying of thirst." She flagged one down and as she turned back a woman came up to their table to talk to Danielle.

"Hello, Sylvia," Danielle said coolly.

"I was going to call you this afternoon and here you are," Sylvia said.

"Yes."

"You know, Danielle, since John died," she paused and Danielle took a little breath and looked warily at Sylvia.

"I hate to dwell in the mundane," Sylvia went on, "but we no longer have a fourth for our Tuesday doubles game. Todd suggested you might like to play."

"Oh," Danielle said, rather robotically, Patti thought, although her face looked flushed beneath her broad brimmed hat.

"Well. Was Todd right?"

Danielle smiled brightly. "Sure. I'd be happy to. Tuesdays at 10:00?"

"That's right. Wonderful. We'll see you, then." Sylvia moved off to make room for the server who was waiting to take their orders.

Danielle picked up her menu and fanned her face. She couldn't catch her breath. Patti finally chose a BLT and glass of Riesling. "Uh. A Caesar," Danielle said to the waiter. "And another one of these." She needed to feel that warm melting in her chest that only came with the second drink.

"I'm telling you, Danielle. I think I am in love! Already, after two weeks, it's so much more than I had with Trevor in seven years. Why did I ever marry him anyway? Why didn't you stop me?"

"There's no stopping you, Patti." Danielle's smile looked like a smirk to Patti but she wasn't going to let Danielle's cynical mood bring her down. Although she decided to change the subject.

"What have you been doing while I was gone?" Patti asked.

Danielle's eyes hardened as she half-smiled and looked out at the water. "Just keeping myself entertained."

"As in?" Patti asked, without her usual interest because she did, in fact, want to get back to the subject of her new boyfriend.

"As in dinners, parties, the club, you know. The kids needed help with their camp projects. Inga is terrible at crafts, though she is a good cook, thank god. What's his name?"

"Jeffery Winslow."

"How do the kids like him?"

"They love him!"

The waiter brought their drinks and food. Danielle took her martini and sat back, looking at the bay and taking a sip. She wondered if the children really loved him or were simply trying to survive the emotional roller coaster. Patti had been "in love" once or twice before since leaving Trevor but it hadn't lasted. Danielle was still having trouble catching her breath but didn't want to start gasping in front of Patti. She took two large swallows of her drink and then finally, there it was, the warm melting that made her feel momentarily okay.

"I need to tell you what Brenna said about Elizabeth. By the way, they're both coming in October."

"Good."

"Have you seen any more of Mark, speaking of Elizabeth?" Patti took a bite of her sandwich.

Danielle tensed and reached for her drink. "Not really."

"This is incredible." Patti put her sandwich on her plate and leaned forward. "Elizabeth told Brenna—well after Elizabeth tried to commit suicide—I guess it was a year ago, Brenna went out to New York to see her. I hadn't realized that."

"Neither had I."

"And while she was there Elizabeth told Brenna that sophomore year at Sanders, when Zooey started flunking all her classes and acting so weird she was seeing a psychiatrist at the health center on campus."

"You're kidding! I can't believe she didn't tell me."

"Elizabeth made her first appointment for her. Because Zooey had gone to the beach with Mark and Sean and they all got really stoned and when she came back she went over to Elizabeth's room and told Elizabeth she was in love with her! Can you believe it?"

"Zooey told Elizabeth she was in love with her?" Danielle wrinkled her nose.

"Yes. And that's when Elizabeth made an appointment for her with the shrink."

Danielle sat back. Oddly, her heart went out to Zooey. She wondered if she hadn't been in Boston that semester if Zooey would have told her about it. "You didn't know about any of this?" she asked Patti. "Weren't you living right down the hall from Zooey?"

"She told me she had mono."

Danielle gave her a doubtful look.

"So she was a queer all that time!" Patti said in a loud whisper. "I thought that Fiona girl seduced her or converted her—when Zooey made that scene at Brenna's wedding and it was all out in the open. But all that time at Sanders she was in love with Elizabeth and hiding it from all of us—hiding that she was a lesbian."

"Well, what choice did she have really?"

"You don't think it's kind of creepy?"

"Having to live a double life?" Danielle had the hard edge in her eyes again and the cynical curve to her mouth.

"I don't know why she didn't just drop out and go live with the rest of them in San Francisco."

"She did."

"Well. That's true," Patti admitted. She picked up her sandwich. "It's too bad. She was such a brain."

"She was sweet in a funny way. I think we would have stayed friends if she hadn't been so … militant … last time I talked to her. Not herself at all."

"It must screw you up, to have to live like that. People hate queers." Patti finished her glass of wine and glanced around for the waiter. "Anyway." She turned back to Danielle. "Elizabeth told all this to Brenna and said it really upset her at the time. She was so relieved when Zooey didn't come back to Sanders."

"I hope she's not blaming Zooey!"

"No, I don't think so. She was just telling Brenna how hard those years were for her. The thing with Mark—" Patti stopped to order another glass of wine. She looked back at Danielle who was gazing at the water and repeated, "So, her thing with Mark."

Danielle turned to Patti, nodding. "Mark. Right. And then there was the weird old poet guy."

Patti laughed. "Oh yeah. Lucius something. But you're right. Brenna said Elizabeth was miserable in general at Sanders."

"Is she still a Catholic?"

"Brenna thinks everyone is a Catholic deep down so I couldn't really tell."

"How does Brenna seem to you? What about your theory that Drew abuses her?"

"Oh, I doubt if he beats her. He just controls her. It's an article of faith he's the authority in the house and she and the kids tiptoe around when he's in one of his moods. He's a master brooder. One night he didn't say a word at dinner. It was like there was a guillotine hanging over our heads waiting to fall. I couldn't wait to get out of there. But I'm so glad I went because the next day I met Jeff!"

"Are you seeing a lot of him?"

"A few nights a week he stays over. He's great with the kids, Danielle. And they rarely see Trevor—I think it's good for them to have Jeff around."

"Yes, probably." Danielle bit her lip and sighed. Then Patti saw that hard gleam in her eyes.

Patti wondered if something were going on with Danielle but she was meeting Jeff in San Rafael in an hour. "Let's get down to business," she said as she put her napkin on her plate and reached for her purse. "We've got to pick a couple dates and tell Brenna and Elizabeth—Elizabeth can only fly out for the weekend."

Danielle lit a cigarette. "What about Zooey?"

"Right. We'll pick some dates and you can call her. I'll get back to Brenna and Elizabeth." She waved away Danielle's offer of a cigarette. Jeff didn't like the smell.

"I can't wait to see what Elizabeth and Zooey look like now. Do you know Brenna already has some gray hair?" Patti thumbed through her calendar. "I hope Zooey doesn't have a crew cut."

In the parking lot Danielle carefully undid the ties of her large straw hat and then got into her silver Mercedes coupe and took down the sunshade from the windshield. She pulled down the visor and examined herself in the mirror then reached for her purse. She brushed her hair out and fluffed it, then decided to pile it on her head and clip it back. She was getting warm so she started the engine and let it run with the air conditioner while she freshened her make up. She had three hours until it was time for Inga to start dinner and she would need to get back for the children. She glanced at her watch. She had fifteen minutes now which is how long it took, so she put the car in reverse and backed out.

As she drove down Blythedale she noticed there was a new Thai restaurant. She didn't like Thai food, though, too foreign. Near the Depot in Mill Valley she turned and drove up toward the hills. She thought of Zooey. All that time, living with that secret. Not telling any of them. Danielle wondered if Sean had smoked marijuana that day at the beach, too. She sincerely doubted it. Sean always said he had never done any drugs. Sean liked beer.

She wondered if it was the marijuana that made Zooey finally reveal herself, tell her frightening secret to Elizabeth. Danielle shuddered. How awful to be so out of control. So messy. No wonder Elizabeth had turned her in, more or less. Or had she planned it—was it a relief for her to finally say it—the way she had nearly shouted it out at Brenna's wedding years later, *I'm a lesbian*. That took guts. Or was it the champagne. Danielle could never picture Zooey as an attention seeker—or a rebel. She was too shy and quirky.

Danielle rounded a curve and then slowed down, looking for the driveway. She thought it was just ahead. She had only been here twice before. As she found it and turned the steering wheel slowly to pull in, she felt her breasts tingle and moistness descending in her vagina. She pulled the car to a stop and sat a moment, feeling the warming in her nipples. It was a delicious sensation. She smiled, lips parted, and let the heat throb through her. She opened the car door. The front door of the shingled house opened and she saw him standing there, his shirt off and his pants slung low on his hips. She walked slowly, watching him, as she moved toward him.

At dinner that evening, after she heard about Sean's golf game, Danielle told him about her lunch with Patti and asked if he knew anyone named Jeff Winslow but he didn't. As she spoke she remembered what Patti said about marijuana at the beach—Sean and Mark and Zooey that day, and almost asked him about it. She was intrigued for a moment to think he might have done something like that and lied to her but then Inga brought their afterdinner drinks and Sean said he thought he'd take his into his den and watch the Giants game.

Danielle went into the family room where the kids were watching television. She told Claire it was time for bed and eventually got her to come upstairs with her. Sean would put Jason to bed later. Once Claire was in her pajamas and had brushed her teeth, Danielle tucked her into her little French provincial bed with a pink canopy and sat down next to her to read a story. They were a third of the way through *Black Beauty*. Sometimes Danielle wondered if Claire was old enough for such a sad book but every time she suggested they save it for another time Claire took the book from her mother's hands and clutched it to her, refusing to let go until Danielle agreed to read a few more pages. Tonight Danielle was only half paying attention as she read and when she finally did glance over at Claire she saw she was asleep. But instead of tiptoeing out of the room as usual, she lie on the bed next to her daughter and put her arm around her. It gave her great comfort, like a mooring when she was adrift in a foggy sea. She lay there for an hour not knowing what else to do. And then she remembered Zooey. She quietly stood up from the bed.

In her own office, Danielle opened the drawer of her desk with her address books labeled by years. She found the one marked 1975–1978. She had no idea if any of the five numbers she had for Zooey would work but she started with the last one. Someone named Krista answered on the third ring. She said Zooey had moved out years before and she had her own place now. Danielle asked for the number but the woman didn't want to give out Zooey's telephone number.

"I was her roommate in college," Danielle said. "She was maid of honor at my wedding."

"But you haven't talked to her in six years?"

"Right," Danielle admitted. It was actually eight. Then she saw in her book she had Zooey's parents' phone number. If they were still there …

"Nevermind. Thanks." She hung up.

Zooey's father was at home. Danielle didn't ask about Mrs. James—she knew she had been ill. Mr. James didn't seem to remember Danielle but he gave her Zooey's phone number. He said he'd just spoken with her last week, which surprised Danielle. Zooey had cut off so much of her past.

She answered on the second ring. "Danielle!" Zooey said when she heard her voice. She always recognized Danielle's voice.

She sounded just the same, Danielle thought. "Hard to track down as ever," she said.

"Are you still in Tiburon?"

"Yes. The same house. There are more of us now, though. Jason and Claire, our kids. They have kept me so busy, Zooey."

"I bet. How old are they?"

"Seven and five."

"So they're in school?"

"Yes. And I do have more time on my hands now. But what are you doing these days? Are you still working for that woman …"

"No. I work for some lawyers—a small office—typing, phones, same stuff."

"Zooey," Danielle said, her voice sad. "You could have *been* a lawyer."

"But I'm glad I'm not. I couldn't get behind the law, argue for the system. There's so much crap."

Danielle heard someone talking in the background. "Is this a bad time, Zooey?"

"Well … there are a couple people here. We thought you were the person who hasn't shown up yet …"

"A political meeting?"

"Yes. But it can wait a few minutes. How are you? Is something …"

"Yes, something. Patti, Brenna, Elizabeth and I are having a reunion in October and we really want you to come. We're picking a date and I'm giving you first dibs on which dates work for you."

"Oh."

"You've got to come and meet my children, Zooey. It's going to be here, at my house."

"Well …"

"Zooey! Aren't you dying to see us all? Aren't you even curious?"

"I am."

"It won't be like the weddings. Those were different. This will be just us."

"All right. Sure. It would be great to see you, Danielle."

October 1985

Danielle glanced at her watch. Five o'clock. She thought Elizabeth had said she was coming early. She'd declined a ride from the airport saying she would take a shuttle, but Elizabeth was usually prompt, if Danielle remembered correctly. Although her plane could have been late. Danielle opened the kitchen door and glanced in. Inga was busy preparing *hors d'ouvres*.

"Everything all right?" Danielle asked her.

"Yes, Ma'am. Shall I serve you and Miss Hammond now?"

"No, no. We'll wait for the others." Danielle walked back through the dining room to the living room where Patti sat on a mauve sofa.

"I thought Elizabeth might be here by now." She walked to the wet bar. "Riesling, Patti?"

"Please. You know, when I think of it, I really didn't know Elizabeth that well. Don't you think she was kind of a cold fish?"

"Oh, I don't know. She seemed aloof sometimes, I guess." Danielle stirred some ice around in the martini shaker.

"I mean, if Zooey had walked into my room at the dorm and told me she was in love with me, the whole dorm would have known about it ten minutes later. I wouldn't have waited *ten years* to tell anyone."

"Maybe that's why Zooey wasn't in love with you."

"Thank god. Come on, Danielle. Doesn't it kind of give you the creeps. And she stayed with you that whole summer you were playing tennis."

"Just because Zooey fell in love with Elizabeth and fell in love with Fiona doesn't mean she's in love with every girl she sees, Patti. Are you in love with every guy you ever talk to or hang out with?" Danielle handed her a glass of wine and sat across from her with her martini.

"It feels like it, sometimes." Patti laughed. "But not since I met Jeff. He is so—"

"Zooey might be here any minute, Patti, and you can't talk about her like that. Be reasonable."

"Spoken from the soul of reason, I suppose."

"I feel like she's coming as a favor to me and I want her to feel perfectly welcome. I'm surprised Elizabeth agreed to come, too, all the way from New York."

"Because she's going to see her brother tomorrow in Malibu. She tries to visit him more since her father died."

"What? I didn't know her father died."

"I told you. Brenna said her father died not long before she … you know … tried to off herself."

"You didn't tell me. So that must have brought up her mother's death all over again. Obviously that had something to do with it."

"I think it was Mark."

Danielle stiffened slightly and said with irritation, "Not everything is about Mark, Patti. But in case you're right, let's not bring him up at all tonight."

"That seems uncharacteristically sensitive of you, Danielle." Patti laughed.

The doorbell rang and Danielle got up to answer it herself since Inga was busy in the kitchen.

It was Elizabeth, wearing a long black wool coat with her dark hair in a neat French twist. She looks exactly the same, Danielle thought. Not a single line in her face. Her amber eyes were still lively.

"Elizabeth!" Danielle gave her a quick hug and brought her into the foyer. "Let me have your coat. Let's get a look at you. It's been, what? Ten years?"

Elizabeth handed Danielle her coat. She was wearing black slacks and a red sweater. "I guess it has."

"You look like you go to the gym every day."

"Thank you." Elizabeth laughed. "You look wonderful, Danielle. Still playing tennis?"

"Yes, I am." As she led her into the living room Danielle felt a slight twinge of envy. Elizabeth looked so chic and East coast and was actually thinner than she had been in college.

"Elizabeth." Patti said as she stood up from the sofa to give her a kiss on the cheek. "Well. You never aged!" Patti looked at Danielle. "Guess we shouldn't have had children, Danielle."

"What will you have to drink, Elizabeth?" Danielle said rushing to fill Elizabeth's surprised silence.

"Oh." She glanced at their drinks on the table. "A glass of wine would be nice." She sat down just as the doorbell rang again.

"Get that, Patti, please," Danielle said. Then she said over her shoulder as she hurried to get Elizabeth a glass of wine, "I'm so happy you could come. How's New York?"

"I'm actually teaching in Massachusetts, now. At a small college. In some ways, it's like a New England version of Sanders."

"I think I know what you mean. When I was in Boston everyone said it was a New England version of San Francisco." She put Elizabeth's wine on the table.

"Zooey! Brenna!" Danielle looked up as they came into the room with Patti, and she and Elizabeth walked over to embrace them.

For a few minutes the five of them stood in the center of the living room all talking and laughing at once and it did feel like they were together again in the dorm getting ready for a night of studying or to go on an adventure. As they moved to sit in a circle on the sofas and chairs by the fireplace, Danielle got Zooey a glass and brought a wine bottle and her martini shaker to the table.

Brenna looked excited and flushed despite being seven months pregnant. She was thrilled, she said, to be with them all again.

"Where are all your kids?" Patti wanted to know. "Don't tell me Drew's taking care of them," she added as Brenna said, "With my mother." And Zooey asked Elizabeth where she was living now, and Danielle told Zooey her hair looked cute that short as Patti gave Danielle a sidelong glance. Brenna thanked Elizabeth for sending her those books and she meant to write when she had a minute and Zooey asked Danielle where Sean was and where were her kids! Brenna asked Patti about her children and Patti pulled out some photographs and then Inga came in and set down two trays of *hors d'ouvres* on the large glass coffee table.

Danielle asked Inga to bring the children down to say hello in a little while and Inga told Danielle that Todd Belmont had called to ask what their court time was Tuesday and Danielle looked flustered and said she'd call later. Then Sean walked in the front door—they all heard him—and all the chatter stopped a minute as each woman except Brenna took a sip of her drink and Sean stood in the arched entrance to the living room. He wore gray chinos and a dark blue polo shirt and looked tan and handsome, his black curly hair much shorter than it had been when they knew him at Sanders.

"Ladies," he greeted them in his affable, generous way. "Everyone's here, I see." He grinned. "Got everything you need?"

They all waved at him and said hello.

"We're fine, hon," Danielle said with a casual smile and Sean waved a friendly good-bye and went up the stairs.

Then they all started talking at once again and looking at photos of Patti's and Brenna's children, finding out that Zooey had a studio apartment in the Haight and worked in a law office, that Elizabeth had bought a house for herself and her two cats in a town in the Berkshires where she taught comparative literature at a small private college, that Drew might be transferred to the Persian Gulf and their whole family would be living in Saudi Arabia—this was the most shocking news—and they all had questions, when, how, exactly where and most importantly how did Brenna feel about it?

"I just hope the baby comes first, before we have to go," she said. "But it's fine. It will be interesting."

"Would you ever consider staying with the kids in San Diego while Drew is stationed over there?" Zooey asked.

Brenna looked at her as if she understood nothing. "No, Zo, that wouldn't be possible."

"Well, I have some news," Patti said. They all looked at her.

"I'm getting married!"

"What? You didn't tell me," Danielle said reprovingly.

"When?" Brenna asked as Elizabeth said, "Congratulations!" and Zooey said, "Another wedding."

Patti heard her. "My first, Zooey. Trevor and I eloped. This time I'm going to do it right and every single one of you has to come. We were all at Brenna's wedding and Danielle's and now you have to come to mine. Otherwise it might not last! I've decided having all of us there is the good luck charm."

"Is it Jeff, Patti?" Brenna asked as Elizabeth said, "Is that how it works," and Zooey poured herself another glass of wine then refilled Patti's and Elizabeth's glasses.

"Yes, Jeff—and I am eternally grateful to you for the day we went to the zoo and I met him, Brenna. He is truly the love of my life."

"More than Rick?" Zooey asked.

Patti shot her a look. "Yes, more than that bastard. Jeff is such a sweetheart. And funny! And so much better in bed than Trevor I can't tell you."

"Please don't," Danielle said.

"Where will it be?"

"San Francisco. In December. And I haven't picked the exact date because I'm waiting to get a commitment from each one of you. Tell me you're not going to Saudi Arabia before then, Brenna, for god's sake."

"You sound like your marriage will depend on it," Brenna said laughing.

"I'm telling you—look at the statistics. The five of us were at your wedding and at Danielle's wedding, and you both are still married. You weren't at my wedding and I'm divorced."

"You didn't have a wedding," Danielle reminded her.

"You could be right," Zooey said. "Fiona and I didn't have a wedding and we're not together anymore either. I've been single ever since."

There was a brief silence and Danielle looked at Zooey to see if she was getting drunk.

"I'll tell you what, Zooey," Patti finally said. "Next time you move in with a girl we'll all throw you a party and then you'll have good luck, too."

"That's a good idea," Danielle said although Brenna and Elizabeth looked uneasy.

"Thanks, Patti," Zooey said. "But, actually, what I really want is a marriage certificate and the health benefits, inheritance, social security—"

"Enough, Zooey," Patti said. "Forget I said it."

"I think if Fiona and I had been married we might still be together."

"Really? How would it have made a difference?" Danielle asked.

"The support of society. We kept trying to—"

"Long distance relationships never work," Elizabeth said.

They looked at her.

"One person has to give up her life—friends, home, family—and enter the other's world and there will always be resentment."

"I don't believe a wedding is what makes a marriage work," Danielle said.

"It's commitment," Brenna said. "Believing in your love for each other, no matter what."

"It's easier when the society doesn't condemn your love," Zooey said.

"That's probably true, Zo," Brenna said sadly. "Marriage is a precious thing."

"Divorce is very hard on kids. I didn't realize how hard it would be on mine," Patti said.

"Really?" Danielle was surprised to hear Patti say this.

"I'm always saying I'm glad to be rid of Trevor but he is the kids' dad. And now they rarely see him."

"A colleague of mine realized, only after her divorce, that it was much more disturbing for her children than she had thought it would be," Elizabeth said.

"Well, remember Sherry at Holy Name, Liz?" Brenna asked. "Her parents were divorced and she had to go back and forth between their two houses and then she had that awful step-mother."

"I remember her. What happened to her?" Zooey asked.

"She went into the convent."

Patti burst out laughing and so did Danielle and eventually even Elizabeth and Brenna started laughing. Zooey said, "There are worse fates," and Elizabeth glanced at her with a frown.

Inga appeared in the living room entrance holding the hands of Jason and Claire.

"Mommy!" Claire cried and came running to her with Jason close behind.

Danielle bit her lip and it looked as if there were tears in her eyes. She put down her drink and leaned to gather them both in her arms, and then moved them gently forward to let her friends meet her children.

November 1985

Danielle stood by the answering machine listening to the clicking sound and then the voice speaking. It was Patti. She picked up the phone. "It's about time. I haven't talked to you since the reunion."

"I know. This past week has been crazy—Halloween, I'm still recovering. Ricky had to be The Hulk and I couldn't find a costume anywhere."

Danielle sat down in a cushioned chair. "Too bad he wasn't Spiderman, they were everywhere. Claire was a princess, I made her costume myself."

"Are you kidding?"

"No. It was fun."

"I didn't know you could thread a needle."

"I like sewing, I've discovered. I'm making a dress for Claire now."

"Danielle. What's going on?"

Danielle gave a light, breathy laugh. "Could you believe Elizabeth? She was drop dead gorgeous."

"I know! And why? It sounds like she goes home to her cats every night."

"Who really knows. She's so private, as always."

"And the way she talks. So formal. Like a professor."

"She is a professor."

"Zooey drinks so much!"

"I know but she holds it well."

"I thought she seemed awfully bitter."

"Well. Fiona didn't work out and she's alone ..."

"It's the political stuff. Imperialists and whatever the hell. She seems mad at the world."

"She probably is."

"I can't believe she finally said she'd come to my wedding. If I didn't have this crazy superstition I wouldn't have cared that much. Do you think she'll really show?"

"I'll call her and work on her."

"Can you picture Brenna and all her kids in Saudi fucking Arabia?"

"God no. She's not going to find many Catholics there."

"And it's a desert! Where are the ships?"

"The Persian Gulf. Protecting the oil, no doubt."

"She's not the beauty she was. All those kids. I'm telling you, Elizabeth is the living proof of how kids change your body—she's like an un-mom."

"Zooey doesn't have kids."

"But she drinks. She smokes. I couldn't tell if she kept leaving the room to smoke out of consideration for Brenna or because she was pissed off."

"She doesn't look so bad. She's certainly thin."

"She always had that fit, athletic look. With her hair that short she looks like a boy."

"Oh, not really."

"You've always had a soft spot for her. You're so maternal, Danielle. And now you're sewing!" Patti laughed. "Listen, that's kind of why I called."

"What?"

"You have to come shopping with me to find a dress for my wedding."

"You don't have a dress yet?"

"I've got six weeks. But what are you doing tomorrow?"

They made a time to meet and Danielle hung up the phone and walked back to the family room where she had a pattern on the long side table and a pretty fabric with tiny blue flowers. She tried to regain her concentration but the ring of the telephone had jarred her and she felt that quickness of breath again. She put down the pinking shears and walked to the window looking out on the bay. It was another dry autumn day. Brilliant light made the water royal blue. A ferry half-way to Angel Island led a dozen wheeling gulls. For an instant she wished she were on the ferry herself with a picnic lunch and a bottle of wine and—she changed the image quickly to a picnic lunch with cookies and sodas and Jason and Claire and smiled to herself. Yes, that was an excellent idea. This Saturday, while Sean was playing golf as usual, she would take the children to Angel Island for a picnic. She wouldn't invite Patti and her kids because she didn't want to drink and besides, she would be seeing Patti tomorrow for lunch and shopping and they would probably cover all the gossip then.

Danielle walked back to her sewing table. Leaning over the pattern, she worked the shears precisely along the dotted lines, pulling out the pins as she went, careful not to miss any.

The telephone rang again and she froze. She had instructed Inga, who was working in the laundry room downstairs, not to answer it for any reason. Danielle put down the shears and hurried to the den where the answering machine clicked and then a voice started to speak. It was a woman from the PTA saying she was delighted Danielle would be joining them and inviting her to a special meeting for new members Thursday night. Danielle took a deep breath and relaxed then turned and went back to her work.

As she picked up the shears again she had to admit, although it was a tremendous relief he wasn't calling her, she was disappointed. He was letting her go that easily. She had told him under no circumstance whatsoever would she continue to see him. But he wasn't even going to call! She felt insulted and angry and put down the shears and went to stand by the window again looking out at the bay.

She remembered the scene again, her determination. It was two days after the reunion, after she had made up her mind that same night that she was insane to be putting her marriage in danger. Sean was a wonderful father. The children adored him. How could she be so selfish as to risk their happiness? Was she turning into her father? Look what her father's selfishness had done to her mother and to her—those awful months in Boston with Sandrine and her aunt. Nothing had ever been the same after he left them. She must have been out of her mind to ever for a minute—in her mind's eye she saw Jason's sweet, trusting face as he told her happily about playing golf with Daddy and then Claire sitting in Sean's lap as he read her a story and the two of them looking up at her and smiling when she came in the room.

That other madness, that crazed adrenalin high of the past two months—it was Patti's influence, probably, although she could hardly blame Patti. She really didn't know what insanity had come over her. But still, you'd think he would call. Was it that easy for him to give her up! He was single, after all. She was the one with children and a family and lives to ruin. What did he have? It certainly wasn't concern about being a homewrecker or he never would have come on to her in the first place. Although it had been almost a fluke—no, she was not going to relive it again, that first meeting she had relived so obsessively for so long that even now she felt her lips part slightly at the thought of it. She slapped her hand hard against the plate glass then jumped back fearful she could have broken it and cut herself and made a huge bloody mess. She was losing her mind.

On the day before Thanksgiving, Danielle sat with Sandrine in her penthouse apartment on Nob Hill in San Francisco. It was pouring rain outside and her mother had the drapes pulled so the near panoramic view was blocked out. The heat was on high. Sandrine's live-in assistant served them vodka collins and shrimp with cocktail sauce for dipping.

"I don't miss Tiburon at all," Sandrine said. "Although it is noisier here. I can hear that awful cable car clanging as it goes by when the skylight is open."

"Really?" Danielle looked up at the skylight above them. Rain was sluicing across it and draining to the roof gutters. The sky was gray and they were up so high they might have been poking right into a raincloud, Danielle thought. The image seemed like something she would see in one of Claire's picture books.

"Yes. But I like taking the cable car downtown occasionally."

"I thought Edward drove you everywhere in the town car."

"Well he does have a day off now and again." Sandrine took a sip of her drink. "He'll be bringing me to dinner tomorrow. Will Sean's parents be there?"

"Yes, Mother." Danielle had already told her this several times but Sandrine's memory wasn't what it once was. She had never been quite the same since Boston. That's how she and Sandrine referred to her mother's breakdown after the divorce: Boston. But after Sandrine's second husband died last winter, and then especially after she had moved here to this apartment two months ago, she seemed more disoriented. Danielle was grateful she had live-in help. She couldn't take on her mother's problems right now.

"And who else?"

"His brother and his wife and their son."

"None of his cousins?"

"No. Definitely not," Danielle said with agitation.

"So there will be ten of us."

Danielle thought a moment. "Yes," she said brightly. Her mother was sharper than she thought. They were on their second drink, after all. Danielle lit a cigarette.

"When did you take up that nasty habit again?" Sandrine said wrinkling her nose.

"Oh, Mother. A few weeks ago, I guess."

"You don't smoke around the children, I hope."

"As I recall, you used to smoke two packs a day."

"Nevermind, then."

"Are you going to be taking that cruise in the Caribbean over Christmas?" Danielle asked.

"Oh yes. It's finalized." Sandrine smiled. "I'm looking forward to Martinique again, especially."

"Does Uncle Remy still have a house there?"

"He does. I got his letter a few days ago and he said I was welcome to stay there, the servants can open it up for me, but of course I'll be staying on the ship."

"But you'll see the house."

"Oh, yes. And Danielle, I was hoping this summer the four of you could stay with me there for a few weeks. I think it would be good for the children to be around French-speaking people. It's never too early to begin learning a language."

Oddly, Danielle found herself responding positively to the idea. It would be different. She wouldn't mind getting away from the house in Tiburon. It sounded almost liberating, even though Sandrine would be with them. But to get out of Tiburon …

"You don't have to make up your mind now."

"No, it's fine. It sounds like a good idea." Danielle took another sip of her drink and then, setting it down, picked up a shrimp and dipped it in the bright red sauce and ate it.

The Sunday after Thanksgiving Sean was late coming home from the club. He usually got in by seven after golf, even after a couple drinks with his friends. It was past eight and Danielle decided to put the children to bed by herself since tomorrow was a school day. It wasn't like Sean and she glanced worriedly at her watch again.

"Where's Daddy?" Jason asked as she sat with him and Claire in her king sized bed to read them a story.

"He had to stay at the club a little longer." Danielle wore her sea green silk pajamas and a pair of gray cashmere sox. She had decided she may as well dress for bed since she had gotten wet helping Claire with her bath. The children wriggled under the bed covers as Danielle opened the large illustrated copy of Bayou Bay. Jason accepted books with pictures if Danielle was reading and this was an adventure story.

"Chapter Four," Danielle began. "When Stella saw the giant sea tortoise swimming toward her …"

She kept reading until nine then decided the children really did have to go to bed and sent Jason to his room saying she would come in a minute to tuck him in. She took Claire into her room down the hall and put her in bed, sitting a few minutes to smooth her hair and sing her a little French song she often sang to her. Then she kissed her goodnight and went down the hall to Jason's room.

At ten o'clock, Danielle wondered if she should be making phone calls. She was sure she could find Gary's number in Sean's den. Sean always called when he was going to be late. That was the thing. It wasn't that he was late, because he was often late—he ran into so and so, he had to stop by the office—and now that Danielle thought of it, she could call the office. But what would he be doing at the office on Sunday night? That was ridiculous. The fact was she was always slightly relieved when he was late, but he didn't usually miss the children's bed time. Usually he spent a lot of time with them on weekends, especially Sundays. She was surprised he played golf today—the club was so crowded on Sundays and Sean could play any day of the week he liked. Let's face it, his job was more nominal than anything else. How many insurance policies had he sold this year? Five? And four of them were to his friends. Stop it, Danielle said to herself. She had really tried to stop being negative about Sean. He was such a good father.

At ten-thirty she heard the garage door open and his car pull in and then she thought she heard the front door opening. But when fifteen minutes went by and he hadn't come upstairs to at least kiss the children she got up and put on her dressing gown.

She found him in his den sitting at his desk with a scotch and water on a coaster beneath the light of the Tiffany lamp. He had a pen in one hand but he was simply sitting there. He looked up startled as she stood in the doorway. "Danielle."

"Why didn't you call? The children were asking for you."

"Oh, the time got away from me. I was at the club." He took a sip of his scotch. He was looking in her direction but not really at her.

"You don't usually forget to say good night to the children, Sean." Danielle sounded more worried than blaming.

"Oh Danielle." Sean put down the pen and leaned his elbows on the desk and put his head in his hands.

Danielle was taken by surprise and stood looking at him, his long graceful fingers woven in between black curls as he clutched the top of his head and looked down at a blank sheet of paper on his desk. To her horror she saw his shoulders begin to shake and she realized he was crying. She stood frozen.

"I'm sorry. I'm sorry, Danielle," he finally said, his voice shaking with tears.

She could not imagine what was going on. Had he lost all their money?

"Sean. Stop it. What's going on?"

With one hand he swiped his nose, his head still resting in his other hand as he refused to look up at her.

She went into the room and sat on the divan across from his desk. She crossed her legs and her arms and vibrated her left foot, waiting for him to collect himself.

Still he wouldn't look at her but he mumbled something.

"What? What!" The words sounded like barks, she realized. She lowered her voice and spoke as if to Jason or Claire. "What is it, Sean."

"I didn't mean it to happen," he said in a miserable voice, although he seemed to have stopped crying.

Danielle suddenly had a vision of herself penniless in some little apartment in San Rafael, or worse, moving in with Sandrine. She realized she was holding her breath.

"It started—we were friends—that's all," Sean was saying.

Danielle's eyes widened. Oh. My. God.

"Just golfing buddies."

Sean was gay!

"She's a great golfer," Sean said apologetically. Finally he looked up but didn't meet Danielle's eyes. "It was because she's—she's with the LPGA. I mean she can outdrive me!" He sounded awed.

"You're having an affair."

"I'm sorry. I'm sorry, Danielle." Sean's face crumpled and he looked as if he might start crying again.

"All right, Sean." Should she tell him about Todd? Would that make it all even? And then they could go back to their hollow marriage?

"We want to get married," he said.

December 1985

Danielle went to the Mark Hopkins alone, or rather she had Sandrine's driver, Edward, bring her in the town car although the hotel was only a block and a half from Sandrine's apartment. Danielle could barely face the evening ahead, Patti's wedding, but the five of them had made a pact at the reunion two months before. Even Zooey was coming, Danielle knew because she and Zooey had lunch together a week earlier. Danielle had to tell someone about Sean, who had bought a condo in Sausalito and was living there, already, with Kitty, the all of twenty-three-year-old female golf pro. He had already put his down payment on the condo a month before that night in his den when he finally had the guts to come clean. Of course, Danielle never told him about Todd Belmont. But Danielle had never planned to move in with Todd. Danielle had broken everything off with Todd at the end of October. And Todd had never pursued it further. Danielle still felt a mixture of shame and anger that he had so matter-of-factly taken her at her word when she said it was over, without the slightest protest! He must have hundreds of these affairs and she was quite replaceable. Except she had thought they had a unique connection—that was the shame she felt thinking about it—their first conversation about John Vertig's death on the tennis court that sunny Tuesday morning. Or was it a Thursday? She felt so confused about everything now, always on the verge of tears. She was taking valium two or three times a day thanks to her family doctor, and the horrible panicky feeling had subsided enough that she could still live her life, take care of her children. That's when she felt rage at Sean, for abandoning the children. Fine, if he abandoned her, because frankly there was not much between them to abandon. But his children. And she had thought he was such a good father. It was this that made her feel most ... she would have to describe it as bitter. And then she had remembered what Patti said about Zooey after the reunion, that Zooey was bitter and that was when Danielle

- 215 -

decided to call her. They had gone to some place in the Haight for lunch—Zooey's idea. It was a little funky, it never would have been Danielle's choice because, for one thing, she had the feeling the dishes weren't clean and it was hard for her to eat. But she had been having a hard time eating, anyway. She'd lost at least ten pounds which was absolutely the *only* positive thing about the past month. The children. Every time she thought of them her heart broke. They simply could not understand why Daddy had left and who this—Kitty—was. It had been a relief to talk to Zooey. She was the only person who seemed to ... listen. Of course, Danielle hadn't told Sandrine yet because she was certain it would bring up Boston for her and Danielle right now was trying not to have a Boston of her own. Patti was absolutely preoccupied with Jeff and her wedding and Danielle could almost swear Patti's biggest concern was that her plan for the five of them at the wedding to be a good luck charm was—now that Sean had left Danielle—a bust.

Edward pulled the car into the circular drive in front of the hotel and a doorman opened Danielle's door. She stepped out making sure not to catch her high heels on anything. She wore a dark green silk sheath and her hair in a perfect French twist. She hoped they wouldn't think she was trying to imitate Elizabeth.

Zooey was in the lobby waiting for her as they had planned. She looked slightly windblown, she must have taken the cable car up the hill. She wore dark purple silk slacks and a black silk blouse. Luckily the pants were loose and long enough to hide her Chinese slippers, those three-dollar shoes you could buy in Chinatown Zooey had on every time Danielle saw her the past twelve years. Although that wasn't very often, unfortunately. She should have stayed in closer touch with Zooey, despite her angry politics, because Zooey under-stood something important—though Danielle couldn't say quite what it was at the moment. She waved and smiled at her as she approached and Zooey stood up from the circular velvet sofa and gave Danielle a careful hug, avoiding her perfect French twist and make-up. Zooey wore no make-up of any kind, but her eyes were big enough and she had enough color that it wasn't too obvious.

"Are you ready for this?" Zooey asked.

"Well. It's Patti's wedding. I can't miss it. I'm glad you came, Zooey."

"I've never been here before." She glanced around. "It seems like it will be more a party than a wedding."

"I think there are only fifty guests. Her parents, her brothers' families ..."

"All of us."

"Right, and Jeff's family. He wanted to get married on the beach and wear a Hawaiian shirt." Danielle laughed as she pushed the up button on the elevator.

"Patti's in charge already?"

"I know."

They stepped in the elevator and Danielle said "Five." Patti had several rooms on the fifth floor for overnight guests and friends to gather before the wedding which would be held in the Room of the Dons on the Lobby Level.

"I'm dreading seeing Brenna and Elizabeth," Danielle said, taking a few shallow breaths. "I haven't told them."

"I'm sure Patti has."

"You're right. She was probably on the phone the minute after I told her."

"That's probably better."

They got off on the fifth floor and found Elizabeth and Brenna already in the room when they opened the door. The four friends exchanged hugs and greetings although because they had just seen each other two months before and because of Danielle's bad news there wasn't the excitement and laughter. Brenna kept her arm around Danielle's waist a minute after they hugged offering wordless support. Danielle didn't seem to mind. And Elizabeth offered her a glass of wine which she accepted. Danielle managed to say, "Elizabeth, whatever happened to your macrobiotic diet?"

"It was so much work. I can hardly even find tofu in our small town."

"Now, why did you become a vegetarian? For your health?"

"More the principle of the thing." Elizabeth shrugged if off, although her topaz eyes looked intense.

Elizabeth was always so intense, Danielle thought, as she sipped her chilled white wine and studied her a moment. She looked just as chic as she had in October and again wore red, a silk blouse this time with a dove gray straight skirt and jacket. She must have bought those clothes in New York, Danielle thought, wondering why Elizabeth—a vegetarian professor at a small college, an unmarried woman who lived alone in the Berkshires—would dress so well. Who was she trying to impress? For an instant Danielle wondered—was it just for herself? What a novelty. Danielle felt the closest thing to a prickling of interest in something other than her own situation since Sean had left.

Brenna looked as if she might give birth that night although she wasn't due for another eight days. She and her family were staying with Drew's parents in Ross. They had driven up from San Diego the day before. And yes, they were moving to Saudi Arabia she told Zooey who was appalled but tried not to show it.

"Will you have to wear a veil, or *chador*?"

"I don't think so. There's an area, like a little American city where everyone lives."

"Where will his ship be?"

Brenna laughed. "There's no ship. Drew is a defense consultant. He'll be working with the oil companies and the Embassy—it's a desk job, really."

"The oil companies are hiring Navy personnel to consult on security?" Elizabeth asked.

"No … I don't know, really, it's all classified, Drew said." Brenna gave them an apologetic look.

Zooey bit her lip. "How long is it for?"

"Two years, then possibly more." Brenna laid her hand on her huge belly beneath her blue silk maternity smock, as if protecting her child, although she didn't seem conscious of the gesture.

"It's a quarter to seven." Elizabeth looked at her sleek silver watch. "Should we start down?"

They all spent a few minutes at the mirror freshening make-up, smoothing pleats and seams, removing lint, brushing hair.

In the hallway they were an attractive group of women in their thirties and Danielle had a quick memory of them walking down the beach in Mazatlan when they weren't even twenty years old to meet Sean and Mark at the restaurant under the *palapas,* and how Sean had come up to her when they arrived and held her hands and gazed at her. She had never, for an instant, doubted his love until that night when he sat at his desk—even when he put his head in his hands, she hadn't doubted his loyalty to her. That's what was so difficult, the absolute shock. And the children. What he was doing to the children. She had given up Todd for the children.

The others were talking about Elizabeth's opportunity to teach in London next year and her need to sublet her house. London! Danielle glanced at Elizabeth, slim and youthful, sophisticated. Patti was right, she was the antithesis of whatever she and Patti were—housewives, she supposed she would have to say. Although, Zooey lived alone. But Danielle could tell, at lunch last week, Zooey understood the heartbreak Danielle felt for her children and she recalled now how, at the time, she realized Zooey would probably have given anything to have children of her own. What a bizarre irony.

The Room of the Dons was elegant and intimate. There were white floral arrangements on prettily set tables and the friends found their seats near the dais where the brief ceremony would take place. On another stage to the side a small dance band had set up. There wouldn't be any procession or maids of honor although Megan and Ricky, Patti's children, would be ring bearers. As Danielle rested her fingertips on the back of her chair waiting for everyone to find their seats, she noticed to her shock she was still wearing her wedding ring, the multiple diamonds and platinum bands had caught the light just so but she couldn't take them off now and risk losing them. They were a small fortune and how could she not have noticed before all this time, over a month, it was embarrassing and confusing. She took a few shallow breaths and saw with relief there was already a bottle of open chilled white wine in a silver ice bucket on the table although what she really wanted was a vodka collins.

"You're all here!" Patti came up in an excited rush, gripping each of them in a quick hug and laughing, saying what a wreck she was and why hadn't they told her how nerve-wracking weddings are. "And Jeff won't let me touch the champagne until after we've done the vows thing. He doesn't want me to start bawling.

"Oh, there he is!" Patti waved at a good-looking guy across the room in a blue suit and yellow silk tie with sun bleached hair a little long in back. Danielle thought again, as she had when she first met Jeff, that he looked like a surfer. Still, Patti's parents accepted him as they hadn't Trevor although Danielle assumed they weren't too thrilled. Or maybe they were happy Patti was with anyone vaguely acceptable and the kids had a father again. Trevor was in Greece now opening a gift shop with a friend and studying the classics. Danielle assumed he was gay and the seminary and then marriage to Patti had been his desperate effort not to be.

Jeff waved back. He had an easy, charming grin and Danielle felt her heart dip in her chest because he reminded her of Sean ten years ago, the boyish grace. Not the Sean who always seemed not quite present—and now she knew why!

Danielle turned to Zooey who was also watching Jeff with a curious, observing gaze.

"Zooey, remember the day you and Mark and Sean went to the Marin headlands. Before you left Sanders?"

Zooey turned her head in surprise and looked at Danielle.

"And you all smoked some grass? Is that what happened? You all smoked grass?"

Zooey saw that day perfectly in her mind—the bright, wild blue water and the spray from the surf in the wind, Mark's face silhouetted against the backdrop of the ocean and she could hear Sean's funny laugh—that's all she remembered hearing—she didn't remember one word of the conversation. But she did remember Sean inhaling deeply on the joint. Had he said something about not telling Danielle? Hadn't he?

"Zooey?"

"I—I'm trying to remember."

"Cut it out. You know."

Someone was dinging a glass, the high pinging sounds of a spoon tapping on crystal. Patti's father. People were clearing their throats and preparing to quiet down.

"Tell me," Danielle nearly hissed.

What did she actually owe Sean now, Zooey wondered, and what did she owe to Danielle—why was it so important to her? But of course she knew: the lie. Well. She nodded her head. "I think he did," she whispered. Why should she lie now?

"Think?"

"He did."

Danielle felt fury rising in her. He was a liar all along! Bastard! With that smarmy, innocent grin, looking like he adored her. What the hell was he really up to for fourteen years.

"I think he was a little afraid of you," Zooey whispered.

Danielle stiffened. *What!* she thought. But of course, it was true. She felt the awful truth of it. Had she known it? Not really, not totally. She felt fury again. As if she were some *ogre*. How unfair!

"… and our beautiful daughter, Patti." Patti's father beamed at her and put his arm around her, hugging her close to his side. He was a stocky man with a fringe of gray hair and a mustache. He seemed full of love for Patti and then he beamed at his wife who was a round little woman with dyed red hair in an emerald green silk suit, matching heels and gold jewelry. "So I think we can begin," Mr. Hammond concluded and Jeff, who was standing close by entered the little family circle and took Patti's hand leading her to the dais where a minister stood with an open book in his hands.

Danielle tried to concentrate on the ceremony. Patti and Jeff were standing ten feet away. Everyone in the room was seated and silent, trying to hear. Danielle thought Patti was sniffling, whether with emotion or allergies she didn't know. She felt so angry at Sean. It was really all she could think about. Though Ricky looked cute, so serious and grown up in his little blue blazer and gray flannels. He handed Jeff Patti's ring with such solemnity, man to man. This made Danielle take a sharp, short breath and tears sprang to her eyes and rolled slowly down her perfectly carved cheeks. Zooey glanced at her. No one else was crying. It wasn't that kind of wedding. Although it did seem Patti was sniffling a bit.

Zooey opened her clutch bag and found an old Kleenex packet still there from her mother's funeral and handed a tissue to Danielle who seemed to be paralyzed by her own reaction. Danielle accepted it with a quick little smile and then surreptitiously patted her eyes. She felt like a fool and prayed her mascara wasn't running. She would run in the restroom the minute this so called "brief" ceremony was over.

At last she saw Jeff turn to Patti and give her a lingering and, she had to admit, sexy kiss. She felt a flame of jealousy and wished she had never come. What an insane thing to be doing right now. And Patti's ridiculous hex or whatever it was wasn't even valid anymore. Danielle stood and excused herself while everyone was applauding and even catcalling and Patti and Jeff turned and grinned at the crowd. Patti's brothers ran up and started flinging rice and the band started playing some Beatles song Patti liked. Danielle hurried toward the exit feeling exhausted.

When she came back to the table they had already finished their salads and were waiting for the first course. She saw Zooey had already finished her wine and then noticed, no, her glass hadn't been used. Danielle sat down and immediately took a sip of what was a very good Pinot Grigio.

"You okay?" Zooey asked.

"I'm fine."

"Doesn't Patti look gorgeous?" Brenna said. "She looks happier than I've seen her in a long time."

"Since Rick."

"Why did she ever marry Trevor?" Brenna asked then laughed. It sounded funny.

"Aren't you drinking, Zooey?" Danielle asked.

"No. I quit."

"You're kidding." Danielle put down her glass as Elizabeth said, "When?" and Brenna said, "That's great, Zooey."

"Thanks," Zooey said with a little smile and shrug.

"But when?"

"Six weeks, as of yesterday. I am counting," Zooey admitted.

"You just—stopped?" Danielle asked.

"I go to AA sometimes."

"Oh, you mean, the twelve steps?" Brenna asked.

"The Higher Power? You believe in a Higher Power?" Elizabeth looked at her with that intense life or death stare.

"And aren't you supposed to discover your inner child?" Brenna asked.

"Let her talk," Danielle said.

"I would say it was more my 'inner piranha.'" Zooey laughed. "I didn't realize how totally angry I was until I quit. It's really different, not drinking."

"Here Here, Zooey!" Brenna cheered her.

"I didn't even notice at lunch last week—" Danielle began.

"Yes, congratulations, Zooey," Elizabeth said.

Danielle sat back in her chair and looked at them happily congratulating Zooey. She saw Brenna wasn't drinking either, of course, and Elizabeth had only a few sips of her wine. She missed Patti suddenly and looked at the table where Patti and Jeff sat with their families. Patti was drinking and talking and laughing happily. She and Jeff were going to Hawaii with the kids and Bettina for a month tomorrow—Patti's idea to compensate for not getting married on a beach. Patti would be gone for a month! And when she came back she would be with Jeff, not calling all the time wanting to do things with Danielle like she had the last few years since her divorce. And there was Elizabeth, Danielle looked at her, on her way to Europe. Brenna, on her way to Saudi Arabia! Zooey—a teetotaler.

Danielle looked down at her own hands holding her empty wine glass and her empty wedding ring. She had never felt so alone in her life.

PART III

January 1995

Zooey put on her glasses and booted up the computer. She tapped her fingers waiting for the screen to fully appear and then all the familiar buzzes and static of the modem connecting. A voice said "you've got mail" and she clicked the mouse and glanced at her watch. Eva would be home in an hour. Zooey wondered what she could make for dinner. Since she was between jobs she did most the cooking—or heating—she was more a microwave handler than a cook, Eva had commented once.

Finally her mailbox opened. A message from Fiona. One from Molly. Three things that looked like junk. She clicked on Fiona's. She and Laura were going to the Palm Springs Film Festival in a few weeks, did Eva and Zooey want to join them? "sounds fun! i'll talk to eva and get back to you" Zooey typed quickly although she doubted Eva could take time off. And although Eva liked movies, she wasn't a film devotée like Zooey and Fiona and Molly. She clicked on Molly's message. She and Greg, her husband, were going to Palm Springs, too. Now Zooey really wanted to go. Maybe she could go without Eva although they didn't have the money for extra, separate vacations. Though Eva wouldn't care. She typed the identical message she'd sent Fiona to Molly then got offline because Eva might call to say she would be late.

Zooey walked into the kitchen and opened the refrigerator. Would grilled cheese sandwiches be too lunch-like? And there was V-8 juice for a vegetable. She looked at her watch again and decided to walk to the grocery store.

As she stopped on the front deck to lock the door she marveled again at their view of the San Francisco skyline. Zooey had never spent time on Potrero Hill until she and Eva bought this house two years before. She still felt lucky, as if she might wake up tomorrow and be back in her little studio in the Haight with an airshaft for a view. And before that, all the rooms in communal houses—with Ruth and Ginny on Guerrero, then very weird Carol on Dolores

Street, that was bad. Then two years in Noe Valley with Alice and Rachel. They were fun but it got messy when Rachel wanted to sleep with her. She was lucky to find that studio.

She waited at the corner for the light to change. Living alone had been so peaceful, she knew it had helped her finally take hold of her life and stop drinking. It had been ten years since she'd quit, and now alcohol looked like poison to her. She had been so in its thrall—she'd always managed to scrape up the money to go to Maud's for a drink. No car, no health insurance, just rent and food and thrift store clothes. She never had more than a foam mattress and a bookshelf.

But that's how they all had lived. It was a point of honor. All the serious political radicals were downwardly mobile. It was inadmissible to be from a wealthy or middle class family and everyone lied about their background, although the truth was often the most militant radicals were the wealthiest. Something about guilt, she imagined, or an entitlement which made them assume they should run the world.

Although Danielle wasn't like that, nor Patti, and they were very wealthy, not just upper-middle class like Brenna and Elizabeth. It was hard to believe ten years had gone by since she had seen any of them, except Danielle whom she saw quite a bit the year or two after her divorce from Sean. Then Danielle somehow disappeared and Zooey started writing a screenplay in her studio and, without really knowing it, saw less of all her friends. And then Fiona moved back to San Francisco with Laura and Zooey didn't want to run into her.

It took a long time for Zooey to get over Fiona. Even though she had a few short relationships, if you could call them that, she hadn't sufficiently fallen out of love with Fiona to make them last. She had still believed if they'd had more money, or hadn't been part of an experimental culture or simply been *married* they could have stayed together.

Zooey ran across the next intersection to make the light. The blessing was, she didn't care anymore. She finally got over Fiona, and part of it was bumping into her at a bus stop on Castro Street in 1987. They both had started laughing, then they met for dinner soon after to catch up on each other's lives. While in New York, Fiona had become successful. She was in demand for portraits and was exhibiting her other work. And now she was exploring cinematography, shooting a short film Molly and Greg were making.

Zooey had told Fiona, then, that she was doing less political work because she had, in essence, lost her faith. Not the way she had at Our Lady of the

Immaculate Conception when she was eighteen—all at once—like Paul at Damascus in reverse: up off the ground, back on his horse, faithless. It was more a gradual widening of her perspective on life.

Fiona thought Zooey seemed much happier. After dinner that night, Zooey met Fiona's partner, Laura, and was surprised by how much she liked her. Zooey and Fiona saw each other often after that. They had the unique friendship that occurs between exlovers—an intimacy without the sexual charge.

Then two years later, Zooey met Eva. Zooey was working with Molly on the Women's Film Festival as she had every year since the '70s. It was the 1989 Festival at the Pacific Film Archive in Berkeley. Molly was going over logistics and both she and Zooey were buzzing with coffee and nerves because one of the directors who was supposed to speak hadn't shown up yet. Then Molly spotted a woman across the lobby, tall with lots of black wavy hair and flashing dark eyes—she was looking sideways at Molly and her quick smile was disarming as she walked by. Then Molly waved at her to come over, a little frantically, for Molly, Zooey thought. The woman looked puzzled an instant then smiled again and approached them. She was wearing a burgundy dress with embroidered sleeves.

"Hi Eva," Molly said, a little breathless, "Listen, is there any way—oh, Eva, this is Zooey James, Zooey—Eva Valero. Could you do us a big favor and give a ten minute q&a on adoption rights? Gina Carson hasn't shown up. She was supposed to take questions after her documentary. She's such a damn introvert," Molly added.

"Oh. Sure." Eva shrugged. "If she doesn't come, introduce me after the film and I'll do it. That's actually what I came to see." The disarming smile again. Her teeth were absolutely perfect, Zooey realized.

"Who is she?" Zooey asked after Eva rejoined her friends—two women and a man, Zooey noticed, all well dressed, sexuality unknown.

"She's a lawyer. She works at a firm downtown but she does a lot of *pro bono* work for the gay community, especially on adoption rights."

"She's gorgeous." Too bad she's a lawyer, Zooey added to herself.

"She's single, Zooey." Molly was more relaxed now that their biggest problem was solved but then she saw the film critic for *The Chronicle* and rushed off.

"Does that mean she's a lesbian?" Zooey asked but Molly was gone.

Zooey loved reliving that evening, seeing that smile the first time. It still got to her. How could she describe it?—it was like a flash of insight, humor, brilliance—sudden and then gone. It didn't happen often, you had to watch for it.

Eva had other smiles, her "happy to meet you" smile, her "I'll be representing you" smile, her "that's nice but get out of my way" smile and many more. But that one smile: the I know you smile was like magic to Zooey.

As Zooey approached their little wooden house built into the hillside, carrying her bag of groceries, she looked around for Eva's car. It didn't look like she was home yet. She'd had a court appearance in San Jose today.

Zooey was puffing by the time she reached the twentieth redwood step to their front door. One more sign of old age, she thought. She hadn't been prepared for the decline of the body after forty. Although she felt healthier than she ever had in her life, not smoking or drinking, taking long walks alone or with Eva. She set the groceries on the counter and marveled at the view out the large window. There were high rolling clouds, the voluptuous kind that looked like a theatre backdrop, portending drama. One thing Zooey loved about life with Eva was the lack of drama. The trust and ease of their relationship. None of the desperate angst-filled scenes she'd been involved in when she was young.

It had been a month after the opening night before she'd seen Eva again. It was one of those rambling days and Zooey had walked out to Ocean Beach and then because it was early kept walking all the way to Fort Funston. It was September, and the light was the hard, stark light of the fall equinox. Everything reflected vivid color and the sky was bright blue. She walked through the fields of ice plant turning yellow and rust, to the edge where the cliffs dropped down to the surf below. It was very hot and dry. She wondered if she could get down the foot path descending in front of her. After Sanders, she had become afraid of heights. She thought now if she sat on her butt and edged down she might be able to. She was just in that position, halfway down the cliff path, when she came upon Eva and a child on an intersecting foot trail also headed for the beach. Eva was picking her way cautiously on her own path and didn't see her at first but then suddenly looked up. She stared at Zooey and didn't seem to recognize her. Zooey tried to gracefully stand up.

"Hi." She smiled and waved.

"Oh. Hi," Eva said. It was her "nice to meet you" smile. Then there was a flash of that other, special smile and she said, "I'm afraid of heights too. This is taking me forever! Rosa's losing patience with me, aren't you? This is my niece, Rosa. And, you are ..."

"Zooey. Zooey James."

"Oh that's right. The film festival."

They talked for a few minutes about the film and Zooey told her how happy they were she stepped in to field questions and what a great job she had done.

Eva was a natural speaker, even though she had since told Zooey she was sick with anxiety every time she stood in front of a crowd.

They continued down the path together and then Eva introduced Zooey to her brother, Luis, and his wife and their new baby. They were there for a picnic for the afternoon and it seemed natural for Zooey to join them. At one point she and Eva took a walk by themselves down the beach and with the film and law and living in San Francisco the conversation was easy. Eventually Eva and her family gave Zooey a ride back to her studio in the Haight.

Zooey looked out the kitchen window at the darkening sky. Lights were going on across the city. She remembered that night after she got home from her unexpected day with Eva, how strange she had felt. Excited and, not like herself. Something had cracked through and she felt herself hatching, like an egg, emerging, scared and awed. She could barely sleep. She and Eva had exchanged phone numbers but she couldn't believe Eva would really call, while at the same time she knew she would—she knew Eva felt what she did.

Eva had called and they saw each other for lunch downtown a few times over the next month and although it was always exciting to see her Zooey began to assume Eva just wanted friendship after all. She found she was losing the sense of possibility and decided the day at Fort Funston had simply been a brilliantly lit afternoon made special by the sun. Then in mid-October, while Zooey was sitting at her desk in her top floor studio in the early evening the floor buckled and the room started swaying and everything fell off her shelves and plaster fell out of the ceiling making a pile of smoking dust on her bed. She ran for the doorway and heard people screaming in the flat below and people running downstairs and she ran out to follow everyone into the street. There was broken glass and a street sign tipping over but all the buildings still stood. Cars had stopped and people were walking around dazed. And suddenly Zooey thought of Eva on the twenty-fifth floor of a downtown highrise and felt terrible panic. Eva! She had to find out if Eva was all right—she went running back into the Victorian and up the stairs two at a time to her studio. Her phone was dead. She realized she must be crazy and ran back down the stairs out into the street. No one seemed to know anything because all the electricity was off. Someone had a white t-shirt stained with blood held against his forehead. People were streaming toward Golden Gate Park. She remembered that's what everyone did in 1906. Huge clouds of gray smoke filled the sky in the north.

Zooey looked out at the sky now, a deep indigo with a few stars managing to shine through the haze and ambient light. She looked at her watch. Where was Eva?

She always felt upset remembering that night of the earthquake, how it was midnight before she finally found a telephone that worked. A mile or so from her house—she had been walking the streets alone—people were sitting on blankets on the sidewalk afraid to go in the buildings and every aftershock made them more determined to stay outside. One group of young people passing around a bottle of bourbon told her the phone in their flat on the second floor worked and she could use it. She ran up the stairs and found the telephone and dialed Eva's number in Twin Peaks.

Eva answered on the first ring. "Zooey!" she said when she heard her voice. "Where are you?" Zooey felt near tears when she heard her voice and then told her where she was and that she was all right. It was a miracle she had gotten through, Eva told her. She told her about the evacuation from her office building, how it swayed and swayed for what seemed forever. She had gotten under her desk like you were supposed to but nothing much had fallen. A colleague had given her a ride home but it took hours because the traffic lights didn't work. Now it was strange being alone in her apartment with just a candle burning. "I wish you were here," she said, "so much." They agreed to meet the next morning out at the beach. A few months later they rented a flat together in the Sunset.

Zooey got up and paced across the room. She shouldn't have relived that night because it still brought tears to her eyes when she remembered Eva's voice on the phone. Where was she? She went in the living room and turned on the television. The news was all about Newt Gingrich and nothing about local traffic but there weren't any disaster reports. Zooey knew she was being silly but she looked at her watch again. It was almost seven and Eva's court time had been early this morning.

She turned her head as she heard a key in the front door and jumped up to open it.

"Hi!" Zooey waited for Eva to get in the door with her big briefcase on wheels before she put an arm around her and kissed her.

Eva kissed her warmly. "Hello sweetheart. Oh that fucking traffic." She shook off her silk scarf. "Those dot-com people in Silicon Valley. All those big SUVs, you know? I can't even see past them to read the signs. I almost went to Oakland."

"And got stuck on the bridge." Zooey headed toward the kitchen to cook the salmon.

"I know." Eva flipped through the mail on the lamp table by the front door.

"How'd it go?" Zooey called from the kitchen.

"We won."

"Great!"

"I'm so glad it's over. The guy, their attorney—I told you what a hardass he is." Eva sat at the kitchen table.

"Is he going to appeal?"

"Probably." Eva sighed.

Zooey put the salad on the table then stood behind Eva's chair and massaged her shoulders.

"Mmm." Eva rolled her head slightly, stretching her neck.

"Do you have much vacation time left?" Zooey asked, remembering Fiona's and Molly's emails.

"Probably." She waited a minute, letting Zooey's fingers work out the stiffness in her shoulders. "Why?"

"Fiona and Molly are going to a film festival in Palm Springs next month and wanted to know if we could go."

"That sounds fun." Eva sat up straight. "Should I do something?"

"No, I've got it." Zooey checked the salmon and then got the Perrier out of the refrigerator. Eva wasn't a drinker although she had an occasional glass of wine.

"Smells good. You've been *cooking*, Zooey."

Zooey grinned. "For you, darling." She set down the platter of grilled salmon.

"Did you work on your script today?"

"Yeah, and Molly has some good ideas for the grant proposal."

"Mmm. Delicious! Chef Zooey." Eva took another bite. "Show it to me when you've got another draft."

"Oh, I will."

"You know what? I didn't get a chance to tell you I was so nuts with this case," Eva said. "I got an email from Lynne and she and Rita are going to China to adopt a baby girl."

"That's not legal, is it?"

"Lynne has to pretend she's single and go to the orphanage alone. She'll adopt the baby in China, then Rita will do a second parent adoption in California."

"How many thousands will that cost?"

"Twenty thousand, I think. We can't even think about it right now."

"Maybe we could refinance the house—interest rates are down."

"That's a good idea. Can you look into it?"

"Sure." Zooey got up from the table. "Do we still have that ice cream?"

"I think so. But you know, it would be so much better if we could adopt a baby here, there are so many teenage girls who are pregnant."

Zooey found the ice cream in the freezer. She felt the same mix she always did when this subject came up—a thrill of possibility, a dread of disappointment and a fear of how actually having a child might change their lives.

"As soon as I've finished the grant, I'll do some research."

Early the next morning Zooey waited for the computer to boot up, trying to decide how to proceed on the grant proposal. Molly said she would raise matching funds from Film Festival donors to produce Zooey's screenplay. She said Zooey should have shown her her script years ago because it was a film that should be made. Fiona agreed to do the cinematography for free, Molly and Greg would be the producers and Zooey would direct.

She got up to make coffee. She couldn't decide how to write the grant because she didn't want to work on it at all.

She looked out the kitchen window—a sunny winter day. She would have loved to walk out the front door and keep walking for hours. Until last month, she hadn't shown anything she'd written to anyone since she was at Sanders. Half a lifetime ago.

She put the kettle on. Was it really half a lifetime? She left Sanders when she was nineteen. Now she was forty-two. *More* than half a lifetime. When she realized how old she was, she wondered about her and Eva's plan to adopt a baby. Although she knew she wanted a child, she didn't know how it might change their lives and they were so happy as they were. Part of her did not want to change anything at all. And, too, she treasured her free time. Some days she still rambled alone around the city, going wherever her inclination took her. She even went to an occasional demonstration if she thought it might do any good, although the left's power to influence policy as it had during the Vietnam war was gone. Now there were ritualistic protests and arrests, everyone going through their paces. Zooey had been arrested several times—in fact she and Eva were surprised they hadn't met years before because Eva often defended demonstrators as a volunteer.

One day, before she met Eva, Zooey was walking by the Federal Building and saw twenty white people in their forties marching in a circle chanting, "Effay Emmay Ellay Ennay," and she knew things had gone too far off course for her. She knew the chant was Spanish for FMLN, the El Salvadorian liberation group, but did all the people walking by, ignoring this arcane group, know or care at all? It sounded ridiculous in that context. The odd thing was, for a second she thought she recognized one of the marchers and was two blocks past before she realized it was Mark Landry!

Things had changed so much she wondered if their Women's Film Festival would last much longer. Women's bookstores and cafés were closing. The women's movement was over for now, she would have to admit. And the right had turned "feminist" into a dirty word. It was like calling someone an idiot to call them a "feminist" or a "liberal".

She sat at the kitchen table, staring at the downtown highrises in the distance. She wondered why Molly and Greg never had children. Years ago Molly had asked how anyone could bring a child into this world that was going to hell. But they could have adopted a child who needed a home. It was more as if the Women's Film Festival was Molly's child. She had conceived it, birthed it, raised it with total devotion for twenty years. Like many women, she didn't really want children. And Greg must not have wanted to be a parent, either. They had their two big, goofy dogs. Greg had once said their brand new living room couch had become the most expensive dog bed in the city.

But Zooey did want a baby. She did want a family. She always had, although she never thought it would be possible and gave up long ago. It was Eva who made everything seem possible. Eva had wanted to have a child since she was a child herself. It was enormously important to her, so much so she dated men all through her twenties hoping to find the ideal husband and father. She never found him and accepted the fact she preferred women but it left her stymied as to how to create a family. By the time she met Zooey she had buried her longing for children. Instead she and Zooey babysat Eva's niece Rosa and little nephew, Sylvio. But now Rosa was fourteen and she had become Sylvio's babysitter. And the fact was, Eva and Zooey wanted their own children. Eva was thirty-nine and could get pregnant but didn't want to go through the process, which often involved taking hormones at her age. There were so many children in the world who were unwanted for whom they could provide all the love and warmth of their home.

Zooey stood up. Now was a good time to research adoption agencies. They shouldn't let anymore months go by.

As she sat at the computer she decided to research agencies then work on the grant. Although first, she would check her email. A message from Molly, her old friend Ruth, some obvious junk and then something she didn't recognize: cryder@prodigy.net, but she decided to open it.

"Zooey, is this you? I got this address off the film festival site. How many Zooey Jameses are working on women's film festivals? Where are you? I tried your old phone number a year ago and some man answered and claimed he never heard of you. Your dad is not at his old number. I hesitate to ask. I finally decided to try Yahoo. Write me ASAP and tell me if I actually found you! Danielle"

Zooey began to type: "you did. i'm living on potrero hill now where are you? who is cryder?"

She hesitated, then added "great to hear from you" and clicked send.

Wow, Danielle. That was a voice from the past. Though wasn't she just thinking of her yesterday? She couldn't not respond to Danielle although she wasn't ready for any more weddings or reunions. She hoped that wasn't what it was about. She quickly read her other email and then settled down to work.

Still, in the back of her mind, she felt curious about Danielle. Was she still single? Still in Tiburon? How were all the rest of them—Brenna, Patti, Elizabeth?

When Zooey sat at the computer again the next morning it was with a feeling of dread. During the night she had awoken with the thought that maybe it wasn't a wedding Danielle wanted to tell her about, maybe it was a funeral. She hadn't heard back from her last night but expected to this morning. And yes there was something from cryder.

"Aha! I found you. I told Patti I would. Listen, Zooey, it's that time again. Ten years since our last reunion. Next month, my house. I'm still in Tiburon. Different address, though. I'm married again, to Alex Ryder. Thus, CRyder. Like the song. Will you come? Elizabeth and Brenna will be here. You have to!"

Zooey laughed. She was relieved they were all well—well enough to come to another reunion. She didn't really want to go, though. What could they possibly have in common now? Danielle's kids were probably in high school. Patti's too. Although Brenna would have younger kids. Zooey wondered how many kids Brenna had now. And if Elizabeth ever married. She must have come back from Europe, or maybe she was only on vacation here. Danielle had a new house and a new husband … Anyway, she had known she would go. She started typing, asking the date and time.

Zooey looked at the San Jacinto mountains from their outdoor table. They were at Greg's favorite Mexican restaurant in Palm Springs. The sun was low in the sky and the mountains changed color dramatically as they watched, pale pink to terra cotta and then a rosy gray.

"I didn't think watching the desert would be as dramatic as watching ocean surf," Eva said. "I was expecting a lot of sand."

Molly laughed. "You mean like in Lawrence of Arabia? All those white dunes in the Sahara." Molly looked almost Greek with her black curly hair and handwoven tabard of black and white wool.

"It's *cold* here at night, though." Eva pulled her short gray jacket tight.

"I know. You should have warned us, Molly." Fiona laughed as she shivered a little in her denim jacket. She wore tight pants and sandals and red polish on her fingers and toes. She looked glamorous in an unorthodox way, Zooey thought, as did Laura with her spiky peroxided hair. Even Greg looked dapper in a black t-shirt, sports coat and jeans. His light brown hair fell in his face nearly touching the top of his glasses. Zooey felt she and Eva were the most mundane, dressed in their usual work clothes. Fiona had teased Zooey about her black Chinese slippers.

"You come here every year?" Laura asked Molly.

Molly nodded. "I think I like the San Francisco festival a little better, though,"

"It's less Hollywood," Greg agreed.

"But this is a good place to meet people. Zooey, we need to be looking for people who can help us with your film."

"I agree," Fiona said. "I met the producer of—what was that short we saw last night?" she glanced at Laura. "They're starting to blur in my mind. Anyway, I didn't pitch her, Zooey, you should do that, but I have her phone number. Have you finished the grant?"

"Almost. I have one more week."

A waiter lit the heat lamp above them and they all ordered more margaritas except for Eva who still had her first and Zooey who was sipping a coke.

"I think the best thing I've seen all weekend was the one about the Danish guy in prison."

"Pretty dark."

"In every way. I loved the lighting—that's hard to do," Fiona said.

"Too much angst for me, but I agree about the lighting," Molly said.

"The best thing I've seen all weekend is the swimming pool. I don't want to go back to the fog," Laura said.

"You're from New York, what are you complaining about," Molly teased.

"It's true, all this light and sun in January! We're staying an extra day to go hiking at Indian Canyon," Eva said.

"The oasis—we went there last year." Greg smiled at her. "It's fantastic."

Monday morning Eva drove her car south on Palm Canyon as Zooey studied the map.

"Can you believe how many gay people there are in this place?" Eva asked.

"Well, the film festival …"

"No, I mean hotels and restaurants. In the middle of nowhere."

They were driving up a gradual hill through open desert now. A roadrunner dashed across the road, his crest exaggerated in a dark shadow cast by the winter sun.

"Look at those mountains. Now they look completely different than yesterday," Eva said.

"I know, it really is all about lighting."

"You and Fiona." Eva laughed.

"I'm so lucky she's going to do the cinematography. If I can just get that grant!"

"If you don't, we'll still find a way, Zooey."

They drove through a gate then negotiated a hairpin turn and steep climb to a cliffside parking lot by a rustic wooden structure—an Indian Trading Post. Inside they wandered from room to room, marveling at the jewelry, pottery, clothing. Eva lingered at a table of hand-crafted toys. Zooey saw the colorful wood and cloth doll and smiled at Eva, resting her hand on her arm a moment then taking it away. Neither of them mentioned the application they had submitted to an adoption agency two weeks before and the long day of interviews. They still hadn't heard anything but they were hopeful.

They emerged from the shop and bought sodas at the small outdoor café. As they finished their drinks and checked their backpack for all the essentials, two hummingbirds hovered above the flowering vine beside their wooden table. "It feels like summer," Eva said as she stood and looked at the hot blue sky.

A steep stone staircase in the cliff face led to the Andreas Creek in the canyon below. The broad sandy creekbed had great pools of flowing water and islands of large palm trees and plants. Giant boulders and rock formations appeared randomly like sculpture.

They made their way along the creekside path, stunned that such lush beauty existed here in the middle of arid desert.

Eva put her hand on Zooey's arm and pointed to a massive slab of striated rock thrusting up from the earth at a sharp angle. Further along, they found a small worn concavity in bedrock by the creek. The map from the Trading Post said there were mortars in the stone once used by the Agua Caliente Indians who were native to the region and still owned this land.

Eva bent and ran her hand slowly along the smoothed bowl shape in the stone. The only sound was an insect buzzing in the heat. Zooey watched Eva's fingers touching the rock and felt the midday heat on her skin. For a moment she could imagine, a century ago, when there was nothing but native life in the desert, the women and children gathered to grind meal—

"Is that Eva and Zooey?" a voice asked in a whisper. Both of them started and looked across the creek in the direction of the voice. The water was low and wide here with sandy islands heavily shaded by groups of palms. Twenty feet away they saw their friends Alisa and Kay sitting on an outcropping of rock in the shade. Alisa had a pack strapped to the front of her and as Eva said, "Alisa. Oh my god!" and started making her way across the creek to them, Zooey realized it was a baby and his little head was poking out of the pack wearing a yellow hat with ear flaps and a big brim.

"He just fell asleep," Alisa mouthed to them as they approached and they nodded and said nothing but gathered around her and looked at the round little face beneath the yellow cap.

"He's beautiful," Eva whispered to Alisa who beamed as Kay smiled at them, too. Zooey and Eva found places on the shelf of rock and the four women sat silently watching the baby boy. He was exquisite.

Zooey knew Alisa had been trying to get pregnant through a clinic and had her baby two months ago. Kay was a lawyer and friend of Eva's. The four of them hadn't gotten together for some months but it was Alisa and Kay, of all their friends, who were the most encouraging when Zooey and Eva talked about adopting a child.

Eva took out bottles of water and passed them around, then went and sat on the other side of Kay to have a whispered conversation. Alisa had leaned back against the boulder and closed her eyes. Zooey thought she seemed more in tune with her baby than anything else around her—the other women, the palm trees, the birds, the creek. It was as if Alisa and her child were in their own invisible force field. She wondered what that must feel like. She prayed she would find out.

Tuesday on the drive back to San Francisco Zooey and Eva were in high spirits. It had been awhile since they'd had a weekend away and this one was filled with friends, art, nature, sun—it couldn't have been better. They drove west to the interstate and headed north through the Central Valley listening to Spanish radio and singing along to *mariachi* songs. After six years with Eva, Zooey knew a lot of the words and they sang at the top of their lungs.

At one point, early in the drive, Eva told Zooey she felt meeting Alisa and Kay and their baby in the oasis was a sign.

"What are the chances?" she said. "That they would be in Palm Springs, they weren't even there for the film festival—just to get some sun. And they were sitting on those rocks just when we arrived?"

"Pretty unlikely," Zooey agreed. Although she felt wary about "signs" she secretly believed Eva was right. It would work out for them. They would create their own family. She believed this with her whole heart.

Late that night, when they finally found a parking spot and dragged themselves and their bags up the steps and into the house, Zooey immediately sorted through the mail and Eva walked to the telephone and checked their messages. There was still no word from the adoption agency.

February 1995

It had been three days and Zooey still felt depressed. She hadn't felt this down in a long time. This hopeless. Eva said they could go to another agency, that this time only Eva would apply, but Zooey knew they didn't have the money for other agencies.

She had just finished her grant proposal and mailed it off when they got the letter from the adoption agency turning them down. It was mainly because of Zooey's arrests during the '70s and '80s for political demonstrations. Maybe one or two would have been okay but there were eleven or twelve and it seemed this made her too weird. That combined with being a lesbian, no doubt. Or she didn't know, but it was her, not Eva, they both believed, that made them get turned down.

As it was, they could barely afford what they would need to buy for a baby and occasional daycare, they would never have tens of thousands to go to China to adopt a child. She knew she shouldn't feel hopeless. There was the option of fostering an older child. There was the possibility of finding a pregnant woman somewhere who did not want her child and would choose them …

Zooey put her head in her hands. She was sitting at the computer preparing to do more research but felt overcome with hopelessness. Something she hadn't felt—not since Eva, certainly—probably not since her days at Sanders. She felt it was her fault, and how terribly disappointed Eva was, and that their lives were being invalidated to the core. They weren't a real family, they weren't even real women. They were dykes, freaks. But that didn't make sense because it was Zooey's arrests, purportedly, that caused their rejection. But somehow, in Zooey's heart, it always came down to being that most hated of minorities. Like they should wear Scarlet L's. She was furious, really. What could she do? Eva was being so calm and practical about it. She seemed to still have faith that it would work out. They would find the money. They would make it work. The laws were changing in their favor. It was a relief to Zooey to see Eva so positive. She stood up and paced a few minutes, back and forth. She glanced out the dining room window and saw the cherry tree below growing in a cement cut-out in the sidewalk. Its branches were covered with pink blossoms. She sighed and sat on a dining room chair. She should call Molly to talk about the festival mailing. At least it was time to start working again. Then she remembered she meant to check her email for a message from Molly.

She had mail but it was from Danielle. She had finally fixed a date for the reunion. Zooey and Danielle had sent a few emails back and forth, catching up, and now Danielle said, "I can't believe you're living with a lawyer! You said the law was a lot of crap. By the way, Alex is a lawyer. At least now I know you won't be telling any lawyer jokes."

Zooey half-smiled despite her mood. Yet the thought of going to the reunion made her feel sick. But she had promised. She could hardly back out now.

March 1995

As Zooey drove up the long curving drive to the top of the hill where Danielle and Alex's house sat behind a high hedge, she noticed a tennis court on a terraced shelf of land by the right wing. Behind it she thought she saw part of a swimming pool that must extend back to the west. She pulled Eva's blue Toyota behind a silver Audi and parked. She sat in the car a moment. She didn't feel quite ready to go in. There were four other expensive cars in the parking area at the side of the front entrance.

Zooey had been to Danielle's other house, on the bay, where she had still lived after her divorce, several times. They had renewed their friendship then and Danielle told Zooey about her affair with the man from the tennis club and how strange it felt to be doing something illicit. She and Zooey talked about the effect prolonged guilt can have but Zooey could never quite explain to Danielle the difference between having a closeted lesbian relationship and a secret adulterous relationship—the moral difference. Zooey never felt immoral when she was in love with Elizabeth, for example. And certainly not with Fiona or Eva. Yet, Danielle said she had thought she was in love with—what was his name? Todd—but it was a forbidden love. Zooey bit her lip. It was hard to explain. She had never really successfully explained who she was to these women, her old Sanders friends. She wondered why she was here. They didn't understand her life and, except for Danielle, probably disapproved. Zooey bent her head to her hand, massaging her forehead with the tips of her fingers. Anyway. She was here.

As she got out of the car she decided, yes, this house was even bigger than the one Danielle lived in with Sean and her children. As far as she knew there were only Alex and Danielle here. Alex was a senior partner in a renowned San Francisco law firm.

Zooey rang the bell and a middle-aged African American woman in a simple blue dress opened the door. She led Zooey across the polished wood floor of the foyer to an expansive living room where she saw everyone had already gathered. Danielle got up from the couch and, smiling happily, walked over to embrace her. She looked exactly the same, Zooey thought—long, perfectly straight cornsilk hair pulled back at the neck with a jeweled clasp. She wore pink and cream silk that made her look elegant yet casual. One by one Zooey moved to embrace her old friends, Patti, who had put on quite a few pounds and was wearing something wild and pretty that looked like a muumuu. Brenna whose once long black hair was shoulder-length and almost entirely gray. She was as warm and sweet as ever but looked very tired. Or more than tired. Zooey didn't have time to really see because Elizabeth—looking not a day over twenty-five—came over to give her a pleasant, gentle embrace. She was wearing black slacks and a topaz blouse that matched her eyes and she still wore her dark hair in a chignon. Zooey realized she had never seen Elizabeth look better, more relaxed. They had changed, actually, all of them, though they were all laughing and talking and saying no one had changed a bit.

Danielle asked Zooey if she was still drinking cokes or wanted something else—tea, coffee, wine. Zooey took a coke and sat on the settee next to Brenna who was drinking Perrier. "How are you?" she asked her when Patti returned to telling Elizabeth what a great cook her husband Jeff was.

"I'm back in San Diego now with the kids."

"Drew got reassigned?"

"No. He's still in Saudi Arabia most of the time. But my son—Jimmy," Brenna's eyes looked pained, then fierce, "has cerebral palsy and I wanted him to be here, in California where we're from. I brought all the kids back."

"Oh I'm sorry, Brenna."

"It's been hard, Zooey. It was so hard to get what we needed for Jimmy and all the kids in the American compound over there. I was so tired of living away from home. Nine years." She looked at Zooey as if she still couldn't accept it had happened.

"How old is Jimmy?"

"Four. Mary Ellen is a great help to me, though. My oldest girl. She was going to start college this year but she's putting it off to help me … Jimmy seems to take all my time. And the twins are only in first grade this year. I hate missing so much of their … but Jimmy's in a wheelchair, you know."

"Why can't you hire someone to help you, Brenna?" Danielle asked as she put down a plate of canapés and sat across from them.

"We have eight kids now, Danielle, and they're all in Catholic schools, except Jimmy of course. Andrew's in his first year at Notre Dame. We're stretching it a little thin not living on the base with Drew."

"Is Drew—does he ever come to San Diego?"

"Oh yes. The holidays. He does what he can but you know it's such a mess over there. After the Gulf War, it's so much more tense … I can't tell you how glad I am to be out of there."

She looked so weary, Zooey wished she could help her somehow.

"Where was Mary Ellen going to go to college?" Elizabeth asked.

"Mount Saint Mary's. I do feel sorry she's stayed at home but she insists she doesn't mind."

"Have you seen a picture of her?" Patti asked Zooey. "She looks exactly like Brenna at that age. Do you have a picture of Mary Ellen, Brenna?"

"I do—we had fun taking pictures to come up here and show you guys." Brenna brightened and looked for her purse. She found a photo book and showed it to Zooey.

"Oh, wow," Zooey said as she looked at a face that could definitely have been Brenna twenty-five years ago. "She looks so much like you, Brenna!" Although, what she didn't say was that the girl looked full of sadness—like Brenna now.

"Will she go to college next year?" Zooey couldn't help asking.

"Drew thinks she should go to a community college near home. Drew's father said he would help with Andrew's tuition at Notre Dame. You know the medical expenses for Jimmy—I never could have imagined."

The other women were clustered around the photo book as Zooey turned the pages and they saw an attractive group of children, some looking more like Brenna, others like Drew, one girl who looked like neither of them and then a little boy in a black motorized wheelchair whose hands curled in at the wrists and who struggled to smile for the camera. His stunning blue eyes looked more like Brenna's than any of the other children's.

"What a beautiful boy," Zooey said and she felt Brenna, next to her, warm and smile to herself.

Brenna's story had sobered them and then Patti said, "Well, are you going to feed us Danielle or let us sit here and starve?"

Danielle smiled cheerfully at Patti, good old Patti. "Dinner is served." She stood, then called toward the kitchen, "Maya?" and turned back to her friends. "Let's adjourn to the dining room."

They followed her through an anteroom to the large formal dining room. The table was set with classic French porcelain and crystal stemware. Zooey wondered if it were Sandrine's. She turned to Patti and asked quietly if Sandrine was still living on Nob Hill?

"No, she's in a home now."

They seated themselves at one end of the mahogany table in high-backed chairs. Maya came from the kitchen to pour chilled wine and serve the salads as Patti started talking about her husband, Jeff, again, with whom she was obviously still in love.

"He is the most laid back guy I've ever known—even more than Sean was," she said to Danielle.

"It turns out Sean wasn't as 'mellow' as he seemed," Danielle said.

"Sean?" Elizabeth asked. "He was so agreeable, and charming."

"You weren't there for the divorce."

"Was it bad? A lot of fighting?" Brenna asked.

"Not really. It was—here one day, gone the next. I'm not kidding. He told me he wanted to marry someone else out of the blue, and the next week he moved in with her."

"The poor kids," Brenna said.

"They took it better than I thought they would. It was strange—after he left, it was like he'd never really been there at all."

"At all?" Patti asked doubtfully.

"You weren't here, Patti, remember? You were on your idyll with Jeff in Hawaii and you were in la-la-land when you came back, too."

"Did you ever think, Patti, at the zoo when that surfer guy started joking with us you would be married to him all these years later?" Brenna asked. "How are your kids doing?"

"Rick is going to Sanders with Jason in the fall. Didn't we tell you?"

"Your boys will be freshmen at Sanders?" Elizabeth looked at Patti and Danielle as Zooey said, "Oh my god." Brenna was silent.

"Ricky needed a little help getting in," Patti admitted, taking a sip of wine. "His grades were not the best. I told Jeff to quit taking him surfing during high school. But they are so close. I am grateful everyday."

"How's Megan?" Zooey asked.

"She smokes a little dope, but otherwise she's all right."

"Smokes dope?" Brenna asked, shocked.

"Oh I saw Sean's wife on television," Patti announced. "One of those pseudo-golf tournaments at the end of the season. She was playing—"

"How did she look?" Danielle asked.

"Oh like they all do, you know. Like a—" she stopped herself.

Danielle glanced at Zooey involuntarily then at no one in particular. "I see her now and then when I take the kids to Sean's. Sean's gained some weight. Have you seen him lately?" she asked Patti.

"Not since we ran into him at the Marina last year. But, hey, we're all getting older." She shrugged. "I had to start touching up my hair years ago." She put a hand to her orange-red hair which Zooey saw—now that she mentioned it—looked like Patti's mother's had at her wedding a decade ago. Patti still had her same laugh, though; that hadn't changed at all over the years.

"But look at us," Patti went on. "Danielle you wear contacts now and are on Xanax. I've gained thirty pounds and dye my hair. Brenna has gone completely gray." She looked at Zooey and then Elizabeth. "You know what? It must be true—that thing they say—that married men are the happiest, and then single women, then unmarried men, then us married women—bottom of the pile. It ages us. Look at Elizabeth and Zooey—still single and they look ten years younger than us. Elizabeth looks like she just graduated from Sanders. Because you've never had kids. It's unbelievable what it does to your body. It's not fair!"

"Not fair?" Zooey said without thinking. "I'd give anything to have a child."

This silenced them again until Brenna said, "I agree, Zooey. Having children is so fulfilling. No matter how it turns out, all the heartbreak. I wouldn't have missed having children. Ever."

"We've been trying to adopt a child," Zooey said.

"You and Eva?"

"Yes. It's legal."

"That's wonderful, Zooey," Danielle said. "There are so many children who need a loving home."

"It's not easy. You have to be approved ..." Zooey's voice trailed off and she wished she hadn't brought it up. She took a bite of salad.

"Has it been disappointing?" Elizabeth asked.

Zooey glanced up. "There've been problems. Because of all my political arrests and ... I don't qualify to go through the agency we can afford. But there are other options. We have to start over."

"A lot of people are adopting girls from China," Danielle said. "They have a 'one child per family' law and since they all want boys they put girls in orphanages. Some of the places are disgusting."

"Oh, I saw that story in the paper. Why don't you do that, Zooey?" Patti asked.

"Too expensive. And they don't let lesbians adopt, although they will let a single woman." Zooey glanced at Elizabeth who was sipping a glass of ice water and watching Zooey with an unreadable, intense gaze.

"Is your father still alive, Zooey?" she asked out of nowhere.

"No, he died a few years after my mother."

"How about Eva's parents?" Patti asked.

"They're both fine, living in Merced."

"What do they think … how do they feel about you and Eva?"

"Well, I'm not their *favorite* daughter-in-law."

Patti laughed. "I'm glad you didn't totally lose your sense of humor when you stopped drinking, Zooey."

"Patti, you should be accompanied by an editor at all times," Danielle said.

"But they're nice to us," Zooey went on. "They love Eva a lot."

"I bet they love you too, Zooey," Brenna said.

"I can't imagine having a baby at this age. They run you ragged. I remember when Megan and Ricky were little, I couldn't wait to get away from them sometimes. I used to look forward to going to the dentist." Patti reached to pour herself another glass of wine and Zooey, watching her, was surprised by how much she craved a glass for herself—it didn't look like poison to her now but comfort. She felt stricken after talking about the adoption and wondered if it would matter so much if she just had one glass of wine. She turned to Danielle.

"Where's Alex tonight?"

"Oh, he went to a *tapas* bar with some friends."

"*What*?" Patti said. "You're kidding!"

"What's wrong with that?"

"A topless bar? I didn't even know there were any left."

They all laughed except Danielle who was still annoyed with Patti for what she had said about Xanax.

Finally, Maya appeared with a small wooden cart bearing the entrées which smelled wonderful—lemon and garlic roasted chicken and something vegetarian for Elizabeth it appeared, as well as warm brioche rolls and French green beans with almonds.

Patti was talking about a new clerk in the bakery at the ferry docks. "She was probably fifteen at the most and her hair was standing straight up, iridescent blue like a peacock, and either she had an orange tongue stud or she'd just eaten a carrot. I couldn't even remember what I'd gone in to buy after one look at her. Who would hire—"

"Maybe she's the owner's daughter," Zooey said as Brenna asked Danielle if Xanax really worked well for her; she had heard it wasn't as effective as Valium and Danielle denied she was "on" Xanax but said she did take it occasionally, for example, when she had to go to the dentist.

Patti stopped talking about the girl in the bakery to join in the Xanax discussion and Elizabeth leaned across the table to ask Zooey if they could have lunch together sometime in the next two weeks before she went back East again. Stunned, Zooey agreed.

Zooey got off the bus at the top of the hill and stood a moment to take in the angular, orange beams of a sculpture in the center of the parking lot. She preferred the neoclassic lines of the balustrade beyond, and then the panorama of downtown skyscrapers, green trees and blue bay. She turned around and faced the Palace of the Legion of Honor and its rows of neoclassic columns leading to a graceful rotunda where the Rodins were showcased. She hadn't been here for years and was glad Elizabeth suggested they meet at the museum café for lunch.

Elizabeth was waiting for her at the entrance to the café overlooking the garden. She looked much the same as she had at the reunion the week before, her dark hair in the neat chignon, her tailored suit fitting her well. Zooey wore her generic black clothes and her new glasses. She was surprised how removed she felt from the moment, as if watching it from an audience rather than living it. She felt cautious and curious as they exchanged smiles and a light embrace. They discussed what they would order as they glanced over the menu and took trays from the little stack at the beginning of the line. They were acting as if they often had lunch, a "ladies' lunch", and were going through the protocols. Although Zooey didn't have these kind of lunches, she could see that Elizabeth did, and she followed suit. They ordered salads and half-sandwiches and coffee and found a table near the windows.

"How's Eva?" Elizabeth launched in.

Zooey wondered if this were more protocol, inquiring after spouses and children, or if she really wanted to know. It was good of her to acknowledge Eva anyway.

"Doing well. Busy." Zooey decided to follow protocol.

"How did you two meet?" Elizabeth asked.

"Oh, well. It's funny," Zooey said, suddenly remembering, "Molly—do you remember Molly DeLuca, she was in my film class at Sanders? In fact, we saw her one day, remember? We were riding the cable car up to Nob Hill—or was it Fisherman's Wharf—and there was a demonstration on Market Street?"

Elizabeth looked blank.

"They were burning bras, remember?"

"I don't. When was this?"

"Oh, well, nevermind. Anyway, Molly—"

"I do remember a girl named Molly you became friends with. Didn't you stay with her after you left Sanders?"

"Right, that was Molly." Zooey nodded. "Well, you know, she introduced me to Fiona."

"Fiona was your first—relationship." Elizabeth gazed at her intensely now.

"Yes. We lived together for three or four years. At the end it was back and forth—she was in New York. But it was also Molly who introduced me to Eva, too, years later."

Elizabeth smiled. "Isn't it interesting how those things happen."

"Well, Molly is a great friend. But it is a coincidence. She wasn't actually trying to fix me up with someone, either time."

"Is she a lesbian?"

"No."

"How long have you and Eva lived together?"

"Six years. We just bought a house a couple years ago. Do you still have your house in the Berkshires?"

"Yes, I do. I rented it out while I was living in England but I'll be moving back into it this summer."

"What made you decide to come back? But—hasn't it been almost a year since you left England?"

Elizabeth picked up her napkin from her lap and carefully wiped her lips and the corners of her mouth.

"Yes. I did come back last summer." She looked at Zooey who sat quietly watching her. "I felt so alone in London."

"You mean—living alone?"

"No, I've lived alone since I left Sanders. It was—you would think England wouldn't be drastically different from Massachusetts or the East Coast of this country, but it is. I felt I never fit in. I wasn't able to make good friends. Some acquaintances, and I had colleagues, there were functions at the college. But I felt too alone."

"That's a long time. Weren't you there eight or nine years?"

"I kept thinking things would gel. I loved the countryside there and the basic sanity of the place. Although there are both absurd and provincial aspects to post-imperial Britain, the people are essentially more civil than they are here."

"Is there a stodginess? Queuing up to cross the street and all that?" That's what Molly and Greg had said after their vacation there.

"Not as much as you might think and the civility is worth it, at least to me."

"But you did decide to come back here. Have you reconnected with old friends?"

"I'm trying to." Elizabeth looked at her as if it were obvious that she were, but Zooey felt there couldn't be much to salvage between herself and Elizabeth—it had been decades …

"I had dinner with Mark Landry the other night. Do you remember him?" Elizabeth said.

Zooey sat back a little. "Of course. How is he?" Then she sat forward. "I thought I saw him at a demonstration in the city about, I don't know, not long after you moved to London I guess. Is he still doing all that?"

"No, he's not. He's a high school teacher in Oakland—an inner-city school. He teaches history and he's married."

"Married! Everyone always said he wasn't the marrying kind."

"Well. People change."

"How was it, seeing him?" Zooey remembered the rumors she'd heard.

"It was fun. He's always fun to be with."

"Did you look him up, or …?"

"Actually, it's a long story."

"Tell me!"

"Well, when I decided to leave London I—I was worn out, with loneliness—that's how I thought of it. I couldn't face going back to my house alone. I felt I had to be part of something social—a community. And you know I'd been studying Eastern religions—Buddhism in particular—for years."

"I heard you say something about it at Danielle's."

"I decided to live at a meditation retreat in upstate New York. I wrote to them and had a series of interviews and then moved there last fall."

"You didn't mention that."

"I wasn't ready for their third degree and commentary. Danielle and Patti used to make fun of us for being Catholics, I could imagine where they would take this."

"But when did you give up Catholicism? At Sanders, you …"

"I stopped going to church once and for all—well I switched from Catholic to Anglican when I moved to London, and then—it was part of the loneliness—it was part of coping with the enormous disappointment I felt with my life as I approached forty. Catholicism and Anglicanism couldn't even touch it. I felt terrible despair."

"I'm sorry, Elizabeth." Zooey remembered that Elizabeth's suicide attempt had been around the time she turned thirty. And also that, at dinner the week before, Elizabeth had asked Zooey if she were "disappointed" about the adoption. That was the word she had used.

"Well, as sometimes happens it turned out to be liberating. I had to find something that explained my life to me—or that freed me to accept my life as it is."

"How did you?"

"I remembered reading *The Razor's Edge* at Sanders and how I loved that book but then I started reading Sartre and Simone de Beauvoir—remember?"

"Yes. We spent hours and hours talking."

"I know."

"But how did—"

"I re-read the book and then began to read some of the same material the protagonist—Larry—read, and then immediately set off on my own reading, you know how one thing leads to another. I found a meditation center in London I began to attend. I took a trip to Thailand and went on a Vipassana retreat there."

"Oh. You've really been doing it, then."

"For the last five years or so."

"And—did it help you—with the disappointment?"

"More than psychotherapy, which I'd also done extensively in my early thirties."

"How?" Zooey was thinking of Dr. Reynolds and then the AA meetings she went to for months.

"It's similar to cognitive therapy in the concept of "reframing" things, or instead of trying to change what you can't control—change your attitude toward it."

"Oh, like the Serenity Prayer, in a way."

"Niebuhr's?" Elizabeth smiled. "Exactly, at least, in terms of acceptance."

"I always thought—'free will' is the ability to believe whatever you want about your fate."

Elizabeth laughed. "I know what you mean."

"But what is it? The essence of what you're doing now, of meditation or—"

"Remember that summer you spent playing tennis with Danielle? When you came back to Sanders you were talking about it and you said the most important thing you learned was not to play the people, but to play the ball."

Zooey bit her lip, looking out the window. She did remember that. How, instead of getting caught up in the mind games or attitudes of her opponent or herself—the stories she told herself about what was going on—she simply focused her entire being on the spinning white ball.

"I always remembered that," Elizabeth said, "and all these years later realized what an excellent metaphor it is for living in the present. The present moment is the ball. That's where our attention is best focused. Not on regrets about the past or fears about the future. That's what was killing me. My fear of being old and alone, a spinster. My regrets about never marrying or having children. I was living in the past and future but, when I was able to simply focus on the present moment—that moment was fine. The great percentage of moments in our lives are actually fine, quite benign or even enjoyable. Meditation is the practice of being present for our lives as they actually are in the moment."

"I'm glad you said the thing about tennis. Because otherwise, I don't think I would know what you mean."

"It is experiential. Doing it is the best way to understand it because it's something beyond language. Ironically, language gets in the way of our being in the present more often than not."

"That is ironic given your career is in language arts."

"I know."

"Is that why you stopped teaching?"

"It's why I've taken a break from it, but I love literature and always will, and I enjoy teaching. I plan to teach one semester a year and live at the meditation center the other seven or eight months of the year."

"Wow."

Elizabeth laughed. Then she said, "I told you it was a long story, but that's how I got back in touch with Mark."

"What?"

"His sister-in-law is part of the Vipassana community—his wife's sister. And he and his wife have been going on retreats themselves." Elizabeth raised her eyebrows and gave Zooey a wry look. "Can you believe it?"

Zooey laughed. "He sounds so tame, now. Is he?"

"He's not nearly as cocky. But I'd have to say he's better company now. I believe he has actually learned to listen."

"I guess I can picture that."

"I think he had some bad health—well, he told me had prostate cancer a few years ago although it's completely in remission now. Danielle knew about it through Sean so I don't think I'm revealing a big secret. I hope not."

"I have no one to tell. But that would explain his changes, I think."

"In part."

"I know, it's also … He was sincere about his politics, his—I don't know—not utopianism but …"

"He is a seeker, but no longer in a flashy way. He looks within now."

"Are you …"

"Still in love with him?"

"Well … were you ever really?"

Elizabeth's lips tightened and she looked away.

"I'm sorry," Zooey said.

"I was, Zooey."

"But—in Mazatlan—" Zooey could hardly believe she was bringing this up all these years later but she couldn't seem to help herself, her voice was strained. "Don't you remember that night after you broke up? You came back to the house and I was there alone and you told me you didn't really love him, he didn't see you or know you."

Elizabeth sighed. "I didn't know if we would or should go back to these things, Zooey. But we seem to be here. And actually … I did want to tell you something. I've wanted to tell you for several years—since I realized it myself. It came to me, through layers and layers of denial, after a week of silent sitting. I was in love with Mark. And I also was in love with you."

Zooey's lips parted, she stopped breathing.

"The fact is, I'm bisexual, there's no denying it anymore. But I couldn't begin to face that then. It was even more ominous and dreadful than the fate of spinsterhood I became so despairing of in London. I'm sorry I never admitted it to you. That I let you, I don't know—hang out to dry."

"I see. I was sure you were as much a lesbian as I am. That's part of why I never believed you were in love with Mark."

"I don't remember that conversation with you in Mazatlan. Was I drunk?"

"Yes."

"But I do remember feeling those things—that Mark didn't see who I was, that he was incapable of really connecting with anyone, he was self-absorbed, all the rest of it. But I was still in love with him. And when we saw each other years later at Danielle's wedding, we started up again, did you know that?"

"Yes, Danielle told me." Zooey remembered Elizabeth and Mark slow dancing, wrapped in each other's arms, at the end of the reception.

"When it ended again—I felt such despair, for years. I even tried to kill myself. Did you know that?"

Zooey nodded. "I did."

"Well, there are no secrets, I guess."

Zooey said nothing.

"It was after my father died. That had something to do with it, too. Not long after that I moved to London. And at first, the novelty and—I am an Anglophile—I was relatively happy until—you know, the biological clock. I guess it's a cliché." She took a sip of water, then looked at Zooey. The intense amber gaze. "But you've wanted children, too."

Zooey frowned. It was still painful to think of, yet why had she given up? It was something about the rejection from the agency—the sense that she was deemed unworthy and would always be so.

"It's hard, isn't it?" Elizabeth watched her.

"We can still try. Eva can. She can adopt as a single parent and we're going to try that as soon as we figure out how and where."

"But it's legal for gays to adopt in California, isn't it?"

"Yes, with certain conditions."

"Do you ever wonder …" Elizabeth hesitated, then went on, "What it would be like to have gay parents?"

"Parents who are loving are always a plus. As opposed to no parents, abusive parents, neglectful parents."

"That's true."

"I'm not saying it isn't hard to live with the stigma. As you know."

Elizabeth bowed her head a moment then looked up. "I was too afraid, Zooey."

"I know," Zooey said. To her surprise, tears came to her eyes, and she looked away. They were quiet a moment.

Finally Elizabeth said, "They say children need a father but when I see Brenna and her children I think they're all better off with Drew out of the picture."

"Is he out of the picture? Do you think they'll get divorced?"

"Not divorced because Brenna is still very Catholic. But she and her eight children are living here and Drew is living in Saudi Arabia. When I visited

Brenna—she's changed. Drew is no longer the center. Jimmy is the center. Her fierce loyalties have become completely focused on him and she told me, Drew resents it."

"I thought her daughter—Mary Ellen—looked so depressed in that photograph."

"I know. It's a tragedy—Jimmy's illness—for their family, in a lot of ways. It's devastated them financially, for one thing."

"The Navy doesn't help?"

"Actually, it does. But Brenna has sought out every possible therapy, alternative and otherwise, and it's taken so much of her time and their resources."

"Patti said her second son, after Andrew—"

"Luke."

"Right. That he wants to be a priest?"

Elizabeth nodded and said nothing.

"What?"

Elizabeth shrugged. "I would guess he's gay."

"Ah."

"Yes, choosing the Catholic way out. It's an insidious prejudice."

"It is," Zooey agreed.

"It's interesting neither you nor Mark is politically active anymore."

"Well." Zooey thought a moment. It seemed sad to her suddenly but then she realized it wasn't entirely true. "I think, if Mark's teaching in an inner-city school—that's his political work now. And it might actually be helping some people, more than demonstrations with zero impact."

Elizabeth smiled. "That's exactly what he said."

"And for me," Zooey went on, "I'm doing 'cultural work'. Remember that term?"

"The art of the left."

"Sort of. I'm focusing on human rights, including gay rights."

"Have you heard about your grant application?"

"Not yet. But it is sad, the big social justice movements have shrunk to nearly nothing. It's leaving a vacuum the Right is going to sweep in and fill. They already are."

"Still, there is progress, Zooey. Think of when we were at Sanders. We weren't even allowed to wear pants on campus—remember the dress code? The women's movement, civil rights, the advances in human rights haven't been taken away."

"But there's more poverty now—the gap between rich and poor is bigger than it was in the seventies. In that way, we're becoming a Third World country."

"Mark said that too. You and he should have lunch sometime."

"I haven't seen him since Danielle's wedding."

Elizabeth looked away a moment and it seemed to Zooey she was remembering that day.

"Are you going to see Danielle or Patti again before you leave?"

"No, I'm leaving the day after tomorrow. In fact," she glanced at her watch. "Do you want to share a cab downtown? I'm expecting a call at my hotel in an hour."

April 1995

Zooey sat at the oak desk in the office at Molly and Greg's house working on the Women's Film Festival that would be in early September this year. As she went through the mail she found her mind drifting to her lunch with Elizabeth as it had often since she saw her last week. Certain moments, sentences she thought would never be spoken ran through her mind as if on a tape-loop. She still felt stunned by the encounter although it was starting to fade. She wondered, too, if she would ever see Elizabeth again. On the long cab ride downtown they talked easily as if no time had passed—as if it were twenty-five years ago and they were still school girls at Holy Name, before the feelings of love became complex.

Although, too, they were still women in their forties and there was a feeling that was bittersweet in the small silences, between the lines. Zooey thought often of what Elizabeth said about her new life, eight months a year living at a meditation retreat. It seemed too austere even for Elizabeth. Yet she seemed genuinely happy about her choice, looking forward to it as if it were a Caribbean cruise. When Zooey thought of the vast silence, the "emptiness" as Elizabeth described it before they parted in front of the St. Francis Hotel—where they stood talking until Elizabeth realized she might miss her call and, after embracing Zooey warmly, disappeared through the revolving doors and Zooey looked around Union Square at the crush of rush hour traffic, honking cars, harried pedestrians—"emptiness" seemed very inviting. Especially since she hadn't been able to shake herself from her funk since the rejection from the adoption agency.

She knew, and Eva had helped her see, it wasn't the end of their hopes—there was something else Zooey was responding to, something the letter was triggering in her. It was as if it resonated with every rejection Zooey had ever received, every slight and insult she had endured for being a lesbian.

Something about this one letter from the agency caused Zooey's hopes and belief in herself—her ability to see herself as a good mother—to implode. As if the government had stamped her as bad, unworthy. Why it affected Zooey this way and not Eva was something they discussed for hours, and in the end Zooey felt it was because she had let her life drift. She never went back to school after the Dr. Reynolds days, it had taken her a decade to get over Fiona, it was basically a lack of drive. She spent years wandering, observing life, recording her observations and feelings in poems or journals. She had written the one screenplay, though, completed it and actually shown it to Molly and the others. And even if she didn't get the grant, her friends said they would find a way to produce the film. This was something.

She looked in her purse for the apple she brought, then sat back in her chair and watched the branches of the loquat tree at the high window above the desk. She took a crunching bite of apple. In fact, she had been very happy the past several years. Her relationship with Eva made her richly happy. And even before, she had enjoyed her wanderings and musings—her inner life. It was a great pleasure.

As she watched the yellow-green leaves change in the afternoon light she realized it was all this striving that made her miserable, actually. It was having goals and failing. Yet, wasn't the absence of goals a little … boring? She had never really abandoned her dreams entirely. Her dream of family, of creative expression. Could she really live without dreams at all? And just "be". Elizabeth had described a joy in silence, beyond language. Rapture, she called it. Could she actually sustain it *eight* months a year?

It seemed so un-American to have no goals. And this might be a good thing. To back off, quit trying to impose oneself on the world with progeny or ideology or products. It was not the leftist solution to ending imperialism but what if a more accepting, yin behavior characterized a society? Then she remembered a film by a Tibetan woman should have come in and began looking for the log.

It was dark when Zooey got home that night after a light supper with Molly and Greg. Eva was in Los Angeles. She had an early court appearance there the next morning. Zooey was breathing heavily when she opened the front door after climbing three blocks uphill from the bus and then their steep staircase. She realized she didn't have the stamina she did in her thirties as she set her purse on the table in the foyer. She found her glasses and picked up the mail to sort through. Her breath caught and her lips parted when she saw the return address of the Foundation, although she had been looking for exactly this letter. It shocked her to actually find it here. She held it a moment and closed her eyes, then tore open the envelope. Scanning the content her heart sank, hard.

ॐ

Dear Ms. James,

Thank you for allowing us to consider your proposal for funding. Although your screenplay is original and engaging and we read it with interest, it does not fit into our current program priorities. We regret that our focus this year precludes our funding your project and wish you the best of luck elsewhere …

Zooey slapped the letter down on the table and walked into the living room and sat on the couch. She could see the lights of the city outside the window and stared, feeling neither the usual pleasure at the sight nor much of anything at all unless bitterness was a feeling. It felt worse, even, than the adoption letter, at least it did at this moment. Although, once again, there were other options—it didn't mean she would never produce the film. It just made it a whole lot harder. And more than anything it was, once again, the invalidation. For some reason she remembered Dr. Reynolds telling her to try not to act smart, to start dating boys, to stop being who she was if she wanted to be accepted—in even the most basic way. She felt her face start to burn and realized she was intensely angry. But who could she blame? So the Foundation wasn't doing queer movies this year. Was that their fault? They said they "read it with interest", it was "engaging". She calmed down a little. Then she felt tears come to her eyes and remembered what she thought of herself earlier. How little drive or resilience she had. And this made her feel ashamed and instantly she had that craving again, that she hadn't in a very long time until, for some reason it had come upon her that evening last month at Danielle's. Just one glass of wine—Of course, it was obvious—it was a drug, it would make her feel better. There was no doubt about it, if she had a couple drinks right now she would calm down, start thinking—"oh what the hell." And if she had only two drinks, she wouldn't be hungover. Or at least she never had in her drinking days. Zooey stood up and headed for the hall to find her purse.

As she walked down the hill in the cool, dark night she realized what she was feeling was despair. It didn't make rational sense but it was unbearable. She had had enough. Anger propelled her quickly the block and a half to the corner store but she kept walking right past it. No fucking way was she going to start drinking again. What would Eva think, for one thing. And then she heard in her mind Elizabeth asking her at the dinner at Danielle's, "Were you disappointed?" She pronounced the word in her mind, "disappointed." That's what she was.

Zooey turned around and started walking back up the hill toward home. She remembered Elizabeth saying how she used to feel so afraid of her future, of living with disappointment. And her regrets about the past. The stories we tell ourselves about ourselves. Because really, what was wrong with this moment now as it was? Zooey was just walking in the city on a cool, spring evening. Not only was it not painful, it was nice, it was fun. She felt her face relax into a smile.

Back at home she was grateful for the exercise, she felt much better. She went into the living room and turned on the lamp and sat on the living room floor with her back against the couch and legs crossed beneath her. She put her open palms on her knees and closed her eyes. In her mind, she pictured a tennis ball, a yellow ball—they were yellow now—and watched it spin in front of her closed eyes until all thought vanished.

August 1995

Zooey picked up the phone on the first ring. "Women's Film," she said.

"Zooey, are you going to your meditation group tonight?" It was Eva.

"I was going to." Eva sounded breathless, in a hurry—she must have to be in court in a minute. Zooey looked at her watch. But it was after 3:00.

"Would you mind coming home instead? We could have dinner and—I have a case I need to talk to you about."

"A case?" Zooey was surprised. She didn't know any law and although sometimes Eva ran a few things by her when she was working out a strategy it was hardly as if she relied on Zooey's opinions or needed to make a special meeting with her to discuss a case.

"Yeah, you know. I've gotta run, Zo. Is it okay? I'll see you at home around 6:00?"

"All right. See you then."

"I love you."

"Me too." Zooey hung up the phone. That was weird. She had been looking forward to going to the sangha to meditate because Thursday nights there were only a few people and it was so quiet, but she could miss it this week. Usually she meditated every morning for an hour after Eva left for work. Elizabeth had been right. It was transformative. Eva saw the difference in Zooey and had started coming with her sometimes to the sangha.

In part, Zooey thought meditation was why she was so calm when they had only three weeks until the festival and there was way too much to do. She wondered for a moment what she would do when it was over. Molly said they should focus on getting funding for Zooey's film but Zooey doubted they would have the energy. Maybe later in the fall. Although the holidays started then. She had let go of it really. Lost interest, or at least lost the urgency she felt last spring when she was writing the grant proposal. What she might do is find temporary work so she and Eva could save for a vacation longer than a weekend.

When Zooey started to put the key in the lock of the front door at home, Eva opened the door. "Hi, love." She gave her a kiss. But she seemed nervous to Zooey. Zooey put her key back in her purse and walked in. Eva had already set the dining room table and apparently bought take-out sushi for dinner. Zooey wondered for a second if it were someone's birthday.

"What is going on with you?" she asked Eva, giving her a teasing look.

"I have some things to tell you," was all Eva would say. The kettle in the kitchen began to whistle and Eva went to make some jasmine tea.

When they were sitting at the table, Zooey held a steaming cup in her hands letting the fragrance fill her senses, waiting for Eva to reveal whatever she had on her mind.

"I don't know how you'll feel about this," Eva began. "It's so unlike us, or me—I hadn't thought it would necessarily get this far, I—"

"What?" Zooey put down her cup. "Say it, Eva."

"You were so upset or depressed after the adoption agency rejected you last winter, and you didn't want to apply anywhere else, although we talked about me doing the process …"

"I know. I'm not sure why we didn't. I guess we've been so busy—"

"Well, I did do it, Zooey. I did it on my own."

"You did?" Zooey was surprised. They discussed everything. At least, everything that affected both their lives, and much that didn't.

"I did." Eva looked closely at Zooey, reading her. "It took me awhile to fit it in because I had that big case but, last April, after you got the letter about the grant and you were doing so well starting meditation and dealing with all the disappointments—I didn't want to bring up anything that would stir up more hope or disappointment. I thought I'd just get my name in and see what happened, it can take years before being matched with a baby. I went to Jillian Rudolph, you know that attorney who does open adoptions," Eva was talking rapidly now, "and filled out all the paperwork. She said it isn't easy to find a birth parent who will choose a single person—"

"Open adoption. But the birth parent knows who you are, they see your home and—you're not single." Zooey's eyes narrowed. This wasn't happening. Eva was breaking up with her so she could adopt a child as a single mother.

"No, no, no, Zooey. Just listen to me. Please?"

Zooey felt as if she might cry. Something huge was happening. "What?"

"I'm sorry I did this without telling you, but listen." Eva looked excited now. "They found a baby for me! A sixteen year-old girl in Sacramento who is pregnant and wants to give up her baby because she wants to go to law school. To be a lawyer. I met her, Zooey."

Zooey felt as if the earth were falling out from under her. How could Eva do this? And yet, hadn't Eva wanted a child more than anything her entire life? Wasn't having a child, in the end, more important even than their relationship.

"And Zooey," Eva didn't even seem aware of what Zooey was feeling, "I took pictures to her. Of our house. Of you and me. I told her about us, Zooey, and she's fine with it! As soon as the baby arrives I will adopt her and then you can do a second-parent adoption. I know we can get it through the judge who's doing them. Zooey!" Eva was crying now. "Can you do it? Do you still want to? Can we do this?"

It was like an explosion in her mind—the realization—Eva wasn't leaving her, they could have a baby, their dream could come true. And even the shame that she had so doubted Eva just now vanished as she welcomed this fantastic news. "Yes! Oh my god. Eva. When?" Both of them stood and hurried around the table so they could embrace each other.

"Oh Zooey. I knew I could count on you," Eva whispered into her hair.

"Of course, darling, of course." Zooey wouldn't tell her how she hadn't returned that faith a moment ago but then, some secrets—like Eva's from her about her single application—were for the best.

"When is the baby due?" Zooey asked and already through her euphoria she was wondering how long she would have to fret about something going wrong.

"September."

"Really! That *soon?*"

"Yes, in three weeks!"

December 1995

Zooey sat in the rocker in the living room holding her sleeping baby in her lap. She could look at her forever. Tess had blonde wisps of hair and curly little eyelashes and her skin smelled of something otherworldly of which only babies smelled. Her perfect tiny hands rested on a soft silk blanket, a gift from Danielle.

Sometimes when Zooey sat for hours holding Tess she thought her entire life up to now, all forty-two years, had been simply to prepare her for this, for mothering Tess. Such thoughts came in the moments she felt most benevolent toward herself, when her life seemed to have sense and purpose, even the hard and crazy times. Maybe especially those. She thought of her phone conversation with Brenna after she and Eva sent out announcements to all their friends and family about Tess. Brenna, who was thrilled for them, said "don't you think it's a lucky break you didn't get that grant, and now you can be there a hundred per cent for your daughter? I can't imagine trying to make a movie and take care of a new baby at the same time!" Zooey hadn't put this together in her mind but it was obviously true. Count on Brenna to find the positive in the negative.

Patti had sent a funny book by a new mother called *Operating Instructions* and an electric foot massager. One day she came by with Danielle to see Tess and not only out of curiosity, Zooey felt, but out of friendship. Neither Danielle nor Patti had met Eva before and yet, after a few halting minutes, they all fell into easy conversation about babies and children and their lives. They were all women, after all.

Elizabeth had sent a lovely congratulatory card and a beautiful smock for Tess. She said she hoped to come and visit next time she was on the West Coast although Zooey doubted it would be anytime soon since she had no family in California now. Some weeks before they sent their announcements, Zooey had received a different package in the mail from Elizabeth. It was a few days before the end of the film festival, before Tess was even born, when a manila envelope with Elizabeth's graceful handwriting arrived in the mail. Zooey opened it with curiosity and found inside a slim volume, a hardback book of poetry called *Winter Light*. It was by Elizabeth Riordan, published by a renowned university press. Zooey remembered how surprised she had been. She had read Elizabeth's poetry at Sanders but wasn't aware—Elizabeth never spoke of writing poetry, much less having a book coming out, at their lunch in the spring. Zooey had looked at the beautifully designed book, turning it over in her hands, then turned the title page and looked at the dedication. "For Jordan". That's all. What? Zooey thought. Who is Jordan? Elizabeth. Forever a mystery. She sat down and read the poems—intense, intelligent, beautiful and at the same time, at peace.

Which exacted the greater price, Zooey wondered—being unconventional? or conforming to convention? Or more importantly, why did society, still at the end of the twentieth century, exact such a high price from those whose truest selves were not conventional?

Epilogue

June 2007

Zooey, Eva and Tess got out of Eva's Toyota Prius. Eva took Tess's hand as they stood on the grass bordering the street. They glanced around them and then up the hill.

"That must be it," Zooey said coming around from the driver's side to stand with them. She looked at the ivory-colored announcement in her hand. "The Brazil Room. Four o'clock." She glanced at her watch. "Right on time." She was slightly nervous. Hadn't she sworn to herself twenty years ago she would never go to another wedding unless it were her own? But she had been to Brenna's, Danielle's and Patti's. She couldn't miss Elizabeth's.

"Let's go!" Tess said. Her large gray eyes looked up at Zooey reflecting Zooey's excitement, agitation, curiosity.

"Sure, honey," Zooey looked around, "I just don't see a path."

"Over there." Tess pointed to a walkway between some trees. Zooey and Eva exchanged a glance. Tess's eyes were better than either of theirs and she was often more observant than Zooey.

"Thank you, sweetheart." The three of them headed toward the large stone building on the crest of the hill. Backed by tall pines, it resembled a mountain lodge.

"What's the Brazilian part?" Eva wanted to know.

Zooey shrugged. They were in Tilden Park in Berkeley—miles of beautiful rolling hills, and Zooey wondered why they so rarely visited it.

As they turned up the path they saw several guests on the large verandah and the lawn in front.

"Where's Elizabeth?" Tess wanted to know. She had never met her or any of Zooey's old Sanders friends, other than when she was a month or two old.

"She's probably somewhere getting ready." Zooey glanced at Tess who was wearing her favorite dress, a green and blue silk kimono that resembled one of Eva's. It looked beautiful on her, accentuating the golden highlights in her honey brown hair which Zooey had spent a long time brushing so it glistened now in the afternoon sun. Realizing none of the guests had seen Tess since she was an infant, other than a photo at Danielle's reunion last fall, made the fact Tess was ten years old seem startling to Zooey. Ten years! She was still a child but soon she would be a teen-ager! Zooey put her arm around Tess and pulled her to her for a second.

"Don't mess up my dress, Mom."

"Sorry, honey."

"Aren't you supposed to find the others before the ceremony?" Eva asked, glancing around. She wasn't thrilled to be here but had of course agreed when Zooey asked her and Tess to come.

"I guess so." Zooey peered at the building then looked in her small bag for her glasses and put them on. Everyone standing and talking outside was beginning to head indoors.

"There's Brenna." Zooey turned to Eva and Tess and gave each a quick kiss. "I'll see you at the reception, then. I guess you can just find seats inside."

Zooey stood in the front of the large craftsman hall surveying the seated guests and waiting expectantly. There were more people than she expected—at least a hundred. Several of Elizabeth's friends and colleagues had flown west for her wedding but most of the people here were Mark's friends, she imagined. Zooey turned and looked at Mark standing next to Sean, his best man, by the dais where the monk who was to perform the ceremony was reviewing his notes. Zooey had been stunned when Elizabeth told her she was marrying Mark. More than stunned, she had been shocked. Elizabeth explained that Mark's wife, whom he had married in the early nineties, had sadly died of breast cancer in 2003 at the age of forty-five. Mark was devastated, Elizabeth told her, and she and he began corresponding. Eventually the email correspondence became visits and now, remarkably, they were here. Zooey still couldn't quite put it all together. Yes, Mark, the love of Elizabeth's life. But what about the meditation center and the austerity, the poetry—the inner life? Zooey looked at Mark now in his gray slacks and indigo embroidered shirt from somewhere in Asia. He was still thin and handsome in his jaunty way although the shock of black hair that fell over his forehead was streaked with gray. He had deep lines around his eyes, laughter and sadness. And as Zooey watched him she saw he seemed more serious and calm and just then, feeling her gaze, Mark looked over at her and then smiled a warm, acknowledging smile. She smiled back at him in kind. Something about this unexpected exchange made it click for Zooey. She understood, without being able to explain—how it made sense for Elizabeth and Mark to marry now.

The music started—Chopin—and Elizabeth, who had been standing with her four friends to one side of the dais, moved toward Mark and they took each other's hands standing closely side by side facing the young monk. After a moment the monk read from the *Diamond Sutra* and the *Upanishads*, Zooey recognized some of the verses. She looked at Elizabeth, whose face she could see only in profile, but who seemed fully engaged, happy. Her white linen floor-length caftan was exquisitely embroidered and made her look something like an angel, Zooey thought, although that was too Christian an image for this occasion.

Zooey looked past Mark and then wondered what it was like for Danielle to be standing here with Sean ten feet away. Thirty years ago it had been the two of them exchanging vows and Mark and Elizabeth standing in attendance. Sean was still good-looking although a certain fleshiness in his face and body made his aging more obvious than his cousin's. Sean's curls were still black but had receded so that his forehead was high and shone with perspiration now. It was warm in the big room on this late June day. And too, when was the last time he had seen Danielle? Years, perhaps. Their children were grown. They were grandparents now. Their daughter Claire had a baby boy. Jason hadn't married but he was not even thirty yet. He was working for Alex, helping manage Rivonnier, the winery, and planning to get an MBA, Danielle had told Zooey. And Patti was a grandmother, too, now. Zooey pictured her as one of those rockin' grandmas with more energy than the grandkids, but she was probably imagining that, because Danielle had told her Patti and Jeff were buying a house in Maui and moving there as soon as Megan got a job and moved out. Jeff had retired but Danielle wasn't sure from what—no one had ever quite figured out what it was Jeff did—something to do with surfboards or windsurfing. But Patti and he were a great couple, Danielle said. "Patti lucked out." So had Danielle, it seemed to Zooey, at least from what she saw at the dinner last fall and their emails since then. Danielle was happy with Alex, and Claire and her husband and baby lived a few miles from Rivonnier. She saw her children often and Zooey believed this affirmed how well she had loved them.

Even Brenna seemed less worn and stressed although Drew, retired from the Navy, was living with her and Jimmy and the twins again. The other children had all moved away. Andrew went into politics after graduate school at Harvard and was someone's assistant in Washington DC. Luke had decided not to join the priesthood but moved to San Francisco and came out as a gay man. Elizabeth's intuition about him had been true. Zooey smiled. Elizabeth's 'gadar' was not a surprise, given everything.

Danielle also told her Drew had mellowed since his retirement and spent a lot of time working on the sailboat he had built. He even helped Brenna with Jimmy's care and took the twins to their high school activities. But he had stopped speaking to Luke. Zooey glanced over her shoulder a moment at the guests behind her. Drew was there somewhere. For an instant an image of Brenna's wedding came to her mind and all those young men in navy blue and their stiff snow-white hats with gold braid like so many dinner plates all touching each other row after row. But now she felt a stirring and realized everyone was looking as Mark and Elizabeth turned to each other and kissed, a tender, dignified kiss. And another wedding scene, Danielle's, appeared in Zooey's mind—Elizabeth and Mark kissing hungrily on the dance floor thirty years ago. It was astonishing. But fast forward now, here they were, stately and graceful as they held each others hands and walked down the center aisle past the guests as a lively Irish tune played, Mark's choice no doubt.

"That was a beautiful ceremony," Eva said to Zooey when Zooey joined her and Tess at a table near the buffet.

"Good, I'm glad you enjoyed it. How was it for you, Tess?"

"Why can't you and Mommy get married?" Tess asked Zooey. "I mean by the law. Hasn't it changed yet?"

"Honey, we're working on it. And then we'll have a big party. It'll be great!"

"It isn't fair," Tess said.

"No, it's not," Eva agreed.

Zooey felt guilty. She should have come alone. Or not at all. But then, that didn't feel right either. Always the balance—between protecting your family from the prejudice or living with it in your face. The 'commitment ceremonies' gay couples held instead of weddings weren't quite the same since legal marriage for gays and lesbians had been so much in the news. Tess was old enough to know the difference.

"Well when I grow up I'm going to be a judge and let gays and lesbians get married."

"Where will you go to law school?" a voice behind them asked. It was Mark. He and Elizabeth were greeting guests and Elizabeth bent to embrace Zooey as Zooey reached up and they held each other a moment. Then she smiled and shook Eva's hand as Zooey introduced them. They had never met and each studied the other a quick moment and smiled pleasantly. "So nice to meet you. I hope we have a chance to get together soon." Then she turned, "Is this Tess?" and reached a hand to Tess who gracefully took it and said, "How do you do?"

Mark pulled out a chair and sat next to Zooey while Elizabeth asked Tess about school and Tess answered in her sweet yet savvy way.

"Good to see you, Zooey," Mark said. "Are you still out there in the streets?"

"There hasn't been much going on, don't you think? Except for the demonstrations before the war. That was incredible."

"Yeah, the largest protests in world history and they ignored it."

"Of course no one reports that. Even though they finally figured out, once again, war is a mistake."

Mark looked off a moment, remembering, then at Zooey. "Can you believe how much it's like Vietnam?"

"I guess we're old enough now to actually watch history repeat itself."

Mark laughed. "Yeah. It's up to the kids now."

"I know. I can't seem to summon the passion I once had."

"I never believed that would happen to me. But I think it really is time to turn it over. It's their generation's turn."

"Although the country's state of decline is so much worse now. I wonder how relevant the United States will be in the world in ten years."

"Mark, my man." Sean came up and put a hand on Mark's shoulder. Mark looked up and then back at Zooey and said, "Later." He stood to talk to Sean and they walked over to an older woman seated at a table by the windows who looked so much like Mark, Zooey was sure it must have been his mother—or Sean's. She turned to Eva who was talking with Elizabeth now as Tess looked around the room, watching.

"But that's the irony of language," Eva was saying.

"Yes. It can create order, or chaos."

"They're calling you," Tess said to Elizabeth. She pointed to where Mark and Sean were seated with the elderly woman, and Mark made a quick small motion with his hand for Elizabeth to join them.

A waiter came by and Zooey and Eva each took a glass of champagne. Zooey had an occasional glass of wine now that it had been twenty years since her drinking days.

"I like her," Eva said.

"Maybe we'll see them again. She's moving to Berkeley to live with Mark."

"And giving up her job?" Eva looked perplexed.

"She had cut back to half time already. She was living in that meditation center half of every year."

"She's in for a change."

"I think they'll do okay," Zooey said, remembering her moment of insight before the ceremony. She looked at them as they sat with Sean and Mark's mother and saw Sean's young wife join them. She looked very fit in the way of an athlete and attractive in her sleek blue dress. Sean seemed to visibly relax as she sat down next to him and he took her hand. All those years everyone thought Sean was so easy-going but, in fact, he wasn't. It hadn't been an act exactly but a way he acted in order to survive. She was glad he was happy now. Then she looked around the room and saw Danielle and Alex and Patti and Jeff standing in line at the buffet laughing and joking. She knew Danielle would miss them a lot if Patti and Jeff actually moved to Hawaii.

"Let's get something to eat," Eva said.

"Yeah, I'm hungry," Tess agreed, and Zooey stood and followed them to the buffet table.

"There she is," Danielle said. She left her place in line and came up to them.

"Is this Tess? And Eva—we met, years ago." She smiled and shook each of their hands.

"This is Danielle," Zooey said to Tess. "My old roommate in college."

"Not that old! We have a few good years left." Danielle laughed. Patti looked over and came to join them. "Hi there." Alex and Jeff seemed engrossed in conversation and kept their places in line at the buffet.

More introductions were made and Danielle asked Tess about school and if she were having a good time.

"This is the first wedding I've been to," Tess said with a touch of irony.

"Oh well ..." Danielle said.

"That's a very pretty dress," Patti said.

"Thank you. One of my moms has one and I really liked it so she made one for me."

"That was nice of her," Patti looked at Zooey who nodded in Eva's direction. Eva smiled. "Thank you."

"And congratulations on your film, Zooey." Danielle looked at Zooey as if seeing her differently—a mix of incredulity and respect. "Elizabeth told me. I went to see it in the city. It's superb. I was going to call you—We'll talk."

"That's right! I can't believe you didn't mention it at the reunion," Patti said. "Elizabeth said it won an award. Listen, everyone in this place would know it if I won an award." She laughed.

"Oh god, there's Sean's mother. I haven't seen her in years, I should say hello—" Danielle said.

"So that's *Sean's* mother, not Mark's." Zooey looked across the room.

"I met her before the ceremony. She enunciates everything very precisely," Patti said.

"She makes a science of self-deprecation," Danielle added.

"Well, I should look so good at her age." Patti turned to them. "Who here still gets her period."

They all laughed but only Eva nodded her head.

"For all I know I'm still having mine and I just forgot. Can you believe this memory loss thing?" Patti said.

"I know, I was so mad when I had to go off HRT. It really did make a difference," Danielle said.

Patti glanced at her husband at the buffet. "Hey, come on, we're losing our places."

"Where are you sitting?" Danielle asked Zooey. "Come and sit with us." She gestured toward the windows. "We're over there with Brenna and Drew."

"I think I might have to boycott Drew," Zooey said quietly.

"Oh god." Danielle pressed her lips together. "I know. Just come and sit at the table next to us, on the side where he isn't."

"Okay. Maybe." Zooey laughed. "Thanks. Anyway, we'll talk later." She moved off with Eva and Tess to get in line for the buffet.

"Who's Drew?" Eva asked as they got in line.

"The son in San Francisco. Remember?" Zooey said, speaking in code because she felt Tess had had enough exposure to prejudice for one day.

"Who?" Tess asked, knowing code when she heard it.

"Just an old friend's husband. He supports the war a lot."

"Oh." Tess knew her parents were against the war.

"Well let's sit over in their vicinity, anyway," Eva said. "I mean, we're here."

When they had their food, Zooey saw to her relief there weren't enough seats left at her friends' table, so she led her family to a table nearby, waving at Danielle, Patti and Brenna. They joined an elderly couple who were delighted to sit with a pretty young child. Once again Tess rose to the occasion, talking with them about school and her interests. Zooey marveled at her poise. Tess was always well-behaved around adults but today she was outdoing herself and

Zooey knew it was for her and Eva. Should a child have that burden? Protecting her parents from prejudice? experiencing it by association herself? But Eva said the world is full of prejudice of all kinds and it is not wrong to teach a child that it exists and how to cope with it. How to work for justice in its place.

Zooey believed this to be true although she worried, remembering how hard it had been for her, remembering Sanders and the years after. And all the lonely years Elizabeth endured, avoiding the stigma.

But Eva also said the one thing that really mattered was that Tess knew she was deeply loved, and that's what really counted for anyone in the world. It was what everyone at heart really wanted. And that Zooey knew to be the truth. She looked at Eva, now, who was talking with the elderly couple in an animated way that had them fully engaged. Her thick black hair, without a trace of gray, swept away from her face and her dark eyes seemed lit from within as she glanced at Zooey and smiled, the 'I know you' smile that made Zooey feel a rush of love for her, Eva, her beloved partner, the love of her life. Zooey was filled with gratitude. It was something no law or prejudice could ever take away.

"Hi Zooey." Brenna stood beside her and put a hand on her shoulder.

Zooey turned quickly and looked up. "Brenna! How are you? I barely got to talk to you before the ceremony."

"I know." Brenna squatted down to be at the same level. "Wasn't it beautiful? Elizabeth looks fantastic. Could you ever have guessed, though.... *Mark?*"

"No. Not until Danielle told me. I can see it though. It makes sense."

"It must." Brenna looked at Eva and Tess. "Is this your family?"

"Yes." Zooey got Tess's attention and introduced her and Eva to Brenna who smiled warmly at each of them.

"I'm so happy to finally meet you," she said. "I hope we'll get a chance to talk later."

"I'm sure we will," Eva said graciously and then turned back to the elderly couple who were talking about their trip to Alaska.

"Zooey, I wanted to ask you something. I'm coming up to see Luke next weekend—"

"You are? Do you want to stay with us?"

"No, I'm staying with him. But, do you think you could meet with us and, maybe meet with him, I mean. I remember at Sanders, that semester, we didn't even know what you were going through."

"It's so different now, Brenna. It's not nearly as bad. Especially if he's living in San Francisco."

"But there wasn't AIDS then."

"That's true."

"But it's that Drew won't talk to him. It hurts Luke so much I think."

"Of course. Call me. We'll figure it out."

Someone was pinging on a glass to get everyone's attention. A member of Mark's family was standing and raising his glass to make a toast.

Brenna rose and bent to hug Zooey then went back to her table.

It was Mark's uncle, on his mother's side the man explained—so *that* was Mark's mother, Zooey realized as she watched a thin elderly woman with sharp dark eyes smiling at her brother as he spoke. He talked about Mark's precociousness as a boy, joked about his 'left-wing' politics, made a tasteful, sad allusion to Mark's first wife and then talked about what a great teacher Mark was and all the people he helped. Then he transitioned to Elizabeth, starting with "the best things in life are worth waiting for" and touching lightly on the times in the past the couple had been together and went on to extol Elizabeth's grace and intellectual gifts, mentioning her poems and career—Zooey wondered for a moment if Mark had written this toast for his uncle—and he finally ended by bestowing the blessing and love of the family. Everyone sipped their champagne and applauded warmly.

Then Sean, who had had several glasses of champagne, stood and raised his glass and began talking about what a great guy Mark was, the great times they had as kids. He made a joke which his family seemed to understand. Then he spoke with great admiration about Elizabeth. Finally he wished them all the happiness in the world. Everyone cheered, caught up in Sean's good will as well as his brevity.

Then Mark stood and gracefully raised his glass to his guests, to his family, to his wife and then set it on the table.

"I know the 'groom' doesn't always make a toast at his own wedding, but you know," he bent his head in the faux-modest, sexy way he had and looked up, "I could never resist a public forum." Everyone laughed and relaxed. "And while I have you captive," Mark went on, "let me say how blessed I feel this day to be joining my life with" he extended his arm, "the exquisite, indescribable Elizabeth—my soulmate." There was silence as everyone looked at Elizabeth who sat watching Mark with an unreadable smile. Something both tender and wry, Zooey thought, but she wasn't sure.

"I cannot tell you how happy I am, that I have finally seen the light." Mark looked at Elizabeth and the light in his eyes, and then hers, told Zooey that there was nothing ironic about it. They are in love, she realized. Then Elizabeth's book came to her mind, *Winter Light*—and particularly one poem that she had not understood. Now she did. It was not, like the others, about the ineffable ... Of course. It was about love late in life.

"... and the next time I raise my glass," Mark was saying, "to toast a loving union ... A marriage. I hope it will be for Zooey and Eva. I hope you'll all join me in making that possible."

Zooey caught her breath and felt her face turning pink as she thought 'he will be an activist until the day he dies' and Eva laughed and then raised her glass up as people turned toward their table and raised their glasses to them in response to Mark's gesture. Zooey recovered and smiled, raising her glass, too, and Tess clapped her hands and grinned, thrilled.

978-0-595-48314-3
0-595-48314-3

Printed in the United States
106531LV00007B/178-186/A

9 780595 483143